THE WAR OF THE WORLDS

THE WAR OF THE WORLDS

H.G. Wells

edited by Martin A. Danahay

broadview literary texts

National Library of Canada Cataloguing in Publication

Wells, H.G. (Herbert George), 1866-1946
    The war of the worlds / H.G. Wells ; edited by Martin A. Danahay

(Broadview literary texts)
Includes bibliographical references.
ISBN 1-55111-353-8

    I. Danahay, Martin A.   II. Title.   III. Series.

PR5774.W3 2003   823'.912   C2003-900407-4

Broadview Press Ltd. is an independent, international publishing house, incorporated in 1985. Broadview believes in shared ownership, both with its employees and with the general public; since the year 2000 Broadview shares have traded publicly on the Toronto Venture Exchange under the symbol BDP.

We welcome comments and suggestions regarding any aspect of our publications – please feel free to contact us at the addresses below or at broadview@broadviewpress.com.

North America
Post Office Box 1243, Peterborough, Ontario, Canada K9J 7H5
3576 California Road, Orchard Park, NY, USA 14127
Tel: (705) 743-8990; Fax: (705) 743-8353;
e-mail: customerservice@broadviewpress.com

UK, Ireland, and continental Europe
Thomas Lyster Ltd., Units 3 & 4a, Old Boundary Way,
Burscough Rd, Ormskirk, Lancashire L39 2YW
Tel: (1695) 575112; Fax: (1695) 570120
email: books@tlyster.co.uk

Australia and New Zealand
UNIREPS, University of New South Wales
Sydney, NSW, 2052
Tel: 61 2 9664 0999; Fax: 61 2 9664 5420
email: info.press@unsw.edu.au

www.broadviewpress.com

Broadview Press Ltd. gratefully acknowledges the financial support of the Government of Canada through the Book Publishing Industry Development Program for our publishing activities.

Series Editor: Professor L.W. Conolly
Advisory editor for this volume: Michel W. Pharand
Typesetting and assembly: True to Type Inc., Mississauga, Canada.

PRINTED IN CANADA

Contents

Acknowledgments

My thanks to Nicholas Ruddick for his advice while I was fashioning this edition, and for the sterling example set by his edition of H.G. Wells's *The Time Machine*. David Clammer, author of *The Victorian Army in Photographs* was generous with both his expertise and his photo of the heliograph operators. The Woking Historical Society provided invaluable assistance and images via email. The Woking History Centre and its staff were extremely helpful during my early research on Woking. The Dean of Graduate Research at the University of Texas at Arlington generously provided funds to pay for the rights for the letters of H.G. Wells, which are reproduced by permission of A.P. Watt on behalf of the Literary Executors of the Estate of H.G. Wells. The staff of the Woodson Research Center, Fondren Library, Rice University were admirably friendly and accommodating during my research on the *Army and Navy Illustrated* in their collection. My thanks to Stacy Thorne and Alyson Dickerman for their aid in the process of assembling the edition.

The production staff at Broadview deserve a medal as well as thanks for work above and beyond the usual call of duty on an early and inferior version of the manuscript. As usual, I am immensely grateful to Don LePan and the staff at Broadview for an excuse to indulge my passion for quirky and esoteric research topics. Many happy hours were spent poring over old maps, photographs of Victorian military men with creative facial hair, and so many photographs of men with big guns that one had to wonder if Herr Freud's newfangled theories might have some basis in fact.

Introduction

H.G. Wells in 1898

When *The War of the Worlds* was published in January 1898, H.G. Wells was a new star in the Victorian literary scene. He had published *The Time Machine: An Invention* in 1895, followed by *The Island of Doctor Moreau* in 1896 and *The Invisible Man* in 1897. While the term "science fiction" had not been coined in 1898, Wells had established himself as the leading figure in what he would have called "scientific romance" with these publications and with *The Stolen Bacillus and Other Stories* (1895). While *The Island of Doctor Moreau* had caused some controversy because of its scenes of vivisection, *The Time Machine* had been enormously successful. As Nicholas Ruddick explains in the Broadview *The Time Machine*, Wells was hailed by one reviewer of the book as a "man of genius," and another termed the story a "powerful imaginative romance" (38).

This critical acclaim continued with the publication of *The War of the Worlds*. Wells was compared by reviewers to Edgar Allan Poe, Robert Louis Stevenson and, by one perceptive critic, to Jules Verne in that his fiction combined science and fantasy to extrapolate events or trends into the future (see Appendix D). Reviewers had difficulty in placing the story in terms of genre, but recognized its power and originality. They showed in their remarks a continued lack of an agreed upon term for this kind of writing, as they had with *The Time Machine* (see Ruddick 35-36). Most critics agreed that like *The Time Machine*, *The War of the Worlds* was a page-turner that gained impact by its reference to the geography of London and its surrounding towns. One dissenting critic objected to Wells's story as being too "cockney" in dealing with "bank clerks and newspaper touts;" this objection seems rooted in class prejudice and the author was reacting to the accurate perception that Wells's background was of a lower class than many contemporary authors.

Wells in 1898 was living in "Heatherlea" in suburban Worcester Park in a large Victorian "villa" (a detached house) when the story was published, having moved there from Woking in 1896. He had started to write *The War of the Worlds* while living in Woking and used his knowledge of the town and surrounding countryside in the story. He had recently married his second wife, Amy Catherine

Robbins (known as "Jane"), after divorcing his first wife, his cousin Isabel Mary Wells. He had given up teaching after suffering a serious lung hemorrhage in 1893 and devoted himself to making a living by writing. It was a tremendous risk, but by 1898 it was clear that the move had been the right one. Wells was producing a prodigious amount of prose, both in fiction and non-fiction, and finding a wide and enthusiastic readership. He had a secure income and showed no signs of letting up in his furious pace of publication. He was also being recognized as a dynamic new voice in the literary world and thanks to his growing reputation was meeting established writers such as George Gissing, Henry James, Joseph Conrad and Ford Madox Ford.

Wells had had extensive training in science, including zoology and biology. This comes across clearly in *The War of the Worlds* in the many learned discussions of the aliens' biology and of the Martian flora that came with the invaders. Wells also shows his interest in telescopes and astronomy, subjects that are also found in his short stories. His story "The Stolen Bacillus" (1895) shows his awareness of the recent advances made in understanding bacteria. As his contemporaries saw, Wells was an imaginative writer who also had a grasp of the fundamental concepts of Victorian science.

The looming presences behind *The War of the Worlds*, as behind *The Time Machine* and *The Island of Doctor Moreau*, are Charles Darwin and T.H. Huxley. Huxley in particular was known as a popularizer and champion of Darwin's theories of evolution. Where in *The Time Machine* and *The Island of Doctor Moreau* Wells had dwelled primarily on the theory of "degeneration" (see Ruddick 31 and Wells "Zoological Retrogression," in Appendix B), in *The War of the Worlds* Wells uses theories of evolution. The aliens not only have superior technology, but have also evolved beyond the need for bodies thanks to their elaborate machinery. Instead of the degeneration and death of a species, Wells shows in the aliens a species that has evolved into what he would regard as a "higher" form of existence.

The species that is threatened with extinction in *The War of the Worlds* is humans, and especially the Victorian English contingent. While Darwin's theories focused on forces of nature, Wells, much like Huxley, was aware of the impact of human intervention on the natural world, especially the eradication of animals by human hunters. Wells extrapolates the horrendous impact of European colonization on the dodo and the bison and imagines a similar fate being visited upon humans. Wells topples his Victorian contemporaries from the "top" of the evolutionary hierarchy to shock them into realizing that the British Empire would not last forever and that their faith in their military technology was too great.

Wells had a dim view of both Victorian religion and politics. Neither the Church nor the State are shown as particularly effective in the face of the alien invasion. The Church is criticized through the figure of the Curate and the State through the initially complacent bulletins of the government, which is brought to its knees within days by the alien onslaught. In fact, the Victorian social structure is shown to be a thin veneer that could be stripped away almost overnight by war and destruction. *The War of the Worlds* shows how disenchanted Wells had become both with the religion that he had been taught by his mother and the social organization in which he was raised. Wells continued to be a social critic for the rest of his life; many of his publications, both fiction and non-fiction, are attempts to influence the shape of society in the future, or as Wells put it, "the shape of things to come."

Biographical Sketch: The Life of H.G. Wells

Herbert George Wells was born on 21 September 1866 in Bromley, Kent, a town ten miles southeast of London. Bromley is now part of Greater London and the process of turning Bromley from a small town into part of a metropolitan area had begun in 1861 when a railway station connecting the town to London was constructed. Wells spent most of his life in and around London, and Woking, the town in which the narrator of *The War of the Worlds* lives, was like Bromley in that it was a small town linked to London by rail. Wells is thus a product of a newly emerging suburban culture that grew with the development of the railway system in Victorian England, and he uses his knowledge of this culture in his story. As one critic noted, his story was populated by middle and lower middle class characters.

His parents, Joseph Wells (1827-1910) and Sarah Wells (née Neal) (1822-1910), were servants who left domestic service and took over a cousin's china shop in 1855. Herbert George was their fourth child, but a daughter, Fanny, had died before he was born so he grew up with two older brothers but no sisters. Their house was both their shop and their home. Owning a shop conferred higher social status than being domestic servants, although the shop was not particularly prosperous and Wells's mother continued to clean houses. Wells's family was thus part of the lower stratum of the middle class and during his childhood and early adulthood lived in an economically precarious situation. In 1880 the family found itself in extreme financial difficulties when Mr. Wells fell off a ladder and broke his thigh. Mr. Wells had supplemented the family's income by playing on local cricket teams, and was really more interested in playing cricket than running a shop. The loss of this supplemental income forced Mrs. Wells to accept the post of housekeeper at Up Park in Sussex, where she had previously worked as a maid.

Wells was nicknamed "Bertie" by his family and was a small, somewhat frail boy. He grew up with his family continually on the edge of poverty. He was educated at a "dame school" (a small, one-room school run by a single teacher) in Bromley and later at Thomas Morley's Academy in Bromley. The Academy aimed to give its pupils a basic education that would supposedly make them part of the "genteel" classes. Wells's main education came from neither of these schools, but from his reading. As a result of being pushed and falling on a tent peg at age seven, he broke his hip, which limited his movement. Laid up with nothing else to do, he read avidly. Wells was later to say that this was the most fortunate accident of his life. He credited the event with beginning his interest in literature and his later choice of writing as a profession.

Wells had to be taken out of school and sent out to work as soon as possible because of the family's financial difficulties. In 1880 he was apprenticed to a draper's firm called Rodgers and Denyer in Windsor. To be a draper's assistant appeared to his family to be a "genteel" occupation. Rodgers and Denyer sold items to the Royal Family and gained status from this connection. Wells hated the job and, either deliberately or through inattention, kept making errors in the account books. Rodgers and Denyer soon dismissed him.

Next, Wells briefly helped a roguish relation, a distant relative referred to as "Uncle" Alfred Williams, by acting as a pupil-teacher in the school that his relative had started in Wookey, Somerset. "Uncle" Alfred, however, had no qualifications and no business sense and the school was closed down by government inspectors after only three months. Wells says that he learned a great deal from his "uncle," who had radical and ironic views on authority and regulations. Wells used this uncle as the basis for one of his earliest books, entitled *Select Conversations with an Uncle* (1895).

Wells then had a respite of some weeks as he lived with his mother at Up Park while he was between jobs. There he had access to a large library and continued his reading. He also reconstructed an old telescope and gazed at the stars. He saw first hand the life of a country house and the people who inhabited Up Park. While there, he wrote a mock newspaper called the *Up Park Alarmist* for the household.

His mother soon organized another job for him, this time with a chemist (i.e., pharmacist) in Midhurst, not far from Up Park. As a chemist's assistant, Wells needed to know Latin, and it was arranged that he should take lessons from the headmaster of the nearby Midhurst Grammar School. It became obvious, however, that Wells could not learn the skills necessary to be a chemist without a great deal of training that his employer was not prepared to undertake. He left the chemist's position and became instead a full-time pupil at Midhurst Grammar School in February 1881. He earned his keep by coaching pupils to pass exams that determined the amount of funding the school would receive. He enjoyed his time at the school tremendously.

In May 1881, however, his mother arranged for him again to become a draper's apprentice in a shop in Southsea, Hampshire. Wells described this move as an imprisonment. He hated the monotonous routines of the retail trade, having to work thirteen-hour days for very little money. Nonetheless, he remained in the business for two years, during which he rejected religion and may even have contemplated suicide as the only way of escaping a future of monotonous jobs. In July 1883 he quit the job in Southsea and walked the 17 miles to Up Park to beg his mother to let him leave the drapery business and find another means of employment.

To escape the life of a drapery shop assistant, Wells at the age of seventeen re-entered Midhurst Grammar School as an assistant teacher. Wells's escape was made possible by the headmaster of the school, who had recognized his talents. Wells found a world of knowledge opened up to him in his new position. In the evenings after school was over, he took continuing education classes with the headmaster, cramming knowledge from textbooks on the sciences. He also took exams based on these courses and passed several of them with first-class results.

Wells's high scores automatically earned him a chance for a place at the Normal School for Science (later the Royal College), including free tuition and a small grant for books and supplies. He moved to London in September 1884 and signed up for, among other courses, biology with T.H. Huxley. The education he was to receive at the Normal School was to train him to be a science teacher. Wells was by now 18 years old and had finally embarked on a course of full-time higher education.

Wells was deeply influenced by Huxley and called him the greatest man he ever met. Through Huxley, Wells became convinced that Darwin's theory of evolution was correct. While at the Normal School he underwent a revolution in his thinking. Having been brought up in a religious and evangelical household, at the Normal School he gradually embraced socialism and adopted science as his creed instead of Christianity. Huxley had coined the term "agnostic," and it applied to Wells's views on religion as well as Huxley's own outlook: there may or may not be a grand designer of the universe, but there is no way of knowing for certain whether this designer exists. Science represented the only certain knowledge in the face of this uncertainty. Also, humanity might be heading for a better existence, but there was no guarantee that this was the case. Only science could help bring about a happy future for humanity. Echoes of Huxley's ideas can be found throughout Wells's science fiction.

After an exhilarating first year, Wells found the lectures in his second year at the Normal School disappointing. He almost failed his second year exams and only barely had his scholarship renewed. Wells had become more interested in various extracurricular activities than in his studies. He began a relationship with a cousin, Isabel Mary Wells, and found himself more and more distracted by his blossoming romance and less and less inclined to attend to his studies. There were also other distractions. He became very involved with the student political movement and participated in the revival of the socialist cause. Wells went to meetings held at the house of William Morris (1834-1896), the well-known author, artist and founder of the Socialist League. Here Wells met people who would later be his peers in the Fabian Society. The Fabian Society was founded in London in 1884, and its members believed in achieving a democratic, socialist state in England through gradual change rather than revolution, which was congenial to Wells's ideas of social evolution. Wells also helped launch a student journal called *Science Schools Journal* that was supposed to link science and politics and for which he was for a while the editor. As politics and journalism started to dominate his consciousness, his studies started to occupy less and less of his attention. In the summer of 1887 he failed the final in geology and left the Normal School.

Despite his lackluster qualifications Wells was able to gain a position as a science teacher at Holt Academy, near Wrexham,

North Wales. Although the school was not very good, with poor amenities for teaching science and with very rough pupils who lacked basic skills, Wells was not unhappy; he even had a brief romance with a local girl, but she broke off with him eventually because he was an atheist and a socialist. However, while playing soccer, Wells was fouled by a student and very badly injured, particularly in his kidneys. He left the school in November and went back to Up Park to recuperate. Wells's letters at this point indicate that he felt he was on the verge of death. The local doctor informed him that he was likely to be an invalid for the rest of his life; although this proved inaccurate, he did suffer a series of serious illnesses over the next twelve years that interrupted his ability to work and to write.

At this point in his life he began to read widely in fiction and experimented with different modes of writing. After eight months of illness, Wells went to London and started scratching out a living writing freelance journalism. He lived for a while in Staffordshire with a friend from the Normal School, William Burton, and began work on what was to become *The Time Machine*. He resumed his courtship of Isabel. In January 1889 he gained a position as a teacher at a private school in Kilburn. He also received an appointment to the University Tutorial College, an early correspondence school. Wells was assigned to correspond with students studying for biology exams and to edit the school newsletter, the *University Correspondent*. Later that year, he passed his B.Sc. exams in zoology, gaining first-class honours. At 24 years old, Wells had finally completed the education he had begun at the Normal School.

Wells appeared to settle into the life of a science teacher. In October 1891, he married Isabel and they moved into a house in Wandsworth, part of Greater London. The marriage did not go well, however, as Wells and Isabel discovered that they had little in common. Moreover, in the autumn of 1892, Wells was finding a student in one of his classes, Amy Catherine Robbins, much more interesting than Isabel. In January 1894, Wells left Isabel and moved in with Amy in a small apartment near Euston, London. Neither of them liked their given names, and she eventually became known to her friends as "Jane" and he as "H.G.," although his family still called him "Bertie."

Wells decided to stop teaching and make a living from writing for magazines and journals. This was provoked in part by another health crisis that convinced him he was too frail physically to earn a living by teaching. In 1894 alone he sold 75 articles and short stories, and he received his first book contract for *Select Conversations with an Uncle* in 1895. Wells's breakthrough, however, came with the publication of his story on time travel. He had been thinking about the possibility of time travel for many years, and he published a story serially in the *New Review* called "The Time Machine." This was published as *The Time Machine* in May 1895, followed by *The Wonderful Visit*, a "comic romance," in September 1895. His final publication that year was *The Stolen Bacillus and Other Stories*. All in all it had been a very happy, lucrative and productive year.

1895 marks the beginning of Wells's career as a famous writer. His books, especially *The Time Machine*, were well received, and for the first time in his life, at 29 years old, he was earning a steady income from his writing. It was during this period that Wells started thinking about and writing the book that was to become *The War of the Worlds*. (See Hughes and Geduld, *A Critical Edition of The War of the Worlds* pp. 1-9 for a complete history of the composition of the text.)

Wells and Jane married on October 27, 1895, after his divorce from Isabel was concluded. They had moved to Woking in the summer before their marriage, and it is this area that provides the setting for *The War of the Worlds*. Cycling was a new national craze, and Wells and Jane would take bike rides together in the afternoon. Eventually they bought their own tandem so that they could pedal together on the same bicycle. The geographical landmarks in the Woking area that Wells used to make *The War of the Worlds* so realistic for his Victorian audience were a product of these bicycle journeys through the surrounding countryside.

The first evidence of the writing of *The War of the Worlds* is a letter of January 22, 1896 to William Morris Colles giving him a synopsis of the work in progress. W.M. Colles was one of the new breed of "literary agents" who were representing aspiring authors. Colles went on to represent Bram Stoker (the author of *Dracula*; ed. Glennis Byron, Broadview 1999) and George Gissing (author of *The Odd Women*; ed. Arlene Young, Broadview 1998), among others. Wells played publishers against each other by making them compete for his manuscripts and he instructed Colles as to which magazines should be offered the chance to run the serial version of *The War of the Worlds*. All of Wells's letters to Colles concern his strategies for obtaining the best terms for publication for his manuscript. Wells also instructed Colles not to offer any stories to *The Graphic* because they had earlier turned down his narrative, *The Wheels of Chance*; he wanted to punish them for this act.

By March 26, Wells had a draft of the story that he felt was not yet ready for publication, but which he sent to Colles. At the same time he was also working on "Intelligence on Mars" which came out in the *Saturday Review* in April 1896. He was also working on *The Invisible Man* (September 1897), which appeared in print before *The War of the Worlds*. Wells was revising *The War of the Worlds* in November 1897, and the text was published in January 1898. As the reviews in Appendix D show, the novel was an immediate success.

With the success of both *The Time Machine* and *The War of the Worlds*, Wells acquired a larger and more dependable income. He and Jane left Woking for a bigger house in Worcester Park called "Heatherlea." In 1896, at the age of 30, Wells was a popular author with a steadily growing income from royalties and from advances on further publications, and could now establish himself in a respectable home. It was a remarkable change in fortune from his position only a few years before. On the strength of his growing reputation, he became friends with other writers such as Henry James, George Gissing, Joseph Conrad, Stephen Crane and Bernard Shaw.

By the end of 1897, Wells had published many of the "scientific romances" for which he is famous. His publications thereafter are remarkable for their diversity. Wells thought of himself as a reporter and social commentator rather than a literary artist. Many of his works were predictions of how society would be changed by science, and reflect his interest in both technology and socialism. He also wrote novels that were social criticism in that they dealt with issues of social class and were extremely critical of British society. He was for a while affiliated with the League of Nations (a precursor to the United Nations organization) founded in 1919 after World War I and disbanded in 1946, for which he wrote research reports on current human social organization and extrapolated demographic trends into the future. He was a fervent supporter of organizations such as the League of Nations as a safeguard against catastrophic wars.

Wells's marital difficulties continued in his relationship with Jane. Just as he lost interest in Isabel earlier, he found himself drawn by other women away from Jane. His affair with a certain Amber Reeves caused a scandal when he eloped to France with her and when she later became pregnant. At the same time he published *Ann Veronica* (1909), a novel that treated sex in a way that was extremely frank for the time, and for a while Wells was publicly accused of being immoral. He eventually reconciled with Jane and the furor died down, but this was not the end of his affairs, which included a long relationship with author Rebecca West; their son Anthony went on to write a book, *H.G. Wells: Aspects of a Life* (1984), about his father.

World War I deepened Wells's pessimism about long-term human progress, and in his later writings he decided that only education and struggle bring about any amelioration of social conditions. He saw his mission as the education of humanity to help prevent its self-annihilation, and used his writing and direct political action to help create a critical mass of visionaries who would lead the species to a higher form of consciousness, or "world brain." To spur social progress, Wells focused on writing non-fiction, polemical texts aimed at the general education of his audience. Like T.H. Huxley before him, Wells became a popularizer of scientific ideas.

After World War I, Wells traveled to Russia and met Lenin and Trotsky, and to America where he met F.D. Roosevelt. His meetings with these leaders were part of his effort to bring about a world government that would prevent further conflicts on the scale of World War I. Wells stood unsuccessfully as a Labour candidate for Parliament in the 1920s as part of his effort to become actively engaged in the political process. During this period he published his ironic *Experiment in Autobiography* (1934) in which he narrated his own life in a comic tone, glossing over many of his marital difficulties. He also published *The Holy Terror* (1939), a study of the psychology of dictators such as Hitler and Mussolini.

The efforts of Wells and others did not, of course, prevent further conflict in the way that he had hoped. The outbreak of World War II confirmed much of his pessimism about the future of humanity. He survived it, refusing to leave his house in London even during the Blitz of 1940-41. Wells died at home in London on 13 August 1946.

Publications

It is difficult to place H.G. Wells in a particular genre or field because he tried so many different approaches and subjects. He also did not like being assigned a particular identity. He wrote fiction, autobiography and a great deal of non-fiction, and in his later works was more interested in social commentary than analyses of character or personality. Even in his fiction he resisted a focus on style and characterization, preferring to think of his stories as vehicles for ideas. He was extremely didactic and polemic in his approach to writing.

Wells's first published book was a *Text-Book of Biology* (1893) which was based upon his teaching experience. His first science fiction book (or "scientific romance" as he would term it) was *The Time Machine* (1895), which was immediately successful. In 1895 he also published *The Wonderful Visit*, a satire in which an angel comes to visit the earth. He wrote the rest of his science fiction works from 1896 to 1914: *The Island of Doctor Moreau* (1896) about a doctor who "speeds up" evolution through vivisection, *The Invisible Man* (1897) about a scientist who discovers invisibility and ends up a murderer, *The War of the Worlds* (1898), *When the Sleeper Wakes* (1899), *The First Men in the Moon* (1901) in which voyagers discover life on the moon, and *The Food of the Gods* (1904) in which scientists discover a food that increases the size of humans by a factor of seven. He also wrote many short stories, which were collected in *The Stolen Bacillus and Other Stories* (1895), *The Plattner Story* (1897), and *Tales of Space and Time* (1899). In his 1903 short story "The Land Ironclads" Wells predicted the use of tanks in modern warfare; in *The War in the Air* (1908) he predicted the widespread use of aircraft in battles; and in *The World Set Free* (1914) he predicted atomic warfare. Through these successful predictions, Wells won for himself the status of prophet of the future.

Wells also wrote comic novels of lower middle-class life, such as *Love and Mr. Lewisham* (1900), *Kipps: The Story of a Simple Soul* (1905), and *The History of Mr. Polly* (1910). In these novels he drew on his personal experience of poverty and his sense of the injustice of the British class system. *Kipps* in particular tells a story very similar to Wells's own; Arthur Kipps lives in relative poverty and works as a draper's apprentice. However, in *Kipps* the protagonist inherits money and tries to move into the upper classes, but fails because of class prejudice (see Appendix E of the Broadview edition of George Gissing's *The Odd Women* for an extract from *Kipps*). These are pointed critiques of the bad effects of the social hierarchy on people, especially on the lower classes.

For a long time Wells was optimistic about the possibilities of social progress through science and education, as can be seen in *Anticipations* (1901), *Mankind in the Making* (1903), and *A Modern Utopia* (1905), in which he expressed hopes for the near-term future (although in the long term he predicted the extinction of the human species). He became an active socialist and in 1903 joined the Fabian Society, though he soon came into conflict with Bernard Shaw and Beatrice Webb over the future of the Society. His clash with them in 1906–07 can be found thinly disguised in his novel *The New Machiavelli* (1911), in which they are parodied mercilessly. He resigned as a member of the Fabian Society in 1908. After about 1906, many of Wells's writings were primarily polemics, although he continued to write novels (such as *Ann Veronica* and *Tono-Bungay*, both 1909) and he published his *Experiment in Autobiography* in 1934.

Between 1924 and 1933 Wells lived in France, in voluntary exile from the English society of which he was so critical. In 1933, Wells published a novel, *The Shape of Things to Come*, on which he based a movie script. Alexander Korda filmed an adaptation of the script, *Things To Come*, in 1935; the film shows some optimism about humanity's long-term prospects. However, Wells was by now ill and aging and, with the outbreak of World War II, he lost all hope in the future. Thus, *Mind at the End of its Tether* (1945) is a bleak vision of a world "completely bankrupt," having used up all its natural resources and in which most humans would perish. It was his last prediction of extinction and sounded some of the same themes on the long-term prospects of the human species as had his writings from the 1890s.

Huxley's Interpretation of Darwinism

T.H. Huxley was born on May 4 1825. Like H.G. Wells he was from a humble background and was largely self-taught. He was apprenticed to a doctor who worked in the slums of London and was shocked by the conditions in which the patients lived. He then studied physiology and organic chemistry while on scholarship at Charing Cross Hospital, where he discovered a new human membrane, now named after him.

In 1851 he was elected a Fellow of the Royal Society of London for the scientific researches he had carried out while an assistant surgeon on a navy ship. Huxley felt thwarted by the patronage system that dominated science, and advocated that it become a profession with decent salaries for its practitioners. He himself finally received a salary when he was appointed to a teaching post at the Government School of Mines in London.

Huxley met Darwin in 1856 and was convinced that the theory of evolution on which Darwin was working was correct. He became known popularly as "Darwin's bulldog" for the often pugnacious way in which he attacked Darwin's opponents and championed evolution. He argued, after Darwin, that humans and apes had a common ancestor, and he cited the newly discovered Neanderthal hominid as an example of evolution in *Evidence as to Man's Place in Nature* (1863). In 1867–68 he showed that birds were descended from dinosaurs.

Huxley argued for, and helped bring about, the amalgamation of the Government School of Mines with the Royal College of Chemistry. This new entity was called the Normal School of Science and was moved to South Kensington. There, Huxley taught the new generation of science teachers appointed as part of England's effort to compete with other industrialized European nations. When Wells entered the Normal School, Huxley was at the end of his long career as a teacher and as an advocate of science, and Wells took the last course that Huxley offered. Huxley was perhaps the best known scientist of his day and his talks were routinely filled to overcrowding, while his writings were widely distributed.

Huxley's thought was congenial to Wells in a number of areas. Huxley's social Darwinism reinforced Wells's often pessimistic view of the possibilities of human progress and cooperation. Huxley felt that nature was largely indifferent to human concerns, rather than a benevolent and guiding force. His image of nature was closer to Tennyson's nightmare vision of a nature "red in tooth and claw" than to Wordsworth's guiding spirit. Huxley coined the word "agnostic" in 1869 to describe an attitude toward nature that asserted that there may or may not be a guiding force behind natural phenomena, and that the matter cannot be determined on a scientific basis. This approach accorded with Wells's own growing rejection of religion and his belief that human progress was neither natural nor inevitable. Finally, Huxley's faith in scientific inquiry accorded with Wells's own belief in the efficacy of science as a way of understanding the world.

Context: Invasion Narratives

H.G. Wells's text was published in the context of many other fictional invasion narratives. Wells's innovation was to use Martians instead of humans as the invading force, but the path the Martians follow in attacking and destroying London is the same as that of many other fictional armies in this period. In these other invasion narratives, France and Germany, either alone or in concert, are the primary villains. Britain was in industrial and colonial competition with these countries, and the invasion narratives expressed the anxiety that this competition would become outright war. Some invasion narratives, such as *The Great War of 189-: A Forecast* (1893), which was written by a consortium of military and naval experts, quite accurately prefigured World War I. A text like *The Great War of 189-: A Forecast* shows the close connection between science fiction, military developments and foreign policy.

The first widely popular invasion narrative was George Chesney's *The Battle of Dorking* (1871). It became a best seller and set the pattern for many subsequent invasion narratives. Chesney wrote as if he were a participant in the struggle against a German invasion force that succeeded in defeating the British army on the battlefield and turning the country into a German subsidiary. Using place names familiar to the English, like the town of Dorking in the county of Surrey, Chesney wanted to dramatize what he saw as the decline of the British armed forces and to scare people into supporting increased military spending. In this he was successful. The book spawned numerous imitators, including the anonymous *The Siege of London* (1871), which was a rebuttal to *The Battle of Dorking*, showing how the brave British forces had in fact defeated the German forces and saved London from destruction.

Invasion narratives enjoyed a resurgence of popularity after a hiatus during the 1880s. Whereas Chesney's story did not discuss military technology, focusing on the horror of the idea of invasion, many of the texts serialized in magazines in the 1890s and published as novels did focus on new developments in military firepower. One of the most successful, William Laird Clowes's *The Captain of the Mary Rose* (1892), was a story of an advanced battleship funded and captained by a wealthy ex-navy man who wanted to update the Royal Navy. Other texts, such as James Eastwick's *The New Centurion: A Tale of Automatic War* (1895), were extremely detailed, and were intended to extrapolate existing military technology, in this case a ship's guns, into the near future. George Griffith's *The Angel of the Revolution* (1895) extended military technology into the air and became a best seller both in its serial and novel forms.

Other invasion narratives such as *The Great War of 189-* (1893) and *How John Bull Lost London* (1882) invariably have as their climax the destruction of London. Since London was the capital city of Britain and the Empire, as well as the center of trade, government and culture, its destruction was seen as the ultimate calamity. Wells follows this pattern also in having the Martians, after they have destroyed Woking and surrounding villages, marching on and occupying London.

Wells's text is closest to these precursor narratives in his use of local places familiar to an English audience and in his portrayal of the destruction of London. Like Chesney, he makes the account a first-person narrative by a survivor of the conflict. Wells's text clearly emerges from the same set of invasion anxieties as expressed in these tales. Wells's text, however, makes the invasion a threat to the human species as a whole. Although the Martians attack England, Wells is implying that all of humanity is under threat. Wells also takes the technological issues much further into the future by giving the Martians military technology completely unknown to the Victorians. His text is also much better written than most of the narratives cited here. His story raises troubling questions about imperialism, technology and violence, and is not aimed solely at sensation and adventure.

Context: Mars in 1898

In 1877, Mars made one of its closest approaches to earth at a time when a new generation of reflector telescopes was aimed at the skies. These telescopes, building upon the first reflector telescope built by Sir William Herschel in the late eighteenth century, were able for the first time to examine features on Mars. Mars is a comparatively small planet and earlier telescopes had not been able to discern much detail. The planet's proximity and the new generation of telescopes aimed at it meant that features were now visible that had never been seen before. The theory of "canals" on Mars dates from this conjunction of the approach of Mars and the new telescopes of the 1870s.

Italian astronomer Giovanni Schiaparelli (1835-1910) in 1877 claimed that he had observed "canali" on the surface of Mars. In Italian this could mean simply "channels," but the word was reported in the English press as "canals," implying the existence of a civilization similar to that of humans. Schiaparelli himself became obsessed with Mars, producing elaborate maps of the features he claimed to be able to discern. He was not alone in this obsession and was joined by, among others, the American astronomer Percival Lowell.

Percival Lowell (1855-1916) was a respected member of the

eminent Lowell family of Massachusetts. Lowell used his personal fortune to construct a telescope, specifically for observations of Mars, in Flagstaff, Arizona. He also published books advocating his theory that the surface of Mars showed signs of intelligent life. From 1894 on, he argued that the "canals" on Mars were built by inhabitants of the dying planet to transport water from the polar caps to irrigate their crops. He interpreted changes in the colour of the Mars surface as signs of vegetation growing and then dying when it was irrigated by these "canals." Like many astronomers, Lowell thought that Mars was an older planet than the Earth, and that it would, therefore, be home to a more advanced civilization.

H.G. Wells joined the speculation on the possibility of intelligent life on Mars with his "Intelligence on Mars" article (1896) (see Appendix B). Wells the sober scientist and zoologist concluded that it was highly unlikely that anything like human intelligence would be found on the planet. Wells the novelist, however, joined Schiaparelli and Lowell in imagining life on Mars and making it more advanced than human culture.

Context: Roentgen Rays

Wilhelm Conrad Roentgen (1845-1923) discovered what we now call X-rays and what were in Wells's time often referred to as "Roentgen Rays." In 1895, while experimenting with electric current flow in tubes containing a partial vacuum, Roentgen noticed that a nearby screen gave off light when the tube was in operation. He theorized that some unknown radiation was being formed that traveled across the room, struck the chemical on the screen, and caused the glow. Further investigation revealed that paper, wood, and aluminum, among other materials, were transparent to this new form of radiation. He also found that it affected photographic plates and that he could take photographs of people's bones. Roentgen thought these rays were different from light, but was uncertain as to their true nature, so he called them "X-radiation." For this reason we now refer to this kind of light as "X-rays." He took the first X-ray photographs of the interiors of metal objects (including his gun) and of the bones in his wife's hand.

News of Roentgen's discovery was broadcast across Europe in 1896. On January 7, the *London Standard* reported that Roentgen had "discovered a light which for the purpose of photography will penetrate wood, flesh, cloth, and most other organic substances." The medical possibilities of X-rays were immediately apparent, since they allowed doctors to see inside the human body. Roentgen's most famous X-ray photograph is the one showing the bones in his wife's hand. However, during the next decade it became obvious that X-rays caused injury to various human tissue and to vision. This new form of ray had the potential to kill its human users. Early speculation about X-rays and their possible military uses may well have been on Wells's mind when he gave the Martians a "heat ray" with which to decimate the English military.

Context: The Victorian Military

The Victorian army would strike a contemporary observer as an odd mixture of the archaic and modern. It was undergoing a modernization of its weapons and procedures in the late nineteenth century, but it also looked back to the "glory days" of the Napoleonic era in its customs and dress. The narrator comes across men from the 8th Hussars, a cavalry regiment that would still have had splendid uniforms and a high status in the army (see Appendix I). The days of the cavalry were numbered, but it was still an important part of the military. Indeed, horses in general remained a crucial means of transportation in those places where the railway could not be used. The primary weapon used against the Martians is horse-drawn "field artillery" that was light enough to be pulled by a team of horses and deployed rapidly across most terrain. Heavier guns, such as the "wire guns" used to defend London, had to be carried by train and took longer to deploy.

The most important piece of military technology in *The War of the Worlds* is artillery. The artillery dominates the military defenses described by Wells, and the soldier he meets is a member of an artillery unit. Artillery was undergoing continual improvement in the late Victorian period. "Wire guns" were a new breed of weapons which, thanks to the wire spiraled in their barrels, could send shells higher and longer than conventional artillery. The Victorian military was continually testing new and more powerful guns and sending shells higher, faster and longer, resulting in various technological breakthroughs. Appendix I includes a photograph of such a test in which shells were fired up to a mile high. The Martians themselves use artillery in that their spacecraft seem to be "shells" fired from huge guns on Mars that produce clouds of smoke and eventually obscure the Martian atmosphere. Rather than rockets, it is artillery that dominates images of space travel in the narrative, as it does in Jules Verne's stories earlier in the century.

The Royal Navy was also updating its fleet, if only sporadically. After the success of the first armour-plated vessels, known as "dreadnoughts," in the American Civil War (1861–1865), the British fleet began fitting all ships with protective plates. All such ships were driven by steam, then increasingly by the new fuel, oil. Torpedo boats were introduced and experiments were conducted with submarines. The guns on these ships, like the artillery deployed by the army, were bigger and had longer ranges as the Victorian period progressed. Indeed, the Navy often had the most powerful guns in the military, and these were sometimes taken off the ships and used on land during sieges, as they were in the Boer War (1899–1902; see Appendix I) for example.

Some aspects of the Royal Navy still seemed archaic. Many ships still had masts and sails alongside their engines. Wells describes the "Thunder Child" as a "ram." Ships from the time of the Greeks had often had a "ram prow," a sharp projection extending out from the ship's bow that could be used to ram an opponent. This was a weapon of last resort, as it could mean the end of both ships. These ram prows were being phased out as the fleet modernized, but Wells gives the "Thunder Child" a ram prow with which to destroy a Martian in a heroic and suicidal last charge.

The army too was modernizing. Wells describes the Maxim gun, an early form of machine gun. However, the army had not embraced more modern forms of communication, and in *The War of the Worlds* still uses the semaphore to flash signals between units. Wells does not, unfortunately, seem aware that the army was experimenting with bicycles as a form of military transportation and was forming special bicycle units. Both the narrator and the artillery man walk to most places, although the narrator's brother does ride a bicycle briefly. Despite his love of bicycles, Wells did not give them a prominent place in his story.

The attention to detail in terms of military technology in *The War of the Worlds* shows Wells's fascination with war and armament. Later in his life Wells played war games with his sons using toy soldiers and artillery pieces that fired little dummy shells. He published a small book on the rules and tactics of such war games in *Little Wars* in 1913. Although Wells was philosophically opposed to war and destruction, he was also fascinated by the military and its technology.

Literary Criticism and H.G. Wells

Criticism of H.G. Wells is confined mainly to two forms: literary biography that examines his works in relation to his life and analysis of his early "scientific romances" as precursors to contemporary science fiction. There are a number of excellent literary biographies that place Wells's texts in the context of his intellectual development, such as Norman and Jeanne Mackenzie's *H.G. Wells: A Biography* (1973), David C. Smith's *H.G. Wells: Desperately Mortal* (1986), and Michael Foot's *H.G.: The History of Mr. Wells* (1995). Some biographies focus on a particular aspect of Wells's life, such as J.R. Hammond's *H.G. Wells and Rebecca West* (1991). For many years Wells was thought interesting because of his life—which included his many extramarital affairs—rather than for his writing. (For Well's own assessment of his life, see his *Experiment in Autobiography*, 1934.)

In the realm of science fiction, however, Wells has always been regarded, along with Jules Verne, as one of the pioneers of the genre. A good example of this kind of analysis is Bernard Bergonzi's *The Early H.G. Wells* (1961), which as its title suggests, deals with earlier science fiction stories rather than his later social critiques. In the 1980s, as science fiction became more widely studied, critical analyses of Wells proliferated. These included Frank McConnell's *The Science Fiction of H.G. Wells* (1981), John Huntington's *The Logic of Fantasy: H.G. Wells and Science Fiction* (1982), and Robert Crossley's *H.G. Wells* (1986). Darko Suvin's *Victorian Science Fiction* (1983) examines Wells in the context of the creation of science fiction as a genre in the Victorian period.

There are some notable book-length treatments of H.G. Wells's works that include sections on *The War of the Worlds*. Peter Kemp's *H.G. Wells and the Culminating Ape: Biological Imperatives and Imaginative Obsessions* (1996), while it is interested in patterns in all of Wells's fiction, has an excellent section that shows how Wells uses reminders of the Victorians' closeness to the animal world to undermine their sense of dominance. Kemp points out that Wells compares humans to "infusoria, monkeys, lemurs, sheep, dodos, cows, ants, frogs, bees, wasps, rabbits, rats, and oxen" in the narrative (23). Kemp also points out that the Martians, since they are more evolved than humans, don't eat but inject themselves with blood. Kemp examines Wells's attitudes toward food, sex, habitats, and individuality in some excellent discussions of these themes in his science fiction.

Patrick Parrinder, as well as editing Wells's literary criticism (*H.G. Wells's Literary Criticism*, 1980, co-edited with Robert M. Philmus) and the critical response to Wells (*H.G. Wells: The Critical Heritage*, 1972), has written a book-length study of his science fiction, *Shadows of the Future: H.G. Wells, Science Fiction and Prophecy* (1995). Parrinder examines Wells as a prophet who successfully foretold social changes over a hundred years ahead of his time. While Parrinder focuses primarily on *The Time Machine*, he makes astute observations on *The War of the Worlds*. Parrinder notes that the story is one of "colonization in reverse," as the Martians visit upon England the same treatment as the Victorians visited on the inhabitants of Tasmania (75).

After the success of his early "scientific romances," Wells went on to write social critiques of the class system and sexual repression in England, and prophesies of the future of social organization. These are not nearly as popular as his early science fiction and have not had the same kind of impact as a text like *The War of the Worlds*. Thus, while Wells is famous as the author of *The Time Machine* and *The War of the Worlds*, he has not been given the iconic status of some of his contemporaries. If Wells had produced a larger corpus of science fiction stories, then his reputation may well have been much greater; however, after World War I he wrote more non-fiction than science fiction. It is a shame that this later writing does not command so much attention, because Wells was, and still is, a unique writer in the way in which he combines science, imagination and social critique. So successful was Wells in combining non-fiction and prophecies of the future (rather than embodying them in a fictional narrative like *The Time Machine* or *The War of the Worlds*) that he became known as "The Man Who Invented Tomorrow."

The War of the Worlds continues to influence readers beyond its Victorian context, touching upon peoples' fears of invasion, the unknown, and of powerful military technology. A dramatic example of this came on October 30, 1938, when Orson Welles adapted *The War of the Worlds* for a performance on the radio by his Mercury Theater of the Air. Welles had the aliens land in Grover's Mill, N.J., and used names from New Jersey and New York that would be familiar to people on the East coast of the United States. He simulated news broadcasts and interviews with real people, as if the events were unfolding with dramatic speed that very night.

Welles carefully announced at the beginning and throughout the production that it was a performance; nonetheless, the show created widespread panic on the East coast because many people believed Welles's imitation of news broadcasts and eyewitness accounts were real. The broadcast is now cited as a textbook example of how the media can be used to manipulate an audience and create hysteria. It is also a testament, however, to the power of H.G. Wells's imagination that he could conceive of a story in 1898 that would still touch peoples' anxieties in 1938 and beyond. For more on the Orson Welles broadcast, see Brian Holmsten and Alex Lubertozzi's *The Complete War of the Worlds: Mars's Invasion from H.G. Wells to Orson Welles* (2001).

The critiques that H.G. Wells leveled at the Victorian English could very easily be leveled at many contemporary societies, because an exaggerated faith in technology and the inevitability of human progress continue to hold sway in popular belief. Wells asked his Victorian audience if the Martians could be criticized for carrying out an invasion when the Tasmanians had suffered a similar fate at the hands of the British military; he would probably pose the same question to the leaders of many present-day countries. *The War of the Worlds*, as the first story to speculate about the effects of aliens with superior technology landing on the earth, informs all subsequent invasion narratives, as the movies *Independence Day* (1996) and *Mars Attacks!* (1996) showed in very different ways. *The War of the Worlds* will undoubtedly continue to exert its influence over science fiction and perceptions of extraterrestrial life well into the future. H.G. Wells continues to be "The Man Who Invented Tomorrow."

H. G. Wells: A Brief Chronology

1866   On September 21 Herbert George Wells born at 47 High
       Street, Bromley, Kent, youngest son of Joseph and Sarah
       Wells.
1871   Attends dame school in Bromley.
1874   Breaks leg and is confined to bed for several weeks.
       In September enters Morley's Academy.
1877   Father breaks leg in accident and financial distress ensues.
1880   Works as draper's assistant at Rodgers and Denyers for one
       month. For three months helps his "Uncle" Williams with
       school in Wookey, Somerset.
1881   One month as chemist's assistant in Midhurst. From
       February to April is a full-time pupil at Midhurst Grammar
       School. In May sent to Hyde's Drapery Emporium,
       Southsea.
1883   Leaves drapery business at end of July. Begins employment
       as a pupil-teacher at Midhurst Grammar School.
1884   In September commences as full-time student at Normal
       School of Science, South Kensington.
1885   Attends lectures by T.H. Huxley. In May meets Isabel Mary
       Wells.
1887   Fails Geology and loses scholarship. In July takes position as
       schoolmaster at Holt Academy, North Wales. In August is
       injured playing football. In November resigns from school
       and travels to Up Park.
1888   In January begins work on "The Chronic Argonauts."
1889   Begins job as assistant schoolmaster at Henley House
       School, London.
1890   In November awarded B.Sc. with first class honours in
       Zoology by London University. Hired by University Tutorial
       College.
1891   Article "Rediscovery of the Unique" published by *Fortnight-
       ly Review* and "Zoological Retrogression" by *Gentleman's
       Magazine*. In October marries Isabel.
1892   In December meets Amy Catherine Robbins for first
       time.
1893   Resigns from teaching because of health concerns. In July
       Text-Book of Biology published. Article "On Extinction" pub-
       lished in *Chamber's Journal*. In November "Man of the Year
       Million" published in *Pall Mall Gazette*.

1894   Moves in with Amy Catherine Robbins (henceforth
        "Jane"). In March *The Time Machine* begins serial publica-
        tion in *National Observer*. In June "The Stolen Bacillus" pub-
        lished in *Pall Mall Budget*. In September "The Extinction of
        Man" published in *Pall Mall Gazette*.

1895   In January divorces Isabel. "The Flying Man" published in
        Pall Mall Gazette. "The Limits of Individual Plasticity" pub-
        lished in *Saturday Review*. In May moves to Woking with
        Jane. *The Time Machine* published as book by Heinemann. In
        November the collection *The Stolen Bacillus* published. In
        December "The Argonauts of the Air" published in *Phil
        May's Annual*.

1896   In January marries Jane. Moves to Worcester Park. In April
        publication of *The Island of Doctor Moreau* and "Intelligence
        on Mars" in *Saturday Review*.

1897   In April "Human Evolution" published in *Natural Science*.
        May publication of *The Plattner Story, and Others*. September
        publication of *The Invisible Man*. Publication of *Certain Per-
        sonal Matters*. In October sends nearly complete manuscript
        of *War of the Worlds* to Heinemann.

1898   In January publication of *The War of the Worlds*.

1899   *When the Sleeper Wakes* published. Publication of *Tales of
        Space and Time*. *Love and Mr. Lewisham* serialized in *Weekly
        Times*.

1900   *Love and Mr. Lewisham* published. In December moves into
        Spade House, Sandgate.

1901   *Anticipations* and *The First Men in the Moon* published. Son
        George Philip Wells born.

1903   Son Frank Richard Wells born. Joins Fabian Society.

1904   Publication of *The Food of the Gods*.

1905   Publication of *A Modern Utopia*. Publication of *Kipps*.
        Death of mother Sarah Wells.

1906   Publication of *In the Days of the Comet*. Conflict with
        Bernard Shaw and Beatrice Webb over the Fabian
        Society.

1908   Resigns from Fabian Society. Publication of *The War in the
        Air*. In June begins relationship with Amber Reeves

1909   Daughter Anna Jane Blanco-White born to Amber Reeves.
        Publication of *Tono-Bungay* and *Ann Veronica*.

1910   Death of father Joseph Wells. Begins affair with Elizabeth
        von Arnim.

1911   Publication of *The New Machiavelli*.

1913   Begins relationship with Rebecca West.

1914   Outbreak of First World War. Publication of *The World Set Free* and *The War to End All Wars*.

1916   Publication of *Mr. Britling Sees it Through* and *What is Coming?*

1917   Publication of *War and the Future*.

1920   Publication of *Outline of History*. Meets Lenin and Trotsky in Russia.

1921   Travels to USA to attend Washington Disarmament Conference.

1922   Publication of *A Short History of the World*. Runs unsuccessfully for seat in Parliament.

1923   Publication of *Men Like Gods*.

1924   Publication of Atlantic Edition of *The Works of H. G. Wells*.

1927   Jane (Amy Catherine Wells) dies.

1928   Publication of *The Way the World is Going*.

1931   Publication of *What Are We to do with Our Lives?* Isabel Mary Wells dies.

1932   Publication of *The Work, Wealth and Happiness of Mankind*.

1933   Publication of *The Shape of Things to Come*.

1934   Publication of *An Experiment in Autobiography*. In May invited to meet President Roosevelt. Travels to USA. In July travels to Moscow and meets Josef Stalin.

1935   In November travels to Hollywood to work on *Things to Come* film.

1936   In February *Things to Come* opens in London. Publication of *The Man Who Could Work Miracles*.

1938   In October Orson Welles radio adaptation of *War of the Worlds* causes panic in USA. Publication of *World Brain*.

1939   Publication of *The Fate of Homo Sapiens*. In September Germany invades Poland, beginning of World War II.

1942   Publication of *The Outlook for Homo Sapiens* and *The Conquest of Time*.

1940   Publication of *The Rights of Man* and *The Commonsense of War and Peace*.

1945   In May end of War in Europe. On August 6 atomic bomb dropped on Hiroshima, on August 9 on Nagasaki. On August 14 World War II ends. Publication of *Mind at the End of its Tether*.

1946   On August 13 death of Herbert George Wells.

A Note on the Text

The War of the Worlds was first serialized in *Pearson's Magazine* from April–December 1897. This early version did not include the chapter entitled "The Man on Putney Hill" or the Epilogue. When it was published in London by William Heinemann in 1898 the text included this chapter and the Epilogue, and this is the text on which this edition is based. The version of *The War of the Worlds* published simultaneously in New York lacked the Epilogue and reflected the spelling conventions of the USA rather than England. Wells carried out minor editing and made small changes for the 1924 Atlantic Edition (Volume III), which is the text used most often for new editions of the story. However, the Atlantic Edition reflects the punctuation of the 1920s, and dispenses with many commas and the capitalizations (such as Red Weed and Fighting Machine) of the 1898 edition. In order to give the reader a sense of the conventions of Victorian prose, the London 1898 edition is used as the basis for this reprint.

The
War of the Worlds

By
H. G. Wells

Author of ' The Time Machine,' ' The Island of Doctor Moreau,'
' The Invisible Man,' etc.

' But who shall dwell in these Worlds if they be inhabited?
. . . Are we or they Lords of the World? . . . And
how are all things made for man?'
KEPLER (quoted in *The Anatomy of Melancholy*) [1]

London
William Heinemann
1898

---

1 The epigraph on the title page, "But who shall dwell...." is a quotation
from Robert Burton's *The Anatomy of Melancholy* (1621). Burton is himself
quoting from a letter by the astronomer Johannes Kepler (1571-1630)
who corresponded with Galileo after reading about his discoveries with
early telescopes. Wells edits Kepler's words to Galileo into a series of dis-
quieting questions prompted by the realization that humans may not be
the center of the universe, and that other forms of life may exist beyond
our own planet.

TO

MY BROTHER

FRANK WELLS,

THIS RENDERING OF HIS IDEA.

BOOK I
THE COMING OF THE MARTIANS

CHAPTER I.
THE EVE OF THE WAR

No one would have believed in the last years of the nineteenth century, that human affairs were being watched keenly and closely by intelligences greater than man's and yet as mortal as his own; that as men busied themselves about their affairs they were scrutinized and studied, perhaps almost as narrowly as a man with a microscope might scrutinize the transient creatures that swarm and multiply in a drop of water.[1] With infinite complacency men went to and fro over this globe about their little affairs, serene in their assurance of their empire over matter. It is possible that the infusoria[2] under the microscope do the same. No one gave a thought to the older worlds of space as sources of human danger, or thought of them only to dismiss the idea of life upon them as impossible or improbable.[3] It is curious to recall some of the mental habits of those departed days. At most, terrestrial men fancied there might be other men upon Mars, perhaps inferior to themselves and ready to welcome a missionary enterprise. Yet across the gulf of space, minds that are to our minds as ours are to those of the beasts that perish, intellects vast and cool and unsympathetic, regarded this earth with envious eyes, and slowly and surely drew their plans against us. And early in the twentieth century came the great disillusionment.

The planet Mars, I scarcely need remind the reader, revolves about the sun at a mean distance of 140,000,000 miles, and the light and heat it receives from the sun is barely half of that received by this world. It must be, if the nebular hypothesis[4] has any truth, older than our world and long before this earth ceased to be molten, life upon its surface must have begun its course. The fact

---

1   Wells was keenly interested in the development of the microscope, even visiting a microscope factory for his article "Through a Microscope" (see Appendix B).

2   Minute organisms, protozoa.

3   Wells is thinking here of the debate over the possibility of intelligent life on Mars; see his article "Intelligence on Mars," in Appendix B, and Percival Lowell's *Mars*, in Appendix G.

4   The idea that the solar system has evolved from hot gaseous matter.

that it is scarcely one-seventh of the volume of the earth must have accelerated its cooling to the temperature at which life could begin. It has air and water, and all that is necessary for the support of animated existence.

Yet so vain is man, and so blinded by his vanity, that no writer, up to the very end of the nineteenth century, expressed any idea that intelligent life might have developed there far, or indeed at all, beyond its earthly level. Nor was it generally understood that since Mars is older than our earth, with scarcely a quarter of the superficial area, and remoter from the sun, it necessarily follows that it is not only more distant from life's beginning but nearer its end.

The secular cooling that must someday overtake our planet has already gone far indeed with our neighbour. Its physical condition is still largely a mystery, but we know now that even in its equatorial region the midday temperature barely approaches that of our coldest winter. Its air is much more attenuated[1] than ours, its oceans have shrunk until they cover but a third of its surface, and as its slow seasons change huge snowcaps gather and melt about either pole and periodically inundate its temperate zones.[2] That last stage of exhaustion, which to us is still incredibly remote, has become a present-day problem for the inhabitants of Mars. The immediate pressure of necessity has brightened their intellects, enlarged their powers, and hardened their hearts. And looking across space, with instruments and intelligences such as we have scarcely dreamt of, they see, at its nearest distance only 35,000,000 of miles sunward of them, a morning star of hope, our own warmer planet, green with vegetation and gray with water, with a cloudy atmosphere eloquent of fertility, with glimpses through its drifting cloud-wisps of broad stretches of populous country and narrow navy-crowded seas.

And we men, the creatures who inhabit this earth, must be to them at least as alien and lowly as are the monkeys and lemurs to us. The intellectual side of man already admits that life is an incessant struggle for existence,[3] and it would seem that this too is the belief of the minds upon Mars. Their world is far gone in its cooling and this world is still crowded with life, but crowded only with

---

1 Less dense, thinner.
2 This is the theory of "melting icecaps" put forward by Lowell in *Mars*; see Appendix G.
3 This phrase derives directly from the evolutionary theories of Darwin and Huxley.

what they regard as inferior animals. To carry warfare sunwar indeed, their only escape from the destruction that generation generation creeps upon them.

And before we judge of them too harshly we must remember what ruthless and utter destruction our own species has wrought, not only upon animals, such as the vanished bison and the dodo,[1] but upon its own inferior races. The Tasmanians, in spite of their human likeness, were entirely swept out of existence in a war of extermination waged by European immigrants, in the space of fifty years.[2] Are we such apostles of mercy as to complain if the Martians warred in the same spirit?

The Martians seem to have calculated their descent with amazing subtlety—their mathematical learning is evidently far in excess of ours—and to have carried out their preparations with a wellnigh perfect unanimity. Had our instruments permitted it, we might have seen the gathering trouble far back in the nineteenth century. Men like Schiaparelli[3] watched the red planet—it is odd, by-the-by, that for countless centuries Mars has been the star of war—but failed to interpret the fluctuating appearances of the markings they mapped so well. All that time the Martians must have been getting ready.

During the opposition of 1894[4] a great light was seen on the illuminated part of the disk, first at the Lick Observatory, then by Perrotin of Nice, and then by other observers. English readers heard of it first in the issue of *Nature* dated August 2d. I am inclined

---

1 The North American bison was on the verge of extinction. The dodo was a large, flightless bird made extinct by English hunters.

2 An island south of Australia whose inhabitants were driven off their lands by English colonists. The island was turned into a prison colony. T.H. Huxley has Tasmania on his mind also when he describes an English garden on the island as a colony in "Evolution and Ethics," in Appendix E.

3 Giovanni Schiaparelli (1835-1910) Italian astronomer who claimed to have observed "canals" on Mars and who helped launch the fascination with the red planet.

4 A year during which Mars and the Earth approach each other most closely, with the Earth between Mars and the sun. The previous closest approach was in 1877 when Schiaparelli made his first observations. The Lick observatory was on Mount Hamilton, California and Henri Joseph Perrotin (1845-1904) was a French astronomer based in Nice, France.

to think that the appearance may have been the casting of the huge gun,[1] the vast pit sunk into their planet, from which their shots were fired at us. Peculiar markings, as yet unexplained, were seen near the site of that outbreak during the next two oppositions.

The storm burst upon us six years ago now. As Mars approached opposition, Lavelle of Java[2] set the wires of the astronomical exchange palpitating with the amazing intelligence of a huge outbreak of incandescent gas upon the planet. It had occurred towards midnight of the 12th, and the spectroscope,[3] to which he had at once resorted, indicated a mass of flaming gas, chiefly hydrogen, moving with an enormous velocity towards this earth. This jet of fire had become invisible about a quarter past twelve. He compared it to a colossal puff of flame suddenly and violently squirted out of the planet, "as flaming gas rushes out of a gun."

A singularly appropriate phrase it proved. Yet the next day there was nothing of this in the papers, except a little note in the *Daily Telegraph*, and the world went in ignorance of one of the gravest dangers that ever threatened the human race. I might not have heard of the eruption at all had I not met Ogilvy, the well-known astronomer, at Ottershaw.[4] He was immensely excited at the news, and in the excess of his feelings invited me up to take a turn with him that night in a scrutiny of the red planet.

In spite of all that has happened since, I still remember that vigil very distinctly: the black and silent observatory, the shadowed lantern throwing a feeble glow upon the floor in the corner, the steady ticking of the clockwork of the telescope, the little slit in the roof—an oblong profundity with the star-dust streaked across it.[5]

---

1 Wells imagines that the Martians were propelled toward the earth from a huge cannon, much like the artillery shown in Appendix I.

2 A fictional character based on the real M. Javelle (not Lavelle) mentioned in Wells's "Intelligence on Mars" in Appendix B. Java is an Indonesian island.

3 An optical instrument for forming and examining spectra (as that of solar light, or those produced by flames), so as to determine the composition of the substance.

4 Ogilvy is another fictitious astronomer; Ottershaw is a real village not far from Woking.

5 The clock governed a mechanism that automatically kept the telescope aligned with the stars as they moved across the sky. This mysterious atmosphere in an observatory is also used by Wells in his short story "In the Avu Observatory."

Ogilvy moved about, invisible but audible. Looking through the telescope, one saw a circle of deep blue and the little round planet swimming in the field. It seemed such a little thing, so bright and small and still, faintly marked with transverse stripes, and slightly flattened from the perfect round. But so little it was, so silvery warm—a pin's head of light! It was as if it quivered a little, but really this was the telescope vibrating with the activity of the clockwork that kept the planet in view.

As I watched the planet seemed to grow larger and smaller, and to advance and recede, but that was simply that my eye was tired. Forty millions of miles it was from us—more than 40,000,000 of miles of void. Few people realize the immensity of vacancy in which the dust of the material universe swims.

Near it in the field, I remember, were three little points of light, three telescopic stars infinitely remote, and all around it was the unfathomable darkness of empty space. You know how that blackness looks on a frosty starlight night. In a telescope it seems far profounder. And invisible to me, because it was so remote and small, flying swiftly and steadily towards me across that incredible distance, drawing nearer every minute by so many thousands of miles, came the Thing they were sending us, the Thing that was to bring so much struggle and calamity and death to the earth. I never dreamt of it then as I watched; no one on earth dreamt of that unerring missile.

That night, too, there was another jetting out of gas from the distant planet. I saw it. A reddish flash at the edge, the slightest projection of the outline just as the chronometer struck midnight, and at that I told Ogilvy, and he took my place. The night was warm and I was thirsty, and I went, stretching my legs clumsily, and feeling my way in the darkness, to the little table where the siphon stood, while Ogilvy exclaimed at the streamer of gas that came out towards us.

That night another invisible missile started on its way to the earth from Mars, just a second or so under twenty-four hours after the first one. I remember how I sat on the table there in the blackness, with patches of green and crimson swimming before my eyes. I wished I had a light to smoke by, little suspecting the meaning of the minute gleam I had seen, and all that it would presently bring me. Ogilvy watched till one, and then gave it up, and we lit the lantern and walked over to his house. Down below in the darkness were Ottershaw and Chertsey,[1] and all their hundreds of people, sleeping in peace.

---

1 The village of Chertsy is described in the extract from *Black's Guide to Surrey*, in Appendix H.

He was full of speculation that night about the condition of Mars, and scoffed at the vulgar idea of its having inhabitants who were signalling us. His idea was that meteorites might be falling in a heavy shower upon the planet, or that a huge volcanic explosion was in progress. He pointed out to me how unlikely it was that organic evolution had taken the same direction in the two adjacent planets.

"The chances against anything man-like on Mars are a million to one," he said.

Hundreds of observers saw the flame that night and the night after about midnight, and again the night after, and so for ten nights, a flame each night. Why the shots ceased after the tenth no one on earth has attempted to explain. It may be the gases of the firing caused the Martians inconvenience. Dense clouds of smoke or dust, visible through a powerful telescope on earth as little gray, fluctuating patches, spread through the clearness of the planet's atmosphere and obscured its more familiar features.

Even the daily papers woke up to the disturbances at last, and popular notes appeared here, there, and everywhere concerning the volcanoes upon Mars. The serio-comic periodical *Punch*,[1] I remember, made a happy use of it in the political cartoon. And, all unsuspected, those missiles the Martians had fired at us drew earthward, rushing now at a pace of many miles a second through the empty gulf of space, hour by hour and day by day, nearer and nearer. It seems to me now almost incredibly wonderful that, with that swift fate hanging over us, men could go about their petty concerns as they did. I remember how jubilant Markham was at securing a new photograph of the planet for the illustrated paper he edited in those days. People in these latter times scarcely realize the abundance and enterprise of our nineteenth-century papers.[2] For my own part, I was much occupied in learning to ride the bicycle, and busy upon a series of papers discussing the probable developments of moral ideas as civilization progressed.[3]

---

1 This Victorian periodical carried a mixture of serious news, parodies and cartoons.
2 The late nineteenth century saw an explosion of new newspapers and magazines, as Wells knew because he was a contributor to several of them.
3 Wells himself was an enthusiastic cyclist and his *Wheels of Chance* (1896) is about cyclists; the article upon which the narrator is working sounds very much like a Wells piece.

One night (the first missile then could scarcely have been 10,000,000 miles away) I went for a walk with my wife. It was starlight, and I explained the Signs of the Zodiac to her, and pointed out Mars, a bright dot of light creeping zenithward, towards which so many telescopes were pointed. It was a warm night. Coming home, a party of excursionists from Chertsey or Isleworth passed us singing and playing music. There were lights in the upper windows of the houses as the people went to bed. From the railway-station in the distance[1] came the sound of shunting trains, ringing and rumbling, softened almost into melody by the distance. My wife pointed out to me the brightness of the red, green, and yellow signal lights, hanging in a framework against the sky. It seemed so safe and tranquil.

II.
THE FALLING STAR

Then came the night of the first falling star. It was seen early in the morning, rushing over Winchester eastward, a line of flame high in the atmosphere. Hundreds must have seen it, and taken it for an ordinary falling star. Albin described it as leaving a greenish streak behind it that glowed for some seconds. Denning, our greatest authority on meteorites, stated that the height of its first appearance was about ninety or one hundred miles. It seemed to him that it fell to earth about one hundred miles east of him.

I was at home at that hour and writing in my study, and although my French windows face towards Ottershaw and the blind was up (for I loved in those days to look up at the night sky), I saw nothing of it. Yet this strangest of all things that ever came to earth from outer space must have fallen while I was sitting there, visible to me had I only looked up as it passed. Some of those who saw its flight say it travelled with a hissing sound. I myself heard nothing of that. Many people in Berkshire, Surrey, and Middlesex must have seen the fall of it, and, at most, have thought that another meteorite had descended.[2] No one seems to have troubled to look for the fallen mass that night.

---

1 This railway station is described in the extract from *Black's Guide to Surrey*, in Appendix H.
2 Berkshire, Surrey, and Middlesex are contiguous English counties; much of the action in the story takes place in Surrey.

But very early in the morning poor Ogilvy, who had seen the shooting-star, and who was persuaded that a meteorite lay somewhere on the common between Horsell, Ottershaw, and Woking, rose early with the idea of finding it. Find it he did, soon after dawn, and not far from the sand-pits. An enormous hole had been made by the impact of the projectile, and the sand and gravel had been flung violently in every direction over the heath and heather, forming heaps visible a mile and a half away. The heather was on fire eastward, and a thin blue smoke rose against the dawn.

The Thing itself lay almost entirely buried in sand, amidst the scattered splinters of a fir-tree it had shivered to fragments in its descent. The uncovered part had the appearance of a huge cylinder, caked over, and its outline softened by a thick, scaly, dun-coloured incrustation. It had a diameter of about thirty yards. He approached the mass, surprised at the size and more so at the shape, since most meteorites are rounded more or less completely. It was, however, still so hot from its flight through the air as to forbid his near approach. A stirring noise within its cylinder he ascribed to the unequal cooling of its surface; for at that time it had not occurred to him that it might be hollow.

He remained standing at the edge of the pit that the thing had made for itself, staring at its strange appearance, astonished chiefly at its unusual shape and colour, and dimly perceiving even then some evidence of design in its arrival. The early morning was wonderfully still, and the sun, just clearing the pine trees towards Weybridge, was already warm. He did not remember hearing any birds that morning, there was certainly no breeze stirring, and the only sounds were the faint movements from within the cindery cylinder. He was all alone on the common.

Then suddenly he noticed with a start that some of the gray clinker,[1] the ashy incrustation that covered the meteorite, was falling off the circular edge of the end. It was dropping off in flakes and raining down upon the sand. A large piece suddenly came off and fell with a sharp noise that brought his heart into his mouth.

For a minute he scarcely realized what this meant, and, although the heat was excessive, he clambered down into the pit close to the bulk to see the Thing more clearly. He fancied even then that the cooling of the body might account for this, but what disturbed that

---

1 Ash that has formed a hard crust.

idea was the fact that the ash was falling only from the end of the cylinder.

And then he perceived that, very slowly, the circular top of the cylinder was rotating on its body. It was such a gradual movement that he discovered it only through noticing that a black mark that had been near him five minutes ago was now at the other side of the circumference. Even then he scarcely understood what this indicated, until he heard a muffled grating sound and saw the black mark jerk forward an inch or so. Then the thing came upon him in a flash. The cylinder was artificial—hollow—with an end that screwed out! Something within the cylinder was unscrewing the top!

"Good heavens!" said Ogilvy. "There's a man in it—men in it! Half roasted to death! Trying to escape!"

At once, with a quick mental leap, he linked the Thing with the flash upon Mars.

The thought of the confined creature was so dreadful to him that he forgot the heat and went forward to the cylinder to help turn. But luckily the dull radiation arrested him before he could burn his hands on the still glowing metal. At that he stood irresolute for a moment, then turned, scrambled out of the pit, and set off running wildly into Woking. The time then must have been somewhere about six o'clock. He met a waggoner and tried to make him understand, but the tale he told and his appearance were so wild—his hat had fallen off in the pit—that the man simply drove on. He was equally unsuccessful with the potman[1] who was just unlocking the doors of the public-house by Horsell Bridge. The fellow thought he was a lunatic at large and made an unsuccessful attempt to shut him into the tap-room.[2] That sobered him a little, and when he saw Henderson, the London journalist, in his garden, he called over the palings and made himself understood.

"Henderson," he called, "you saw that shooting star last night?"

"Well?" said Henderson.

"It's out on Horsell Common now."

"Good Lord!" said Henderson. "Fallen meteorite! That's good."

"But it's something more than a meteorite. It's a cylinder—an artificial cylinder, man! And there's something inside."

---

1   A bartender opening the public house (pub) for the day.
2   The pub room where beer is served "on tap."

Henderson stood up with his spade in his hand.

"What's that?" he said. He is deaf in one ear.

Ogilvy told him all that he had seen. Henderson was a minute or so taking it in. Then he dropped his spade, snatched up his jacket, and came out into the road. The two men hurried back at once to the common, and found the cylinder still lying in the same position. But now the sounds inside had ceased, and a thin circle of bright metal showed between the top and the body of the cylinder. Air was either entering or escaping at the rim with a thin, sizzling sound.

They listened, rapped on the scaly burnt metal with a stick, and, meeting with no response, they both concluded the man or men inside must be insensible or dead.

Of course the two were quite unable to do anything. They shouted consolation and promises, and went off back to the town again to get help. One can imagine them, covered with sand, excited and disordered, running up the little street in the bright sunlight, just as the shop folks were taking down their shutters and people were opening their bedroom windows. Henderson went into the railway station at once, in order to telegraph the news to London. The newspaper articles had prepared men's minds for the reception of the idea.

By eight o'clock a number of boys and unemployed men had already started for the common to see the "dead men from Mars." That was the form the story took. I heard of it first from my newspaper boy, about a quarter to nine when I went out to get my *Daily Chronicle*. I was naturally startled, and lost no time in going out and across the Ottershaw bridge to the sand-pits.

III.

ON HORSELL COMMON

I found a little crowd of perhaps twenty people surrounding the huge hole in which the cylinder lay. I have already described the appearance of that colossal bulk, embedded in the ground. The turf and gravel about it seemed charred as if by a sudden explosion. No doubt its impact had caused a flash of fire. Henderson and Ogilvy were not there. I think they perceived that nothing was to be done for the present, and had gone away to breakfast at Henderson's house.

There were four or five boys sitting on the edge of the pit, with their feet dangling, and amusing themselves—until I stopped them—by throwing stones at the giant mass. After I had spoken to them about it, they began playing at "touch" in and out of the group of bystanders.

Among these were a couple of cyclists, a jobbing gardener[1] I employed sometimes, a girl carrying a baby, Gregg the butcher and his little boy, and two or three loafers and golf caddies who were accustomed to hang about the railway station. There was very little talking. Few of the common people in England had anything but the vaguest astronomical ideas in those days. Most of them were staring quietly at the big table-like end of the cylinder, which was still as Ogilvy and Henderson had left it. I fancy the popular expectation of a heap of charred corpses was disappointed at this inanimate bulk. Some went away while I was there, and other people came. I clambered into the pit and fancied I heard a faint movement under my feet. The top had certainly ceased to rotate.

It was only when I got thus close to it that the strangeness of this object was at all evident to me. At the first glance it was really no more exciting than an overturned carriage or a tree blown across the road. Not so much so, indeed. It looked like a rusty gas-float[2] half buried more than anything else in the world. It required a certain amount of scientific education to perceive that the gray scale of the thing was no common oxide, that the yellowish-white metal that gleamed in the crack between the lid and the cylinder had an unfamiliar hue. "Extra-terrestrial" had no meaning for most of the onlookers.

At that time it was quite clear in my own mind that the Thing had come from the planet Mars, but I judged it improbable that it contained any living creature. I thought the unscrewing might be automatic. In spite of Ogilvy, I still believed that there were men in Mars. My mind ran fancifully on the possibilities of its containing manuscript, on the difficulties in translation that might arise, whether we should find coins and models in it, and so forth. Yet it was a little too large for assurance on this idea. I felt an impatience to see it opened. About eleven, as nothing seemed happening, I walked back, full of such thoughts, to my home in Maybury. But I found it difficult to get to work upon my abstract investigations.

---

1   A gardener who does occasional work for different people.
2   A hollow metallic ball or tube that floats.

In the afternoon the appearance of the common had altered very much. The early editions of the evening papers had startled London with enormous headlines:

"A MESSAGE RECEIVED FROM MARS,"
"REMARKABLE STORY FROM WOKING,"

and so forth. In addition, Ogilvy's wire to the Astronomical Exchange had roused every observatory in the three kingdoms.[1]

There were half a dozen flys[2] or more from the Woking station standing in the road by the sand-pits, a basket-chaise[3] from Chobham, and a rather lordly carriage. Besides that, there was quite a heap of bicycles. In addition, a large number of people must have walked, in spite of the heat of the day, from Woking and Chertsey, so that there was altogether quite a considerable crowd—one or two gaily dressed ladies among the others.

It was glaringly hot, not a cloud in the sky nor a breath of wind, and the only shadow was that of the few scattered pine-trees. The burning heather had been extinguished, but the level ground towards Ottershaw was blackened as far as one could see, and still giving off vertical streamers of smoke. An enterprising sweetstuff dealer in the Chobham Road had sent up his son with a barrow-load of green apples and ginger-beer.

Going to the edge of the pit, I found it occupied by a group of about half a dozen men—Henderson, Ogilvy, and a tall, fair-haired man that I afterwards learned was Stent, the Astronomer Royal,[4] with several workmen wielding spades and pickaxes. Stent was giving directions in a clear, high-pitched voice. He was standing on the cylinder, which was now evidently much cooler; his face was crimson and streaming with perspiration, and something seemed to have irritated him.

A large portion of the cylinder had been uncovered, though its lower end was still embedded. As soon as Ogilvy saw me among the staring crowd on the edge of the pit he called to me to come down, and asked me if I would mind going over to see Lord Hilton, the lord of the manor.

---

1 England, Scotland, and Wales.
2 A "fly" was a two-wheeled carriage pulled by a horse.
3 Another kind of small carriage.
4 The chief astronomer in England.

The growing crowd, he said, was becoming a serious impediment to their excavations, especially the boys. They wanted a light railing put up, and help to keep the people back. He told me that a faint stirring was occasionally still audible within the case, but that the workmen had failed to unscrew the top, as it afforded no grip to them. The case appeared to be enormously thick, and it was possible that the faint sounds we heard represented a noisy tumult in the interior.

I was very glad to do as he asked, and so become one of the privileged spectators within the contemplated enclosure. I failed to find Lord Hilton at his house, but I was told he was expected from London by the six o'clock train from Waterloo; and as it was then about a quarter past five, I went home, had some tea, and walked up to the station to waylay him.

IV.
THE CYLINDER OPENS

When I returned to the common the sun was setting. Scattered groups were hurrying from the direction of Woking, and one or two persons were returning. The crowd about the pit had increased, and stood out black against the lemon-yellow of the sky—a couple of hundred people, perhaps. There were a number of voices raised, and some sort of struggle appeared to be going on about the pit. Strange imaginings passed through my mind. As I drew nearer I heard Stent's voice:

"Keep back! Keep back!"

A boy came running towards me.

"It's a-movin'," he said to me as he passed; "a-screwin' and a-screwin' out. I don't like it. I'm a-goin' 'ome, I am."

I went on to the crowd. There were really, I should think, two or three hundred people elbowing and jostling one another, the one or two ladies there being by no means the least active.

"He's fallen in the pit!" cried someone.

"Keep back!" said several.

The crowd swayed a little, and I elbowed my way through. Everyone seemed greatly excited. I heard a peculiar humming sound from the pit.

"I say!" said Ogilvy; "help keep these idiots back. We don't know what's in the confounded thing, you know!"

I saw a young man, a shop assistant in Woking I believe he was, standing on the cylinder and trying to scramble out of the hole again. The crowd had pushed him in.

The end of the cylinder was being screwed out from within. Nearly two feet of shining screw projected.[1] Somebody blundered against me, and I narrowly missed being pitched on to the top of the screw. I turned, and as I did so the screw must have come out, for the lid of the cylinder fell upon the gravel with a ringing concussion. I stuck my elbow into the person behind me, and turned my head towards the Thing again. For a moment that circular cavity seemed perfectly black. I had the sunset in my eyes.

I think everyone expected to see a man emerge—possibly something a little unlike us terrestrial men, but in all essentials a man. I know I did. But, looking, I presently saw something stirring within the shadow—grayish billowy movements, one above another, and then two luminous discs like eyes. Then something resembling a little gray snake, about the thickness of a walking stick, coiled up out of the writhing middle, and wriggled in the air towards me—and then another.

A sudden chill came over me. There was a loud shriek from a woman behind. I half turned, keeping my eyes fixed upon the cylinder still, from which other tentacles were now projecting, and began pushing my way back from the edge of the pit. I saw astonishment giving place to horror on the faces of the people about me. I heard inarticulate exclamations on all sides.

There was a general movement backward. I saw the shopman struggling still on the edge of the pit. I found myself alone, and saw the people on the other side of the pit running off, Stent among them. I looked again at the cylinder, and ungovernable terror gripped me. I stood petrified and staring.

A big grayish rounded bulk, the size, perhaps, of a bear, was rising slowly and painfully out of the cylinder. As it bulged up and caught the light, it glistened like wet leather.

Two large dark-coloured eyes were regarding me steadfastly. It was rounded, and had, one might say, a face. There was a mouth under the eyes, the lipless brim of which quivered and panted, and dropped saliva. The body heaved and pulsated convulsively. A lank tentacular appendage gripped the edge of the cylinder, another swayed in the air.

---

1   The newly exposed and shiny thread underneath the unscrewing end of the cylinder.

Those who have never seen a living Martian can scarcely imagine the strange horror of its appearance. The peculiar V-shaped mouth with its pointed upper lip, the absence of brow ridges, the absence of a chin beneath the wedge-like lower lip, the incessant quivering of this mouth, the Gorgon groups of tentacles,[1] the tumultuous breathing of the lungs in a strange atmosphere, the evident heaviness and painfulness of movement due to the greater gravitational energy of the earth—above all, the extraordinary intensity of the immense eyes—culminated in an effect akin to nausea. There was something fungoid in the oily brown skin, something in the clumsy deliberation of their tedious movements unspeakably terrible. Even at this first encounter, this first glimpse, I was overcome with disgust and dread.

Suddenly the monster vanished. It had toppled over the brim of the cylinder and fallen into the pit, with a thud like the fall of a great mass of leather. I heard it give a peculiar thick cry, and forthwith another of these creatures appeared darkly in the deep shadow of the aperture.

At that my rigour of terror passed away. I turned and, running madly, made for the first group of trees, perhaps a hundred yards away; but I ran slantingly and stumbling, for I could not avert my face from these things.

There, among some young pine-trees and furze bushes,[2] I stopped, panting, and waited further developments. The common round the sand-pits was dotted with people, standing like myself in a half-fascinated terror, staring at these creatures, or rather at the heaped gravel at the edge of the pit in which they lay. And then, with a renewed horror, I saw a round, black object bobbing up and down on the edge of the pit. It was the head of the shopman who had fallen in, but showing as a little black object against the hot western sun. Now he got his shoulder and knee up, and again he seemed to slip back until only his head was visible. Suddenly he vanished, and I could have fancied a faint shriek had reached me. I had a momentary impulse to go back and help him that my fears overruled.

Everything was then quite invisible, hidden by the deep pit and the heap of sand that the fall of the cylinder had made. Anyone

---

1 Any of three snake-haired sisters in Greek mythology who had the power to turn people into stone.
2 Low-growing spiny shrubs.

coming along the road from Chobham or Woking would have been amazed at the sight—a dwindling multitude of perhaps a hundred people or more standing in a great irregular circle, in ditches, behind bushes, behind gates and hedges, saying little to one another and that in short, excited shouts, and staring, staring hard at a few heaps of sand. The barrow of ginger-beer stood, a queer derelict, black against the burning sky, and in the sand-pits was a row of deserted vehicles with their horses feeding out of nose-bags or pawing the ground.

V.

THE HEAT-RAY

After the glimpse I had had of the Martians emerging from the cylinder in which they had come to the earth from their planet, a kind of fascination paralyzed my actions. I remained standing knee-deep in the heather, staring at the mound that hid them. I was a battle-ground of fear and curiosity.

I did not dare to go back towards the pit, but I felt a passionate longing to peer into it. I began walking, therefore, in a big curve, seeking some point of vantage and continually looking at the sand heaps that hid these new-comers to our earth. Once a leash of thin black whips, like the arms of an octopus, flashed across the sunset and was immediately withdrawn, and afterwards a thin rod rose up, joint by joint, bearing at its apex a circular disk that spun with a wobbling motion. What could be going on there?

Most of the spectators had gathered in one or two groups— one a little crowd towards Woking, the other a knot of people in the direction of Chobham. Evidently they shared my mental conflict. There were few near me. One man I approached—he was, I perceived, a neighbour of mine, though I did not know his name—and accosted.[1] But it was scarcely a time for articulate conversation.

"What ugly *brutes!*" he said. "Good God! What ugly brutes!" He repeated this over and over again.

"Did you see a man in the pit?" I said; but he made no answer to that. We became silent, and stood watching for a time side by side, deriving, I fancy, a certain comfort in one another's company.

---

1 Spoke to or grabbed hold of.

Then I shifted my position to a little knoll[1] that gave me the advantage of a yard or more of elevation and when I looked for him presently he was walking towards Woking.

The sunset faded to twilight before anything further happened. The crowd far away on the left, towards Woking, seemed to grow, and I heard now a faint murmur from it. The little knot of people towards Chobham dispersed. There was scarcely an intimation of movement from the pit.

It was this, as much as anything, that gave people courage, and I suppose the new arrivals from Woking also helped to restore confidence. At any rate, as the dusk came on, a slow, intermittent movement upon the sand-pits began, a movement that seemed to gather force as the stillness of the evening about the cylinder remained unbroken. Vertical black figures in twos and threes would advance, stop, watch, and advance again, spreading out as they did so in a thin irregular crescent that promised to enclose the pit in its attenuated[2] horns. I, too, on my side began to move towards the pit.

Then I saw some cabmen and others had walked boldly into the sand-pits, and heard the clatter of hoofs and the grind of wheels. I saw a lad trundling off the barrow of apples. And then, within thirty yards of the pit, advancing from the direction of Horsell, I noted a little black knot of men, the foremost of whom was waving a white flag.

This was the Deputation. There had been a hasty consultation, and since the Martians were evidently, in spite of their repulsive forms, intelligent creatures, it had been resolved to show them, by approaching them with signals, that we, too, were intelligent.

Flutter, flutter, went the flag, first to the right, then to the left. It was too far for me to recognize anyone there, but afterwards I learned that Ogilvy, Stent, and Henderson were with others in this attempt at communication. This little group had in its advance dragged inward, so to speak, the circumference of the now almost complete circle of people, and a number of dim black figures followed it at discreet distances.

Suddenly there was a flash of light, and a quantity of luminous greenish smoke came out of the pit in three distinct puffs, which drove up, one after the other, straight into the still air.

---

1   A small mound, smaller than a hill.
2   Thin.

This smoke (or flame, perhaps, would be the better word for it) was so bright that the deep blue sky overhead and the hazy stretches of brown common towards Chertsey, set with black pine-trees, seemed to darken abruptly as these puffs arose, and to remain the darker after their dispersal. At the same time a faint hissing sound became audible.

Beyond the pit stood the little wedge of people with the white flag at its apex, arrested by these phenomena, a little knot of small vertical black shapes upon the black ground. As the green smoke rose, their faces flashed out pallid green, and faded again as it vanished. Then slowly the hissing passed into a humming, into a long, loud, droning noise. Slowly a humped shape rose out of the pit, and the ghost of a beam of light seemed to flicker out from it.

Forthwith flashes of actual flame, a bright glare leaping from one to another, sprang from the scattered group of men. It was as if some invisible jet[1] impinged upon them and flashed into white flame. It was as if each man were suddenly and momentarily turned to fire.

Then, by the light of their own destruction, I saw them staggering and falling, and their supporters turning to run.

I stood staring, not as yet realizing that this was death leaping from man to man in that little distant crowd. All I felt was that it was something very strange. An almost noiseless and blinding flash of light, and a man fell headlong and lay still; and as the unseen shaft of heat passed over them, pine-trees burst into fire, and every dry furze-bush became with one dull thud a mass of flames. And far away towards Knaphill I saw the flashes of trees and hedges and wooden buildings suddenly set alight.

It was sweeping round swiftly and steadily, this flaming death, this invisible, inevitable sword of heat. I perceived it coming towards me by the flashing bushes it touched, and was too astounded and stupefied to stir. I heard the crackle of fire in the sand-pits and the sudden squeal of a horse that was as suddenly stilled. Then it was as if an invisible yet intensely heated finger were drawn through the heather between me and the Martians, and all along a curving line beyond the sand-pits the dark ground smoked and crackled. Something fell with a crash, far away to the left where the road from Woking Station opens out on the common. Forthwith

1 Stream or ray.

the hissing and humming ceased, and the black, dome-like object sank slowly out of sight into the pit.

All this had happened with such swiftness that I had stood motionless, dumfounded and dazzled by the flashes of light. Had that death swept through a full circle, it must inevitably have slain me in my surprise. But it passed and spared me, and left the night about me suddenly dark and unfamiliar.

The undulating common seemed now dark almost to blackness, except where its roadways lay gray and pale under the deep-blue sky of the early night. It was dark, and suddenly void of men. Overhead the stars were mustering,[1] and in the west the sky was still a pale, bright, almost greenish blue. The tops of the pine-trees and the roofs of Horsell came out sharp and black against the western after-glow. The Martians and their appliances were altogether invisible, save for that thin mast upon which their restless mirror wobbled. Patches of bush and isolated trees here and there smoked and glowed still, and the houses towards Woking station were sending up spires of flame into the stillness of the evening air.

Nothing was changed save for that and a terrible astonishment. The little group of black specks with the flag of white had been swept out of existence, and the stillness of the evening, so it seemed to me, had scarcely been broken.

It came to me that I was upon this dark common, helpless, unprotected, and alone. Suddenly, like a thing falling upon me from without, came—Fear.

With an effort I turned and began a stumbling run through the heather.

The fear I felt was no rational fear, but a panic terror not only of the Martians, but of the dusk and stillness all about me. Such an extraordinary effect in unmanning me it had that I ran weeping silently as a child might do. Once I had turned, I did not dare to look back.

I remember I felt an extraordinary persuasion that I was being played with, that presently, when I was upon the very verge of safety, this mysterious death—as swift as the passage of light—would leap after me from the pit about the cylinder and strike me down.

---

1 Literally collecting together, but here figuratively meaning becoming more numerous.

VI.

THE HEAT-RAY IN THE CHOBHAM ROAD

It is still a matter of wonder how the Martians are able to slay men so swiftly and so silently. Many think that in some way they are able to generate an intense heat in a chamber of practically absolute non-conductivity. This intense heat they project in a parallel beam against any object they choose, by means of a polished parabolic[1] mirror of unknown composition, much as the parabolic mirror of a light-house projects a beam of light. But no one has absolutely proved these details. However it is done, it is certain that a beam of heat is the essence of the matter. Heat, and invisible, instead of visible light. Whatever is combustible flashes into flame at its touch, lead runs like water, it softens iron, cracks and melts glass, and when it falls upon water, incontinently[2] that explodes into steam.

That night nearly forty people lay under the starlight about the pit, charred and distorted beyond recognition, and all night long the common from Horsell to Maybury was deserted and brightly ablaze.

The news of the massacre probably reached Chobham, Woking, and Ottershaw about the same time. In Woking the shops had closed when the tragedy happened, and a number of people, shop-people and so forth, attracted by the stories they had heard, were walking over the Horsell Bridge and along the road between the hedges that runs out at last upon the common. You may imagine the young people brushed up after the labours of the day, and making this novelty, as they would make any novelty, the excuse for walking together and enjoying a trivial flirtation. You may figure to yourself the hum of voices along the road in the gloaming[3] ....

As yet, of course, few people in Woking even knew that the cylinder had opened, though poor Henderson had sent a messenger on a bicycle to the post office with a special wire to an evening paper.

As these folks came out by twos and threes upon the open, they found little knots of people talking excitedly and peering at the spinning mirror over the sand-pits, and the new-comers were, no doubt, soon infected by the excitement of the occasion.

---

1 Bowl shaped.
2 Immediately.
3 Twilight.

By half past eight, when the Deputation was destroyed, there may have been a crowd of three hundred people or more at this place, besides those who had left the road to approach the Martians nearer. There were three policemen too, one of whom was mounted, doing their best, under instructions from Stent, to keep the people back and deter them from approaching the cylinder. There was some booing from those more thoughtless and excitable souls to whom a crowd is always an occasion for noise and horse-play.

Stent and Ogilvy, anticipating some possibilities of a collision, had telegraphed from Horsell to the barracks as soon as the Martians emerged, for the help of a company of soldiers to protect these strange creatures from violence. After that they returned to lead that ill-fated advance. The description of their death, as it was seen by the crowd, tallies very closely with my own impressions: the three puffs of green smoke, the deep humming note, and the flashes of flame.

But that crowd of people had a far narrower escape than mine. Only the fact that a hummock of heathery sand intercepted the lower part of the Heat-Ray saved them. Had the elevation of the parabolic mirror been a few yards higher, none could have lived to tell the tale. They saw the flashes, and the men falling and an invisible hand, as it were, lit the bushes as it hurried towards them through the twilight. Then, with a whistling note that rose above the droning of the pit, the beam swung close over their heads, lighting the tops of the beech trees that line the road, and splitting the bricks, smashing the windows, firing the window-frames, and bringing down in crumbling ruin a portion of the gable of the house nearest the corner.

In the sudden thud, hiss, and glare of the igniting trees, the panic-stricken crowd seems to have swayed hesitatingly for some moments. Sparks and burning twigs began to fall into the road, and single leaves like puffs of flame. Hats and dresses caught fire. Then came a crying from the common. There were shrieks and shouts, and suddenly a mounted policeman came galloping through the confusion with his hands clasped over his head, screaming.

"They're coming!" a woman shrieked, and incontinently everyone was turning and pushing at those behind, in order to clear their way to Woking again. They must have bolted as blindly as a flock of sheep. Where the road grows narrow and black between the high banks the crowd jammed, and a desperate struggle occurred. All that crowd did not escape; three persons at least, two women and a little boy, were crushed and trampled there, and left to die amid the terror and the darkness.

VII.
HOW I REACHED HOME

For my own part, I remember nothing of my flight except the stress of blundering against trees and stumbling through the heather. All about me gathered the invisible terrors of the Martians; that pitiless sword of heat seemed whirling to and fro, flourishing overhead before it descended and smote me out of life. I came into the road between the cross-roads and Horsell, and ran along this to the cross-roads.

At last I could go no further; I was exhausted with the violence of my emotion and of my flight, and I staggered and fell by the wayside. That was near the bridge that crosses the canal by the gasworks. I fell and lay still.

I must have remained there some time. I sat up, strangely perplexed. For a moment, perhaps, I could not clearly understand how I came there. My terror had fallen from me like a garment. My hat had gone, and my collar had burst away from its stud.[1] A few minutes before there had only been three real things before me – the immensity of the night and space and nature, my own feebleness and anguish, and the near approach of death. Now it was as if something turned over, and the point of view altered abruptly. There was no sensible transition from one state of mind to the other. I was immediately the self of every day again, a decent, ordinary citizen. The silent common, the impulse of my flight, the starting flames, were as if it were a dream. I asked myself had these latter things indeed happened? I could not credit it.

I rose and walked unsteadily up the steep incline of the bridge. My mind was blank wonder. My muscles and nerves seemed drained of their strength. I dare say I staggered drunkenly. A head rose over the arch, and the figure of a workman carrying a basket appeared. Beside him ran a little boy. He passed me, wishing me good night. I was minded to speak to him, and did not. I answered his greeting with a meaningless mumble and went on over the bridge.

---

1 Victorian collars were not part of the shirt but instead were fastened to it by buttons or studs.

Over the Maybury arch a train, a billowing tumult of white, firelit smoke, and a long caterpillar of lighted windows, went flying south: clatter, clatter, clap, rap, and it had gone. A dim group of people talked in the gate of one of the houses in the pretty little row of gables that was called Oriental Terrace. It was all so real and so familiar. And that behind me! It was frantic, fantastic! Such things, I told myself, could not be.

Perhaps I am a man of exceptional moods. I do not know how far my experience is common. At times I suffer from the strangest sense of detachment from myself and the world about me; I seem to watch it all from the outside, from somewhere inconceivably remote, out of time, out of space, out of the stress and tragedy of it all. This feeling was very strong upon me that night. Here was another side to my dream.

But the trouble was the blank incongruity of this serenity and the swift death flying yonder, not two miles away. There was a noise of business from the gas-works, and the electric-lamps were all alight. I stopped at the group of people.

"What news from the common?" said I.

There were two men and a woman at the gate.

"Eh?" said one of the men, turning.

"What news from the common?" I said.

"'Ain't yer just *been* there?" asked the men.

"People seem fair silly about the common," said the woman over the gate. "What's it all abart?"[1]

"Haven't you heard of the men from Mars?" said I—"the creatures from Mars?"

"Quite enough," said the woman over the gate. "Thenks;" and all three of them laughed.

I felt foolish and angry. I tried and found I could not tell them what I had seen. They laughed again at my broken sentences.

"You'll hear more yet," I said, and went on to my home.

I startled my wife at the doorway, so haggard was I. I went into the dining room, sat down, drank some wine, and so soon as I could collect myself sufficiently I told her the things I had seen. The dinner, which was a cold one, had already been served, and remained neglected on the table while I told my story.

"There is one thing," I said, to allay the fears I had aroused— "they are the most sluggish things I ever saw crawl. They may keep

---

1 About. Wells is imitating a broad London accent.

the pit and kill people who come near them, but they cannot get out of it.... But the horror of them!"

"Don't, dear!" said my wife, knitting her brows and putting her hand on mine.

"Poor Ogilvy!" I said. "To think he may be lying dead there!"

My wife at least did not find my experience incredible. When I saw how deadly white her face was, I ceased abruptly.

"They may come here," she said again and again.

I pressed her to take wine, and tried to reassure her.

"They can scarcely move," I said.

I began to comfort her and myself by repeating all that Ogilvy had told me of the impossibility of the Martians establishing themselves on the earth. In particular I laid stress on the gravitational difficulty. On the surface of the earth the force of gravity is three times what it is on the surface of Mars. A Martian, therefore, would weigh three times more than on Mars, albeit his muscular strength would be the same. His own body would be a cope[1] of lead to him. That, indeed, was the general opinion. Both the *Times* and the *Daily Telegraph*, for instance, insisted on it the next morning, and both overlooked, just as I did, two obvious modifying influences.

The atmosphere of the earth, we now know, contains far more oxygen or far less argon[2] (whichever way one likes to put it) than does Mars. The invigorating influences of this excess of oxygen upon the Martians indisputably did much to counterbalance the increased weight of their bodies. And, in the second place, we all overlooked the fact that such mechanical intelligence as the Martian possessed was quite able to dispense with muscular exertion at a pinch.

But I did not consider these points at the time, and so my reasoning was dead against the chances of the invaders. With wine and food, the confidence of my own table, and the necessity of reassuring my wife, I grew by insensible degrees courageous and secure.

"They have done a foolish thing," said I, fingering my wineglass. "They are dangerous because, no doubt, they are mad with terror.

---

1 A cloak or cape.
2 An inert gas found in trace amounts in Earth's atmosphere. Argon was not isolated from the air until 1894, and Wells wrote articles on the discovery of the pure form of the gas.

Perhaps they expected to find no living things—certainly no intelligent living things.

"A shell in the pit" said I, "if the worst comes to the worst will kill them all."

The intense excitement of the events had no doubt left my perceptive powers in a state of erethism.[1] I remember that dinnertable with extraordinary vividness even now. My dear wife's sweet, anxious face peering at me from under the pink lamp-shade, the white cloth with its silver and glass table furniture—for in those days even philosophical writers had many little luxuries—the crimson-purple wine in my glass, are photographically distinct. At the end of it I sat, tempering nuts with a cigarette, regretting Ogilvy's rashness, and denouncing the shortsighted timidity of the Martians.

So some respectable dodo in the Mauritius might have lorded it in his nest, and discussed the arrival of that shipful of pitiless sailors in want of animal food. "We will peck them to death to-morrow, my dear."

I did not know it, but that was the last civilized dinner I was to eat for very many strange and terrible days.

VIII.

FRIDAY NIGHT

The most extraordinary thing to my mind, of all the strange and wonderful things that happened upon that Friday, was the dovetailing of the commonplace habits of our social order with the first beginnings of the series of events that was to topple that social order headlong. If on Friday night you had taken a pair of compasses and drawn a circle with a radius of five miles round the Woking sand-pits, I doubt if you would have had one human being outside it, unless it were some relation of Stent or of the three or four cyclists or London people lying dead on the common, whose emotions or habits were at all affected by the new-comers. Many people had heard of the cylinder, of course, and talked about it in their leisure, but it certainly did not make the sensation that an ultimatum to Germany would have done.[2]

---

1 A state of abnormal excitement or hyperactivity.
2 Wells compares the opening of the "war" with the Martians to the reaction that would have accompanied a declaration of war against another country like Germany.

In London that night poor Henderson's telegram describing the gradual unscrewing of the shot was judged to be a canard,[1] and his evening paper, after wiring for authentication from him and receiving no reply—the man was killed—decided not to print a special edition.

Within the five-mile circle even the great majority of people were inert. I have already described the behaviour of the men and women to whom I spoke. All over the district people were dining and supping; working-men were gardening after the labours of the day, children were being put to bed, young people were wandering through the lanes love-making, students sat over their books.

Maybe there was a murmur in the village streets, a novel and dominant topic in the public-houses, and here and there a messenger, or even an eye-witness of the later occurrences, caused a whirl of excitement, a shouting, and a running to and fro; but for the most part the daily routine of working, eating, drinking, sleeping, went on as it had done for countless years—as though no planet Mars existed in the sky. Even at Woking Station and Horsell and Chobham that was the case.

In Woking Junction, until a late hour, trains were stopping and going on, others were shunting on the sidings, passengers were alighting and waiting, and everything was proceeding in the most ordinary way. A boy from the town, trenching on Smith's monopoly, was selling papers with the afternoon's news.[2] The ringing and impact of trucks, the sharp whistle of the engines from the junction, mingled with their shouts of "Men from Mars!" Excited men came into the station about nine o'clock with incredible tidings, and caused no more disturbance than drunkards might have done. People rattling Londonwards peered into the darkness outside the carriage windows, and saw only a rare, flickering, vanishing spark dance up from the direction of Horsell, a red glow and a thin veil of smoke driving across the stars, and thought that nothing more serious than a heath fire was happening. It was only round the edge of the common that any disturbance was perceptible. There were half a dozen villas[3] burning on the Woking border. There were

---

1 A joke or hoax.
2 A young boy is attempting to sell reading material to train commuters, a market already dominated by W.H. Smith's chain of booksellers. He is therefore "trenching" or trespassing on Smith's business.
3 The Victorian term for any large detached modern house.

lights in all the houses on the common side of the three villages, and the people there kept awake till dawn.

A curious crowd lingered restlessly, people coming and going but the crowd remaining, both on the Chobham and Horsell bridges. One or two adventurous souls, it was afterwards found, went into the darkness and crawled quite near the Martians; but they never returned, for now and again a light-ray, like the beam of a warship's searchlight, swept the common, and the Heat-Ray was ready to follow. Save for such, that big area of common was silent and desolate, and the charred bodies lay about on it all night under the stars, and all the next day. A noise of hammering from the pit was heard by many people.

So you have the state of things on Friday night. In the centre, sticking into the skin of our old planet Earth like a poisoned dart, was this cylinder. But the poison was scarcely working yet. Around it was a patch of silent common, smouldering in places, and with a few dark, dimly seen objects lying in contorted attitudes here and there. Here and there was a burning bush or tree. Beyond was a fringe of excitement, and further than that fringe the inflammation had not crept as yet. In the rest of the world the stream of life still flowed as it had flowed for immemorial years. The fever of war that would presently clog vein and artery, deaden nerve and destroy brain, had still to develop.

All night long the Martians were hammering and stirring, sleepless, indefatigable, at work upon the machines they were making ready, and ever and again a puff of greenish-white smoke whirled up to the starlit sky.

About eleven a company of soldiers came through Horsell, and deployed along the edge of the common to form a cordon. Later a second company marched through Chobham to deploy on the north side of the common. Several officers from the Inkerman barracks[1] had been on the common earlier in the day, and one, Major Eden, was reported to be missing. The Colonel of the regiment came to the Chobham bridge and was busy questioning the crowd at midnight. The military authorities were certainly alive to the seriousness of the business. About eleven, the next morning's

---

1 Nearby army barracks named after the Battle of Inkerman, 1854, in which combined British and French forces defeated the Russian army during the Crimean War (1853-56).

papers were able to say, a squadron of hussars,[1] two Maxims,[2] and about 400 men of the Cardigan[3] regiment started from Aldershot.

A few seconds after midnight the crowd in the Chertsey road, Woking, saw a star fall from heaven into the pine-woods to the northwest. It fell with a greenish light, causing a flash of light like summer lightning. This was the second cylinder.

IX.
THE FIGHTING BEGINS

Saturday lives in my memory as a day of suspense. It was a day of lassitude[4] too, hot and close, with, I am told, a rapidly fluctuating barometer. I had slept but little, though my wife had succeeded in sleeping, and I rose early. I went into my garden before breakfast and stood listening, but towards the common there was nothing stirring but a lark.

The milkman came as usual. I heard the rattle of his chariot[5] and I went round to the side-gate to ask the latest news. He told me that during the night the Martians had been surrounded by troops, and that guns were expected. Then—a familiar, reassuring note—I heard a train running towards Woking.

"They aren't to be killed," said the milkman, "if that can possibly be avoided."

I saw my neighbour gardening, chatted with him for a time, and then strolled in to breakfast. It was a most unexceptional morning. My neighbour was of opinion that the troops would be able to capture or to destroy the Martians during the day.

"It's a pity they make themselves so unapproachable," he said. "It would be curious to learn how they live on another planet; we might learn a thing or two."

He came up to the fence and extended a handful of strawberries, for his gardening was as generous as it was enthusiastic. At the same time he told me of the burning of the pine-woods about the Byfleet Golf Links.

---

1 Light cavalry, shown in a photograph in Appendix I.
2 A Maxim-Vickers gun, the first true machine gun. A photo of this machine gun can be found in Appendix I.
3 A Regiment named after James Thomas Cardigan, 7th Earl of Brudenell (1797-1868).
4 Weariness, lack of energy.
5 A word for cart.

"They say," said he, "that there's another of those blessed things fallen there—number two. But one's enough, surely. This lot'll cost the insurance people a pretty penny before everything's settled." He laughed with an air of the greatest good-humour as he said this. The woods, he said, were still burning, and pointed out a haze of smoke to me. "They will be hot under foot for days on account of the thick soil of pine-needles and turf," he said, and then grew serious over "poor Ogilvy."

After breakfast, instead of working, I decided to walk down towards the common. Under the railway-bridge I found a group of soldiers—sappers,[1] I think, men in small round caps, dirty red jackets unbuttoned, and showing their blue shirts, dark trousers, and boots coming to the calf. They told me no one was allowed over the canal, and, looking along the road towards the bridge, I saw one of the Cardigan men standing sentinel there. I talked with these soldiers for a time; I told them of my sight of the Martians on the previous evening. None of them had seen the Martians, and they had but the vaguest ideas of them, so that they plied me with questions. They said that they did not know who had authorized the movements of the troops; their idea was that a dispute had arisen at the Horse Guards.[2] The ordinary sapper is a great deal better educated than the common soldier, and they discussed the peculiar conditions of the possible fight with some acuteness. I described the Heat-Ray to them, and they began to argue among themselves.

"Crawl up under cover and rush 'em, say I," said one.

"Get aht!,"[3] said another. "What's Cover against this 'ere 'eat? Sticks to cook yer! What we got to do is to go as near as the ground'll let us, and then drive a trench."

"Blow yer trenches! You always want trenches; you ought to ha' been born a rabbit, Snippy."

"'Ain't they got any necks, then?" said a third, abruptly—a little, contemplative, dark man, smoking a pipe.

I repeated my description.

"Octopuses," said he, "that's what I calls 'em. Talk about fishers of men—fighters of fish it is this time!"

---

1   Engineers who built bridges, forts and any other structures the army might need.
2   The Royal Horse Guards, one of the élite cavalry units of the British army.
3   Get out. Again Wells is imitating a broad London accent.

"It ain't no murder killing beasts like that," said the first speaker. "Why not shell the darned things strite off[1] and finish 'em?" said the little dark man. "You carn tell what they might do."

"Where's your shells?" said the first speaker. "There ain't no time. Do it in a rush, that's my tip, and do it at once."

So they discussed it. After a while I left them, and went on to the railway station to get as many morning papers as I could.

But I will not weary the reader with a description of that long morning and of the longer afternoon. I did not succeed in getting a glimpse of the common, for even Horsell and Chobham church towers were in the hands of the military authorities. The soldiers I addressed didn't know anything; the officers were mysterious as well as busy. I found people in the town quite secure again in the presence of the military, and I heard for the first time from Marshall, the tobacconist, that his son was among the dead on the common. The soldiers had made the people on the outskirts of Horsell lock up and leave their houses.

I got back to lunch about two, very tired for, as I have said, the day was extremely hot and dull, and in order to refresh myself I took a cold bath in the afternoon. About half-past four I went up to the railway station to get an evening paper, for the morning papers had contained only a very inaccurate description of the killing of Stent, Henderson, Ogilvy, and the others. But there was little I didn't know. The Martians did not show an inch of themselves. They seemed busy in their pit, and there was a sound of hammering and an almost continuous streamer of smoke. Apparently they were busy getting ready for a struggle. "Fresh attempts have been made to signal, but without success," was the stereotyped formula of the papers. A sapper told me it was done by a man in a ditch with a flag on a long pole. The Martians took as much notice of such advances as we should of the lowing of a cow.

I must confess the sight of all this armament, all this preparation, greatly excited me. My imagination became belligerent, and defeated the invaders in a dozen striking ways; something of my school-boy dreams of battle and heroism came back. It hardly seemed a fair fight to me at that time. They seemed very helpless in that pit of theirs.

About three o'clock there began the thud of a gun at measured intervals from Chertsey or Addlestone. I learned that the smoul-

---

1 Straight off, meaning right away.

dering pine-wood into which the second cylinder had fallen was being shelled, in the hope of destroying that object before it opened. It was only about five, however, that a field-gun[1] reached Chobham for use against the first body of Martians.

About six in the evening, as I sat at tea with my wife in the summer-house talking vigorously about the battle that was lowering upon us, I heard a muffled detonation from the common, and immediately after a gust of firing. Close on the heels of that came a violent rattling crash, quite close to us, that shook the ground; and, starting out upon the lawn, I saw the tops of the trees about the Oriental College[2] burst into smoky red flame, and the tower of the little church beside it slide down into ruin. The pinnacle of the mosque had vanished, and the roof-line of the college itself looked as if a hundred-ton gun had been at work upon it. One of our chimneys cracked as if a shot had hit it, flew, and a piece of it came clattering down the tiles and made a heap of broken red fragments upon the flower-bed by my study window.

I and my wife stood amazed. Then I realized that the crest of Maybury Hill must be within range of the Martians' Heat-Ray now that the college was cleared out of the way.

At that I gripped my wife's arm, and without ceremony ran her out into the road. Then I fetched out the servant, telling her I would go upstairs myself for the box she was clamouring for.

"We can't possibly stay here," I said; and as I spoke the firing reopened for a moment upon the common.

"But where are we to go?" said my wife in terror.

I thought, perplexed. Then I remembered her cousins at Leatherhead.

"Leatherhead!" I shouted above the sudden noise.

She looked away from me downhill. The people were coming out of their houses, astonished.

"How are we to get to Leatherhead?" she said.

Down the hill I saw a bevy[3] of hussars ride under the railway-bridge; three galloped through the open gates of the Oriental College; two others dismounted, and began running from house to

---

1 A piece of mobile artillery, usually pulled by horses. See the photograph in Appendix I.

2 The Oriental Institute described in *Black's Guide to Surrey*, in Appendix H.

3 A large group.

house. The sun, shining through the smoke that drove up from the tops of the trees, seemed blood red, and threw an unfamiliar lurid light upon everything.

"Stop here," said I; "you are safe here;" and I started off at once for the Spotted Dog,[1] for I knew the landlord had a horse and dog-cart.[2] I ran, for I perceived that in a moment everyone upon this side of the hill would be moving. I found him in his bar, quite unaware of what was going on behind his house. A man stood with his back to me, talking to him.

"I must have a pound," said the landlord, "and I've no one to drive it."

"I'll give you two," said I, over the stranger's shoulder.

"What for?"

"And I'll bring it back by midnight," I said.

"Lord!" said the landlord; "what's the hurry? I'm selling my bit of a pig. Two pounds, and you bring it back? What's going on now?"

I explained hastily that I had to leave my home, and so secured the dogcart. At the time it did not seem to me nearly so urgent that the landlord should leave his. I took care to have the cart there and then, drove it off down the road, and, leaving it in charge of my wife and servant, rushed into my house and packed a few valuables, such plate as we had, and so forth. The beech-trees below the house were burning while I did this, and the palings up the road glowed red. While I was occupied in this way, one of the dismounted hussars came running up. He was going from house to house, warning people to leave. He was going on as I came out of my front-door, lugging my treasures, done up in a table-cloth. I shouted after him:

"What news?"

He turned, stared, bawled something about "crawling out in a thing like a dish cover,"[3] and ran on to the gate of the house at the crest. A sudden whirl of black smoke driving across the road hid him for a moment. I ran to my neighbour's door and rapped to satisfy myself of what I already knew, that his wife had gone to London with him and had locked up their house. I went in again according to my promise to get my servant's box, lugged it out,

---

1 The name of a pub.
2 A small open cart.
3 A large metal cover used to keep food hot.

clapped it beside her on the tail of the dogcart, and then caught the reins and jumped up into the driver's seat beside my wife. In another moment we were clear of the smoke and noise, and spanking[1] down the opposite slope of Maybury Hill towards Old Woking.

In front was a quiet sunny landscape, a wheat-field ahead on either side of the road, and the Maybury Inn with its swinging sign. I saw the doctor's cart ahead of me. At the bottom of the hill I turned my head to look at the hillside I was leaving. Thick streamers of black smoke shot with threads of red fire were driving up into the still air, and throwing dark shadows upon the green tree-tops eastward. The smoke already extended far away to the east and west—to the Byfleet pine-woods eastward, and to Woking on the west. The road was dotted with people running towards us. And very faint now, but very distinct through the hot, quiet air, one heard the whirr of a machine-gun that was presently stilled, and an intermittent cracking of rifles. Apparently the Martians were setting fire to everything within range of their Heat-Ray.

I am not an expert driver, and I had immediately to turn my attention to the horse. When I looked back again the second hill had hidden the black smoke. I slashed the horse with the whip, and gave him a loose rein until Woking and Send lay between us and that quivering tumult. I overtook and passed the doctor between Woking and Send.

X.
IN THE STORM

Leatherhead is about twelve miles from Maybury Hill. The scent of hay was in the air through the lush meadows beyond Pyrford, and the hedges on either side were sweet and gay with multitudes of dog-roses.[2] The heavy firing that had broken out while we were driving down Maybury Hill ceased as abruptly as it began, leaving the evening very peaceful and still. We got to Leatherhead without misadventure about nine o'clock, and the horse had an hour's rest while I took supper with my cousins and commended my wife to their care.

---

1 Speeding.
2 A small, wild rose.

My wife was curiously silent throughout the drive, and seemed oppressed with forebodings of evil. I talked to her reassuringly, pointing out that the Martians were tied to the pit by sheer heaviness, and at the utmost could but crawl a little out of it; but she answered only in monosyllables. Had it not been for my promise to the innkeeper, she would, I think, have urged me to stay in Leatherhead that night. Would that I had! Her face, I remember, was very white as we parted.

For my own part, I had been feverishly excited all day. Something very like the war-fever that occasionally runs through a civilized community had got into my blood, and in my heart I was not so very sorry that I had to return to Maybury that night. I was even afraid that that last fusillade[1] I had heard might mean the extermination of our invaders from Mars. I can best express my state of mind by saying that I wanted to be in at the death.

It was nearly eleven when I started to return. The night was unexpectedly dark; to me, walking out of the lighted passage of my cousins' house, it seemed indeed black, and it was as hot and close as the day. Overhead the clouds were driving fast, albeit not a breath stirred the shrubs about us. My cousins' man lit both lamps. Happily, I knew the road intimately. My wife stood in the light of the doorway, and watched me until I jumped up into the dogcart. Then abruptly she turned and went in, leaving my cousins side by side wishing me good hap.[2]

I was a little depressed at first with the contagion of my wife's fears, but very soon my thoughts reverted to the Martians. At that time I was absolutely in the dark as to the course of the evening's fighting. I did not know even the circumstances that had precipitated the conflict. As I came through Ockham (for that was the way I returned, and not through Send and Old Woking) I saw along the western horizon a blood-red glow, which as I drew nearer, crept slowly up the sky. The driving clouds of the gathering thunderstorm mingled there with masses of black and red smoke.

Ripley Street was deserted, and except for a lighted window or so the village showed not a sign of life; but I narrowly escaped an accident at the corner of the road to Pyrford, where a knot of people stood with their backs to me. They said nothing to me as I passed. I do not know what they knew of the things happening

---

1 A round of coordinated fire by a body of soldiers.
2 Good luck.

beyond the hill, nor do I know if the silent houses I passed on my way were sleeping securely, or deserted and empty, or harassed and watching against the terror of the night.

From Ripley until I came through Pyrford I was in the valley of the Wey, and the red glare was hidden from me. As I ascended the little hill beyond Pyrford Church the glare came into view again, and the trees about me shivered with the first intimation of the storm that was upon me. Then I heard midnight pealing out[1] from Pyrford Church behind me, and then came the silhouette of Maybury Hill, with its tree-tops and roofs black and sharp against the red.

Even as I beheld this a lurid green glare lit the road about me, and showed the distant woods towards Addlestone. I felt a tug at the reins. I saw that the driving clouds had been pierced as it were by a thread of green fire, suddenly lighting their confusion and falling into the field to my left. It was the Third Falling Star!

Close on its apparition, and blindingly violet by contrast, danced out the first lightning of the gathering storm, and the thunder burst like a rocket overhead. The horse took the bit between his teeth and bolted.

A moderate incline runs towards the foot of Maybury Hill, and down this we clattered. Once the lightning had begun, it went on in as rapid a succession of flashes as I have ever seen. The thunder-claps, treading one on the heels of another and with a strange crackling accompaniment, sounded more like the working of a gigantic electric machine than the usual detonating reverberations. The flickering light was blinding and confusing, and a thin hail smote[2] gustily at my face as I drove down the slope.

At first I regarded little but the road before me, and then abrupt-ly my attention was arrested by something that was moving rapid-ly down the opposite slope of Maybury Hill. At first I took it for the wet roof of a house, but one flash following another showed it to be in swift rolling movement. It was an elusive vision—a moment of bewildering darkness, and then, in a flash like daylight, the red masses of the Orphanage near the crest of the hill, the green tops of the pine-trees, and this problematical object came out clear and sharp and bright.

---

1   Church bells ringing.
2   Struck or hit.

And this thing I saw! How can I describe it? A monstrous tri-pod,[1] higher than many houses, striding over the young pine-trees, and smashing them aside in its career;[2] a walking engine of glit-tering metal, striding now across the heather; articulate[3] ropes of steel dangling from it, and the clattering tumult of its passage min-gling with the riot of the thunder. A flash, and it came out vividly, heeling over one way with two feet in the air, to vanish and reap-pear almost instantly as it seemed, with the next flash, a hundred yards nearer. Can you imagine a milking-stool tilted and bowled violently along the ground? That was the impression those instant flashes gave. But instead of a milking-stool imagine it a great body of machinery on a tripod stand.

Then suddenly the trees in the pine-wood ahead of me were parted, as brittle reeds are parted by a man thrusting through them; they were snapped off and driven headlong, and a second huge tri-pod appeared, rushing, as it seemed, headlong towards me. And I was galloping hard to meet it! At the sight of the second monster my nerve went altogether. Not stopping to look again, I wrenched the horse's head hard round to the right and in another moment the dogcart had heeled over upon the horse; the shafts smashed noisily, and I was flung sideways and fell heavily into a shallow pool of water.

I crawled out almost immediately, and crouched, my feet still in the water, under a clump of furze. The horse lay motionless (his neck was broken, poor brute!) and by the lightning flashes I saw the black bulk of the overturned dogcart and the silhouette of the wheel still spinning slowly. In another moment the colossal mech-anism went striding by me, and passed uphill towards Pyrford.

Seen nearer, the Thing was incredibly strange, for it was no mere insensate[4] machine driving on its way. Machine it was, with a ring-ing metallic pace, and long, flexible, glittering tentacles (one of which gripped a young pine-tree) swinging and rattling about its strange body. It picked its road as it went striding along, and the brazen hood that surmounted it moved to and fro with the inevitable suggestion of a head looking about it. Behind the main body was a huge thing of white metal like a gigantic fisherman's

---

1 The Martians' machines walk on three legs.
2 In its path.
3 Jointed, able to bend and move.
4 Without consciousness.

basket, and puffs of green smoke squirted out from the joints of the limbs as the monster swept by me. And in an instant it was gone.

So much I saw then, all vaguely for the flickering of the lightning, in blinding highlights and dense black shadows.

As it passed it set up an exultant deafening howl that drowned the thunder—"Aloo! Aloo!"—and in another minute it was with its companion, half a mile away, stooping over something in the field. I have no doubt this thing in the field was the third of the ten cylinders they had fired at us from Mars.

For some minutes I lay there in the rain and darkness watching, by the intermittent light, these monstrous beings of metal moving about in the distance over the hedge-tops. A thin hail was now beginning, and as it came and went their figures grew misty and then flashed into clearness again. Now and then came a gap in the lightning, and the night swallowed them up.

I was soaked with hail above and puddle water below. It was some time before my blank astonishment would let me struggle up the bank to a drier position, or think at all of my imminent peril.

Not far from me was a little one-roomed squatter's[1] hut of wood, surrounded by a patch of potato-garden. I struggled to my feet at last, and, crouching and making use of every chance of cover, I made a run for this. I hammered at the door, but I could not make the people hear (if there were any people inside), and after a time I desisted, and, availing myself of a ditch for the greater part of the way, succeeded in crawling, unobserved by these monstrous machines, into the pine-wood towards Maybury.

Under cover of this I pushed on, wet and shivering now, towards my own house. I walked among the trees trying to find the footpath. It was very dark indeed in the wood, for the lightning was now becoming infrequent, and the hail, which was pouring down in a torrent, fell in columns through the gaps in the heavy foliage.

If I had fully realized the meaning of all the things I had seen I should have immediately worked my way round through Byfleet to Street Cobham, and so gone back to rejoin my wife at Leatherhead. But that night the strangeness of things about me, and my physical wretchedness, prevented me, for I was bruised, weary, wet to the skin, deafened and blinded by the storm.

---

1   A person living in a building without paying rent.

I had a vague idea of going on to my own house, and that was as much motive as I had. I staggered through the trees, fell into a ditch and bruised my knees against a plank, and finally splashed out into the lane that ran down from the College Arms. I say splashed, for the storm water was sweeping the sand down the hill in a muddy torrent. There in the darkness a man blundered into me and sent me reeling back.

He gave a cry of terror, sprung sideways, and rushed on before I could gather my wits sufficiently to speak to him. So heavy was the stress[1] of the storm just at this place that I had the hardest task to win my way up the hill. I went close up to the fence on the left and worked my way along its palings.

Near the top I stumbled upon something soft, and, by a flash of lightning, saw between my feet a heap of black broadcloth and a pair of boots. Before I could distinguish clearly how the man lay, the flicker of light had passed. I stood over him waiting for the next flash. When it came, I saw that he was a sturdy man, cheaply but not shabbily dressed; his head was bent under his body, and he lay crumpled up close to the fence, as though he had been flung violently against it.

Overcoming the repugnance natural to one who had never before touched a dead body, I stooped and turned him over to feel for his heart. He was quite dead. Apparently his neck had been broken. The lightning flashed for a third time, and his face leapt upon me. I sprang to my feet. It was the landlord of the Spotted Dog, whose conveyance I had taken.

I stepped over him gingerly and pushed on up the hill. I made my way by the police station and the College Arms towards my own house. Nothing was burning on the hillside, though from the common there still came a red glare and a rolling tumult of ruddy smoke beating up against the drenching hail. So far as I could see by the flashes, the houses about me were mostly uninjured. By the College Arms a dark heap lay in the road.

Down the road towards Maybury Bridge there were voices and the sound of feet, but I had not the courage to shout or to go to them. I let myself in with my latch-key, closed, locked and bolted the door, staggered to the foot of the staircase, and sat down. My imagination was full of those striding metallic monsters, and of the dead body smashed against the fence.

---

1 Force.

I crouched at the foot of the staircase with my back to the wall, shivering violently.

XI

AT THE WINDOW

I have said already that my storms of emotion have a trick of exhausting themselves. After a time I discovered that I was cold and wet, and with little pools of water about me on the stair-carpet. I got up almost mechanically, went into the dining room and drank some whisky, and then I was moved to change my clothes.

After I had done that I went upstairs to my study, but why I did so I do not know. The window of my study looks over the trees and the railway towards Horsell Common. In the hurry of our departure this window had been left open. The passage was dark, and, by contrast with the picture the window frame enclosed, the side of the room seemed impenetrably dark. I stopped short in the doorway.

The thunderstorm had passed. The towers of the Oriental College and the pine-trees about it had gone, and very far away, lit by a vivid red glare, the common about the sand-pits was visible. Across the light, huge black shapes, grotesque and strange, moved busily to and fro.

It seemed indeed as if the whole country in that direction was on fire—a broad hill-side set with minute tongues of flame, swaying and writhing with the gusts of the dying storm, and throwing a red reflection upon the cloud-scud above. Every now and then a haze of smoke from some nearer conflagration drove across the window and hid the Martian shapes. I could not see what they were doing, nor the clear form of them, nor recognize the black objects they were busied upon. Neither could I see the nearer fire, though the reflections of it danced on the wall and ceiling of the study. A sharp, resinous twang of burning was in the air.

I closed the door noiselessly and crept towards the window. As I did so, the view opened out until, on the one hand, it reached to the houses about Woking Station, and on the other to the charred and blackened pine-woods of Byfleet. There was a light down below the hill, on the railway, near the arch, and several of the houses along the Maybury road and the streets near the station were glowing ruins. The light upon the railway puzzled me at first; there were a black heap and a vivid glare, and to the right of that a row of yellow oblongs. Then I perceived this was a wrecked train, the fore part smashed and on fire, the hinder carriages still upon the rails.

Between these three main centres of light, the houses, the train, and the burning county towards Chobham, stretched irregular patches of dark country, broken here and there by intervals of dimly glowing and smoking ground. It was the strangest spectacle, that black expanse set with fire. It reminded me, more than anything else, of the Potteries[1] seen at night. Of people at first I could distinguish none, though I peered intently for them. Later I saw against the light of Woking Station a number of black figures hurrying one after the other across the line.

And this was the little world in which I had been living securely for years, this fiery chaos! What had happened in the last seven hours I still did not know; nor did I know, though I was beginning to guess, the relation between these mechanical colossi and the sluggish lumps I had seen disgorged from the cylinder. With a queer feeling of impersonal interest I turned my desk-chair to the window, sat down, and stared at the blackened country, and particularly at the three gigantic black things that were going to and fro in the glare about the sand-pits.

They seemed amazingly busy. I began to ask myself what they could be. Were they intelligent mechanisms? Such a thing I felt was impossible. Or did a Martian sit within each, ruling, directing, using, much as a man's brain sits and rules in his body? I began to compare the things to human machines, to ask myself for the first time in my life how an ironclad[2] or a steam engine would seem to an intelligent lower animal.

The storm had left the sky clear, and over the smoke of the burning land the little fading pin-point of Mars was dropping into the west, when the soldier came into my garden. I heard a slight scraping at the fence, and rousing myself from the lethargy that had fallen upon me, I looked down and saw him dimly, clambering over the palings. At the sight of another human being my torpor passed, and I leaned out of the window eagerly.

"Hist!" said I, in a whisper.

---

1 An area of central England with a large number of china factories and their furnaces.
2 A battleship. Both the ironclad and the steam engine for Victorians were symbols of technological progress. The Martians' technology is represented as more "advanced" than that of the Victorians.

He stopped astride of the fence in doubt. Then he came over and across the lawn to the corner of the house. He bent down and stepped softly.

"Who's there?" he said, also whispering, standing under the window and peering up.

"Where are you going?" I asked.

"God knows."

"Are you trying to hide?"

"That's it."

"Come into the house," I said.

I went down, unfastened the door, and let him in, and locked the door again. I could not see his face. He was hatless, and his coat was unbuttoned.

"My God!" he said, as I drew him in.

"What has happened?" I asked.

"What hasn't?" In the obscurity I could see he made a gesture of despair. "They wiped us out—simply wiped us out," he repeated again and again.

He followed me, almost mechanically, into the dining-room.

"Take some whisky," I said, pouring out a stiff dose.

He drank it. Then abruptly he sat down before the table, put his head on his arms, and began to sob and weep like a little boy, in a perfect passion of emotion, while I, with a curious forgetfulness of my own recent despair, stood beside him, wondering.

It was a long time before he could steady his nerves to answer my questions, and then he answered perplexingly and brokenly. He was a driver in the artillery, and had only come into action about seven. At that time firing was going on across the common, and it was said the first party of Martians were crawling slowly towards their second cylinder under cover of a metal shield.

Later this shield staggered up on tripod legs and became the first of the Fighting Machines I had seen. The gun he drove had been unlimbered near Horsell, in order to command the sand-pits, and its arrival it was that had precipitated the action. As the limber[1] gunners went to the rear, his horse trod in a rabbit hole and came down, throwing him into a depression of the ground. At the same moment the gun exploded behind him, the ammunition blew up,

---

1   The part of the carriage on which the gun is pulled, and from which it has to be "unlimbered" or detached.

there was fire all about him, and he found himself lying under a heap of charred dead men and dead horses.

"I lay still," he said, "scared out of my wits, with the fore-quarter of a horse atop of me. We'd been wiped out. And the smell—good God! Like burnt meat! I was hurt across the back by the fall of the horse, and there I had to lie until I felt better. Just like parade it had been a minute before—then stumble, bang, swish!"

"Wiped out!" he said.

He had hid under the dead horse for a long time, peeping out furtively across the common. The Cardigan men had tried a rush, in skirmishing order, at the pit, simply to be swept out of existence. Then the monster had risen to its feet and had begun to walk leisurely to and fro across the common among the few fugitives, with its headlike hood turning about exactly like the head of a cowled human being. A kind of arm carried a complicated metallic case, about which green flashes scintillated, and out of the funnel of this there smote the Heat-Ray.

In a few minutes there was, so far as the soldier could see, not a living thing left upon the common, and every bush and tree upon it that was not already a blackened skeleton was burning. The hussars had been on the road beyond the curvature of the ground, and he saw nothing of them. He heard the Maxims rattle for a time and then become still. The giant saved Woking Station and its cluster of houses until the last; then in a moment the Heat-Ray was brought to bear, and the town became a heap of fiery ruins. Then the thing shut off the Heat-Ray, and turning its back upon the artilleryman, began to waddle away towards the smouldering pine-woods that sheltered the second cylinder. As it did so a second glittering Titan built itself up out of the pit.

The second monster followed the first, and at that the artilleryman began to crawl very cautiously across the hot heather ash towards Horsell. He managed to get alive into the ditch by the side of the road, and so escaped to Woking. There his story became ejaculatory.[1] The place was impassable. It seems there were a few people alive there, frantic for the most part and many burnt and scalded. He was turned aside by the fire, and hid among some almost scorching heaps of broken wall as one of the Martian giants returned. He saw this one pursue a man, catch him up in one of its steely tentacles, and knock his head against the trunk of a pine-

---

1   Disjointed, told in short erratic bursts.

tree. At last, after nightfall, the artilleryman made a rush for it and got over the railway embankment.

Since then he had been skulking along towards Maybury, in the hope of getting out of danger Londonward. People were hiding in trenches and cellars, and many of the survivors had made off towards Woking Village and Send. He had been consumed with thirst until he found one of the water mains near the railway arch smashed, and the water bubbling out like a spring upon the road.

That was the story I got from him bit by bit. He grew calmer telling me and trying to make me see the things he had seen. He had eaten no food since mid-day, he told me early in his narrative, and I found some mutton and bread in the pantry and brought it into the room. We lit no lamp for fear of attracting the Martians, and ever and again our hands would touch upon bread or meat. As he talked, things about us came darkly out of the darkness, and the trampled bushes and broken rose-trees outside the window grew distinct. It would seem that a number of men or animals had rushed across the lawn. I began to see his face, blackened and haggard, as no doubt mine was also.

When we had finished eating we went softly up-stairs to my study, and I looked again out of the open window. In one night the valley had become a valley of ashes. The fires had dwindled now. Where flames had been there were now streamers of smoke; but the countless ruins of shattered and gutted houses and blasted and blackened trees that the night had hidden stood out now gaunt and terrible in the pitiless light of dawn. Yet here and there some object had had the luck to escape—a white railway signal here, the end of a greenhouse there, white and fresh amid the wreckage. Never before in the history of warfare had destruction been so indiscriminate and so universal. And, shining with the growing light of the east, three of the metallic giants stood about the pit, their cowls[1] rotating as though they were surveying the desolation they had made.

It seemed to me that the pit had been enlarged, and ever and again puffs of vivid green vapour streamed up and out of it towards the brightening dawn—streamed up, whirled, broke, and vanished.

Beyond were the pillars of fire about Chobham. They became pillars of bloodshot smoke at the first touch of day.

---

1 The hood of a monk's garment.

XII

WHAT I SAW OF THE DESTRUCTION OF WEYBRIDGE AND SHEPPERTON

As the dawn grew brighter we withdrew ourselves from the window from which we had watched the Martians, and went very quietly down-stairs.

The artilleryman agreed with me that the house was no place to stay in. He proposed, he said, to make his way Londonward, and thence rejoin his battery—No. 12, of the Horse Artillery. My plan was to return at once to Leatherhead, and so greatly had the strength of the Martians impressed me that I had determined to take my wife to Newhaven, and go with her out of the country forthwith. For I already perceived clearly that the country about London must inevitably be the scene of a disastrous struggle before such creatures as these could be destroyed.

Between us and Leatherhead, however, lay the third cylinder, with its guarding giants. Had I been alone, I think I should have taken my chance and struck across country. But the artilleryman dissuaded me: "It's no kindness to the right sort of wife," he said, "to make her a widow;" and in the end I agreed to go with him, under cover of the woods, northward as far as Street Cobham before I parted with him. Thence I would make a big detour by Epsom to reach Leatherhead.

I should have started at once, but my companion had been in active service and he knew better than that. He made me ransack the house for a flask, which he filled with whisky; and we lined every available pocket with packets of biscuits and slices of meat. Then we crept out of the house, and ran as quickly as we could down the ill-made road by which I had come overnight. The houses seemed deserted. In the road lay a group of three charred bodies close together, struck dead by the Heat-Ray; and here and there were things that people had dropped—a clock, a slipper, a silver spoon, and the like poor valuables. At the corner turning up towards the post office a little cart, filled with boxes and furniture, and horseless, heeled over on a broken wheel. A cash box had been hastily smashed open and thrown under the débris.

Except the lodge at the Orphanage, which was still on fire, none of the houses had suffered very greatly here. The Heat-Ray had shaved the chimney tops and passed. Yet, save ourselves, there did not seem to be a living soul on Maybury Hill. The majority of the inhabitants had escaped, I suppose, by way of the Old Woking road—the road I had taken when I drove to Leatherhead—or they had hidden.

We went down the lane, by the body of the man in black, sodden now from the overnight hail, and broke into the woods at the foot of the hill. We pushed through these towards the railway, without meeting a soul. The woods across the line were but the scarred and blackened ruins of woods; for the most part the trees had fallen, but a certain proportion still stood, dismal gray stems, with dark brown foliage instead of green.

On our side the fire had done no more than scorch the nearer trees; it had failed to secure its footing. In one place the woodmen had been at work on Saturday; trees, felled and freshly trimmed, lay in a clearing, with heaps of sawdust by the sawing-machine and its engine. Hard by was a temporary hut, deserted. There was not a breath of wind this morning, and everything was strangely still. Even the birds were hushed, and as we hurried along, I and the artilleryman talked in whispers, and looked now and again over our shoulders. Once or twice we stopped to listen.

After a time we drew near the road, and as we did so we heard the clatter of hoofs and saw through the tree-stems three cavalry soldiers riding slowly towards Woking. We hailed them, and they halted while we hurried towards them. It was a lieutenant and a couple of privates of the 8th Hussars, with a stand like a theodolite,[1] which the artilleryman told me was a heliograph.[2]

"You are the first men I've seen coming this way this morning," said the lieutenant. "What's brewing?"

His voice and face were eager. The men behind him stared curiously. The artilleryman jumped down the bank into the road and saluted.

"Gun destroyed last night, sir. Have been hiding. Trying to rejoin battery, sir. You'll come in sight of the Martians, I expect, about half a mile along this road."

"What the dickens are they like?" asked the lieutenant.

"Giants in armour, sir. Hundred feet high. Three legs and a body like 'luminium, with a mighty great head in a hood, sir."

"Get out!" said the lieutenant. "What confounded nonsense!"

---

1 A mirror mounted on a pole, used in this situation to communicate the whereabouts of the Martians and warn the artillery of their approach.
2 An apparatus for telegraphing by means of the sun's rays flashed from a mirror. See Appendix I for a photograph of heliograph operators.

"You'll see, sir. They carry a kind of box, sir, that shoots fire and strikes you dead."

"What d'ye mean—a gun?"

"No, sir," and the artilleryman began a vivid account of the Heat-Ray. Halfway through, the lieutenant interrupted him and looked up at me. I was still standing on the bank by the side of the road.

"It's perfectly true," I said.

"Well," said the lieutenant, "I suppose it's my business to see it too. Look here"—to the artilleryman—"we're detailed here clearing people out of their houses. You'd better go along and report yourself to Brigadier-General Marvin, and tell him all you know. He's at Weybridge. Know the way?"

"I do," I said; and he turned his horse southward again.

"Half a mile, you say?" said he.

"At most," I answered, and pointed over the tree-tops southward. He thanked me and rode on, and we saw them no more.

Further along we came upon a group of three women and two children in the road, busy clearing out a labourer's cottage. They had got hold of a little hand-truck, and were piling it up with unclean-looking bundles and shabby furniture. They were all too assiduously[1] engaged to talk to us as we passed.

By Byfleet Station we emerged from the pine-trees, and found the country calm and peaceful under the morning sunlight. We were far beyond the range of the Heat-Ray there, and had it not been for the silent desertion of some of the houses, the stirring movement of packing in others, and the knot of soldiers standing on the bridge over the railway and staring down the line towards Woking, the day would have seemed very like any other Sunday.

Several farm waggons and carts were moving creakily along the road to Addlestone, and suddenly through the gate of a field we saw, across a stretch of flat meadow, six twelve-pounders,[2] standing neatly at equal distances pointing towards Woking. The gunners stood by the guns waiting, and the ammunition waggons were at a business-like distance. The men stood almost as if under inspection.

"That's good!" said I. "They will get one fair shot, at any rate."

---

1 Busily.
2 Artillery, heavier than the field guns described previously. See Appendix I.

The artilleryman hesitated at the gate.

"I shall go on," he said.

Further on towards Weybridge, just over the bridge, there were a number of men in white fatigue jackets throwing up a long rampart,[1] and more guns behind.

"It's bows and arrows against the lightning, anyhow," said the artilleryman. "They 'aven't seen that fire-beam yet."

The officers who were not actively engaged stood and stared over the treetops southwestward, and the men digging would stop every now and again to stare in the same direction.

Byfleet was in a tumult, people packing, and a score of hussars, some of them dismounted, some on horseback, were hunting them about. Three or four black government waggons, with crosses in white circles, and an old omnibus,[2] among other vehicles, were being loaded in the village street. There were scores of people, most of them sufficiently Sabbatical[3] to have assumed their best clothes. The soldiers were having the greatest difficulty in making them realize the gravity of their position. We saw one shrivelled old fellow with a huge box and a score or more of flower-pots containing orchids, angrily expostulating with the corporal who would leave them behind. I stopped and gripped his arm.

"Do you know what's over there?" I said, pointing at the pine-tops that hid the Martians.

"Eh?" said he, turning. "I was explainin' these is vallyble."

"Death!" I shouted. "Death is coming! Death!" and leaving him to digest that if he could, I hurried on after the artilleryman. At the corner I looked back. The soldier had left him, and he was still standing by his box, with the pots of orchids on the lid of it, and staring vaguely over the trees.

No one in Weybridge could tell us where the headquarters were established; the whole place was in such confusion as I had never seen in any town before. Carts, carriages everywhere, the most astonishing miscellany of conveyances and horseflesh. The respectable inhabitants of the place, men in golf and boating costumes, wives prettily dressed, were packing, riverside loafers energetically helping, children excited, and, for the most part, highly

---

1 A broad embankment raised as a fortification.
2 A bus, horse-drawn in this period.
3 Literally means day of worship; people are dressed as if for going to church on Sunday.

delighted at this astonishing variation of their Sunday experiences. In the midst of it all the worthy vicar was very pluckily holding an early celebration, and his bell was jangling out above the excitement.

I and the artilleryman, seated on the step of the drinking fountain, made a very passable meal upon what we had brought with us. Patrols of soldiers—here no longer hussars, but grenadiers[1] in white—were warning people to move now or to take refuge in their cellars as soon as the firing began. We saw as we crossed the railway bridge that a growing crowd of people had assembled in and about the railway-station, and the swarming platform was piled with boxes and packages. The ordinary traffic had been stopped, I believe, in order to allow of the passage of troops and guns to Chertsey, and I have heard since that a savage struggle occurred for places in the special trains that were put on at a later hour.

We remained at Weybridge until mid-day, and at that hour we found ourselves at the place near Shepperton Lock where the Wey and Thames join. Part of the time we spent helping two old women to pack a little cart. The Wey has a treble mouth, and at this point boats are to be hired, and there was a ferry across the river. On the Shepperton side was an inn, with a lawn, and beyond that the tower of Shepperton Church—it has been replaced by a spire—rose above the trees.

Here we found an excited and noisy crowd of fugitives. As yet the flight had not grown to a panic, but there were already far more people than all the boats going to and fro could enable to cross. People came panting along under heavy burdens; one husband and wife were even carrying a small outhouse door between them, with some of their household goods piled thereon. One man told us he meant to try to get away from Shepperton Station.

There was a lot of shouting, and one man was even jesting. The idea people seemed to have here was that the Martians were simply formidable human beings, who might attack and sack the town, to be certainly destroyed in the end. Every now and then people would glance nervously across the Wey, at the meadows towards Chertsey, but everything over there was still.

Across the Thames, except just where the boats landed, everything was quiet, in vivid contrast with the Surrey side. The people who landed there from the boats went tramping off down the lane.

---

1 Originally "grenade throwers," but by this time an élite army regiment.

The big ferry-boat had just made a journey. Three or four soldiers stood on the lawn of the inn, staring and jesting at the fugitives, without offering to help. The inn was closed, as it was now within prohibited hours.[1]

"What's that?" cried a boatman, and "Shut up, you fool!" said a man near me to a yelping dog. Then the sound came again, this time from the direction of Chertsey, a muffled thud—the sound of a gun.

The fighting was beginning. Almost immediately unseen batteries across the river to our right, unseen because of the trees, took up the chorus, firing heavily one after the other. A woman screamed. Everyone stood arrested by the sudden stir of battle, near us and yet invisible to us. Nothing was to be seen save flat meadows, cows feeding unconcernedly for the most part, and silvery pollard willows motionless in the warm sunlight.

"The sojers'll stop 'em," said a woman beside me, doubtfully. A haziness rose over the tree-tops.

Then suddenly we saw a rush of smoke far away up the river, a puff of smoke that jerked up into the air, and hung, and forthwith the ground heaved under foot and a heavy explosion shook the air, smashing two or three windows in the houses near, and leaving us astonished.

"Here they are!" shouted a man in a blue jersey. "Yonder! D'yer see them? Yonder!"

Quickly, one after the other, one, two, three, four of the armoured Martians appeared, far away over the little trees, across the flat meadows that stretch towards Chertsey, and striding hurriedly towards the river. Little cowled figures they seemed at first, going with a rolling motion and as fast as flying birds.

Then, advancing obliquely towards us, came a fifth. Their armoured bodies glittered in the sun as they swept swiftly forward upon the guns, growing rapidly larger as they drew nearer. One on the extreme left, the remotest that is, flourished a huge case high in the air, and the ghostly, terrible Heat-Ray I had already seen on Friday night smote towards Chertsey, and struck the town.

At sight of these strange, swift, and terrible creatures the crowd near the water's edge seemed to me to be for a moment horror-struck. There was no screaming or shouting, but a silence. Then a

---

1 Inns and pubs were allowed to sell alcohol only during particular hours specified by law.

hoarse murmur and a movement of feet—a splashing from the water. A man, too frightened to drop the portmanteau[1] he carried on his shoulder, swung round and sent me staggering with a blow from the corner of his burden. A woman thrust at me with her hand and rushed past me. I turned too with the rush of the people, but I was not too terrified for thought. The terrible Heat-Ray was in my mind. To get under water! That was it!

"Get under water!" I shouted unheeded.

I faced about again, and rushed towards the approaching Martian—rushed right down the gravelly beach and headlong into the water. Others did the same. A boatload of people putting back came leaping out as I rushed past. The stones under my feet were muddy and slippery, and the river was so low that I ran perhaps twenty feet scarcely waist-deep. Then, as the Martian towered overhead scarcely a couple of hundred yards away, I flung myself forward under the surface. The splashes of the people in the boats leaping into the river sounded like thunderclaps in my ears. People were landing hastily on both sides of the river.

But the Martian machine took no more notice for the moment of the people running this way and that than a man would of the confusion of ants in a nest against which his foot has kicked. When, half suffocated, I raised my head above water, the Martian's hood pointed at the batteries that were still firing across the river, and as it advanced it swung loose what must have been the generator of the Heat-Ray.

In another moment it was on the bank, and in a stride wading half-way across. The knees of its foremost legs bent at the further bank, and in another moment it had raised itself to its full height again, close to the village of Shepperton. Forthwith the six guns which, unknown to anyone on the right bank, had been hidden behind the outskirts of that village, fired simultaneously. The sudden near concussion, the last close upon the first, made my heart jump. The monster was already raising the case generating the Heat-Ray as the first shell burst six yards above the hood.

I gave a cry of astonishment. I saw and thought nothing of the other four Martian monsters; my attention was riveted upon the nearer incident. Simultaneously two other shells burst in the air near the body as the hood twisted round in time to receive, but not in time to dodge, the fourth shell.

---

1   A large traveling bag.

The shell burst clean in the face of the thing. The hood bulged, flashed, was whirled off in a dozen tattered fragments of red flesh and glittering metal.

"Hit!" shouted I, with something between a scream and a cheer.

I heard answering shouts from the people in the water about me. I could have leaped out of the water with that momentary exultation.

The decapitated colossus reeled like a drunken giant; but it did not fall over. It recovered its balance by a miracle, and, no longer heeding its steps and with the camera[1] that fired the Heat-Ray now rigidly upheld, it reeled swiftly upon Shepperton. The living intelligence, the Martian within the hood, was slain and splashed to the four winds of heaven, and the thing was now but a mere intricate device of metal whirling to destruction. It drove along in a straight line, incapable of guidance. It struck the tower of Shepperton Church, smashing it down as the impact of a battering ram might have done, swerved aside, blundered on and collapsed with tremendous force into the river out of my sight.

A violent explosion shook the air, and a spout of water, steam, mud, and shattered metal shot far up into the sky. As the camera of the Heat-Ray hit the water, the latter had incontinently flashed into steam. In another moment a huge wave, like a muddy tidal bore, but almost scaldingly hot, came sweeping round the bend upstream. I saw people struggling shorewards, and heard their screaming and shouting faintly above the seething and roar of the Martian's collapse.

For a moment I heeded nothing of the heat, forgot the patent need of self-preservation. I splashed through the tumultuous water, pushing aside a man in black to do so, until I could see round the bend. Half a dozen deserted boats pitched aimlessly upon the confusion of the waves. The fallen Martian came into sight downstream, lying across the river, and for the most part submerged.

Thick clouds of steam were pouring off the wreckage, and through the tumultuously whirling wisps I could see, intermittently and vaguely, the gigantic limbs churning the water and flinging a splash and spray of mud and froth into the air. The tentacles

---

1   The first portable camera was invented by George Eastmann in 1888. These were very large, box-like cameras. Wells himself was an enthusiastic amateur photographer.

swayed and struck like living arms, and, save for the helpless pur-poselessness of these movements, it was as if some wounded thing were struggling for its life amid the waves. Enormous quantities of a ruddy-brown fluid were spurting up in noisy jets out of the machine.

My attention was diverted from this death flurry by a furious yelling, like that of the thing called a siren in our manufacturing towns. A man, knee-deep near the towing path, shouted inaudi-bly to me and pointed. Looking back, I saw the other Martians advancing with gigantic strides down the riverbank from the direction of Chertsey. The Shepperton guns spoke this time unavailingly.

At that I ducked at once under water, and, holding my breath until movement was an agony, blundered painfully ahead under the surface as long as I could. The water was in a tumult about me, and rapidly growing hotter.

When for a moment I raised my head to take breath and throw the hair and water from my eyes, the steam was rising in a whirling white fog that at first hid the Martians altogether. The noise was deafening. Then I saw them dimly, colossal figures of gray, magni-fied by the mist. They had passed by me, and two were stooping over the frothing, tumultuous ruins of their comrade.

The third and fourth stood beside him in the water, one per-haps two hundred yards from me, the other towards Laleham. The generators of the Heat-Rays waved high, and the hissing beams smote down this way and that.

The air was full of sound, a deafening and confusing conflict of noises, the clangorous[1] din of the Martians, the crash of falling houses, the thud of trees, fences, sheds flashing into flame, and the crackling and roaring of fire. Dense black smoke was leaping up to mingle with the steam from the river, and as the Heat-Ray went to and fro over Weybridge, its impact was marked by flashes of incandescent white, that gave place at once to a smoky dance of lurid flames. The nearer houses still stood intact, awaiting their fate, shadowy, faint and pallid in the steam, with the fire behind them going to and fro.

For a moment, perhaps, I stood there, breast-high in the almost boiling water, dumbfounded at my position, hopeless of escape. Through the reek I could see the people who had been with me

---

1 A loud, metallic ringing sound.

in the river scrambling out of the water through the reeds, like little frogs hurrying through grass from the advance of a man, or running to and fro in utter dismay on the towing-path.

Then suddenly the white flashes of the Heat-Ray came leaping towards me. The houses caved in as they dissolved at its touch, and darted out flames; the trees changed to fire with a roar. It flickered up and down the towing-path, licking off the people who ran this way and that, and came down to the water's edge not fifty yards from where I stood. It swept across the river to Shepperton, and the water in its track rose in a boiling weal crested with steam. I turned shoreward.

In another moment the huge wave, well-nigh at the boiling-point had rushed upon me. I screamed aloud, and scalded, half blinded, agonized, I staggered through the leaping, hissing water towards the shore. Had my foot stumbled, it would have been the end. I fell helplessly, in full sight of the Martians, upon the broad, bare gravelly spit that runs down to mark the angle of the Wey and Thames. I expected nothing but death.

I have a dim memory of the foot of a Martian coming down within a score of yards of my head, driving straight into the loose gravel, whirling it this way and that and lifting again; of a long suspense, and then of the four carrying the débris of their comrade between them, now clear and then presently faint, through a veil of smoke, receding interminably, as it seemed to me, across a vast space of river and meadow. And then, very slowly, I realized that by a miracle I had escaped.

XIII.

HOW I FELL IN WITH THE CURATE[1]

After giving this sudden lesson in the power of terrestrial weapons, the Martians retreated to their original position upon Horsell Common, and in their haste, and encumbered with the débris of their smashed companion, they no doubt overlooked many such a stray and unnecessary victim as myself. Had they left their comrade and pushed on forthwith, there was nothing at that time between them and London but batteries of twelve-pounder guns, and they would certainly have reached the capital in advance of the tidings

---

1   A member of the clergy who is either in charge of a parish or who is serving as an assistant in a parish.

of their approach; as sudden, dreadful, and destructive their advent would have been as the earthquake that destroyed Lisbon a century ago.[1]

But they were in no hurry. Cylinder followed cylinder on its interplanetary flight; every twenty-four hours brought them reinforcement. And, meanwhile, the military and naval authorities, now fully alive to the tremendous power of their antagonists, worked with furious energy. Every minute a fresh gun came into position until, before twilight, every copse, every row of suburban villas on the hilly slopes about Kingston and Richmond, masked an expectant black muzzle. And through the charred and desolated area—perhaps twenty square miles altogether—that encircled the Martian encampment on Horsell Common, through charred and ruined villages among the green trees, through the blackened and smoking arcades that had been but a day ago pine spinneys,[2] crawled the devoted scouts with the heliographs that were presently to warn the gunners of the Martian approach. But the Martians now understood our command of artillery and the danger of human proximity, and not a man ventured within a mile of either cylinder, save at the price of his life.

It would seem that these giants spent the earlier part of the afternoon in going to and fro, transferring everything from the second and third cylinders—the second in Addlestone Golf Links, and the third at Pyrford—to their original pit on Horsell Common. Over that, above the blackened heather and ruined buildings that stretched far and wide, stood one as sentinel, while the rest abandoned their vast Fighting-Machines and descended into the pit. They were hard at work there far into the night, and the towering pillar of dense green smoke that rose therefrom could be seen from the hills about Merrow, and even, it is said, from Banstead and Epsom Downs.

And while the Martians behind me were thus preparing for their next sally, and in front of me Humanity gathered for the battle, I made my way with infinite pains and labour from the fire and smoke of burning Weybridge towards London.

I saw an abandoned boat, very small and remote, drifting downstream, and throwing off the most of my sodden clothes, I went after

---

1   Lisbon, the capital of Portugal, was almost completely destroyed by a devastating earthquake in 1755.
2   Small clumps of trees, not large enough to be a wood.

it, gained it, and so escaped out of that destruction. There were no oars in the boat, but I contrived to paddle, as much as my parboiled hands would allow, down the river towards Halliford and Walton, going very tediously and continually looking behind me, as you may well understand. I followed the river, because I considered that the water gave me my best chance of escape should these giants return.

The hot water from the Martian's overthrow drifted downstream with me, so that for the best part of a mile I could see little of either bank. Once, however, I made out a string of black figures hurrying across the meadows from the direction of Weybridge. Halliford, it seemed, was quite deserted, and several of the houses facing the river were on fire. It was strange to see the place quite tranquil, quite desolate under the hot blue sky, with the smoke and little threads of flame going straight up into the heat of the afternoon. Never before had I seen houses burning without the accompaniment of an inconvenient crowd. A little further on the dry reeds up the bank were smoking and glowing, and a line of fire inland was marching steadily across a late field of hay.

For a long time I drifted, so painful and weary was I after the violence I had been through, and so intense the heat upon the water. Then my fears got the better of me again, and I resumed my paddling. The sun scorched my bare back. At last, as the bridge at Walton was coming into sight round the bend, my fever and faintness overcame my fears, and I landed on the Middlesex bank and lay down, deadly sick, amidst the long grass. I suppose the time was then about four or five o'clock. I got up presently, walked perhaps half a mile without meeting a soul, and then lay down again in the shadow of a hedge. I seem to remember talking wonderingly to myself during that last spurt. I was also very thirsty, and bitterly regretful I had drunk no more water. It is a curious thing that I felt angry with my wife; I cannot account for it, but my impotent desire to reach Leatherhead worried me excessively.

I do not clearly remember the arrival of the curate, so that I probably dozed. I became aware of him as a seated figure in soot-smudged shirt sleeves, and with his upturned clean-shaven face staring at a faint flickering that danced over the sky. The sky was what is called a mackerel sky,[1] rows and rows of faint down-plumes of cloud, just tinted with the midsummer sunset.

---

1 A mackerel is a seawater fish that has rows of dark markings on its back. The rows of clouds resemble these markings.

I sat up, and at the rustle of my motion he looked at me quickly.

"Have you any water?" I asked abruptly. He shook his head.

"You have been asking for water for the last hour," he said.

For a moment we were silent, taking stock of each other. I dare say he found me a strange enough figure, naked, save for my water-soaked trousers and socks, scalded, and my face and shoulders blackened by the smoke. His face was a fair weakness, his chin retreated,[1] and his hair lay in crisp, almost flaxen curls on his low forehead; his eyes were rather large, pale blue, and blankly staring. He spoke abruptly, looking vacantly away from me.

"What does it mean?" he said. "What do these things mean?"

I stared at him and made no answer.

He extended a thin white hand and spoke in almost a complaining tone.

"Why are these things permitted? What sins have we done? The morning service was over, I was walking through the roads to clear my brain for the afternoon, and then—fire, earthquake, death! As if it were Sodom and Gomorrah![2] All our work undone, all the work—What are these Martians?"

"What are we?" I answered, clearing my throat.

He gripped his knees and turned to look at me again. For half a minute, perhaps, he stared silently.

"I was walking through the roads to clear my brain," he said. "And suddenly, fire, earthquake, death!"

He relapsed into silence, with his chin now sunken almost to his knees.

Presently he began waving his hand.

"All the work—all the Sunday-schools—What have we done—what has Weybridge done? Everything gone—everything destroyed. The church! We rebuilt it only three years ago. Gone!—swept out of existence! Why?"

Another pause, and he broke out again like one demented.

"The smoke of her burning goeth up for ever and ever!"[3] he shouted.

---

1 His chin does not stick out, but instead recedes under his mouth. Some Victorians believed that the shape of the head indicated moral character-istics, and Wells's description implies that the curate is weak.

2 In Genesis 18:20-28 these cities are destroyed by fire because of the sins of the people.

3 Revelations 6:16-17 describes the end of the world in these terms.

His eyes flamed, and he pointed a lean finger in the direction of Weybridge.

By this time I was beginning to take his measure. The tremendous tragedy in which he had been involved—it was evident he was a fugitive from Weybridge—had driven him to the very verge of his reason.

"Are we far from Sunbury?" I said, in a matter-of-fact tone.

"What are we to do?" he asked. "Are these creatures everywhere? Has the earth been given over to them?"

"Are we far from Sunbury?"

"Only this morning I officiated at early celebration?....."

"Things have changed," I said, quietly. "You must keep your head. There is still hope."

"Hope!"

"Yes; Plentiful hope—for all this destruction!"

I began to explain my view of our position. He listened at first, but as I went on the interest in his eyes gave place to their former stare, and his regard wandered from me.

"This must be the beginning of the end," he said, interrupting me. "The end! The great and terrible day of the Lord! When men shall call upon the mountains and the rocks to fall upon them and hide them—hide them from the face of Him that sitteth upon the throne!"

I began to understand the position. I ceased my laboured reasoning, struggled to my feet, and, standing over him, laid my hand on his shoulder.

"Be a man" said I. "You are scared out of your wits! What good is religion if it collapses at calamity? Think of what earthquakes and floods, wars and volcanoes, have done before to men. Did you think God had exempted Weybridge....? He is not an insurance agent, man."

For a time he sat in blank silence.

"But how can we escape?" he asked, suddenly. "They are invulnerable, they are pitiless...."

"Neither the one nor, perhaps, the other," I answered. "And the mightier they are the more sane and wary should we be. One of them was killed yonder not three hours ago."

"Killed!" he said, staring about him. "How can God's ministers be killed?"

"I saw it happen." I proceeded to tell him. "We have chanced to come in for the thick of it," said I, "and that is all."

"What is that flicker in the sky?" he asked abruptly.

I told him it was the heliograph signalling—that it was the sign of human help and effort in the sky.

"We are in the midst of it," I said, "quiet as it is. That flicker in the sky tells of the gathering storm. Yonder, I take it, are the Martians, and Londonward, where those hills rise about Richmond and Kingston, and the trees give cover, earthworks are being thrown up and guns are being laid. Presently the Martians will be coming this way again...."

And even as I spoke he sprang to his feet and stopped me by a gesture.

"Listen!" he said.

From beyond the low hills across the water came the dull resonance of distant guns and a remote, weird crying. Then everything was still. A cockchafer[1] came droning over the hedge and past us. High in the west the crescent moon hung faint and pale, above the smoke of Weybridge and Shepperton and the hot still splendour of the sunset.

"We had better follow this path," I said, "northward."

XIV.
IN LONDON

My younger brother was in London when the Martians fell at Woking. He was a medical student, working for an imminent examination, and he heard nothing of the arrival until Saturday morning. The morning papers on Saturday contained, in addition to lengthy special articles on the planet Mars, on life in the planets, and so forth, a brief and vaguely-worded telegram, all the more striking for its brevity.

The Martians, alarmed by the approach of a crowd, had killed a number of people with a quick-firing gun, so the story ran. The telegram concluded with the words: "Formidable as they seem to be, the Martians have not moved from the pit into which they have fallen, and, indeed, seem incapable of doing so. Probably this is due to the relative strength of the earth's gravitational energy." On that last text their leader-writers expanded very comfortingly.

Of course all the students in the crammer's[2] biology class, to which my brother went that day, were intensely interested, but

---

1 European large flying beetle.
2 Somebody who helps students "cram" for their exams. This was usually a graduate student or somebody with an advanced degree; Wells himself worked as a "crammer" preparing students for science exams.

there were no signs of any unusual excitement in the streets. The afternoon papers puffed scraps of news under big headlines. They had nothing to tell beyond the movements of troops about the common, and the burning of the pine-woods between Woking and Weybridge, until eight. Then the *St. James's Gazette*, in an extra special edition, announced the bare fact of the interruption of telegraphic communication. This was thought to be due to the falling of burning pine-trees across the line. Nothing more of the fighting was known that night, the night of my drive to Leatherhead and back.

My brother felt no anxiety about us, as he knew from the description in the papers that the cylinder was a good two miles from my house. He made up his mind to run down that night to me, in order, as he says, to see the things before they were killed. He despatched a telegram, which never reached me, about four o'clock, and spent the evening at a music-hall.[1]

In London, also, on Saturday night there was a thunderstorm, and my brother reached Waterloo in a cab. On the platform from which the midnight train usually starts he learnt, after some waiting, that an accident prevented trains from reaching Woking that night. The nature of the accident he could not ascertain; indeed, the railway authorities did not clearly know at that time. There was very little excitement in the station, as the officials, failing to realize that anything further than a breakdown between Byfleet and Woking junction had occurred, were running the theatre trains which usually passed through Woking round by Virginia Water or Guildford. They were busy making the necessary arrangements to alter the route of the Southampton and Portsmouth Sunday League excursions.[2] A nocturnal newspaper reporter, mistaking my brother for the traffic manager, whom he does to a slight resemble, waylaid and tried to interview him. Few people, excepting the railway officials, connected the breakdown with the Martians.

I have read, in another account of these events, that on Sunday morning "all London was electrified by the news from Woking." As a matter of fact, there was nothing to justify that very extravagant phrase. Plenty of people in London did not hear of

---

1 A vaudeville type of entertainment in a theater comprised of singing, comedy and dancing.
2 Groups opposed to opening the pubs on Sundays organized wholesome alternatives such as excursions.

the Martians until the panic of Monday morning. Those who did took some time to realize all that the hastily worded telegrams in the Sunday papers conveyed. The majority of people in London do not read Sunday papers.

The habit of personal security, moreover, is so deeply fixed in the Londoner's mind, and startling intelligence so much a matter of course in the papers, that they could read without any personal tremors: "About seven o'clock last night the Martians came out of the cylinder, and, moving about under an armour of metallic shields, have completely wrecked Woking Station with the adjacent houses, and massacred an entire battalion of the Cardigan Regiment. No details are known. Maxims have been absolutely useless against their armour; the field-guns have been disabled by them. Flying hussars have been galloping into Chertsey. The Martians appear to be moving slowly towards Chertsey or Windsor. Great anxiety prevails in West Surrey, and earthworks are being thrown up to check the advance Londonwards." That was how the Sunday *Sun* put it, and a clever and remarkably prompt "hand-book" article in the *Referee* compared the affair to a menagerie[1] suddenly let loose in a village.

No one in London knew positively of the nature of the armoured Martians, and there was still a fixed idea that these monsters must be sluggish: "crawling," "creeping painfully"—such expressions occurred in almost all the earlier reports. None of the telegrams could have been written by an eye-witness of their advance. The Sunday papers printed separate editions as further news came to hand, some even in default of it. But there was practically nothing more to tell people until late in the afternoon, when the authorities gave the press agencies the news in their possession. It was stated that the people of Walton and Weybridge, and all that district, were pouring along the roads Londonward, and that was all.

My brother went to church at the Foundling Hospital in the morning, still in ignorance of what had happened on the previous night. There he heard allusions made to the invasion, and a special prayer for peace. Coming out, he bought a *Referee*. He became alarmed at the news in this, and went again to Waterloo Station to find out if communication were restored. The omnibuses, carriages, cyclists, and innumerable people walking in their best

---

1   A collection of wild or foreign animals kept for exhibition.

clothes, seemed scarcely affected by the strange intelligence that the news-vendors were disseminating. People were interested, or, if alarmed, alarmed only on account of the local residents. At the station he heard for the first time that the Windsor and Chertsey lines were now interrupted. The porters told him that several remarkable telegrams had been received in the morning from Byfleet and Chertsey Stations, but that these had abruptly ceased. My brother could get very little precise detail out of them. "There's fighting going on about Weybridge" was the extent of their information.

The train service was now very much disorganized. Quite a number of people, who had been expecting friends from places on the South-Western network, were standing about the station. One gray-headed old gentleman came and abused the South-Western Company bitterly to my brother. "It wants showing up," he said.

One or two trains came in from Richmond, Putney, and Kingston, containing people who had gone out for a day's boating, and found the locks closed and a feeling of panic in the air. A man in a blue and white blazer addressed my brother, full of strange tidings.

"There's hosts of people driving into Kingston in traps[1] and carts and things, with boxes of valuables and all that," he said. "They come from Molesey and Weybridge and Walton, and they say there's been guns heard at Chertsey, heavy firing, and that mounted soldiers have told them to get off at once because the Martians are coming. We heard guns firing at Hampton Court Station, but we thought it was thunder. What the dickens does it all mean? The Martians can't get out of their pit, can they?"

My brother could not tell him.

Afterwards he found that the vague feeling of alarm had spread to the clients of the underground railway, and that the Sunday excursionists began to return from all over the South-Western "lungs"[2]—Barnes, Wimbledon, Richmond Park, Kew, and so forth—at unnaturally early hours; but not a soul had anything more than vague hearsay to tell of. Everyone connected with the terminus seemed ill-tempered.

---

1 Small two-wheeled carriages.
2 Green spaces supposed to act like "lungs" providing clean air for the rest of London.

About five o'clock the gathering crowd in the station was immensely excited by the opening of the line of communication, which is almost invariably closed, between the South-Eastern and the South-Western stations, and the passage of carriage-trucks bearing huge guns and carriages crammed with soldiers. These were the guns that were brought up from Woolwich and Chatham to cover Kingston. There was an exchange of pleasantries: "You'll get eaten!" "We're the beast-tamers!" and so forth. A little while after that a squad of police came into the station and began to clear the public off the platforms, and my brother went out into the street again.

The church bells were ringing for evensong,[1] and a squad of Salvation Army[2] lasses[3] came singing down Waterloo Road. On the bridge a number of loafers were watching a curious brown scum that came drifting down the stream in patches. The sun was just setting, and the Clock Tower and the Houses of Parliament rose against one of the most peaceful skies it is possible to imagine, a sky of gold, barred with long transverse stripes of reddish-purple cloud. There was talk of a floating body. One of the men there, a reservist[4] he said he was, told my brother he had seen the heliograph flickering in the west.

In Wellington Street my brother met a couple of sturdy roughs,[5] who had just rushed out of Fleet Street with still wet newspapers and staring placards. "Dreadful catastrophe!" they bawled one to the other down Wellington Street. "Fighting at Weybridge! Full description! Repulse of the Martians! London said to be in danger!" He had to give threepence[6] for a copy of that paper.

Then it was, and then only, that he realized something of the full power and terror of these monsters. He learned that they were not merely a handful of small sluggish creatures, but that they were minds swaying vast mechanical bodies, and that they could move swiftly and smite with such power that even the mightiest guns could not stand against them.

---

1   Evening prayer.
2   William Booth had founded the Salvation Army in 1878.
3   Young women.
4   Somebody in the army reserve force.
5   Working-class young men.
6   Wells is implying that newspapers were exploiting the situation by making their newspapers unusually expensive.

They were described as "vast spider-like machines, nearly a hundred feet high, capable of the speed of an express-train, and able to shoot out a beam of intense heat." Masked batteries, chiefly of field-guns, had been planted in the country about Horsell Common, and especially between the Woking district and London. Five of the machines had been seen moving towards the Thames, and one, by a freak of chance, had been destroyed. In the other cases the shells had missed, and the batteries had been at once annihilated by the Heat-Rays. Heavy losses of soldiers were mentioned, but the tone of the despatch was optimistic.

The Martians had been repulsed; they were not invulnerable. They had retreated to their triangle of cylinders again, in the circle about Woking. Signallers with heliographs were pushing forward upon them from all sides. Guns were in rapid transit from Windsor, Portsmouth, Aldershot, Woolwich—even from the north; among others, long wire-guns[1] of ninety-five tons from Woolwich. Altogether one hundred and sixteen were in position or being hastily laid, chiefly covering London. Never before in England had there been such a vast or rapid concentration of military material.

Any further cylinders that fell, it was hoped, could be destroyed at once by high explosives, which were being rapidly manufactured and distributed. No doubt, ran the report, the situation was of the strangest and gravest description, but the public was exhorted to avoid and discourage panic. No doubt the Martians were strange and terrible in the extreme, but at the outside there could not be more than twenty of them against our millions.

The authorities had reason to suppose, from the size of the cylinders, that at the outside there could not be more than five in each cylinder—fifteen altogether. And one at least was disposed of—perhaps more. The public would be fairly warned of the approach of danger, and elaborate measures were being taken for the protection of the people in the threatened south-western suburbs. And so, with reiterated assurances of the safety of London, and the confidence of the authorities to cope with the difficulty, this quasi-proclamation closed.

This was printed in enormous type on paper so fresh that it was still wet, and there had been no time to add a word of comment. It was curious, my brother said, to see how ruthlessly the other

---

1 Artillery with wire wound in the barrels that increased their power and range.

contents of the paper had been hacked and taken out to give this place.

All down Wellington Street people could be seen fluttering out the pink sheets and reading, and the Strand was suddenly noisy with the voices of an army of hawkers[1] following these pioneers. Men came scrambling off buses to secure copies. Certainly this news excited people intensely, whatever their previous apathy. The shutters of a map-shop in the Strand were being taken down, my brother said, and a man in his Sunday raiment, lemon-yellow gloves even, was visible inside the window, hastily fastening maps of Surrey to the glass.

Going on along the Strand to Trafalgar Square, the paper in his hand, my brother saw some of the fugitives from West Surrey. There was a man with his wife and two boys and some articles of furniture driving a cart such as green-grocers use. He was driving from the direction of Westminster Bridge, and close behind him came a hay-waggon with five or six respectable-looking people in it, and some boxes and bundles. The faces of these people were haggard, and their entire appearance contrasted conspicuously with the Sabbath-best appearance of the people on the omnibuses. People in fashionable clothing peeped at them out of cabs. They stopped at the Square as if undecided which way to take, and finally turned eastward along the Strand. Some way after these came a man in workday clothes, riding one of those old-fashioned tricycles with a small front-wheel. He was dirty and white in the face.

My brother turned down towards Victoria, and met a number of such people. He had a vague idea that he might see something of me. He noticed an unusual number of police regulating the traffic. Some of the refugees were exchanging news with the people on the omnibuses. One was professing to have seen the Martians. "Boilers on stilts, I tell you, striding along like men." Most of them were excited and animated by their strange experience.

Beyond Victoria the public-houses were doing a lively trade with these arrivals. At all the street corners groups of people were reading papers, talking excitedly, or staring at these unusual Sunday visitors. They seemed to increase as night drew on, until at last the roads, my brother said, were like Epsom High Street on a Derby Day. My brother addressed several of these fugitives and got unsatisfactory answers from most.

---

1 People who sold in the streets by shouting out the name of their product.

None of them could tell him any news of Woking except one man, who assured him that Woking had been entirely destroyed on the previous night.

"I come from Byfleet," he said. "A man on a bicycle came through the place in the early morning, and ran from door to door warning us to come away. Then came soldiers. We went out to look, and there were clouds of smoke to the south—nothing but smoke, and not a soul coming that way. Then we heard the guns at Chertsey, and folks coming from Weybridge. So I've locked up my house and come on."

At the time there was a strong feeling in the streets that the authorities were to blame for their incapacity to dispose of the invaders without all this inconvenience.

About eight o'clock a noise of heavy firing was distinctly audible all over the south of London. My brother could not hear it for the traffic in the main streets, but by striking through the quiet back streets to the river he was able to distinguish it quite plainly.

He walked from Westminster to his apartments, near Regent's Park, about two. He was now very anxious on my account, and disturbed at the evident magnitude of the trouble. His mind was inclined to run, even as mine had run on Saturday, on military details. He thought of all those silent expectant guns, of the suddenly nomadic countryside; he tried to imagine "boilers on stilts" a hundred feet high.

There were one or two cartloads of refugees passing along Oxford Street, and several in the Marylebone Road, but so slowly was the news spreading that Regent Street and Portland Place were full of their usual Sunday-night promenaders,[1] albeit they talked in groups, and along the edge of Regent's Park there were as many silent couples "walking out" together under the scattered gas-lamps as ever there had been. The night was warm and still, and a little oppressive, the sound of guns continued intermittently, and after midnight there seemed to be sheet lightning in the south.

He read and re-read the paper, fearing the worst had happened to me. He was restless, and after supper prowled out again aimlessly. He returned and tried to divert his attention to his examination notes in vain. He went to bed a little after midnight, and he was awakened out of some lurid dreams in the small hours of Monday by the sound of door-knockers, feet running in the street, distant

---

1 People dressed in their best clothes out for a stroll.

drumming, and a clamour of bells. Red reflections danced on the ceiling. For a moment he lay astonished, wondering whether day had come or the world gone mad. Then he jumped out of bed and ran to the window.

His room was an attic, and as he thrust his head out, up and down the street there were a dozen echoes to the noise of his window-sash, and heads in every kind of night disarray appeared. Inquiries were being shouted. "They are coming!" bawled a policeman, hammering at the door; "the Martians are coming!" and hurried to the next door.

The noise of drumming and trumpeting came from the Albany Street Barracks, and every church within earshot was hard at work killing sleep with a vehement disorderly tocsin.[1] There was a noise of doors opening, and window after window in the houses opposite flashed from darkness into yellow illumination.

Up the street came galloping a closed carriage, bursting abruptly into noise at the corner, rising to a clattering climax under the window, and dying away slowly in the distance. Close on the rear of this came a couple of cabs, the forerunners of a long procession of flying vehicles, going for the most part to Chalk Farm Station, where the North-Western special trains were loading up, instead of coming down the gradient into Euston.

For a long time my brother stared out of the window in blank astonishment, watching the policemen hammering at door after door, and delivering their incomprehensible message. Then the door behind him opened, and the man who lodged across the landing came in, dressed only in shirt, trousers, and slippers, his braces loose about his waist, his hair disordered from his pillow.

"What the devil is it?" he asked. "A fire? What a devil of a row!"

They both craned their heads out of the window, straining to hear what the policemen were shouting. People were coming out of the side streets, and standing in groups at the corners talking.

"What the devil is it all about?" said my brother's fellow-lodger.

My brother answered him vaguely and began to dress, running with each garment to the window in order to miss nothing of the growing excitement of the streets. And presently men selling unnaturally early newspapers came bawling into the street:

"London in danger of suffocation! The Kingston and Richmond defences forced! Fearful massacres in the Thames Valley!"

---

1 Alarm bell or warning signal.

And all about him—in the rooms below, in the houses on either side and across the road, and behind in the Park Terraces and in the hundred other streets of that part of Marleybone, and the West-bourne Park district and St. Pancras, and westward and northward in Kilburn and St. John's Wood and Hampstead, and eastward in Shoreditch and Highbury and Haggerston and Hoxton, and, indeed, through all the vastness of London from Ealing to East Ham—people were rubbing their eyes, and opening windows to stare out and ask aimless questions, and dressing hastily as the first breath of the coming storm of Fear blew through the streets. It was the dawn of the great panic. London, which had gone to bed on Sunday night stupid and inert, was awakened, in the small hours of Monday morning to a vivid sense of danger.

Unable from his window to learn what was happening, my brother went down and out into the street, just as the sky between the parapets of the houses grew pink with the early dawn. The fly-ing people on foot and in vehicles grew more numerous every moment. "Black Smoke!" he heard people crying, and again "Black Smoke!" The contagion of such a unanimous fear was inevitable. As my brother hesitated on the doorstep, he saw another news-vendor approaching, and got a copy forthwith. The man was run-ning away with the rest, and selling his papers as he ran for a shilling each[1]—a grotesque mingling of profit and panic.

And from this paper my brother read that catastrophic despatch of the Commander-in-Chief:

The Martians are able to discharge enormous clouds of a black and poisonous vapour[2] by means of rockets. They have smoth-ered our batteries, destroyed Richmond, Kingston, and Wim-bledon, and are advancing slowly towards London, destroying everything on the way. It is impossible to stop them. There is no safety from the Black Smoke but in instant flight.

That was all, but it was enough. The whole population of the great six-million city was stirring, slipping, running; presently it would be pouring *en masse*[3] northward.

1　The price of a newspaper has now risen from threepence to a shilling, or twelve pence.
2　Wells's vision of the use of poison gas, which was used as a weapon for the first time in World War I.
3　In one huge mass.

"Black Smoke!" the voices cried. "Fire!"

The bells of the neighbouring church made a jangling tumult, a cart carelessly driven smashed, amidst shrieks and curses, against the water-trough up the street. Sickly yellow light went to and fro in the houses, and some of the passing cabs flaunted unextinguished lamps. And overhead the dawn was growing brighter, clear and steady and calm.

He heard footsteps running to and fro in the rooms, and up and down stairs behind him. His landlady came to the door, loosely wrapped in dressing gown and shawl; her husband followed, ejaculating.

As my brother began to realize the import of all these things, he turned hastily to his own room, put all his available money—some ten pounds altogether—into his pockets, and went out again into the streets.

XV.
WHAT HAD HAPPENED IN SURREY

It was while the curate had sat and talked so wildly to me under the hedge in the flat meadows near Halliford, and while my brother was watching the fugitives stream over Westminster Bridge, that the Martians had resumed the offensive. So far as one can ascertain from the conflicting accounts that have been put forth, the majority of them remained busied with preparations in the Horsell pit until nine that night, hurrying on some operation that disengaged huge volumes of green smoke.

But three certainly came out about eight o'clock and, advancing slowly and cautiously, made their way through Byfleet and Pyrford towards Ripley and Weybridge, and so came in sight of the expectant batteries against the setting sun. These Martians did not advance in a body, but in a line, each perhaps a mile and a half from his nearest fellow. They communicated with one another by means of siren-like howls, running up and down the scale from one note to another.

It was this howling and the firing of the guns at Ripley and St. George's Hill that we had heard at Upper Halliford. The Ripley gunners, unseasoned artillery volunteers who ought never to have been placed in such a position, fired one wild, premature, ineffectual volley, and bolted on horse and foot through the deserted village, while the Martian walked over their guns serenely without using his Heat-Ray, stepped gingerly among them, passed in front of them, and so came unexpectedly upon the guns in Painshill Park, which he destroyed.

The St. George's Hill men, however, were better led or of a better mettle. Hidden by a pine-wood as they were, they seem to have been quite unsuspected by the Martian nearest to them. They laid their guns[1] as deliberately as if they had been on parade, and fired at about a thousand yards range.

The shells flashed all round the Martian, and they saw him advance a few paces, stagger, and go down. Everybody yelled together, and the guns were reloaded in frantic haste. The overthrown Martian set up a prolonged ululation,[2] and immediately a second glittering giant, answering him, appeared over the trees to the south. It would seem that a leg of the tripod had been smashed by one of the shells. The whole of the second volley flew wide of the Martian on the ground, and, simultaneously, both his companions brought their Heat-Rays to bear on the battery. The ammunition blew up, the pine-trees all about the guns flashed into fire, and only one or two of the men who were already running over the crest of the hill escaped.

After this it would seem that the three took counsel together and halted, and the scouts who were watching them report that they remained absolutely stationary for the next half-hour. The Martian who had been overthrown crawled tediously out of his hood, a small brown figure, oddly suggestive from that distance of a speck of blight, and apparently engaged in the repair of his support. About nine he had finished, for his cowl was then seen above the trees again.

It was a few minutes past nine that night when these three sentinels were joined by four other Martians, each carrying a thick black tube. A similar tube was handed to each of the three, and the seven proceeded to distribute themselves at equal distances along a curved line between St. George's Hill, Weybridge, and the village of Send, south-west of Ripley.

A dozen rockets sprang out of the hills before them so soon as they began to move, and warned the waiting batteries about Ditton and Esher. At the same time four of their Fighting Machines, similarly armed with tubes, crossed the river, and two of them, black against the western sky, came into sight of myself and the

---

1 Prepared to fire at the Martians.
2 A high-pitched cry that goes up and down the scale.

curate as we hurried wearily and painfully along the road that runs northward out of Halliford. They moved, as it seemed to us, upon a cloud, for a milky mist covered the fields and rose to a third of their height.

At this sight the curate cried faintly in his throat, and began running; but I knew it was no good running from a Martian, and I turned aside and crawled through dewy nettles and brambles into the broad ditch by the side of the road. He looked back, saw what I was doing, and turned to join me.

The two Martians halted, the nearer to us standing and facing Sunbury, the remoter being a grey indistinctness towards the evening star, away towards Staines.

The occasional howling of the Martians had ceased; they took up their positions in the huge crescent about their cylinders in absolute silence. It was a crescent with twelve miles between its horns. Never since the devising of gunpowder was the beginning of a battle so still. To us and to an observer about Ripley it would have had precisely the same effect—the Martians seemed in solitary possession of the darkling night, lit only as it was by the slender moon, the stars, the after-glow of the daylight, and the ruddy glare from St. George's Hill and the woods of Painshill.

But facing that crescent everywhere—at Staines, Hounslow, Ditton, Esher, Ockham, behind hills and woods south of the river, and across the flat grass meadows to the north of it, wherever a cluster of trees or village houses gave sufficient cover—the guns were waiting. The signal rockets burst and rained their sparks through the night and vanished, and the spirit of all those watching batteries rose to a tense expectation. The Martians had but to advance into the line of fire, and instantly those motionless black forms of men, those guns glittering so darkly in the early night, would explode into a thunderous fury of battle.

No doubt the thought that was uppermost in a thousand of those vigilant minds, even as it was uppermost in mine, was the riddle—how much they understood of us. Did they grasp that we in our millions were organized, disciplined, working together? Or did they interpret our spurts of fire, the sudden stinging of our shells, our steady investment of their encampment, as we should the furious unanimity of onslaught in a disturbed hive of bees? Did they dream they might exterminate us? (At that time no one knew what food they needed.) A hundred such questions struggled together in my mind as I watched that vast sentinel shape. And in the back of my mind was the sense of all the huge unknown and hidden forces Londonward. Had they prepared pitfalls? Were the powder-mills at Hounslow ready as a snare? Would the Londoners have the heart and courage to make a greater Moscow[1] of their mighty province of houses?

Then, after an interminable time, as it seemed to us, crouching and peering through the hedge, came a sound like the distant concussion of a gun. Another nearer, and then another. And then the Martian beside us raised his tube on high and discharged it, gunwise, with a heavy report that made the ground heave. The one towards Staines answered him. There was no flash, no smoke, simply that loaded detonation.

I was so excited by these heavy minute-guns[2] following one another that I so far forgot my personal safety and my scalded hands as to clamber up into the hedge and stare towards Sunbury. As I did so a second report followed, and a big projectile hurtled overhead towards Hounslow. I expected at least to see smoke or fire, or some such evidence of its work. But all I saw was the deep-blue sky above, with one solitary star, and the white mist spreading wide and low beneath. And there had been no crash, no answering explosion. The silence was restored; the minute lengthened to three.

"What has happened?" said the curate, standing up beside me.

"Heaven knows!" said I.

A bat flickered by and vanished. A distant tumult of shouting began and ceased. I looked again at the Martian, and saw he was now moving eastward along the riverbank, with a swift, rolling motion.

Every moment I expected the fire of some hidden battery to spring upon him; but the evening calm was unbroken. The figure of the Martian grew smaller as he receded, and presently the mist and the gathering night had swallowed him up. By a common impulse we clambered higher. Towards Sunbury was a dark appearance, as though a conical hill had suddenly come into being there, hiding our view of the further country; and then, remoter across the river, over Walton, we saw another such summit. These hill-like forms grew lower and broader even as we stared.

---

1 When Napoleon invaded Russia in 1812 he was finally stopped at Moscow.

2 Rapid-fire guns that could be fired every minute.

Moved by a sudden thought, I looked northward, and there I perceived a third of these cloudy black kopjes[1] had risen.

Everything had suddenly become very still. Far away to the southeast, marking the quiet, we heard the Martians hooting to one another, and then the air quivered again with the distant thud of their guns. But the earthly artillery made no reply.

Now at the time we could not understand these things, but later I was to learn the meaning of these ominous kopjes that gathered in the twilight. Each of the Martians, standing in the great crescent I have described, had discharged at some unknown signal, by means of the gun-like tube he carried, a huge canister over whatever hill, copse, cluster of houses, or other possible cover for guns, chanced to be in front of him. Some fired only one of these, some two—as in the case of the one we had seen; the one at Ripley is said to have discharged no fewer than five at that time. These canisters smashed on striking the ground—they did not explode—and incontinently disengaged an enormous volume of heavy, inky vapour, coiling and pouring upward in a huge and ebony cumulus cloud, a gaseous hill that sank and spread itself slowly over the surrounding country. And the touch of that vapour, the inhaling of its pungent wisps, was death to all that breathes.

It was heavy, this vapour, heavier than the densest smoke, so that, after the first tumultuous uprush and outflow of its impact, it sank down through the air and poured over the ground in a manner rather liquid than gaseous, abandoning the hills, and streaming into the valleys and ditches and water-courses even as I have heard the carbonic-acid gas that pours from volcanic clefts is wont to do. And where it came upon water some chemical action occurred, and the surface would be instantly covered with a powdery scum that sank slowly and made way for more. The scum was absolutely insoluble, and it is a strange thing, seeing the instant effect of the gas, that one could drink the water from which it had been strained without hurt. The vapour did not diffuse as a true gas would do. It hung together in banks, flowing sluggishly down the slope of the land and driving reluctantly before the wind, and very slowly it combined with the mist and moisture of the air, and sank to the earth in the form of dust. Save that an unknown element giving a group of four lines in the blue of the spectrum is concerned, we are still entirely ignorant of the nature of this substance.

---

1   A small hill.

Once the tumultuous upheaval of its dispersion was over, the black smoke clung so closely to the ground, even before its precipitation, that fifty feet up in the air, on the roofs and upper stories of high houses and on great trees, there was a chance of escaping its poison altogether, as was proved even that night at Street Cobham and Ditton.

The man who escaped at the former place tells a wonderful story of the strangeness of its coiling flow, and how he looked down from the church spire and saw the houses of the village rising like ghosts out of its inky nothingness. For a day and a half he remained there, weary, starving and sun-scorched, the earth under the blue sky and against the prospect of the distant hills a velvet black expanse, with red roofs, green trees, and, later, black-veiled shrubs and gates, barns, out-houses, and walls, rising here and there into the sunlight.

But that was at Street Cobham, where the black vapour was allowed to remain until it sank of its own accord into the ground. As a rule the Martians, when it had served its purpose, cleared the air of it again by wading into it and directing a jet of steam upon it.

That they did with the vapour-banks near us, as we saw in the starlight from the window of a deserted house at Upper Halliford, whither we had returned. From there we could see the searchlights on Richmond Hill and Kingston Hill going to and fro, and about eleven the windows rattled, and we heard the sound of the huge siege guns that had been put in position there. These continued intermittently for the space of a quarter of an hour, sending chance shots at the invisible Martians at Hampton and Ditton, and then the pale beams of the electric light vanished, and were replaced by a bright red glow.

Then the fourth cylinder fell—a brilliant green meteor—as I learned afterwards, in Bushey Park.[1] Before the guns on the Richmond and Kingston line of hills began, there was a fitful cannonade[2] far away in the south-west, due, I believe, to guns being fired haphazard before the black vapour could overwhelm the gunners.

So, setting about it as methodically as men might smoke out a wasps' nest, the Martians spread this strange stifling vapour over the

---

1 A large park, part of Greater London.
2 A heavy fire of artillery.

Londonward country. The horns of the crescent slowly moved apart, until at last they formed a line from Hanwell to Coombe and Malden. All night through their destructive tubes advanced. Never once, after the Martian at St. George's Hill was brought down, did they give the artillery the ghost of a chance against them. Wherever there was a possibility of guns being laid for them unseen, a fresh canister of the black vapour was discharged, and where the guns were openly displayed the Heat-Ray was brought to bear.

By midnight the blazing trees along the slopes of Richmond Park, and the glare of Kingston Hill threw their light upon a network of black smoke, blotting out the whole Valley of the Thames and extending as far as the eye could reach. And through this two Martians slowly waded, and turned their hissing steam jets this way and that.

The Martians were sparing of the Heat-Ray that night, either because they had but a limited supply of material for its production, or because they did not wish to destroy the country, but only to crush and overawe the opposition they had aroused. In the latter aim they certainly succeeded. Sunday night was the end of the organized opposition to their movements. After that no body of men would stand against them, so hopeless was the enterprise. Even the crews of the torpedo boats and destroyers[1] that had brought their quick-firers[2] up the Thames refused to stop, mutinied, and went down again. The only offensive operation men ventured upon after that night was the preparation of mines and pitfalls, and even in that men's energies were frantic and spasmodic.

One has to imagine the fate of those batteries towards Esher, waiting so tensely in the twilight as well as one may. Survivors there were none. One may picture the orderly expectation, the officers alert and watchful, the gunners ready, the ammunition piled to hand, the limber gunners with their horses and waggons, the groups of civilian spectators standing as near as they were permitted, the evening stillness; the ambulances and hospital tents with the burnt and wounded from Weybridge; then the dull resonance of the shots the Martians fired, and the clumsy projectile whirling over the trees and houses, and smashing amid the neighbouring fields.

---

1   New forms of warships were created in the 1880s and 1890s thanks to the combination of steam power and metal plating of hulls.
2   Rapid-fire artillery like minute-guns.

One may picture, too, the sudden shifting of the attention, the swiftly spreading coils and bellyings of that blackness advancing headlong, towering heavenward, turning the twilight to a palpable darkness, a strange and horrible antagonist of vapour striding upon its victims, men and horses near it seen dimly, running, shrieking, falling headlong, shouts of dismay, the guns suddenly abandoned, men choking and writhing on the ground, and the swift broadening out of the opaque cone of smoke. And then, night and extinction—nothing but a silent mass of impenetrable vapour hiding its dead.

Before dawn the black vapour was pouring through the streets of Richmond, and the disintegrating organism of government was, with a last expiring effort, rousing the population of London to the necessity of flight.

XVI.
THE EXODUS FROM LONDON

So you understand the roaring wave of fear that swept through the greatest city in the world just as Monday was dawning—the stream of flight rising swiftly to a torrent, lashing in a foaming tumult round the railway-stations, banked up into a horrible struggle about the shipping in the Thames, and hurrying by every available channel northward and east-ward. By ten o'clock the police organisation, and by mid-day even the railway organisations, were losing coherency, losing shape and efficiency, guttering, softening, running at last in that swift liquefaction of the social body.

All the railway lines north of the Thames and the South-Eastern people at Cannon Street had been warned by midnight on Sunday, and trains were being filled, people were fighting savagely for standing-room in the carriages, even at two o'clock. By three, people were being trampled and crushed even in Bishopsgate Street, a couple of hundred yards, or more, from Liverpool Street Station; revolvers were fired, people stabbed, and the policemen who had been sent to direct the traffic, exhausted and infuriated, were breaking the heads of the people they were called out to protect.

And as the day advanced and the engine drivers and stokers refused to return to London, the pressure of the flight drove the people in an ever-thickening multitude away from the stations and along the northward-running roads. By mid-day a Martian had been seen at Barnes, and a cloud of slowly sinking black vapour drove along the Thames and across the flats of Lambeth, cutting off all escape over the bridges in its sluggish advance. Another bank drove over Ealing, and surrounded a little island of survivors on Castle Hill, alive, but unable to escape.

After a fruitless struggle to get aboard a North-Western train at Chalk Farm—the engines of the trains that had loaded in the goods yard there *ploughed* through shrieking people, and a dozen stalwart men fought to keep the crowd from crushing the driver against his furnace—my brother emerged upon the Chalk Farm road, dodged across through a hurrying swarm of vehicles, and had the luck to be foremost in the sack[1] of a cycle shop. The front tyre of the machine he got was punctured in dragging it through the window, but he got up and off, notwithstanding, with no further injury than a cut wrist. The steep foot of Haverstock Hill was impassable owing to several overturned horses, and my brother struck into Belsize Road.

So he got out of the fury of the panic, and, skirting the Edgware Road, reached Edgware about seven, fasting and wearied, but well ahead of the crowd. Along the road people were standing in the roadway, curious, wondering. He was passed by a number of cyclists, some horsemen, and two motor-cars. A mile from Edgware the rim of the wheel broke, and the machine became unridable. He left it by the roadside and trudged through the village. There were shops half opened in the main street of the place, and people crowded on the pavement and in the doorways and windows, staring astonished at this extraordinary procession of fugitives that was beginning. He succeeded in getting some food at an inn.

For a time he remained in Edgware not knowing what next to do. The flying people increased in number. Many of them, like my brother, seemed inclined to stop in the place. There was no fresh news of the invaders from Mars.

At that time the road was crowded, but as yet far from congested. Most of the fugitives at that hour were mounted on cycles, but there were soon motor-cars, hansom cabs,[2] and carriages hurrying along, and the dust hung in heavy clouds along the road to St. Albans.

---

1 Looting.
2 Two-wheeled cabs in which the driver sat in a raised seat behind the cab; these were frequently for hire on the streets of London like taxis.

It was perhaps a vague idea of making his way to Chelmsford, where some friends of his lived, that at last induced my brother to strike into a quiet lane running eastward. Presently he came upon a stile,[1] and, crossing it, followed a footpath north-eastward. He passed near several farm-houses and some little places whose names he did not learn. He saw few fugitives until, in a grass lane towards High Barnet, he happened upon two ladies who became his fellow travellers. He came upon them just in time to save them.

He heard their screams, and, hurrying round the corner, saw a couple of men struggling to drag them out of the little pony-chaise[2] in which they had been driving, while a third with difficulty held the frightened pony's head. One of the ladies, a short woman dressed in white, was simply screaming; the other, a dark, slender figure, slashed at the man who gripped her arm with a whip she held in her disengaged hand.

My brother immediately grasped the situation, shouted, and hurried towards the struggle. One of the men desisted and turned towards him, and my brother, realizing from his antagonist's face that a fight was unavoidable, and being an expert boxer, went into him forthwith and sent him down against the wheel of the chaise.

It was no time for pugilistic[3] chivalry and my brother laid him quiet with a kick, and gripped the collar of the man who pulled at the slender lady's arm. He heard the clatter of hoofs, the whip stung across his face, a third antagonist struck him between the eyes, and the man he held wrenched himself free and made off down the lane in the direction from which he had come.

Partly stunned, he found himself facing the man who had held the horse's head, and became aware of the chaise receding from him down the lane, swaying from side to side, and with the women in it looking back. The man before him, a burly rough, tried to close, and he stopped him with a blow in the face. Then, realizing that he was deserted, he dodged round and made off down the lane after the chaise, with the sturdy man close behind him, and the fugitive, who had turned now, following remotely.

Suddenly he stumbled and fell; his immediate pursuer went headlong, and he rose to his feet to find himself with a couple of

---

1   A step or set of steps for passing over a fence or wall.
2   A small carriage light enough to be pulled by a pony.
3   Of or pertaining to boxing.

antagonists again. He would have had little chance against them had not the slender lady very pluckily pulled up and returned to his help. It seems she had had a revolver all this time, but it had been under the seat when she and her companion were attacked. She fired at six yards' distance, narrowly missing my brother. The less courageous of the robbers made off, and his companion followed him, cursing his cowardice. They both stopped in sight down the lane, where the third man lay insensible.[1]

"Take this!" said the slender lady, and she gave my brother her revolver.

"Go back to the chaise," said my brother, wiping the blood from his split lip.

She turned without a word—they were both panting – and they went back to where the lady in white struggled to hold back the frightened pony.

The robbers had evidently had enough of it. When my brother looked again they were retreating.

"I'll sit here," said my brother, "if I may;" and he got upon the empty front seat. The lady looked over her shoulder.

"Give me the reins," she said, and laid the whip along the pony's side. In another moment a bend in the road hid the three men from my brother's eyes.

So, quite unexpectedly, my brother found himself, panting, with a cut mouth, a bruised jaw, and bloodstained knuckles, driving along an unknown lane with these two women.

He learned they were the wife and the younger sister of a surgeon living at Stanmore, who had come in the small hours from a dangerous case at Pinner, and heard at some railway-station on his way of the Martian advance. He had hurried home, roused the women—their servant had left them two days before—packed some provisions, put his revolver under the seat—luckily for my brother—and told them to drive on to Edgware, with the idea of getting a train there. He stopped behind to tell the neighbours. He would overtake them, he said, at about half past four in the morning, and now it was nearly nine and they had seen nothing of him since. They could not stop in Edgware because of the growing traffic through the place, and so they had come into this side-lane.

---

1 Unconscious.

That was the story they told my brother in fragments when presently they stopped again, nearer to New Barnet. He promised to stay with them, at least until they could determine what to do, or until the missing man arrived, and professed to be an expert shot with the revolver—a weapon strange to him—in order to give them confidence.

They made a sort of encampment by the wayside, and the pony became happy in the hedge. He told them of his own escape out of London, and all that he knew of these Martians and their ways. The sun crept higher in the sky, and after a time their talk died out and gave place to an uneasy state of anticipation. Several wayfarers came along the lane, and of these my brother gathered such news as he could. Every broken answer he had deepened his impression of the great disaster that had come on humanity, deepened his persuasion of the immediate necessity for prosecuting[1] this flight. He urged the matter upon them.

"We have money," said the slender woman, and hesitated.

Her eyes met my brother's, and her hesitation ended.

"So have I," said my brother.

She explained that they had as much as thirty pounds in gold, besides a five-pound note, and suggested that with that they might get upon a train at St. Albans or New Barnet. My brother thought that was hopeless, seeing the fury of the Londoners to crowd upon the trains, and broached his own idea of striking across Essex towards Harwich and thence escaping from the country altogether.

Mrs. Elphinstone—that was the name of the woman in white—would listen to no reasoning, and kept calling upon "George;" but her sister-in-law was astonishingly quiet and deliberate, and at last agreed to my brother's suggestion. So, they went on towards Barnet designing to cross the Great North Road, my brother leading the pony, to save it as much as possible.

As the sun crept up the sky the day became excessively hot, and under foot a thick, whitish sand grew burning and blinding, so that they travelled only very slowly. The hedges were gray with dust. And as they advanced towards Barnet, a tumultuous murmuring grew stronger.

They began to meet more people. For the most part these were staring before them, murmuring indistinct questions, jaded, hag-

---

1 Proceeding with.

gard, unclean. One man in evening dress passed them on foot, his eyes on the ground. They heard his voice, and, looking back at him, saw one hand clutched in his hair and the other beating invisible things. His paroxysm[1] of rage over, he went on his way without once looking back.

As my brother's party went on towards the crossroads to the south of Barnet, they saw a woman approaching the road across some fields on their left, carrying a child and with two other children; and then a man in dirty black, with a thick stick in one hand and a small portmanteau in the other, passed. Then round the corner of the lane, from between the villas that guarded it at its confluence with the high road, came a little cart drawn by a sweating black pony and driven by a sallow youth in a bowler hat, gray with dust. There were three girls like East End factory girls, and a couple of little children, crowded in the cart.

"This'll tike us rahnd Edgware?" asked the driver, wild-eyed, white-faced; and when my brother told him it would if he turned to the left, he whipped up at once without the formality of thanks.

My brother noticed a pale gray smoke or haze rising among the houses in front of them, and veiling the white facade of a terrace beyond the road that appeared between the backs of the villas. Mrs. Elphinstone suddenly cried out at a number of tongues of smoky red flame leaping up above the houses in front of them against the hot, blue sky. The tumultuous noise resolved itself now into the disorderly mingling of many voices, the gride[2] of many wheels, the creaking of waggons, and the staccato of hoofs. The lane came round sharply not fifty yards from the cross-roads.

"Good heavens!" cried Mrs. Elphinstone. "What is this you are driving us into?"

My brother stopped.

For the main road was a boiling stream of people, a torrent of human beings rushing northward, one pressing on another. A great bank of dust, white and luminous in the blaze of the sun, made everything within twenty feet of the ground gray and indistinct and was perpetually renewed by the hurrying feet of a dense crowd

---

1 A sudden violent emotion.
2 A grating, grinding sound.

of horses and men and women on foot, and by the wheels of vehicles of every description.

"Way!" my brother heard voices crying. "Make way!"

It was like riding into the smoke of a fire to approach the meeting-point of the lane and road; the crowd roared like a fire, and the dust was hot and pungent. And, indeed, a little way up the road a villa was burning and sending rolling masses of black smoke across the road to add to the confusion.

Two men came past them. Then a dirty woman, carrying a heavy bundle and weeping. A lost retriever dog, with hanging tongue, circled dubiously round them, scared and wretched, and fled at my brother's threat.

So much as they could see of the road Londonward between the houses to the right was a tumultuous stream of dirty, hurrying people, pent in between the villas on either side; the black heads, the crowded forms, grew into distinctness as they rushed towards the corner, hurried past, and merged their individuality again in a receding multitude that was swallowed up at last in a cloud of dust.

"Go on! Go on!" cried the voices. "Way! Way!"

One man's hands pressed on the back of another. My brother stood at the pony's head. Irresistibly attracted, he advanced slowly, pace by pace, down the lane.

Edgware had been a scene of confusion, Chalk Farm a riotous tumult, but this was a whole population in movement. It is hard to imagine that host. It had no character of its own. The figures poured out past the corner, and receded with their backs to the group in the lane. Along the margin came those who were on foot, threatened by the wheels, stumbling in the ditches, blundering into one another.

The carts and carriages crowded close upon one another, making little way for those swifter and more impatient vehicles that darted forward every now and then when an opportunity showed itself of doing so, sending the people scattering against the fences and gates of the villas.

"Push on!" was the cry. "Push on! They are coming!"

In one cart stood a blind man in the uniform of the Salvation Army, gesticulating with his crooked fingers and bawling, "Eternity! Eternity!" His voice was hoarse and very loud so that my brother could hear him long after he was lost to sight in the southward dust. Some of the people who crowded in the carts whipped stupidly at their horses and quarrelled with other drivers; some sat motionless, staring at nothing with miserable eyes; some gnawed their hands with thirst, or lay prostrate in the bottoms of their conveyances. The horses' bits[1] were covered with foam, their eyes bloodshot.

There were cabs, carriages, shop-carts, waggons, beyond counting; a mail-cart, a road-cleaner's cart marked "Vestry of St. Pancras," a huge timber-waggon crowded with roughs. A brewer's dray[2] rumbled by with its two near wheels splashed with recent blood.

"Clear the way!" cried the voices. "Clear the way!"

"Eter-nity! Eter-nity!" came echoing up the road.

There were sad, haggard women tramping by, well dressed, with children that cried and stumbled, their dainty clothes smothered in dust, their weary faces smeared with tears. With many of these came men, sometimes helpful, sometimes lowering and savage. Fighting side by side with them pushed some weary street outcast in faded black rags, wide-eyed, loud-voiced, and foul-mouthed. There were sturdy workmen thrusting their way along, wretched unkempt men clothed like clerks or shop-men, struggling spasmodically; a wounded soldier my brother noticed, men dressed in the clothes of railway porters, one wretched creature in a nightshirt with a coat thrown over it.

But, varied as its composition was, certain things all that host had in common. There was fear and pain on their faces, and fear behind them. A tumult up the road, a quarrel for a place in a waggon, sent the whole host of them quickening their pace; even a man so scared and broken that his knees bent under him was galvanized[3] for a moment into renewed activity. The heat and dust had already been at work upon this multitude. Their skins were dry, their lips black and cracked. They were all thirsty, weary, and footsore. And amid the various cries one heard disputes, reproaches, groans of weariness and fatigue; the voices of most of them were hoarse and weak. Through it all ran a refrain:

"Way! Way! The Martians are coming!"

Few stopped and came aside from that flood. The lane opened slantingly into the main road with a narrow opening, and had a delusive appearance of coming from the direction of London. Yet a

---

1   Pieces of metal that form part of the reins and fit in the horse's mouth.
2   A large cart used by beer breweries to deliver beer.
3   The Italian scientist Luigi Galvani (1737–98) passed electricity through dead animal tissue to make it move; this kind of involuntary movement became know as galvanism.

kind of eddy of people drove into its mouth; weaklings elbowed out of the stream, who for the most part rested but a moment before plunging into it again. A little way down the lane, with two friends bending over him, lay a man with a bare leg, wrapped about with bloody rags. He was a lucky man to have friends.

A little old man, with a gray military moustache and a filthy black frock-coat, limped out and sat down beside the trap, removed his boot—his sock was blood-stained—shook out a pebble, and hobbled on again; and then a little girl of eight or nine, all alone, threw herself under the hedge close by my brother, weeping.

"I can't go on! I can't go on!"

My brother woke from his torpor of astonishment and lifted her up, speaking gently to her, and carried her to Miss Elphinstone. So soon as my brother touched her she became quite still, as if frightened.

"Ellen!" shrieked a woman in the crowd, with tears in her voice. "Ellen!" And the child suddenly darted away from my brother, crying "Mother!"

"They are coming," said a man on horseback, riding past along the lane.

"Out of the way, there!" bawled a coachman, towering high; and my brother saw a closed carriage turning into the lane.

The people crushed back on one another to avoid the horse. My brother pushed the pony and chaise back into the hedge, and the man drove by and stopped at the turn of the way. It was a carriage, with a pole for a pair of horses, but only one was in the traces.

My brother saw dimly through the dust that two men lifted out something on a white stretcher and put it gently on the grass beneath the privet hedge.

One of the men came running to my brother.

"Where is there any water?" he said. "He is dying fast, and very thirsty. It is Lord Garrick."

"Lord Garrick!" said my brother; "the Chief Justice?"

"The water?" he said.

"There may be a tap," said my brother, "in some of the houses. We have no water. I dare not leave my people."

The man pushed against the crowd towards the gate of the corner house.

"Go on!" said the people, thrusting at him. "They are coming! Go on!"

Then my brother's attention was distracted by a bearded, eagle-faced man lugging a small hand-bag, which split even as my brother's eyes rested on it and disgorged[1] a mass of sovereigns[2] that seemed to break up into separate coins as it struck the ground. They rolled hither and thither among the struggling feet of men and horses. The man stopped and looked stupidly at the heap, and the shaft of a cab struck his shoulder and sent him reeling. He gave a shriek and dodged back, and a cartwheel shaved him narrowly.

"Way!" cried the men all about him. "Make way!"

So soon as the cab had passed, he flung himself, with both hands open, upon the heap of coins, and began thrusting handfuls in his pocket. A horse rose close upon him, and in another moment he had risen, and he had been borne down under the horse's hoofs.

"Stop!" screamed my brother, and pushing a woman out of his way, tried to clutch the bit of the horse.

Before he could get to it, he heard a scream under the wheels, and saw through the dust the rim passing over the poor wretch's back. The driver of the cart slashed his whip at my brother, who ran round behind the cart. The multitudinous shouting confused his ears. The man was writhing in the dust among his scattered money, unable to rise, for the wheel had broken his back, and his lower limbs lay limp and dead. My brother stood up and yelled at the next driver, and a man on a black horse came to his assistance.

"Get him out of the road," said he; and, clutching the man's collar with his free hand, my brother lugged him sideways. But he still clutched after his money, and regarded my brother fiercely, hammering at his arm with a handful of gold. "Go on! Go on!" shouted angry voices behind. "Way! Way!"

There was a smash as the pole of a carriage crashed into the cart that the man on horseback stopped. My brother looked up, and the man with the gold twisted his head round and bit the wrist that held his collar. There was a concussion, and the black horse came staggering sideways, and the cart-horse pushed beside it. A hoof missed my brother's foot by a hair's breadth. He released his grip on the fallen man and jumped back. He saw anger change to terror on the face of the poor wretch on the ground, and in a moment he was hidden and my brother was borne backward and

---

1 Spilled out.
2 Gold coins worth over two pounds each; the man has a lot of very heavy money in his bag.

carried past the entrance of the lane, and had to fight hard in the torrent to recover it.

He saw Miss Elphinstone covering her eyes, and a little child, with all a child's want of sympathetic imagination, staring with dilated eyes at a dusty something that lay black and still, ground and crushed under the rolling wheels. "Let us go back!" he shouted, and began turning the pony round. "We cannot cross this—hell," he said and they went back a hundred yards the way they had come, until the fighting crowd was hidden. As they passed the bend in the lane my brother saw the face of the dying man in the ditch under the privet, deadly white and drawn, and shining with perspiration. The two women sat silent, crouching in their seat and shivering.

Then beyond the bend my brother stopped again. Miss Elphinstone was white and pale, and her sister-in-law sat weeping, too wretched even to call upon "George." My brother was horrified and perplexed. So soon as they had retreated he realized how urgent and unavoidable it was to attempt this crossing. He turned to Miss Elphinstone, suddenly resolute.

"We must go that way," he said, and led the pony round again.

For the second time that day this girl proved her quality. To force their way into the torrent of people, my brother plunged into the traffic and held back a cab horse, while she drove the pony across its head. A waggon locked wheels for a moment and ripped a long splinter from the chaise. In another moment they were caught and swept forward by the stream. My brother, with the cabman's whip marks red across his face and hands, scrambled into the chaise and took the reins from her.

"Point the revolver at the man behind," he said, giving it to her, "if he presses us too hard. No!—point it at his horse."

Then he began to look out for a chance of edging to the right across the road. But once in the stream he seemed to lose volition, to become a part of that dusty rout. They swept through Chipping Barnet with the torrent; they were nearly a mile beyond the centre of the town before they had fought across to the opposite side of the way. It was din and confusion indescribable; but in and beyond the town the road forks repeatedly, and this to some extent relieved the stress.

They struck eastward through Hadley, and there on either side of the road, and at another place further on, they came upon a great multitude of people drinking at the stream, some fighting to come at the water. And further on, from a hill near East Barnet, they saw two trains running slowly one after the other without signal or order—trains swarming with people, with men even among the coals behind the engines—going northward along the Great Northern Railway. My brother supposes they must have filled outside London, for at that time the furious terror of the people had rendered the central termini impossible.

Near this place they halted for the rest of the afternoon, for the violence of the day had already utterly exhausted all three of them. They began to suffer the beginnings of hunger, the night was cold, and none of them dared to sleep. And in the evening many people came hurrying along the road nearby their stopping-place, fleeing from unknown dangers before them, and going in the direction from which my brother had come.

XVII.
THE "THUNDER CHILD".

Had the Martians aimed only at destruction, they might on Monday have annihilated the entire population of London, as it spread itself slowly through the home counties.[1] Not only along the road through Barnet, but also through Edgware and Waltham Abbey, and along the roads eastward to Southend and Shoeburyness, and south of the Thames to Deal and Broadstairs, poured the same frantic rout. If one could have hung that June morning in a balloon in the blazing blue above London, every northward and eastward road running out of the infinite tangle of streets would have seemed stippled black with the streaming fugitives, each dot a human agony of terror and physical distress. I have set forth at length in the last chapter my brother's account of the road through Chipping Barnet, in order that my readers may realize how that swarming of black dots appeared to one of those concerned. Never before in the history of the world had such a mass of human beings moved and suffered together. The legendary hosts of Goths and Huns,[2] the hugest armies Asia has ever seen, would have been but a drop in that current. And this was no disciplined march; it was a stampede—a stampede gigantic and terrible—without order and without a goal, six million people unarmed and unprovisioned, driving

---

1 The collective name for the counties south of London.
2 Large armies of barbarians who overran the Roman Empire.

headlong. It was the beginning of the rout of civilization, of the massacre of mankind.

Directly below him the balloonist would have seen the network of streets far and wide, houses, churches, squares, crescents, gardens—already derelict—spread out like a huge map, and in the southward *blotted*. Over Ealing, Richmond, Wimbledon, it would have seemed as if some monstrous pen had flung ink upon the chart. Steadily, incessantly, each black splash grew and spread, shooting out ramifications[1] this way and that, now banking itself against rising ground, now pouring swiftly over a crest into a new-found valley, exactly as a gout[2] of ink would spread itself upon blotting paper.

And beyond, over the blue hills that rise southward of the river, the glittering Martians went to and fro, calmly and methodically spreading their poison-cloud over this patch of country and then over that, laying it again with their steam-jets when it had served its purpose, and taking possession of the conquered country. They do not seem to have aimed at extermination so much as at complete demoralisation and the destruction of any opposition. They exploded any stores of powder they came upon, cut every telegraph, and wrecked the railways here and there. They were hamstringing[3] mankind. They seemed in no hurry to extend the field of their operations, and did not come beyond the central part of London all that day. It is possible that a very considerable number of people in London stuck to their houses through Monday morning. Certain it is that many died at home, suffocated by the Black Smoke.

Until about mid-day the Pool of London[4] was an astonishing scene. Steamboats and shipping of all sorts lay there, tempted by the enormous sums of money offered by fugitives, and it is said that many who swam out to these vessels were thrust off with boat-hooks and drowned. About one o'clock in the afternoon the thinning remnant of a cloud of the black vapour appeared between the arches of Blackfriars Bridge. At that the Pool became a scene of mad confusion, fighting and collision, and for some time a multitude of boats and barges jammed in the northern arch of the Tower

---

1 New branches of "black smoke."
2 Blob.
3 If you cut the hamstring, the human leg will no longer work.
4 The area of the Thames in London where ships gather.

Bridge, and the sailors and lightermen[1] had to fight savagely against the people who swarmed upon them from the river front. People were actually clambering down the piers of the bridge from above.

When, an hour later, a Martian appeared beyond the Clock Tower and waded down the river, nothing but wreckage floated above Limehouse.

Of the falling of the fifth cylinder I have presently to tell. The sixth star fell at Wimbledon.[2] My brother, keeping watch beside the women in the chaise in a meadow, saw the green flash of it far beyond the hills. On Tuesday the little party, still set upon getting across the sea, made its way through the swarming country towards Colchester. The news that the Martians were now in possession of the whole of London was confirmed. They had been seen at Highgate, and even, it was said, at Neasdon. But they did not come into my brother's view until the morrow.

That day the scattered multitudes began to realize the urgent need of provisions. As they grew hungry the rights of property ceased to be regarded. Farmers were out to defend their cattlesheds, granaries, and ripening root crops with arms in their hands. A number of people now, like my brother, had their faces eastward, and there were some desperate souls even going back towards London to get food. These were chiefly people from the northern suburbs, whose knowledge of the Black Smoke came by hearsay. He heard that about half the members of the Government had gathered at Birmingham, and that enormous quantities of high explosives were being prepared to be used in automatic mines across the Midland counties.

He was also told that the Midland Railway Company had replaced the desertions of the first day's panic, had resumed traffic, and was running northward trains from St. Albans to relieve the congestion of the home counties. There was also a placard in Chipping Ongar announcing that large stores of flour were available in the northern towns, and that within twenty-four hours bread would be distributed among the starving people in the neighbourhood. But this intelligence did not deter him from the plan of escape he had formed, and the three pressed eastward all day, and saw no more of the bread distribution than this promise. Nor, as a matter of fact, did anyone else see more of it. That night fell the

---

1 The crew of a barge or cargo ship.
2 The cylinders are now falling on London itself.

seventh star, falling upon Primrose Hill. It fell while Miss Elphin-stone was watching, for she took that duty alternately with my brother. She saw it.

On Wednesday the three fugitives—they had passed the night in a field of unripe wheat—reached Chelmsford, and there a body of the inhabitants, calling itself the Committee of Public Supply, seized the pony as provisions, and would give nothing in exchange for it but the promise of a share in it the next day. Here there were rumours of Martians at Epping, and news of the destruction of Waltham Abbey Powder Mills in a vain attempt to blow up one of the invaders.

People were watching for Martians here from the church tow-ers. My brother, very luckily for him as it chanced, preferred to push on at once to the coast rather than wait for food, although all three of them were very hungry. By mid-day they passed through Tillingham, which, strangely enough, seemed to be quite silent and deserted, save for a few furtive plunderers hunting for food. Near Tillingham they suddenly came in sight of the sea, and the most amazing crowd of shipping of all sorts that it is possible to imag-ine.

For after the sailors could no longer come up the Thames, they came on to the Essex coast, to Harwich and Walton and Clacton, and afterwards to Foulness and Shoebury, to bring off the people. They lay in a huge sickle-shaped curve that vanished into mist at last towards the Naze.[1] Close inshore was a multitude of fishing-smacks[2]—English, Scotch, French, Dutch, and Swedish; steam-launches from the Thames, yachts, electric boats; and beyond were ships of larger burthen, a multitude of filthy colliers,[3] trim mer-chantmen, cattle-ships, passenger-boats, petroleum-tanks, ocean tramps, an old white transport even, neat white and gray liners from Southampton and Hamburg; and along the blue coast across the Blackwater my brother could make out dimly a dense swarm of boats chaffering[4] with the people on the beach, a swarm which also extended up the Blackwater almost to Maldon.

About a couple of miles out lay an ironclad, very low in the water, almost, to my brother's perception, like a water-logged ship.

---

1 A promontory that sticks out into the sea north of London.
2 Small fishing boats.
3 Ships that specialized in hauling coal.
4 Haggling, in this case about fare with passengers.

This was the ram *Thunder Child*.[1] It was the only warship in sight, but far away to the right over the smooth surface of the sea—for that day there was a dead calm—lay a serpent of black smoke to mark the next ironclads of the Channel Fleet, which hovered in an extended line, steam up and ready for action, across the Thames estuary[2] during the course of the Martian conquest, vigilant and yet powerless to prevent it.

At the sight of the sea, Mrs. Elphinstone, in spite of the assurances of her sister-in-law, gave way to panic. She had never been out of England before, she would rather die than trust herself friendless in a foreign country, and so forth. She seemed, poor woman! to imagine that the French and the Martians might prove very similar. She had been growing increasingly hysterical, fearful, and depressed during the two days' journeyings. Her great idea was to return to Stanmore. Things had been always well and safe at Stanmore. They would find George at Stanmore.

It was with the greatest difficulty they could get her down to the beach, where presently my brother succeeded in attracting the attention of some men on a paddle-steamer from the Thames. They sent a boat and drove a bargain for thirty-six pounds for the three. The steamer was going, these men said, to Ostend.[3]

It was about two o'clock when my brother, having paid their fares at the gangway, found himself safely aboard the steamboat with his charges. There was food aboard, albeit at exorbitant prices, and the three of them contrived to eat a meal on one of the seats forward.

There were already a couple of score of passengers aboard, some of whom had expended their last money in securing a passage, but the captain lay off the Blackwater until five in the afternoon, picking up passengers until the seated decks were even dangerously crowded. He would probably have remained longer had it not been for the sound of guns that began about that hour in the south. As if in answer, the ironclad seaward fired a small gun and hoisted a string of flags. A jet of smoke sprang out of her funnels.

Some of the passengers were of opinion that this firing came from Shoeburyness, until it was noticed that it was growing loud-

---

1 A ship with a reinforced prow for sinking enemy ships by ramming them. See Appendix I.
2 The mouth of a river where it meets the sea.
3 A Belgian port.

er. At the same time, far away in the south-east the masts and upper-works of three ironclads rose one after the other out of the sea, beneath clouds of black smoke. But my brother's attention speedily reverted to the distant firing in the south. He fancied he saw a column of smoke rising out of the distant gray haze.

The little steamer was already flapping her way eastward of the big crescent of shipping, and the low Essex coast was growing blue and hazy, when a Martian appeared, small and faint in the remote distance, advancing along the muddy coast from the direction of Foulness. At that the captain on the bridge swore at the top of his voice with fear and anger at his own delay, and the paddles seemed infected with his terror. Every soul aboard stood at the bulwarks[1] or on the seats of the steamer and stared at that distant shape, higher than the trees or church towers inland, and advancing with a leisurely parody of a human stride.

It was the first Martian my brother had seen, and he stood, more amazed than terrified, watching this Titan advancing deliberately towards the shipping, wading farther and farther into the water as the coast fell away. Then, far away beyond the Crouch, came another striding over some stunted trees, and then yet another, still further off, wading deeply through a shiny mud-flat that seemed to hang halfway up between sea and sky. They were all stalking seaward, as if to intercept the escape of the multitudinous vessels that were crowded between Foulness and the Naze. In spite of the throbbing exertions of the engines of the little paddle-boat, and the pouring foam that her wheels flung behind her, she receded with terrifying slowness from this ominous advance.

Glancing northwestward, my brother saw the large crescent of shipping already writhing with the approaching terror; one ship passing behind another, another coming round from broadside to end on, steamships whistling and giving off volumes of steam, sails being let out, launches rushing hither and thither. He was so fascinated by this and by the creeping danger away to the left that he had no eyes for anything seaward. And then a swift movement of the steamboat (she had suddenly come round to avoid being run down) flung him headlong from the seat upon which he was standing. There was a shouting all about him, a trampling of feet, and a cheer that seemed to be answered faintly. The steam-boat lurched and rolled him over upon his hands.

---

1   Sides of a ship above the upper deck.

He sprang to his feet and saw to starboard, and not a hundred yards from their heeling, pitching boat, a vast iron bulk like the blade of a plough tearing through the water, tossing it on either side in huge waves of foam that leapt towards the steamer, flinging her paddles helplessly in the air, and then sucking her deck down almost to the water-line.

A douche[1] of spray blinded my brother for a moment. When his eyes were clear again he saw the monster had passed and was rushing landward. Big iron upper-works rose out of this headlong structure, and from that twin funnels projected and spat a smoking blast shot with fire into the air. It was the torpedo-ram, *Thunder Child*, steaming headlong, coming to the rescue of the threatened shipping.

Keeping his footing on the heaving deck by clutching the bulwarks, my brother looked past this charging leviathan[2] at the Martians again, and he saw the three of them now close together, and standing so far out to sea that their tripod supports were almost entirely submerged. Thus sunken, and seen in remote perspective, they appeared far less formidable than the huge iron bulk in whose wake the steamer was pitching so helplessly. It would seem they were regarding this new antagonist with astonishment. To their intelligence, it may be, the giant was even such another as themselves. The *Thunder Child* fired no gun, but simply drove full speed towards them. It was probably her not firing that enabled her to get so near the enemy as she did. They did not know what to make of her. One shell, and they would have sent her to the bottom forthwith with the Heat-Ray.

She was steaming at such a pace that in a minute she seemed halfway between the steamboat and the Martians—a diminishing black bulk against the receding horizontal expanse of the Essex coast.

Suddenly the foremost Martian lowered his tube and discharged a canister of the black gas at the ironclad. It hit her larboard side and glanced off in an inky jet that rolled away to seaward, an unfolding torrent of Black Smoke, from which the ironclad drove clear. To the watchers from the steamer, low in the water and with the sun in their eyes, it seemed as though she were already among the Martians.

---

1 Shower.
2 A mythical huge sea beast.

They saw the gaunt figures separating and rising out of the water as they retreated shoreward, and one of them raised the camera-like generator of the Heat-Ray. He held it pointing obliquely downward, and a bank of steam sprang from the water at its touch. It must have driven through the iron of the ship's side like a white-hot iron rod through paper.

A flicker of flame went up through the rising steam, and then the Martian reeled and staggered. In another moment he was cut down, and a great body of water and steam shot high in the air. The guns of the *Thunder Child* sounded through the reek, going off one after the other, and one shot splashed the water high close by the steamer, ricocheted towards the other flying ships to the north, and smashed a smack to matchwood.

But no one heeded that very much. At the sight of the Martian's collapse, the captain on the bridge yelled inarticulately, and all the crowding passengers on the steamer's stern shouted together. And then they yelled again. For, surging out beyond the white tumult, drove something long and black, the flames streaming from its middle parts, its ventilators and funnels spouting fire.

She was alive still; the steering gear, it seems, was intact and her engines working. She headed straight for a second Martian, and was within a hundred yards of him when the Heat-Ray came to bear. Then with a violent thud, a blinding flash, her decks, her funnels, leaped upward. The Martian staggered with the violence of her explosion, and in another moment the flaming wreckage, still driving forward with the impetus of its pace, had struck him and crumpled him up like a thing of card-board. My brother shouted involuntarily. A boiling tumult of steam hid everything again.

"Two!" yelled the captain.

Everyone was shouting. The whole steamer from end to end rang with frantic cheering that was taken up first by one and then by all in the crowding multitude of ships and boats that was driving out to sea.

The steam hung upon the water for many minutes, hiding the third Martian and the coast altogether. And all this time the boat was paddling steadily out to sea and away from the fight; and when at last the confusion cleared, the drifting bank of black vapour intervened, and nothing of the *Thunder Child* could be made out, nor could the third Martian be seen. But the ironclads to seaward were now quite close and standing in towards shore past the steamboat.

The little vessel continued to beat its way seaward, and the iron-clads receded slowly towards the coast, which was hidden still by a marbled bank of vapour, part steam, part black gas, eddying and combining in the strangest ways. The fleet of refugees was scattering to the northeast; several smacks were sailing between the iron-clads and the steamboat. After a time, and before they reached the sinking cloud bank, the warships turned northward, and then abruptly went about and passed into the thickening haze of evening southward. The coast grew faint, and, at last, indistinguishable amid the low banks of clouds that were gathering about the sinking sun.

Then suddenly out of the golden haze of the sunset came the vibration of guns, and a form of black shadows moving. Everyone struggled to the rail of the steamer and peered into the blinding furnace of the west, but nothing was to be distinguished clearly. A mass of smoke rose slanting and barred the face of the sun. The steamboat throbbed on its way through an interminable suspense.

The sun sank into gray clouds, the sky flushed and darkened, the evening star trembled into sight. It was deep twilight when the captain cried out and pointed. My brother strained his eyes. Something[1] rushed up into the sky out of the grayness, rushed slantingly upward and very swiftly into the luminous clearness above the clouds in the western sky; something flat and broad, and very large, that swept round in a vast curve, grew smaller, sank slowly, and vanished again into the gray mystery of the night. And as it flew it rained down darkness upon the land.

---

1 Flight was still a dream when Wells wrote this, and so he is vague about how exactly the Martians' flying machines operate.

BOOK II
THE EARTH UNDER THE MARTIANS

I.

UNDER FOOT

In the first book I have wandered so much from my own adventures to tell of the experiences of my brother that all through the last two chapters I and the curate have been lurking in the empty house at Halliford whither we fled to escape the Black Smoke. There I will resume. We stopped there all Sunday night and all the next day—the day of the panic—in a little island of daylight, cut off by the Black Smoke from the rest of the world. We could do nothing but wait in aching inactivity during those two weary days.

My mind was occupied by anxiety for my wife. I figured her at Leatherhead, terrified, in danger, mourning me already as a dead man. I paced the rooms and cried aloud when I thought of how I was cut off from her, of all that might happen to her in my absence. My cousin I knew was brave enough for any emergency, but he was not the sort of man to realize danger quickly, to rise promptly. What was needed now was not bravery, but circumspection. My only consolation was to believe that the Martians were moving Londonward and away from her. Such vague anxieties keep the mind sensitive and painful. I grew very weary and irritable with the curate's perpetual ejaculations, I tired of the sight of his selfish despair. After some ineffectual remonstrance I kept away from him, staying in a room—evidently a children's school-room—containing globes, forms, and copy-books.[1] When at last he followed me thither, I went to a box-room[2] at the top of the house and locked myself in, in order to be alone with my aching miseries.

We were hopelessly hemmed in by the Black Smoke all that day and the morning of the next. There were signs of people in the next house on Sunday evening—a face at a window and moving lights, and later the slamming of a door. But I do not know who these people were, nor what became of them. We saw nothing of them next day. The Black Smoke drifted slowly riverward all through Monday morning, creeping nearer and nearer to us, driving at last along the roadway outside the house that hid us.

---

1 Books for schoolchildren to practice handwriting.
2 An attic or storage area.

A Martian came across the fields about midday, laying the stuff with a jet of superheated steam that hissed against the walls, smashed all the windows it touched, and scalded the curate's hand as he fled out of the front room. When at last we crept across the sodden rooms and looked out again, the country northward was as though a black snowstorm had passed over it. Looking towards the river, we were astonished to see an unaccountable redness mingling with the black of the scorched meadows.

For a time we did not see how this change affected our position, save that we were relieved of our fear of the Black Smoke. But later I perceived that we were no longer hemmed in, that now we might get away. So soon as I realized that the way of escape was open, my dream of action returned. But the curate was lethargic, unreasonable.

"We are safe here," he repeated—"safe here."

I resolved to leave him—would that I had! Wiser now for the artilleryman's teaching, I sought out food and drink. I had found oil and rags for my burns, and I also took a hat and a flannel shirt that I found in one of the bedrooms. When it was clear to him that I meant to go alone, had reconciled myself to going alone, he suddenly roused himself to come. And, all being quiet throughout the afternoon, we started, as I should judge, about five along the blackened road to Sunbury.

In Sunbury, and at intervals along the road, were dead bodies lying in contorted attitudes—horses as well as men—overturned carts and luggage, all covered thickly with black dust. That pall of cindery powder made me think of what I had read of the destruction of Pompeii.[1] We got to Hampton Court without misadventure, our minds full of strange and unfamiliar appearances, and at Hampton Court our eyes were relieved to find a patch of green that had escaped the suffocating drift. We went through Bushey Park, with its deer going to and fro under the chestnuts, and some men and women hurrying in the distance towards Hampton, and so we came to Twickenham. These were the first people we saw.

Away across the road the woods beyond Ham and Petersham were still afire. Twickenham was uninjured by either Heat-Ray or

---

1 The Roman city of Pompeii was destroyed by a volcanic eruption in 79 A.D. Archeologists found citizens of Pompeii who had been overcome by the ash from the eruption preserved where they had fallen.

Black Smoke, and there were more people about here, though none could give us news. For the most part, they were like ourselves, taking advantage of a lull to shift their quarters. I have an impression that many of the houses here were still occupied by scared inhabitants, too frightened even for flight. Here, too, the evidence of a hasty rout was abundant along the road. I remember most vividly three smashed bicycles in a heap, pounded into the road by the wheels of subsequent carts. We crossed Richmond Bridge about half-past eight. We hurried across the exposed bridge, of course, but I noticed floating down the stream a number of red masses, some many feet across. I did not know what these were—there was no time for scrutiny—and I put a more horrible interpretation on them than they deserved. Here again, on the Surrey side, were black dust that had once been smoke, and dead bodies—a heap near the approach to the station; but we caught not a sight of the Martians until we were some way towards Barnes.

We saw in the blackened distance a group of three people running down a side-street towards the river, but otherwise it seemed deserted. Up the hill Richmond town was burning briskly; outside the town of Richmond there was no trace of the Black Smoke.

Then suddenly, as we approached Kew, came a number of people running, and the upper-works of a Martian Fighting Machine loomed in sight over the housetops, not a hundred yards away from us. We stood aghast at our danger, and had he looked down we must immediately have perished. We were so terrified that we dared not go on, but turned aside and hid in a shed in a garden. There the curate crouched, weeping silently, and refusing to stir again.

But my fixed idea of reaching Leatherhead would not let me rest, and in the twilight I ventured out again. I went through a shrubbery, and along a passage beside a big house standing in its own grounds, and so emerged upon the road towards Kew. The curate I left in the shed, but he came hurrying after me.

That second start was the most foolhardy thing I ever did. For it was manifest the Martians were about us. Scarcely had he overtaken me than we saw either the Fighting Machine we had seen before or another, far away across the meadows in the direction of Kew Lodge. Four or five little black figures hurried before it across the green-gray of the field, and in a moment it was evident this Martian pursued them. In three strides he was among them, and they ran radiating from his feet in all directions. He used no

Heat-Ray to destroy them, but picked them up one by one. Apparently he tossed them into the great metallic carrier which projected behind him, much as a workman's basket hangs over his shoulder.

It was the first time I realized that the Martians might have any other purpose than destruction with defeated humanity. We stood for a moment petrified, then turned and fled through a gate behind us into a walled garden, fell into rather than found a fortunate ditch, and lay there, scarce daring to whisper to each other until the stars were out.

I suppose it was nearly eleven at night before we gathered courage to start again, no longer venturing into the road, but sneaking along hedgerows and through plantations, and watching keenly through the darkness, he on the right and I on the left, for the Martians, who seemed to be all about us. In one place we blundered upon a scorched and blackened area, now cooling and ashen, and a number of scattered dead bodies of men, burned horribly about the heads and trunks but with their legs and boots mostly intact; and of dead horses, fifty feet, perhaps, behind a line of four ripped guns and smashed gun-carriages.

Sheen, it seemed, had escaped destruction, but the place was silent and deserted. Here we happened on no dead, though the night was too dark for us to see into the side-roads of the place. In Sheen my companion suddenly complained of faintness and thirst, and we decided to try one of the houses.

The first house we entered, after a little difficulty with the window, was a small semi-detached villa, and I found nothing eatable left in the place but some mouldy cheese. There was, however, water to drink, and I took a hatchet, which promised to be useful in our next house-breaking.

We then crossed to a place where the road turns towards Mortlake. Here there stood a white house within a walled garden, and in the pantry of this we found a store of food—two loaves of bread in a pan, an uncooked steak, and the half of a ham. I give this catalogue so precisely because, as it happened, we were destined to subsist upon this store for the next fortnight. Bottled beer stood under a shelf, and there were two bags of haricot beans and some limp lettuces. This pantry opened into a kind of wash-up kitchen, and in this was firewood and a cupboard in which we found nearly a dozen of burgundy, tinned soups and salmon, and two tins of biscuits.

We sat in the adjacent kitchen in the dark—for we dared not strike a light—and ate bread and ham, and drank beer out of one bottle. The curate, who was still timorous and restless, was now oddly enough for pushing on, and I was urging him to keep up his strength by eating, when the thing that was to imprison us happened.

"It can't be midnight yet," I said, and then came a blinding glare of vivid green light. Everything in the kitchen leapt out, clearly visible in green and black, and vanished then again. And then followed such a concussion as I have never heard before or since. So close on the heels of this as to seem instantaneous came a thud behind me, a clash of glass, a crash and rattle of falling masonry all about us, and incontinently the plaster of the ceiling came down upon us, smashing into a multitude of fragments upon our heads. I was knocked headlong across the floor against the oven handle and stunned. I was insensible for a long time, the curate told me, and when I came to we were in darkness again, and he, with a face wet as I found afterwards with blood from a cut forehead, was dabbing water over me.

For some time I could not recollect what had happened. Then things came to me slowly. A bruise on my temple asserted itself.

"Are you better?" asked the curate, in a whisper.

At last I answered him. I sat up.

"Don't move," he said. "The floor is covered with smashed crockery from the dresser. You can't possibly move without making a noise, and I fancy *they* are outside."

We both sat quite silent, so that we could scarcely hear each other breathing. Everything seemed deadly still, though once something near us, some plaster or broken brickwork, slid down with a rumbling sound. Outside and very near was an intermittent, metallic rattle.

"That!" said the curate, when presently it happened again.

"Yes," I said. "But what is it?"

"A Martian!" said the curate.

I listened again.

"It was not like the Heat-Ray," I said, and for a time I was inclined to think one of the great Fighting Machines had stumbled against the house, as I had seen one stumble against the tower of Shepperton Church.

Our situation was so strange and incomprehensible that for three or four hours, until the dawn came, we scarcely moved. And then the light filtered in, not through the window, which remained black, but through a triangular aperture between a beam and a heap of broken bricks in the wall behind us. The interior of the kitchen we now saw grayly for the first time.

The window had been burst in by a mass of garden mould, which flowed over the table upon which we had been sitting and lay about our feet. Outside, the soil was banked high against the house. At the top of the window-frame we could see an uprooted drain-pipe. The floor was littered with smashed hardware; the end of the kitchen towards the house was broken into, and since the daylight shone in there, it was evident the greater part of the house had collapsed. Contrasting vividly with this ruin was the neat dresser, stained in the fashion, pale green, and with a number of copper and tin vessels below it, the wall-paper imitating blue and white tiles, and a couple of coloured supplements[1] fluttering from the walls above the kitchen range.

As the dawn grew clearer, we saw through the gap in the wall the body of a Martian, standing sentinel, I suppose, over the still glowing cylinder. At the sight of that we crawled as circumspectly as possible out of the twilight of the kitchen into the darkness of the scullery.

Abruptly the right interpretation dawned upon my mind.

"The fifth cylinder," I whispered, "the fifth shot from Mars, has struck this house and buried us under the ruins!"

For a time the curate was silent, and then he whispered:

"God have mercy upon us!"

I heard him presently whimpering to himself.

Save for that sound we lay quite still in the scullery;[2] I for my part scarce dared breathe, and sat with my eyes fixed on the faint light of the kitchen door. I could just see the curate's face, a dim oval shape, and his collar and cuffs. Outside there began a metallic hammering, then a violent hooting, and then, after a quiet interval, a hissing, like the hissing of an engine. These noises, for the most part problematical, continued intermittently, and seemed, if anything, to increase in number as time wore on. Presently a measured thudding, and a vibration that made everything about us quiver and the vessels in the pantry ring and shift, began and continued. Once the light was eclipsed, and the ghostly kitchen doorway

---

1 Posters provided by newspapers reproducing works of art that people would put on their walls.
2 A room for cleaning and storing dishes and culinary utensils.

became absolutely dark. For many hours we must have crouched there, silent and shivering, until our tired attention failed....

At last I found myself awake and very hungry. I am inclined to believe we must have been the greater portion of a day before that awakening. My hunger was at a stride so insistent that it moved me to action. I told the curate I was going to seek food, and felt my way towards the pantry. He made me no answer, but so soon as I began eating the faint noise I made stirred him to action and I heard him crawling after me.

II.
WHAT WE SAW FROM THE RUINED HOUSE

After eating we crept back to the scullery, and there I must have dozed again, for when presently I stirred I was alone. The thudding vibration continued with wearisome persistence. I whispered for the curate several times, and at last felt my way to the door of the kitchen. It was still daylight, and I perceived him across the room, lying against the triangular hole that looked out upon the Martians. His shoulders were hunched, so that his head was hidden from me.

I could hear a number of noises, almost like those in an engine-shed,[1] and the place rocked with that beating thud. Through the aperture in the wall I could see the top of a tree touched with gold, and the warm blue of a tranquil evening sky. For a minute or so I remained watching the curate, and then I advanced, crouching and stepping with extreme care amid the broken crockery that littered the floor.

I touched the curate's leg, and he started so violently that a mass of plaster went sliding down outside and fell with a loud impact. I gripped his arm, fearing he might cry out, and for a long time we crouched motionless. Then I turned to see how much of our rampart remained. The detachment of the plaster had left a vertical slit open in the débris, and by raising myself cautiously across a beam I was able to see out of this gap into what had been overnight a quiet suburban roadway. Vast indeed was the change that we beheld.

---

1 A workshop in which machinery is being manufactured, often applied to railroads.

The fifth cylinder must have fallen right into the midst of the house we had first visited. The building had vanished, completely smashed, pulverized and dispersed by the blow. The cylinder lay now far beneath the original foundations, deep in a hole, already vastly larger than the pit I had looked into at Woking. The earth all round it had splashed under that tremendous impact—"splashed" is the only word—and lay in heaped piles that hid the masses of the adjacent houses. It had behaved exactly like mud under the violent blow of a hammer. Our house had collapsed backward; the front portion, even on the ground floor, had been destroyed completely; by a chance, the kitchen and scullery had escaped, and stood buried now under soil and ruins, closed in by tons of earth on every side, save towards the cylinder. Over that aspect we hung now on the very verge of the great circular pit the Martians were engaged in making. The heavy beating sound was evidently just behind us, and ever and again a bright green vapour drove up like a veil across our peephole.

The cylinder was already opened in the centre of the pit, and on the further edge of the pit, amid the smashed and gravel-heaped shrubbery, one of the great Fighting Machines, deserted by its occupant, stood stiff and tall against the evening sky. At first I scarcely noticed the pit or the cylinder, although it has been convenient to describe them first, on account of the extraordinary glittering mechanism I saw, busy in the excavation, and on account of the strange creatures that were crawling slowly and painfully across the heaped mould near it.

The mechanism it certainly was held my attention first. It was one of those complicated fabrics that have since been called Handling Machines, and the study of which has already given such an enormous impetus to terrestrial invention. As it dawned upon me first it presented a sort of metallic spider with five jointed, agile legs, and with an extraordinary number of jointed levers, bars, and reaching and clutching tentacles about its body. Most of its arms were retracted, but with three long tentacles it was fishing out a number of rods, plates and bars which lined the covering of, and apparently strengthened the walls of, the cylinder. These, as it extracted them, were lifted out and deposited upon a level surface of earth behind it.

Its motion was so swift, complex, and perfect that at first I did not see it as a machine, in spite of its metallic glitter. The Fighting Machines were coordinated and animated to an extraordinary pitch, but nothing to compare with this. People who have never seen these structures, and have only the ill-imagined efforts of artists or the imperfect descriptions of such eye-witnesses as myself to go upon, scarcely realize that living quality.

I recall particularly the illustration of one of the first pamphlets to give a consecutive account of the war. The artist had evidently made a hasty study of one of the Fighting Machines, and there his knowledge ended. He presented them as tilted, stiff tripods, without either flexibility or subtlety, and with an altogether misleading monotony of effect. The pamphlet containing these renderings had a considerable vogue, and I mention them here simply to warn the reader against the impression they may have created. They were no more like the Martians I saw in action than a Dutch doll is like a human being. To my mind, the pamphlet would have been much better without them.

At first, I say, the Handling Machine did not impress me as a machine, but as a crab-like creature with a glittering integument,[1] the controlling Martian, whose delicate tentacles actuated its movements, seeming to be simply the equivalent of the crab's cerebral portion. But then I perceived the resemblance of its gray-brown, shiny, leathery integument to that of the other sprawling bodies beyond, and the true nature of this dexterous workman dawned upon me. With that realization my interest shifted to those other creatures, the real Martians. Already I had had a transient impression of these, and the first nausea no longer obscured my observation. Moreover, I was concealed and motionless, and under no urgency of action.

They were, I now saw, the most unearthly creatures it is possible to conceive. They were huge round bodies—or, rather, heads—about four feet in diameter, each body having in front of it a face. This face had no nostrils—indeed, the Martians do not seem to have had any sense of smell—but it had a pair of very large dark-coloured eyes, and just beneath this a kind of fleshy beak. In the back of this head or body—I scarcely know how to speak of it—was the single tight tympanic[2] surface, since known to be anatomically an ear, though it must have been almost useless in our denser air. In a group round the mouth were sixteen slender, almost whip-like tentacles, arranged in two bunches of eight each. These bunches have since been named rather aptly, by that distinguished

---

1 An enveloping layer of an organism like a skin or shell.
2 A tympan is a drum, so the Martian skin here is like a drum.

anatomist, Professor Howes, the *hands*. Even as I saw these Martians for the first time they seemed to be endeavouring to raise themselves on these hands, but of course, with the increased weight of terrestrial conditions, this was impossible. There is reason to suppose that on Mars they may have progressed upon them with some facility.

The internal anatomy, I may remark here, dissection has since shown, was almost equally simple. The greater part of the structure was the brain, sending enormous nerves to the eyes, ear and tactile tentacles.[1] Besides this were the complex lungs, into which the mouth opened, and the heart and its vessels. The pulmonary distress caused by the denser atmosphere and greater gravitational attraction was only too evident in the convulsive movements of the outer skin.

And this was the sum of the Martian organs. Strange as it may seem to a human being, all the complex apparatus of digestion, which makes up the bulk of our bodies, did not exist in the Martians. They were heads, merely heads. Entrails they had none. They did not eat, much less digest. Instead, they took the fresh, living blood of other creatures, and *injected* it into their own veins. I have myself seen this being done, as I shall mention in its place. But, squeamish as I may seem, I cannot bring myself to describe what I could not endure even to continue watching. Let it suffice to say, blood obtained from a still living animal, in most cases from a human being, was run directly by means of a little pipette[2] into the recipient canal....

The bare idea of this is no doubt horribly repulsive to us, but at the same time I think that we should remember how repulsive our carnivorous habits would seem to an intelligent rabbit.

The physiological advantages of the practice of injection are undeniable, if one thinks of the tremendous waste of human time and energy occasioned by eating and the digestive process. Our bodies are half made up of glands and tubes and organs, occupied in turning heterogeneous food into blood. The digestive processes and their reaction upon the nervous system sap our strength, colour our minds. Men go happy or miserable as they have

---

1 The Martians are all brain, in keeping with Wells's theory that the bodies of "advanced" creatures would atrophy through disuse.
2 A small glass tube used by chemists to move liquid from one area to another.

healthy or unhealthy livers,[1] or sound gastric glands. But the Martians were lifted above all these organic fluctuations of mood and emotion.

Their undeniable preference for men as their source of nourishment is partly explained by the nature of the remains of the victims they had brought with them as provisions from Mars. These creatures, to judge from the shriveled remains that have fallen into human hands, were bipeds with flimsy, silicious[2] skeletons (almost like those of the silicious sponges) and feeble musculature, standing about six feet high and having round, erect heads, and large eyes in flinty sockets. Two or three of these seem to have been brought in each cylinder, and all were killed before earth was reached. It was just as well for them, for the mere attempt to stand upright upon our planet would have broken every bone in their bodies.

And while I am engaged in this description, I may add in this place certain further details which, although they were not all evident to us at the time, will enable the reader who is unacquainted with them to form a clearer picture of these offensive creatures.

In three other points their physiology differed strangely from ours. Their organisms did not sleep, any more than the heart of man sleeps. Since they had no extensive muscular mechanism to recuperate, that periodical extinction was unknown to them. They had little or no sense of fatigue, it would seem. On earth they could never have moved without effort, yet even to the last they kept in action. In twenty-four hours they did twenty-four hours of work, as even on earth is perhaps the case with the ants.

In the next place, wonderful as it seems in a sexual world, the Martians were absolutely without sex, and therefore without any of the tumultuous emotions that arise from that difference among men. A young Martian, there can now be no dispute, was really born upon earth during the war, and it was found attached to its parent, partially *budded* off, just as young lily-bulbs[3] bud off, or like the young animals in the fresh-water polyp.[4]

---

1 Wells himself suffered from liver problems.
2 Crystalline, made of silica or sand.
3 The bulbs of a lily that reproduce by budding off from each other through the process of fission, a form of asexual reproduction.
4 A sedentary type of animal form characterized by a more or less fixed base, columnar body, and free end with mouth and tentacles.

In man, in all the higher terrestrial animals, such a method of increase has disappeared; but even on this earth it was certainly the primitive method. Among the lower animals, up even to those first cousins of the vertebrated animals, the Tunicates,[1] the two processes occur side by side, but finally the sexual method superseded its competitor altogether. On Mars, however, just the reverse has apparently been the case.

It is worthy of remark that a certain speculative writer[2] of quasi-scientific repute, writing long before the Martian invasion, did forecast for man a final structure not unlike the actual Martian condition. His prophecy, I remember, appeared in November or December, 1893, in a long defunct publication, the *Pall Mall Budget*, and I recall a caricature of it in a pre-Martian periodical called *Punch*. He pointed out—writing in a foolish facetious tone—that the perfection of mechanical appliances must ultimately supersede limbs, the perfection of chemical devices, digestion—that such organs as hair, external nose, teeth, ears, and chin were no longer essential parts of the human being, and that the tendency of natural selection would lie in the direction of their steady diminution through the coming ages. The brain alone remained a cardinal necessity. Only one other part of the body had a strong case for survival, and that was the hand, "teacher and agent of the brain." While the rest of the body dwindled, the hands would grow larger.

There is many a true word written in jest, and here in the Martians we have beyond dispute the actual accomplishment of such a suppression of the animal side of the organism by the intelligence. To me it is quite credible that the Martians may be descended from beings not unlike ourselves, by a gradual development of brain and hands (the latter giving rise to the two bunches of delicate tentacles at last) at the expense of the rest of the body. Without the body the brain would, of course, become a mere selfish intelligence, without any of the emotional substratum of the human being.

The last salient point in which the systems of these creatures differed from ours was in what one might have thought a very trivial particular. Micro-organisms, which cause so much disease and

---

1 A subspecies of sea animals that have saclike bodies and minimal digestive systems.
2 This is Wells himself; see "The Man of the Year Million," in Appendix B.

pain on earth, have either never appeared upon Mars, or Martian sanitary science eliminated them ages ago. A hundred diseases, all the fevers and contagions of human life, consumption,[1] cancers, tumours and such morbidities,[2] never enter the scheme of their life. And speaking of the differences between the life on Mars and terrestrial life, I may allude here to the curious suggestions of the Red Weed.

Apparently the vegetable kingdom in Mars, instead of having green for a dominant colour, is of a vivid blood-red tint. At any rate, the seeds which the Martians (intentionally or accidentally) brought with them gave rise in all cases to red-coloured growths. Only that known popularly as the Red Weed, however, gained any footing in competition with terrestrial forms. The Red Creeper was quite a transitory growth, and few people have seen it growing. For a time, however, the Red Weed grew with astonishing vigour and luxuriance. It spread up the sides of the pit by the third or fourth day of our imprisonment, and its cactus-like branches formed a carmine[3] fringe to the edges of our triangular window. And afterwards I found it broadcast throughout the country, and especially wherever there was a stream of water.

The Martians had what appears to have been an auditory organ, a single round drum at the back of the head-body, and eyes with a visual range not very different from ours except that, according to Philips, blue and violet were as black to them. It is commonly supposed that they communicated by sounds and tentacular gesticulations;[4] this is asserted, for instance, in the able but hastily compiled pamphlet (written evidently by someone not an eye-witness of Martian actions) to which I have already alluded, and which, so far, has been the chief source of information concerning them. Now, no surviving human being saw so much of the Martians in action as I did. I take no credit to myself for an accident, but the fact is so. And I assert that I watched them closely time after time, and that I have seen four, five, and (once) six of them sluggishly performing the most elaborately complicated operations together without either sound or gesture. Their peculiar hooting invariably preceded feeding; it had no modulation, and was, I believe, in no sense a

---

1 Tuberculosis.
2 Things that cause death.
3 Bright red.
4 Gestures.

signal, but merely the expiration of air preparatory to the suction-al[1] operation. I have a certain claim to at least an elementary knowledge of psychology, and in this matter I am convinced—as firmly as I am convinced of anything—that the Martians interchanged thoughts without any physical intermediation. And I have been convinced of this in spite of strong preconceptions. Before the Martian invasion, as an occasional reader here or there may remember, I had written with some little vehemence, against the telepathic theory.

The Martians wore no clothing. Their conceptions of ornament and decorum were necessarily different from ours; and not only were they evidently much less sensible of changes of temperature than we are, but changes of pressure do not seem to have affected their health at all seriously. But if they wore no clothing, yet it was in the other artificial additions to their bodily resources, certainly, that their great superiority over man lay. We men, with our bicycles and road-skates, our Lilienthal soaring-machines,[2] our guns and sticks and so forth, are just in the beginning of the evolution that the Martians have worked out. They have become practically mere brains, wearing different bodies according to their needs, just as men wear suits of clothes and take a bicycle in a hurry or an umbrella in the wet. And of their appliances, perhaps nothing is more wonderful to a man than the curious fact that what is the dominant feature of almost all human devices in mechanism is absent—the *wheel* is absent; amongst all the things they brought to earth there is no trace or suggestion of their use of wheels. One would have at least expected it in locomotion. And in this connection it is curious to remark that even on this earth Nature has never hit upon the wheel, or has preferred other expedients to its development. And not only did the Martians either not know of (which is incredible), or abstain from the wheel, but in their apparatus singularly little use is made of the fixed pivot, or relatively fixed pivot, with circular motions thereabout confined to one plane. Almost all the joints of the machinery present a complicated system of sliding parts moving over small but beautifully curved friction bearings. And while upon this matter of detail, it is remarkable that the long leverages of their machines are in most cases actuated by a sort of sham musculature of discs in an elastic sheath;

---

1 Sucking.
2 Gliders invented by Otto Lilienthal (1849-1896), a German engineer.

these discs become polarised and drawn closely and powerfully together when traversed by a current of electricity. In this way the curious parallelism to animal motions, which was so striking and disturbing to the human beholder, was attained. Such quasi–muscles abounded in the crab-like Handling Machine which I watched unpacking the cylinder, on my first peeping out of the slit. It seemed infinitely more alive than the actual Martians lying beyond it in the sunset light, panting, stirring ineffectual tentacles, and moving feebly after their vast journey across space.

While I was still watching their feeble motions in the sunlight, and noting each strange detail of their form, the curate reminded me of his presence by pulling violently at my arm. I turned to a scowling face, and silent, eloquent lips. He wanted the slit, which permitted only one of us to peep through; and so I had to forego watching them for a time while he enjoyed that privilege.

When I looked again, the busy Handling Machine had already put together several of the pieces of apparatus it had taken out of the cylinder into a shape having an unmistakable likeness to its own; and down on the left a busy little digging mechanism had come into view, emitting jets of green vapour and working its way round the pit, excavating and embanking in a methodical and discriminating manner. This it was which had caused the regular beating noise, and the rhythmic shocks that had kept our ruinous refuge quivering. It piped and whistled as it worked. So far as I could see, the thing was without a directing Martian at all.

III.
THE DAYS OF IMPRISONMENT

The arrival of a second Fighting Machine drove us from our peep-hole into the scullery, for we feared that from his elevation the Martian might see down upon us behind our barrier. At a later date we began to feel less in danger of their eyes, for to an eye in the dazzle of the sunlight outside our refuge must have seemed a blind of blackness, but at first the slightest suggestion of approach drove us into the scullery in heart throbbing retreat. Yet terrible as was the danger we incurred, the attraction of peeping was for both of us irresistible. And I recall now with a sort of wonder that, in spite of the infinite danger in which we were between starvation and a still more terrible death, we could yet struggle bitterly for that horrible privilege of sight. We would race across the kitchen in a grotesque pace between eagerness and the dread of making a noise, and strike one another, and thrust and kick, within a few inches of exposure.

The fact is that we had absolutely incompatible dispositions and habits of thought and action, and our danger and isolation only accentuated the incompatibility. At Halliford I had already come to hate his trick of helpless exclamation, his stupid rigidity of mind. His endless muttering monologue vitiated[1] every effort I made to think out a line of action, and drove me at times, thus pent up and intensified, almost to the verge of craziness. He was as lacking in restraint as a silly woman. He would weep for hours together, and I verily believe that to the very end this spoilt child of life thought his weak tears in some way efficacious.[2] And I would sit in the darkness unable to keep my mind off him by reason of his importunities. He ate more than I did, and it was in vain I pointed out that our only chance of life was to stop in the house until the Martians had done with their pit, that in that long patience a time might presently come when we should need food. He ate and drank impulsively in heavy meals at long intervals. He slept little.

As the days wore on, his utter carelessness of any consideration so intensified our distress and danger that I had, much as I loathed doing it, to resort to threats, and at last to blows. That brought him to reason for a time. But he was one of those weak creatures, full of a shifty cunning, who face neither God nor man, who face not even themselves, void of pride, timorous,[3] anaemic,[4] hateful souls.

It is disagreeable for me to recall and write these things, but I set them down that my story may lack nothing. Those who have escaped the dark and terrible aspects of life will find my brutality, my flash of rage in our final tragedy, easy enough to blame; for they know what is wrong as well as any, but not what is possible to tortured men. But those who have been under the shadow, who have gone down at last to elemental things, will have a wider charity.

And while within we fought out our dark, dim contest of whispers, snatched food and drink, and gripping hands and blows,

---

1 Made ineffective or weak.
2 Effective.
3 Fearful.
4 Literally a deficiency in red blood cells, but figuratively meaning weak.

without in the pitiless sunlight of that terrible June, was the strange wonder, the unfamiliar routine of the Martians in the pit. Let me return to those first new experiences of mine. After a long time I ventured back to the peep-hole, to find that the new-comers had been reinforced by the occupants of no fewer than three of the Fighting Machines. These last had brought with them certain fresh appliances that stood in an orderly manner about the cylinder. The second Handling Machine was now completed, and was busied in serving one of the novel contrivances the big machine had brought. This was a body resembling a milk-can[1] in its general form above which oscillated a pear-shaped receptacle, and from which a stream of white powder flowed into a circular basin below.

The oscillatory motion was imparted to this by one tentacle of the Handling Machine. With two spatulate[2] hands the Handling Machine was digging out and flinging masses of clay into the pear-shaped receptacle above, while with another arm it periodically opened a door and removed rusty and blackened clinkers from the middle part of the machine. Another steely tentacle directed the powder from the basin along a ribbed channel towards some receiver that was hidden from me by the mound of bluish dust. From this unseen receiver a little thread of green smoke rose vertically into the quiet air. As I looked, the Handling Machine, with a faint and musical clinking, extended, telescopic fashion, a tentacle that had been a moment before a mere blunt projection, until its end was hidden behind the mound of clay. In another second it had lifted a bar of white aluminium into sight, untarnished as yet, and shining dazzlingly, and deposited it in a growing stack of bars that stood at the side of the pit. Between sunset and starlight this dexterous machine must have made more than a hundred such bars out of the crude clay, and the mound of bluish dust rose steadily until it topped the side of the pit.

The contrast between the swift and complex movements of these contrivances and the inert, panting clumsiness of their masters was acute, and for days I had to tell myself repeatedly that these latter were indeed the living of the two things.

The curate had possession of the slit when the first men were brought to the pit. I was sitting below, crouched together, listening

---

1 A very large container used by dairies to transport milk.
2 Shaped like a spatula; having a handle with a flat end.

with all my ears. He made a sudden movement backward, and I, fearful that we were observed, crouched in a spasm of terror. He came sliding down the rubbish and crouched beside me in the darkness, inarticulate, gesticulating, and for a moment I shared his terror. His gesture suggested a resignation of the slit, and after a little while my curiosity gave me courage, and I rose up, stepped across him, and clambered up to it. At first I could see no reason for his terror. The twilight had now come, the stars were little and faint, but the pit was illuminated by the flickering green fire that came from the aluminium making. The whole picture was a flickering scheme of green gleams and shifting rusty black shadows, strangely trying to the eyes. Over and through it all went the bats, heeding it not at all. The sprawling Martians were no longer to be seen, the mound of blue-green powder had risen to cover them from sight, and a Fighting Machine, with its legs contracted, crumpled, and abbreviated, stood across the corner of the pit. And then, amidst the clangour of the machinery, came a drifting suspicion of human voices, that I entertained at first only to dismiss.

I crouched, watching this Fighting Machine closely, satisfying myself now for the first time that the hood did indeed contain a Martian. As the green flames lifted I could see the oily gleam of his integument and the brightness of his eyes. And suddenly I heard a yell, and saw a long tentacle reaching over the shoulder of the machine to the little cage that hunched upon its back. Then something—something struggling violently—was lifted high against the sky, a black, vague enigma against the starlight; and as this black object came down again, I saw by the green brightness that it was a man. For an instant he was clearly visible. He was a stout, ruddy, middle-aged man, well dressed; three days before, he must have been walking the world, a man of considerable consequence. I could see his staring eyes and gleams of light on his studs and watch-chain. He vanished behind the mound, and for a moment there was silence. And then began a shrieking and a sustained and cheerful hooting from the Martians.

I slid down the rubbish, struggled to my feet, clapped my hands over my ears and bolted into the scullery. The curate, who had been crouching silently with his arms over his head, looked up as I passed, cried out quite loudly at my desertion of him, and came running after me.

That night, as we lurked in the scullery, balanced between our horror and the horrible fascination this peeping had, although I felt an urgent need of action, I tried in vain to conceive some plan of escape; but afterwards, during the second day, I was able to consider our position with great clearness. The curate, I found, was quite incapable of discussion; strange terrors had already made him a creature of violent impulses, had robbed him of reason and forethought. Practically he had already sunk to the level of an animal. But, as the saying goes, I gripped myself with both hands. It grew upon my mind, once I could face the facts, that terrible as our position was, there was as yet no justification for absolute despair. Our chief chance lay in the possibility of the Martians making the pit nothing more than a temporary encampment. Or even if they kept it permanently, they might not consider it necessary to guard it, and a chance of escape might be afforded us. I also weighed very carefully the possibility of our digging a way out in a direction away from the pit, but the chances of our emerging within sight of some sentinel Fighting Machine seemed at first too great. And I should have had to do all the digging myself. The curate would certainly have failed me.

It was on the third day, if my memory serves me right, that I saw the lad killed. It was the only occasion on which I actually saw the Martians feed. After that experience I avoided the hole in the wall for the better part of a day. I went into the scullery, removed the door, and spent some hours digging with my hatchet as silently as possible; but when I had made a hole about a couple of feet deep the loose earth collapsed noisily, and I did not dare continue. I lost heart, and lay down on the scullery floor for a long time, having no spirit even to move. And after that I abandoned altogether the idea of escaping by excavation.

It says much for the impression the Martians had made upon me that at first I entertained little or no hope of our escape being brought about by their overthrow through any human effort. But on the fourth or fifth night I heard a sound like heavy guns.

It was very late in the night, and the moon was shining brightly. The Martians had taken away the Excavating Machine, and, save for a Fighting Machine that stood in the remoter bank of the pit and a Handling Machine that was buried out of my sight in a corner of the pit immediately beneath my peep-hole, the place was deserted by them. Except for the pale glow from the Handling Machine and the bars and patches of white moonlight the pit was in darkness, and, except for the clinking of the Handling Machine, quite still. That night was a beautiful serenity; save for one planet, the moon seemed to have the sky to herself. I heard a dog howling, and that familiar sound it was that made me listen. Then I heard quite distinctly a booming exactly like the sound of great guns. Six distinct reports I counted, and after a long interval six again. And that was all.

IV.
THE DEATH OF THE CURATE

It was on the sixth day of our imprisonment that I peeped for the last time, and presently found myself alone. Instead of keeping close to me and trying to oust me from the slit, the curate had gone back into the scullery. I was struck by a sudden thought. I went back quickly and quietly into the scullery. In the darkness I heard the curate drinking. I snatched in the darkness, and my fingers caught a bottle of burgundy.

For a few minutes there was a tussle. The bottle struck the floor and broke, and I desisted and rose. We stood panting and threatening each other. In the end I planted myself between him and the food, and told him of my determination to begin a discipline. I divided the food in the pantry into rations to last us ten days. I would not let him eat any more that day. In the afternoon he made a feeble effort to get at the food. I had been dozing, but in an instant I was awake. All day and all night we sat face to face, I weary but resolute, and he weeping and complaining of his immediate hunger. It was, I know, a night and a day, but to me it seemed—it seems now—an interminable length of time.

And so our widened incompatibility ended at last in open conflict. For two vast days we struggled in undertones and wrestling contests. There were times when I beat and kicked him madly, times when I cajoled and persuaded him, and once I tried to bribe him with the last bottle of burgundy, for there was a rain-water pump from which I could get water. But neither force nor kindness availed; he was indeed beyond reason. He would neither desist from his attacks on the food nor from his noisy babbling to himself. The rudimentary precautions to keep our imprisonment endurable he would not observe. Slowly I began to realize the complete overthrow of his intelligence, to perceive that my sole companion in this close and sickly darkness was a man insane.

From certain vague memories I am inclined to think my own mind wandered at times. I had strange and hideous dreams whenever I slept. It sounds strange, but I am inclined to think that the weakness and insanity of the curate warned me, braced me and kept me a sane man.

On the eighth day he began to talk aloud instead of whisper, and nothing I could do would moderate his speech.

"It is just, O God!" he would say, over and over again. "It is just. On me and mine be the punishment laid. We have sinned, we have fallen short. There was poverty, sorrow; the poor were trodden in the dust, and I held my peace. I preached acceptable folly—my God, what folly!—when I should have stood up, though I died for it, and called upon them to repent—repent! ... Oppressors of the poor and needy...! The wine-press of God!"[1]

Then he would suddenly revert to the matter of the food I withheld from him, praying, begging, weeping, at last threatening. He began to raise his voice—I prayed him not to. He perceived a hold on me—he threatened he would shout and bring the Martians upon us. For a time that scared me; but any concession would have shortened our chance of escape beyond estimating. I defied him, although I felt no assurance that he might not do this thing. But that day, at any rate, he did not. He talked with his voice rising slowly, through the greater part of the eighth and ninth days—threats, entreaties, mingled with a torrent of half-sane and always frothy repentance for his vacant sham of God's service, such as made me pity him. Then he slept awhile, and began again with renewed strength, so loudly that I must needs make him desist.

"Be still!" I implored.

He rose to his knees, for he had been sitting in the darkness near the copper.[2]

"I have been still too long," he said, in a tone that must have reached the pit, "and now I must bear my witness. Woe unto this unfaithful city! Woe! Woe! Woe! Woe! Woe! To the inhabitants of the earth by reason of the other voices of the trumpet—"

"Shut up!" I said, rising to my feet, and in a terror lest the Martians should hear us. "For God's sake—"

"Nay," shouted the curate, at the top of his voice, standing likewise and extending his arms. "Speak! The word of the Lord is upon me!"

In three strides he was at the door leading into the kitchen.

"I must bear my witness! I go! It has already been too long delayed."

---

1 See Isaiah 63:3.
2 A large kettle.

I put out my hand and felt the meat chopper hanging to the wall. In a flash I was after him. I was fierce with fear. Before he was half-way across the kitchen I had overtaken him. With one last touch of humanity I turned the blade back and struck him with the butt. He went headlong forward and lay stretched on the ground. I stumbled over him and stood panting. He lay still.

Suddenly I heard a noise without, the run and smash of slipping plaster, and the triangular aperture in the wall was darkened. I looked up and saw the lower surface of a Handling Machine coming slowly across the hole. One of its gripping limbs curled amidst the débris; another limb appeared, feeling its way over the fallen beams. I stood petrified, staring. Then I saw through a sort of glass plate near the edge of the body the face, as we may call it, and the large dark eyes of a Martian, peering, and then a long metallic snake of tentacle came feeling slowly through the hole.

I turned by an effort, stumbled over the curate, and stopped at the scullery door. The tentacle was now some way, two yards or more, in the room, and twisting and turning, with queer sudden movements, this way and that. For a while I stood fascinated by that slow, fitful advance. Then, with a faint, hoarse cry, I forced myself across the scullery. I trembled violently; I could scarcely stand upright. I opened the door of the coal cellar, and stood there in the darkness staring at the faintly lit doorway into the kitchen, and listening. Had the Martian seen me? What was it doing now?

Something was moving to and fro there, very quietly; every now and then it tapped against the wall, or started on its movements with a faint metallic ringing, like the movements of keys on a split-ring. Then a heavy body—I knew too well what—was dragged across the floor of the kitchen towards the opening. Irresistibly attracted, I crept to the door and peeped into the kitchen. In the triangle of bright outer sunlight I saw the Martian, in its Briareus[1] of a Handling Machine, scrutinizing the curate's head. I thought at once that it would infer my presence from the mark of the blow I had given him.

I crept back to the coal-cellar, shut the door, and began to cover myself up as much as I could, and as noiselessly as possible in the darkness, among the firewood and coal therein. Every now and then I paused rigid, to hear if the Martian had thrust its tentacles through the opening again.

---

1 In mythology, a monster with a hundred hands.

Then the faint metallic jingle returned. I traced it slowly feeling over the kitchen. Presently I heard it nearer—in the scullery, as I judged. I thought that its length might be insufficient to reach me. I prayed copiously. It passed, scraping faintly across the cellar door. An age of almost intolerable suspense intervened; then I heard it fumbling at the latch! It had found the door! The Martian understood doors!

It worried at the catch for a minute, perhaps, and then the door opened.

In the darkness I could just see the thing—like an elephant's trunk more than anything else—waving towards me and touching and examining the wall, coals, wood and ceiling. It was like a black worm swaying its blind head to and fro.

Once, even, it touched the heel of my boot. I was on the verge of screaming; I bit my hand. For a time it was silent. I could have fancied it had been withdrawn. Presently, with an abrupt click, it gripped something—I thought it had me!—and seemed to go out of the cellar again. For a minute I was not sure. Apparently, it had taken a lump of coal to examine.

I seized the opportunity of slightly shifting my position, which had become cramped, and then listened. I whispered passionate prayers for safety.

Then I heard the slow, deliberate sound creeping towards me again. Slowly, slowly it drew near, scratching against the walls and tapping the furniture.

While I was still doubtful, it rapped smartly against the cellar door and closed it. I heard it go into the pantry, and the biscuit-tins rattled and a bottle smashed, and then came a heavy bump against the cellar door. Then silence that passed into an infinity of suspense.

Had it gone?

At last I decided that it had.

It came into the scullery no more; but I lay all the tenth day in the close darkness, buried among coals and firewood, not daring even to crawl out for the drink for which I craved. It was the eleventh day before I ventured so far from my security.

V.

THE STILLNESS

My first act, before I went into the pantry, was to fasten the door between the kitchen and the scullery. But the pantry was empty; every scrap of food had gone. Apparently, the Martian had taken it all on the previous day. At that discovery I despaired for the first time. I took no food and no drink either on the eleventh or the twelfth day.

At first my mouth and throat were parched, and my strength ebbed sensibly. I sat about in the darkness of the scullery, in a state of despondent wretchedness. My mind ran on eating. I thought I had become deaf, for the noises of movement I had been accustomed to hear from the pit ceased absolutely. I did not feel strong enough to crawl noiselessly to the peephole, or I would have gone there.

On the twelfth day my throat was so painful that, taking the chance of alarming the Martians, I attacked the creaking rain-water pump that stood by the sink, and got a couple of glassfuls of blackened and tainted rain-water. I was greatly refreshed by this, and emboldened by the fact that no inquiring tentacle followed the noise of my pumping.

During these days I thought much of the curate and of the manner of his death, in a rambling, inconclusive manner.

On the thirteenth day I drank some more water, and dozed and thought disjointedly of eating and of vague impossible plans of escape. Whenever I dozed I dreamt of horrible phantasms,[1] of the death of the curate, or of sumptuous dinners; but, sleeping or awake, I felt a keen pain that urged me to drink again and again. The light that came into the scullery was no longer grey but red. To my disordered imagination it seemed the colour of blood.

On the fourteenth day I went into the kitchen, and I was surprised to find that the fronds of the Red Weed had grown right across the hole in the wall, turning the half-light of the place into a crimson-coloured obscurity.

It was early on the fifteenth day that I heard a curious, familiar sequence of sounds in the kitchen, and, listening, identified it as the snuffing and scratching of a dog. Going into the kitchen, I saw a dog's nose peering in through a break among the ruddy fronds. This greatly surprised me. At the scent of me he barked shortly.

I thought if I could induce him to come into the place quietly I should be able, perhaps, to kill and eat him, and in any case, it would be advisable to kill him, lest his actions attracted the attention of the Martians.

---

1 Ghosts.

I crept forward, saying "Good dog!" very softly; but he suddenly withdrew his head and disappeared.

I listened—I was not deaf—but certainly the pit was still. I heard a sound like the flutter of a bird's wings, and a hoarse croaking, but that was all.

For a long while I lay close to the peep-hole, but not daring to move aside the red plants that obscured it. Once or twice I heard a faint pitter-patter like the feet of the dog going hither and thither on the sand far below me, and there were more birdlike sounds, but that was all. At length, encouraged by the silence, I looked out.

Except in the corner, where a multitude of crows hopped and fought over the skeletons of the dead the Martians had consumed, there was not a living thing in the pit.

I stared about me, scarcely believing my eyes. All the machinery had gone. Save for the big mound of grayish-blue powder in one corner, certain bars of aluminium in another, the black birds and the skeletons of the killed, the place was merely an empty circular pit in the sand.

Slowly I thrust myself out through the Red Weed, and stood upon the mound of rubble. I could see in any direction save behind me, to the north, and neither Martian nor sign of Martian were to be seen. The pit dropped sheerly from my feet, but a little way along the rubbish afforded a practicable slope to the summit of the ruins. My chance of escape had come. I began to tremble.

I hesitated for some time, and then, in a gust of desperate resolution, and with a heart that throbbed violently, I scrambled to the top of the mound in which I had been buried so long.

I looked about again. To the northward, too, no Martian was visible.

When I had last seen this part of Sheen in the daylight it had been a straggling street of comfortable white and red houses, interspersed with abundant shady trees. Now I stood on a mound of smashed brickwork, clay, and gravel, over which spread a multitude of red cactus-shaped plants, knee-high, without a solitary terrestrial growth to dispute their footing. The trees near me were dead and brown, but further a network of red thread scaled the still living stems.

The neighbouring houses had all been wrecked, but none had been burned; their walls stood, sometimes to the second story, with smashed windows and shattered doors. The Red Weed grew tumultuously in their roofless rooms. Below me was the great pit, with the crows struggling for its refuse. A number of other birds hopped about among the ruins. Far away I saw a gaunt[1] cat slink crouchingly along a wall, but traces of men there were none.

The day seemed, by contrast with my recent confinement, dazzlingly bright, the sky a glowing blue. A gentle breeze kept the Red Weed that covered every scrap of unoccupied ground gently swaying. And oh! the sweetness of the air!

VI.

THE WORK OF FIFTEEN DAYS

For some time I stood tottering on the mound regardless of my safety. Within that noisome den from which I had emerged I had thought with a narrow intensity only of our immediate security. I had not realized what had been happening to the world, had not anticipated this startling vision of unfamiliar things. I had expected to see Sheen in ruins—I found about me the landscape, weird and lurid, of another planet.

For that moment I touched an emotion beyond the common range of men, yet one that the poor brutes we dominate know only too well. I felt as a rabbit might feel returning to his burrow and suddenly confronted by the work of a dozen busy navvies[2] digging the foundations of a house. I felt the first inkling of a thing that presently grew quite clear in my mind, that oppressed me for many days, a sense of dethronement, a persuasion that I was no longer a master, but an animal among the animals, under the Martian heel. With us it would be as with them, to lurk and watch, to run and hide; the fear and empire of man had passed away.

But so soon as this strangeness had been realized it passed, and my dominant motive became the hunger of my long and dismal fast. In the direction away from the pit I saw, beyond a red-covered wall, a patch of garden ground unburied. This gave me a hint, and I went knee-deep, and sometimes neck-deep, in the Red Weed. The density of the weed gave me a reassuring sense of hiding. The wall was some six feet high and when I attempted to clamber it I found I could not lift my feet to the crest. So I went along by the side of it, and came to a corner and a rockwork that enabled me to get to the top, and tumble into the garden I coveted. Here I found some young onions, a couple of gladiolus bulbs, and a quantity of

---

1 Skeletal, half starved.
2 Manual labourers.

immature carrots, all of which I secured, and, scrambling over a ruined wall, went on my way through scarlet and crimson trees towards Kew—it was like walking through an avenue of gigantic blood-drops—possessed with two ideas: to get more food, and to limp, as soon and as far as my strength permitted, out of this accursed unearthly region of the pit.

Some way further, in a grassy place, was a group of mushrooms which also I devoured, and then I came upon a brown sheet of flowing shallow water, where meadows used to be. These fragments of nourishment served only to whet my hunger. At first I was surprised at this flood in a hot, dry summer, but afterwards I discovered that it was caused by the tropical exuberance of the Red Weed. Directly this extraordinary growth encountered water, it straightway became gigantic and of unparalleled fecundity.[1] Its seeds were simply poured down into the water of the Wey and Thames, and its swiftly-growing and Titanic water-fronds speedily choked both those rivers.

At Putney, as I afterwards saw, the bridge was almost lost in a tangle of this weed, and at Richmond, too, the Thames water poured in a broad and shallow stream across the meadows of Hampton and Twickenham. As the waters spread the weed followed them, until the ruined villas of the Thames Valley were for a time lost in this red swamp, whose margin I explored, and much of the desolation the Martians had caused was concealed.

In the end the Red Weed succumbed almost as quickly as it had spread. A cankering disease, due, it is believed, to the action of certain bacteria, presently seized upon it. Now by the action of natural selection, all terrestrial plants have acquired a resisting power against bacterial diseases—they never succumb without a severe struggle, but the Red Weed rotted like a thing already dead. The fronds became bleached, and then shrivelled and brittle. They broke off at the least touch, and the waters that had stimulated their early growth carried their last vestiges out to sea.

My first act on coming to this water was, of course, to slake[2] my thirst. I drank a great deal of it and, moved by an impulse, gnawed some fronds of Red Weed; but they were watery, and had a sickly, metallic taste. I found the water was sufficiently shallow for me to wade securely, although the Red Weed impeded my feet a little; but

---

1 Fertility.
2 Quench, to drink until no longer thirsty.

the flood evidently got deeper towards the river, and I turned back to Mortlake. I managed to make out the road by means of occasional ruins of its villas and fences and lamps, and so presently I got out of this spate and made my way to the hill going up towards Roehampton, and came out on Putney Common.

Here the scenery changed from the strange and unfamiliar to the wreckage of the familiar; patches of ground exhibited the devastation of a cyclone, and in a few score yards I would come upon perfectly undisturbed spaces, houses with their blinds trimly drawn and doors closed, as if they had been left for a day by the owners, or as if their inhabitants slept within. The Red Weed was less abundant; the tall trees along the lane were free from the red creeper. I hunted for food among the trees, finding nothing, and I also raided a couple of silent houses, but they had already been broken into and ransacked. I rested for the remainder of the daylight in a shrubbery, being, in my enfeebled condition, too fatigued to push on.

All this time I saw no human beings, and no signs of the Martians. I encountered a couple of hungry-looking dogs, but both hurried circuitously away from the advances I made them. Near Roehampton I had seen two human skeletons—not bodies, but skeletons, picked clean—and in the wood by me I found the crushed and scattered bones of several cats and rabbits and the skull of a sheep. But though I gnawed parts of these in my mouth, there was nothing to be got from them.

After sunset I struggled on along the road towards Putney, where I think the Heat-Ray must have been used for some reason. And in a garden beyond Roehampton I got a quantity of immature potatoes, sufficient to stay my hunger. From this garden one looked down upon Putney and the river. The aspect of the place in the dusk was singularly desolate: blackened trees, blackened, desolate ruins, and down the hill the sheets of the flooded river, red-tinged with the weed. And over all—silence. It filled me with indescribable terror to think how swiftly that desolating change had come.

For a time I believed that mankind had been swept out of existence, and that I stood there alone, the last man left alive. Hard by the top of Putney Hill I came upon another skeleton, with the arms dislocated and removed several yards from the rest of the body. As I proceeded I became more and more convinced that the extermination of mankind was, save for such stragglers as myself, already accomplished in this part of the world. The Martians, I thought, had gone on and left the country desolated, seeking food elsewhere. Perhaps even now they were destroying Berlin or Paris, or it might be they had gone northward.

VII.
THE MAN ON PUTNEY HILL

I spent that night in the inn that stands at the top of Putney Hill, sleeping in a made bed for the first time since my flight to Leatherhead. I will not tell the needless trouble I had breaking into that house—afterwards I found the front door was on the latch—nor how I ransacked every room for food, until just on the verge of despair, in what seemed to me to be a servant's bedroom, I found a rat-gnawed crust and two tinned pineapples. The place had been already searched and emptied. In the bar I afterwards found some biscuits and sandwiches that had been overlooked. The latter I could not eat, but the former not only stayed my hunger, but filled my pockets. I lit no lamps, fearing some Martian might come beating that part of London for food in the night. Before I went to bed I had an interval of restlessness, and prowled from window to window, peering out for some sign of these monsters. I slept little. As I lay in bed I found myself thinking consecutively[1]—a thing I do not remember to have done since my last argument with the curate. During all the intervening time my mental condition had been a hurrying succession of vague emotional states, or a sort of stupid receptivity. But in the night my brain, reinforced, I suppose, by the food I had eaten, grew clear again, and I thought.

Three things struggled for possession of my mind: the killing of the curate, the whereabouts of the Martians, and the possible fate of my wife. The former gave me no sensation of horror or remorse to recall; I saw it simply as a thing done, a memory infinitely disagreeable but quite without the quality of remorse. I saw myself then as I see myself now, driven step by step towards that hasty blow, the creature of a sequence of accidents leading inevitably to that. I felt no condemnation; yet the memory, static, unprogressive, haunted me. In the silence of the night, with that sense of the nearness of God that sometimes comes into the stillness and the darkness, I stood my trial, my only trial, for that moment of wrath and fear. I retraced every step of our conversation from the moment

---

1   Rationally.

when I had found him crouching beside me, heedless of my thirst, and pointing to the fire and smoke that streamed up from the ruins of Weybridge. We had been incapable of co-operation—grim chance had taken no heed of that. Had I foreseen, I should have left him at Halliford. But I did not foresee; and crime is to foresee and do. And I set this down as I have set all this story down, as it was. There were no witnesses—all these things I might have concealed. But I set it down, and the reader must form his judgment as he will.

And when, by an effort, I had set aside that picture of a prostrate body, I faced the problem of the Martians and the fate of my wife. For the former I had no data; I could imagine a hundred things, and so, unhappily, I could for the latter. And suddenly that night became terrible. I found myself sitting up in bed, staring at the dark. I found myself praying that the Heat-Ray may have suddenly and painlessly struck her out of being. Since the night of my return from Leatherhead I had not prayed. I had uttered prayers, fetich prayers,[1] had prayed as heathens mutter charms when I was in extremity; but now I prayed indeed, pleading steadfastly and sanely, face to face with the darkness of God. Strange night! Strangest in this, that so soon as dawn had come, I, who had talked with God, crept out of the house like a rat leaving its hiding place—a creature scarcely larger, an inferior animal, a thing that for any passing whim of our masters might be hunted and killed. Perhaps they also prayed confidently to God. Surely, if we have learned nothing else, this war has taught us pity—pity for those witless souls that suffer our dominion.

The morning was bright and fine, and the eastern sky glowed pink, and was fretted with little golden clouds. In the road that runs from the top of Putney Hill to Wimbledon was a number of pitiful vestiges of the panic torrent that must have poured London-ward on the Sunday night after the fighting began. There was a little two-wheeled cart inscribed with the name of Thomas Lobb, Green-grocer, New Malden, with a smashed wheel and an abandoned tin trunk; there was a straw hat trampled into the now hardened mud, and at the top of West Hill a lot of blood-stained glass about the overturned water-trough. My movements were languid, my plans of the vaguest. I had an idea of going to Leatherhead, though I knew that there I had the poorest chance of finding my

---

1 "Fetish" or superstitious prayers to an idol.

wife. Certainly, unless death had overtaken them suddenly, my cousins and she would have fled thence; but it seemed to me I might find or learn there whither the Surrey people had fled. I knew I wanted to find my wife, that my heart ached for her and the world of men, but I had no clear idea how the finding might be done. I was also clearly aware now of my intense loneliness. From the corner I went, under cover of a thicket of trees and bushes, to the edge of Wimbledon Common, stretching wide and far.

That dark expanse was lit in patches by yellow gorse and broom;[1] there was no Red Weed to be seen, and as I prowled, hesitating, on the verge of the open, the sun rose, flooding it all with light and vitality. I came upon a busy swarm of little frogs in a swampy place among the trees. I stopped to look at them, drawing a lesson from their stout resolve to live. And presently, turning suddenly, with an odd feeling of being watched, I beheld something crouching amid a clump of bushes. I stood regarding this. I made a step towards it, and it rose up and became a man armed with a cutlass. I approached him slowly. He stood silent and motionless, regarding me.

As I drew nearer I perceived he was dressed in clothes as dusty and filthy as my own; he looked, indeed, as though he had been dragged through a culvert.[2] Nearer, I distinguished the green slime of ditches mixing with the pale drab of dried clay and shiny, coaly patches. His black hair fell over his eyes, and his face was dark and dirty and sunken, so that at first I did not recognize him. There was a red cut across the lower part of his face.

"Stop!" he cried, when I was within ten yards of him, and I stopped. His voice was hoarse. "Where do you come from?" he said.

I thought, surveying him.

"I come from Mortlake," I said. "I was buried near the pit the Martians made about their cylinder. I have worked my way out and escaped."

"There is no food about here," he said. "This is my country. All this hill down to the river, and back to Clapham, and up to the edge of the Common. There is only food for one. Which way are you going?"

---

1 European shrubs.
2 A drainage ditch.

I answered slowly.

"I don't know," I said. "I have been buried in the ruins of a house thirteen or fourteen days. I don't know what has happened."

He looked at me doubtfully, then started, and looked with a changed expression.

"I've no wish to stop about here," said I. "I think I shall go to Leatherhead, for my wife was there."

He shot out a pointing finger.

"It is you," said he. "The man from Woking. And you weren't killed at Weybridge?"

I recognized him at the same moment.

"You are the artilleryman who came into my garden."

"Good luck!" he said. "We are lucky ones! Fancy *you!*" He put out a hand, and I took it. "I crawled up a drain," he said. "But they didn't kill everyone. And after they went away I got off towards Walton across the fields. But—It's not sixteen days altogether—and your hair is gray." He looked over his shoulder suddenly. "Only a rook," he said. "One gets to know that birds have shadows these days. This *is* a bit open. Let us crawl under those bushes and talk."

"Have you seen any Martians?" I said. "Since I crawled out—"

"They've gone away across London," he said. "I guess they've got a bigger camp there. Of a night, all over there, Hampstead way, the sky is alive with their lights. It's like a great city, and in the glare you can just see them moving. By daylight you can't. But nearer—I haven't seen them—" (he counted on his fingers) "five days. Then I saw a couple across Hammersmith way carrying something big. And the night before last"—he stopped and spoke impressively—"it was just a matter of lights, but it was something up in the air. I believe they've built a flying-machine, and are learning to fly."

I stopped, on hands and knees, for we had come to the bushes.

"Fly!"

"Yes," he said, "fly."

I went on into a little bower, and sat down.

"It is all over with humanity," I said. "If they can do that they will simply go round the world...."

He nodded.

"They will. But—It will relieve things over here a bit. And besides—" He looked at me. "Aren't you satisfied it *is* up with humanity? I am. We're down; we're beat."

I stared. Strange as it may seem, I had not arrived at this fact—

a fact perfectly obvious so soon as he spoke. I had still held a vague hope; rather, I had kept a lifelong habit of mind. He repeated his words, "We're beat." They carried absolute conviction.

"It's all over," he said. "They've lost *one*—just *one*. And they've made their footing good and crippled the greatest power in the world. They've walked over us. The death of that one at Weybridge was an accident. And these are only pioneers. They kept on coming. These green stars—I've seen none these five or six days, but I've no doubt they're falling somewhere every night. Nothing's to be done. We're under! We're beat!"

I made him no answer. I sat staring before me, trying in vain to devise some countervailing thought.

"This isn't a war," said the artilleryman. "It never was a war, any more than there's war between man and ants."

Suddenly I recalled the night in the observatory.

"After the tenth shot they fired no more—at least, until the first cylinder came."

"How do you know?" said the artilleryman. I explained. He thought. "Something wrong with the gun," he said. "But what if there is? They'll get it right again. And even if there's a delay, how can it alter the end? It's just men and ants. There's the ants builds their cities, live their lives, have wars, revolutions, until the men want them out of the way, and then they go out of the way. That's what we are now—just ants. Only—"

"Yes," I said.

"We're eatable ants."

We sat looking at each other.

"And what will they do with us?" I said.

"That's what I've been thinking," he said—"that's what I've been thinking. After Weybridge I went south—thinking. I saw what was up. Most of the people were hard at it squealing and exciting themselves. But I'm not so fond of squealing. I've been in sight of death once or twice; I'm not an ornamental soldier, and at the best and worst, death—it's just death. And it's the man that keeps on thinking comes through. I saw everyone tracking away south. Says I, 'Food won't last this way,' and I turned right back. I went for the Martians like a sparrow goes for man.[1] All round"—

---

1 Just as small birds like sparrows live off food dropped by humans, the artilleryman decides to act the same way with the Martians.

he waved a hand to the horizon—"they're starving in heaps, bolting, treading on each other...."

He saw my face, and halted awkwardly.

"No doubt lots who had money have gone away to France," he said. He seemed to hesitate whether to apologize, met my eyes, and went on: "There's food all about here. Canned things in shops; wines, spirits, mineral waters; and the water mains and drains are empty. Well, I was telling you what I was thinking. 'Here's intelligent things,' I said, 'and it seems they want us for food. First, they'll smash us up—ships, machines, guns, cities, all the order and organization. All that will go. If we were the size of ants we might pull through. But we're not. It's all too bulky to stop. That's the first certainty.' Eh?"

I assented.

"It is; I've thought it out. Very well, then, next: at present we're caught as we're wanted. A Martian has only to go a few miles to get a crowd on the run. And I saw one, one day, out by Wandsworth, picking houses to pieces and routing among the wreckage. But they won't keep on doing that. So soon as they've settled all our guns and ships, and smashed our railways, and done all the things they are doing over there, they will begin catching us systematic, picking the best and storing us in cages and things. That's what they will start doing in a bit. Lord! They haven't begun on us yet. Don't you see that?"

"Not begun!" I exclaimed.

"Not begun. All that's happened so far is through our not having the sense to keep quiet—worrying them with guns and such foolery. And losing our heads, and rushing off in crowds to where there wasn't any more safety than where we were. They don't want to bother us yet. They're making their things—making all the things they couldn't bring with them, getting things ready for the rest of their people. Very likely that's why the cylinders have stopped for a bit, for fear of hitting those who are here. And instead of our rushing about blind, on the howl, or getting dynamite on the chance of busting them up, we've got to fix ourselves up according to the new state of affairs. That's how I figure it out. It isn't quite according to what a man wants for his species, but it's about what the facts point to. And that's the principle I acted upon. Cities, nations, civilization, progress—it's all over. That game's up. We're beat."

"But if that is so, what is there to live for?"

The artilleryman looked at me for a moment.

"There won't be any more blessed concerts for a million years or so; there won't be any Royal Academy of Arts, and no nice little feeds at restaurants. If it's amusement you're after, I reckon the game is up. If you've got any drawing-room manners or a dislike to eating peas with a knife or dropping aitches,[1] you'd better chuck 'em away. They ain't no further use."

"You mean—"

"I mean that men like me are going on living—for the sake of the breed. I tell you, I'm grim set on living. And if I'm not mistaken, you'll show what insides *you've* got, too, before long. We aren't going to be exterminated. And I don't mean to be caught either, and tamed and fattened and bred like a thundering ox. Ugh! Fancy those brown creepers!"

"You don't mean to say—"

"I do. I'm going on. Under their feet. I've got it planned; I've thought it out. We men are beat. We don't know enough. We've got to learn before we've got a chance. And we've got to live and keep independent while we learn. See? That's what has to be done."

I stared, astonished, and stirred profoundly by the man's resolution.

"Great God!" cried I. "But you are a man indeed!" And suddenly I gripped his hand.

"Eh!" he said, with his eyes shining. "I've thought it out, eh?"

"Go on," I said.

"Well, those who mean to escape their catching must get ready. I'm getting ready. Mind you, it isn't all of us that are made for wild beasts; and that's what it's got to be. That's why I watched you. I had my doubts. You're thin and slender. I didn't know that it was you, you see, or just how you'd been buried. All these—the sort of people that lived in these houses, and all those damn little clerks that used to live down *that* way—they'd be no good. They haven't any spirit in them—no proud dreams and no proud lusts; and a man who hasn't one or the other—Lord! What is he but funk[2] and precautions? They just used to skedaddle[3] off to work—I've seen hundreds of 'em, bit of breakfast in hand, running wild and shin-

---

1   Not pronouncing the "h" at the beginning of a word, like the other things mentioned, was a class marker. The artilleryman is predicting the end of the class system as the Victorians knew it.
2   Cowardice.
3   To hurry, scurry or run.

ing to catch their little season-ticket[1] train, for fear they'd get dismissed if they didn't; working at businesses they were afraid to take the trouble to understand; skedaddling back for fear they wouldn't be in time for dinner; keeping indoors after dinner for fear of the back-streets, and sleeping with the wives they married, not because they wanted them, but because they had a bit of money that would make for safety in their one little miserable skedaddle through the world. Lives insured and a bit invested for fear of accidents. And on Sundays—fear of the hereafter. As if hell was built for rabbits! Well, the Martians will just be a godsend to these. Nice roomy cages, fattening food, careful breeding, no worry. After a week or so chasing about the fields and lands on empty stomachs, they'll come and be caught cheerful. They'll be quite glad after a bit. They'll wonder what people did before there were Martians to take care of them. And the bar-loafers,[2] and mashers,[3] and singers—I can imagine them. I can imagine them," he said, with a sort of sombre gratification. "There'll be any amount of sentiment and religion loose among them. There's hundreds of things I saw with my eyes that I've only begun to see clearly these last few days. There's lots will take things as they are, fat and stupid; and lots will be worried by a sort of feeling that it's all wrong, and that they ought to be doing something. Now, whenever things are so that a lot of people feel they ought to be doing something, the weak, and those who go weak with a lot of complicated thinking, always make for a sort of do-nothing religion, very pious and superior, and submit to persecution and the will of the Lord. Very likely you've seen the same thing. It's energy in a gale of funk, and turned clean inside out. These cages will be full of psalms and hymns and piety. And those of a less simple sort will work in a bit of—what is it?—eroticism."

He paused.

"Very likely these Martians will make pets of some of them; train them to do tricks—who knows?—get sentimental over the pet boy who grew up and had to be killed. And some, maybe, they will train to hunt us."

"No," I cried, "that's impossible! No human being—"

---

1 Train pass that allowed unlimited rail travel for a specified period; usually used by commuters because it is cheaper than purchasing individual tickets.

2 Men who spent all their time in bars.

3 Men who spent all their time chasing after women.

"What's the good of going on with such lies?" said the artillery-man. "There's men who'd do it cheerful. What nonsense to pretend there isn't!"

And I succumbed to his conviction.

"If they come after me," he said; "Lord, if they come after me!" and subsided into a grim meditation.

I sat contemplating these things. I could find nothing to bring against this man's reasoning. In the days before the invasion no one would have questioned my intellectual superiority to his—I, a professed and recognized writer on philosophical themes, and he, a common soldier; and yet he had already formulated a situation that I had scarcely realized.

"What are you doing?" I said presently. "What plans have you made?"

He hesitated.

"Well, it's like this," he said. "What have we to do? We have to invent a sort of life where men can live and breed, and be sufficiently secure to bring the children up. Yes—wait a bit, and I'll make it clearer what I think ought to be done. The tame ones will go like all tame beasts; in a few generations they'll be big, beautiful, rich-blooded, stupid—rubbish! The risk is that we who keep wild will go savage—degenerate into a sort of big, savage rat....You see, how I mean to live is underground.[1] I've been thinking about the drains. Of course, those who don't know drains think horrible things; but under this London are miles and miles—hundreds of miles—and a few days' rain and London empty will leave them sweet and clean. The main drains are big enough and airy enough for anyone. Then there's cellars, vaults, stores, from which bolting passages may be made to the drains. And the railway tunnels and subways. Eh? You begin to see? And we form a band—able-bodied, clean-minded men. We're not going to pick up any rubbish that drifts in. Weaklings go out again."

"As you meant me to go?"

"Well—I parleyed,[2] didn't I?"

"We won't quarrel about that. Go on."

"Those who stop, obey orders. Able-bodied, clean-minded women we want also—mothers and teachers. No lackadaisical

---

1 In *The Time Machine* the Morlochs live underground and have "degenerated."

2 A "parley" was a conversation held under a flag of truce between warring armies.

ladies—no blasted rolling eyes. We can't have any weak or silly. Life is real again, and the useless and cumbersome and mischievous have to die. They ought to die. They ought to be willing to die. It's a sort of disloyalty, after all, to live and taint the race. And they can't be happy. Moreover, dying's none so dreadful—it's the funking makes it bad. And in all those places we shall gather. Our district will be London. And we may even be able to keep a watch, and run about in the open when the Martians keep away. Play cricket, perhaps. That's how we shall save the race. Eh? It's a possible thing? But saving the race is nothing in itself. As I say, that's only being rats. It's saving our knowledge and adding to it is the thing. There men like you come in. There's books, there's models. We must make great safe places down deep, and get all the books we can; not novels and poetry swipes,[1] but ideas, science books. That's where men like you come in. We must go to the British Museum and pick all those books through. Especially we must keep up our science—learn more. We must watch these Martians. Some of us must go as spies. When it's all working, perhaps I will. Get caught, I mean. And the great thing is, we must leave the Martians alone. We mustn't even steal. If we get in their way, we clear out. We must show them we mean no harm. Yes, I know. But they're intelligent things, and they won't hunt us down if they have all they want, and think we're just harmless vermin."

The artilleryman paused and laid a brown hand upon my arm.

"After all, it may not be so much we may have to learn before—Just imagine this: Four or five of their Fighting Machines suddenly starting off—Heat-Rays right and left, and not a Martian in 'em. Not a Martian in 'em, but men—men who have learnt the way how. It may be in my time, even—those men. Fancy having one of them lovely things, with its Heat-Ray wide and free! Fancy having it in control! What would it matter if you smashed to smithereens at the end of the run, after a bust like that? I reckon the Martians'll open their beautiful eyes! Can't you see them, man? Can't you see them hurrying, hurrying—puffing and blowing and hooting to their other mechanical affairs? Something out of gear in every case. And swish, bang, rattle, swish! Just as they are fumbling over it, *swish* comes the Heat-Ray, and, behold! Man has come back to his own."

---

1 Watered down stuff, especially beer.

For a while the imaginative daring of the artilleryman, and the tone of assurance and courage he assumed, completely dominated my mind. I believed unhesitatingly both in his forecast of human destiny and in the practicability of his astonishing scheme, and the reader who thinks me susceptible and foolish must contrast his position, reading steadily with all his thoughts about his subject, and mine, crouching fearfully in the bushes and listening, distracted by apprehension.[1] We talked in this manner through the early morning time, and later crept out of the bushes, and, after scanning the sky for Martians, hurried precipitately to the house on Putney Hill where he had made his lair. It was the coal-cellar of the place, and when I saw the work he had spent a week upon— it was a burrow scarcely ten yards long, which he designed to reach to the main drain on Putney Hill—I had my first inkling of the gulf between his dreams and his powers. Such a hole I could have dug in a day. But I believed in him sufficiently to work with him all that morning until past mid-day at his digging. We had a garden-barrow and shot[2] the earth we removed against the kitchen range. We refreshed ourselves with a tin of mock-turtle soup and wine from the neighbouring pantry. I found a curious relief from the aching strangeness of the world in this steady labour. As we worked, I turned his project over in my mind, and presently objections and doubts began to arise; but I worked there all the morning, so glad was I to find myself with a purpose again. After working an hour, I began to speculate on the distance one had to go before the cloaca[3] was reached, the chances we had of missing it altogether. My immediate trouble was why we should dig this long tunnel, when it was possible to get into the drain at once down one of the manholes, and work back to the house. It seemed to me, too, that the house was inconveniently chosen, and required a needless length of tunnel. And just as I was beginning to face these things, the artilleryman stopped digging, and looked at me.

"We're working well," he said. He put down his spade. "Let us knock off a bit," he said. "I think it's time we reconnoitred from the roof of the house."

I was for going on, and after a little hesitation he resumed his

---

1 Anxiety.
2 Dumped.
3 Sewer.

spade; and then suddenly I was struck by a thought. I stopped, and so did he at once.

"Why were you walking about the Common," I said, "instead of being here?"

"Taking the air," he said. "I was coming back. It's safer by night."

"But the work?"

"Oh, one can't always work," he said, and in a flash I saw the man plain. He hesitated, holding his spade. "We ought to recon- noitre now," he said, "because if any come near they may hear the spades and drop upon us unawares."

I was no longer disposed to object. We went together to the roof and stood on a ladder peeping out of the roof door. No Martians were to be seen, and we ventured out on the tiles, and slipped down under shelter of the parapet.

From this position a shrubbery hid the greater portion of Put- ney, but we could see the river below, a bubbly mass of Red Weed, and the low parts of Lambeth flooded and red. The red creeper swarmed up the trees about the old palace,[1] and their branches stretched gaunt and dead, and set with shrivelled leaves, from amidst its clusters. It was strange how entirely dependent both these things were upon flowing water for their propagation. About us neither had gained a footing; laburnums, pink mays, snowballs, and trees of arbor-vitae, rose out of laurels and hydrangeas, green and brilliant, into the sunlight.[2] Beyond Kensington dense smoke was rising, and that and a blue haze hid the northward hills.

The artilleryman began to tell me of the sort of people who still remained in London.

"One night last week," he said, "some fools got the electric light in order, and there was all Regent's Street and the Circus ablaze, crowded with painted and ragged drunkards, men and women, dancing and shouting till dawn. A man who was there told me. And as the day came they became aware of a Fighting Machine stand- ing near by the Langham, and looking down at them. Heaven knows how long he had been there. He came down the road towards them, and picked up nearly a hundred too drunk or fright- ened to run away."

Grotesque gleam of a time no history will ever fully describe!

---

1 Lambeth Palace, the residence of the Archbishop of Canterbury, the head of the Church of England.
2 The plants described can all be seen flowering in England in the spring.

From that, in answer to my questions, he came round to his grandiose plans again. He grew enthusiastic. He talked so eloquently of the possibility of capturing a Fighting Machine that I more than half believed in him again. But now that I was beginning to understand something of his quality, I could divine the stress he laid on doing nothing precipitately.[1] And I noted that now there was no question that he personally was to capture and fight the great machine.

After a time we went down to the cellar. Neither of us seemed disposed to resume digging, and when he suggested a meal, I was nothing loath.[2] He became suddenly very generous, and when we had eaten he went away, and returned with some excellent cigars. We lit these, and his optimism glowed. He was inclined to regard my coming as a great occasion.

"There's some champagne in the cellar," he said.

"We can dig better on this Thames-side burgundy,"[3] said I.

"No," said he; "I am host to-day. Champagne! Great God! We've a heavy enough task before us! Let us take a rest, and gather strength while we may. Look at these blistered hands!"

And pursuant to this idea of a holiday, he insisted upon playing cards after we had eaten. He taught me euchre,[4] and after dividing London between us, I taking the northern side and he the southern, we played for parish points. Grotesque and foolish as this will seem to the sober reader, it is absolutely true, and what is more remarkable, I found the card game and several others we played extremely interesting.

Strange mind of man! that, with our species upon the edge of extermination or appalling degradation, with no clear prospect before us but the chance of a horrible death, we could sit following the chance of this painted pasteboard, and playing the "joker" with vivid delight. Afterwards he taught me poker, and I beat him at three tough chess games. When dark came we were so interested that we decided to take the risk, and lit a lamp.

After an interminable string of games, we supped,[5] and the artilleryman finished the champagne. We continued smoking the

---

1 Immediately.
2 Didn't object, was willing to do so.
3 A cheap wine, as opposed to champagne.
4 A card game.
5 Had supper.

cigars. He was no longer the energetic regenerator of his species I had encountered in the morning. He was still optimistic, but it was a less kinetic,[1] a more thoughtful optimism. I remember he wound up with my health, proposed in a speech of small variety and considerable intermittence.[2] I took a cigar, and went upstairs to look at the lights that he had spoken of that blazed so greenly along the Highgate hills.

At first I stared across the London valley unintelligently. The northern hills were shrouded in darkness; the fires near Kensington glowed redly, and now and then an orange-red tongue of flame flashed up and vanished in the deep blue night. All the rest of London was black. Then, nearer, I perceived a strange light, a pale, violet-purple fluorescent glow, quivering under the night breeze. For a space I could not understand it, and then I knew that it must be the Red Weed from which this faint irradiation proceeded. With that realization my dormant sense of wonder, my sense of the proportion of things, awoke again. I glanced from that to Mars, red and clear, glowing high in the west, and then gazed long and earnestly at the darkness of Hampstead and Highgate.

I remained a very long time upon the roof, wondering at the grotesque changes of the day. I recalled my mental states from the midnight prayer to the foolish card-playing. I had a violent revulsion of feeling. I remember I flung away the cigar with a certain wasteful symbolism. My folly came to me with glaring exaggeration. I seemed a traitor to my wife and to my kind; I was filled with remorse. I resolved to leave this strange undisciplined dreamer of great things to his drink and gluttony, and to go on into London. There, it seemed to me, I had the best chance of learning what the Martians and my fellow-men were doing. I was still upon the roof when the late moon rose.

VIII.
DEAD LONDON

After I had parted from the artilleryman, I went down the hill, and by the High Street across the bridge to Lambeth. The Red Weed was tumultuous at that time, and nearly choked the bridge road-

---

1 Manic.
2 As he is drunk, the artilleryman's speech is short, pointless and full of pauses.

way, but its fronds were already whitened in patches by the spreading disease that presently removed it so swiftly.

At the corner of the lane that runs to Putney Bridge Station I found a man lying. He was as black as a sweep with the black dust, alive, but helplessly and speechlessly drunk. I could get nothing from him but curses and furious lunges at my head. I think I should have stayed by him but for the brutal type of his face.

There was black dust along the roadway from the bridge onwards, and it grew thicker in Fulham. The streets were horribly quiet. I got food—sour, hard, and mouldy, but quite eatable—in a baker's shop here. Some way towards Walham Green the streets became clear of powder, and I passed a white terrace of houses on fire; the noise of the burning was an absolute relief. Going on towards Brompton, the streets were quiet again.

Here I came once more upon the black powder in the streets and upon dead bodies. I saw altogether about a dozen in the length of the Fulham Road. They had been dead many days, so that I hurried quickly past them. The black powder covered them over, and softened their outlines. One or two had been disturbed by dogs.

Where there was no black powder, it was curiously like a Sunday in the City,[1] with the closed shops, the houses locked up and the blinds drawn, the desertion, and the stillness. In some places plunderers had been at work, but rarely at other than the provision and wine-shops. A jeweller's window had been broken open in one place, but apparently the thief had been disturbed, and a number of gold chains and a watch lay scattered on the pavement. I did not trouble to touch them. Further on was a tattered woman in a heap on a doorstep; the hand that hung over her knee was gashed and bled down her rusty brown dress, and a smashed magnum of champagne formed a pool across the pavement. She seemed asleep, but she was dead.

The further I penetrated into London, the profounder grew the stillness. But it was not so much the stillness of death—it was the stillness of suspense, of expectation. At any time the destruction that had already singed the north-western borders of the Metropolis, and had annihilated Ealing and Kilburn, might strike among these houses and leave them smoking ruins. It was a city condemned and derelict....

---

1 The central part of London that contains many important financial and governmental buildings that would normally be closed on a Sunday.

In South Kensington the streets were clear of dead and of black powder. It was near South Kensington that I first heard the howling. It crept almost imperceptibly upon my senses. It was a sobbing alternation of two notes, "Ulla, ulla, ulla, ulla," keeping on perpetually. When I passed streets that ran northward it grew in volume, and houses and buildings seemed to deaden and cut it off again. It came in a full tide down Exhibition Road. I stopped, staring towards Kensington Gardens, wondering at this strange, remote wailing. It was as if that mighty desert of houses had found a Voice for its fear and solitude.

"Ulla, ulla, ulla, ulla," wailed that superhuman note—great waves of sound sweeping down the broad, sunlit roadway, between the tall buildings on either side. I turned northwards, marvelling, towards the iron gates of Hyde Park. I had half a mind to break into the Natural History Museum and find my way up to the summits of the towers, in order to see across the park. But I decided to keep to the ground, where quick hiding was possible, and so went on up the Exhibition Road. All the large mansions on either side of the road were empty and still, and my footsteps echoed against the sides of the houses. At the top, near the park gate, I came upon a strange sight—a 'bus overturned, and the skeleton of a horse picked clean. I puzzled over this for a time, and then went on to the bridge over the Serpentine. The Voice grew stronger and stronger, though I could see nothing above the housetops on the north side of the park, save a haze of smoke to the northwest.

"Ulla, ulla, ulla, ulla," cried the Voice, coming, as it seemed to me, from the district about Regent's Park. The desolating cry worked upon my mind. The mood that had sustained me passed. The wailing took possession of me. I found I was intensely weary, footsore, and now again hungry and thirsty.

It was already past noon. Why was I wandering alone in this city of the dead? Why was I alone when all London was lying in state, and in its black shroud? I felt intolerably lonely. My mind ran on old friends that I had forgotten for years. I thought of the poisons in the chemists' shops, of the liquors the wine-merchants stored; I recalled the two sodden creatures of despair, who so far as I knew, shared the city with myself....

I came into Oxford Street by the Marble Arch, and here again were black powder and several bodies, and an evil, ominous smell from the gratings of the cellars of some of the houses. I grew very thirsty after the heat of my long walk. With infinite trouble I managed to break into a public-house and get food and drink. I was weary after eating, and went into the parlour behind the bar, and slept on a black horse-hair sofa I found there.

I awoke to find that dismal howling still in my ears, "Ulla, ulla, ulla, ulla." It was now dusk, and after I had routed out some biscuits and a cheese in the bar—there was a meat-safe, but it contained nothing but maggots—I wandered on through the silent residential squares to Baker Street—Portman Square is the only one I can name—and so came out at last upon Regent's Park. And as I emerged from the top of Baker Street, I saw far away over the trees in the clearness of the sunset the hood of the Martian giant from which this howling proceeded. I was not terrified. I came upon him as if it were a matter of course. I watched him for some time, but he did not move. He appeared to be standing and yelling, for no reason that I could discover.

I tried to formulate a plan of action. That perpetual sound of "Ulla, ulla, ulla, ulla," confused my mind. Perhaps I was too tired to be very fearful. Certainly I was rather curious to know the reason of this monotonous crying than afraid. I turned back away from the park and struck into Park Road, intending to skirt the park, went along under the shelter of the terraces, and got a view of this stationary howling Martian from the direction of St. John's Wood. A couple of hundred yards out of Baker Street I heard a yelping chorus, and saw, first a dog with a piece of putrescent[1] red meat in his jaws coming headlong towards me, and then a pack of starving mongrels in pursuit of him. He made a wide curve to avoid me, as though he feared I might prove a fresh competitor. As the yelping died away down the silent road, the wailing sound of "Ulla, ulla, ulla, ulla," reasserted itself.

I came upon the wrecked Handling Machine halfway to St. John's Wood Station. At first I thought a house had fallen across the road. It was only as I clambered among the ruins that I saw, with a start, this mechanical Samson lying, with its tentacles bent and smashed and twisted, among the ruins it had made. The forepart was shattered. It seemed as if it had driven blindly straight at the house, and had been overwhelmed in its overthrow. It seemed to me then that this might have happened by a Handling Machine escaping from the guidance of its Martian. I could not clamber among the ruins to see it, and the twilight was now so far

---

1 Rotting.

advanced that the blood with which its seat was smeared, and the gnawed gristle of the Martian that the dogs had left, were invisible to me.

Wondering still more at all that I had seen, I pushed on towards Primrose Hill. Far away, through a gap in the trees, I saw a second Martian, as motionless as the first, standing in the park towards the Zoological Gardens, and silent. A little beyond the ruins about the smashed Handling Machine I came upon the Red Weed again, and found Regent's Canal a spongy mass of dark-red vegetation.

As I crossed the bridge, the sound of "Ulla, ulla, ulla, ulla" ceased. It was, as it were, cut off. The silence came like a thunderclap.

The dusky houses about me stood faint, and tall and dim; the trees towards the park were growing black. All about me the Red Weed clambered among the ruins, writhing to get above me in the dimness. Night, the Mother of Fear and mystery, was coming upon me. But while that Voice sounded the solitude, the desolation, had been endurable; by virtue of it London had still seemed alive, and the sense of life about me had upheld me. Then suddenly a change, the passing of something—I knew not what—and then a stillness that could be felt. Nothing but this gaunt quiet.

London about me gazed at me spectrally. The windows in the white houses were like the eye-sockets of skulls. About me my imagination found a thousand noiseless enemies moving. Terror seized me, a horror of my temerity.[1] In front of me the road became pitchy black as though it was tarred, and I saw a contorted shape lying across the pathway. I could not bring myself to go on. I turned down St. John's Wood Road, and ran headlong from this unendurable stillness towards Kilburn. I hid from the night and the silence, until long after midnight, in a cabmen's shelter in Harrow Road. But before the dawn my courage returned, and while the stars were still in the sky I turned once more towards Regent's Park. I missed my way among the streets, and presently saw down a long avenue, in the half-light of the early dawn, the curve of Primrose Hill. On the summit, towering up to the fading stars, was a third Martian, erect and motionless like the others.

An insane resolve possessed me. I would die and end it. And I would save myself even the trouble of killing myself. I marched on recklessly towards this Titan, and then, as I drew nearer and the

---

1 Recklessness.

light grew, I saw that a multitude of black birds was circling and clustering about the hood. At that my heart gave a bound, and I began running along the road.

I hurried through the Red Weed that choked St. Edmund's Terrace (I waded breast-high across a torrent of water that was rushing down from the waterworks towards the Albert Road), and emerged upon the grass before the rising of the sun. Great mounds had been heaped about the crest of the hill, making a huge redoubt[1] of it—it was the final and largest place the Martians had made—and from behind these heaps there rose a thin smoke against the sky. Against the skyline an eager dog ran and disappeared. The thought that had flashed into my mind grew real, grew credible. I felt no fear, only a wild, trembling exultation, as I ran up the hill towards the motionless monster. Out of the hood hung lank shreds of brown at which the hungry birds pecked and tore.

In another moment I had scrambled up the earthen rampart and stood upon its crest, and the interior of the redoubt was below me. A mighty space it was, with gigantic machines here and there within it, huge mounds of material and strange shelter-places. And, scattered about it, some in their overturned war-machines, some in the now rigid Handling Machines, and a dozen of them stark and silent and laid in a row, were the Martians—*dead!*—slain by the putrefactive and disease bacteria against which their systems were unprepared; slain as the Red Weed was being slain; slain, after all man's devices had failed, by the humblest things that God, in His wisdom, has put upon this earth.

For so it had come about, as indeed I and many men might have foreseen had not terror and disaster blinded our minds. These germs of disease have taken toll of humanity since the beginning of things—taken toll of our pre-human ancestors since life began here. But by virtue of this natural selection of our kind we have developed resisting-power; to no germs do we succumb without a struggle, and to many—those that cause putrefaction in dead matter, for instance—our living frames are altogether immune. But there are no bacteria in Mars, and directly these invaders arrived, directly they drank and fed, our microscopic allies began to work their overthrow. Already when I watched them they were irrevocably doomed, dying and rotting even as they went to and fro. It

---

1   A fort put up before a battle to protect troops and artillery.

was inevitable. By the toll of a billion deaths man has bought his birthright of the earth, and it is his against all comers; it would still be his were the Martians ten times as mighty as they are. For neither do men live nor die in vain.

Here and there they were scattered, nearly fifty altogether, in that great gulf they had made, overtaken by a death that must have seemed to them as incomprehensible as any death could be. To me also at that time this death was incomprehensible. All I knew was that these things that had been alive and so terrible to men were dead. For a moment I believed that the destruction of Sennacherib[1] had been repeated, that God had repented, that the Angel of Death had slain them in the night.

I stood staring into the pit, and my heart lightened gloriously, even as the rising sun struck the world to fire about me with his rays. The pit was still in darkness; the mighty engines, so great and wonderful in their power and complexity, so unearthly in their tortuous forms, rose weird and vague and strange out of the shadows towards the light. A multitude of dogs, I could hear, fought over the bodies that lay darkly in the depth of the pit, far below me. Across the pit on its farther lip, flat and vast and strange, lay the great flying-machine with which they had been experimenting upon our denser atmosphere when decay and death arrested them. Death had come not a day too soon. At the sound of a cawing overhead I looked up at the huge Fighting Machine that would fight no more for ever, at the tattered red shreds of flesh that dripped down upon the overturned seats on the summit of Primrose Hill.

I turned and looked down the slope of the hill to where, enhaloed[2] now in birds, stood those other two Martians that I had seen overnight, just as death had overtaken them. The one had died, even as it had been crying to its companions; perhaps it was the last to die, and its Voice had gone on perpetually until the force of its machinery was exhausted. They glittered now, harmless tripod towers of shining metal, in the brightness of the rising sun....

All about the pit, and saved as by a miracle from everlasting destruction, stretched the great Mother of Cities. Those who have only seen London veiled in her sombre robes of smoke can scarce-

---

1   Reference to II Kings:19 in which an entire army is wiped out by God in one night.
2   The birds form circular patterns like a halo.

ly imagine the naked clearness and beauty of the silent wilderness of houses.

Eastward, over the blackened ruins of the Albert Terrace and the splintered spire of the church, the sun blazed dazzling in a clear sky, and here and there some facet in the great wilderness of roofs caught the light and glared with a white intensity. It touched even that round store place for wines by the Chalk Farm Station, and the vast railway yards, marked once with a graining of black rails, but red-lined now with the quick rusting of a fortnight's disuse, with something of the mystery of beauty.

Northward were Kilburn and Hampsted, blue and crowded with houses; westward the great city was dimmed; and southward, beyond the Martians, the green waves of Regent's Park, the Langham Hotel, the dome of the Albert Hall, the Imperial Institute, and the giant mansions of the Brompton Road, came out clear and little in the sunrise, the jagged ruins of Westminster rising hazily beyond. Far away and blue were the Surrey hills, and the towers of the Crystal Palace glittered like two silver rods. The dome of St. Paul's was dark against the sunrise, and injured, I saw for the first time, by a huge gaping cavity on its western side.

And as I looked at this wide expanse of houses and factories and churches, silent and abandoned; as I thought of the multitudinous hopes and efforts, the innumerable hosts of lives that had gone to build this human reef, and of the swift and ruthless destruction that had hung over it all; when I realized that the shadow had been rolled back, and that men might still live in the streets, and this dear vast dead city of mine be once more alive and powerful, I felt a wave of emotion that was near akin to tears.

The torment was over. Even that day the healing would begin. The survivors of the people scattered over the country—leaderless, lawless, foodless, like sheep without a shepherd—the thousands who had fled by sea, would begin to return; the pulse of life, growing stronger and stronger, would beat again in the empty streets and pour across the vacant squares. Whatever destruction was done, the hand of the destroyer was stayed. All the gaunt wrecks, the blackened skeletons of houses that stared so dismally at the sunlit grass of the hill, would presently be echoing with the hammers of the restorers and ringing with the tapping of the trowels. At the thought I extended my hands towards the sky and began thanking God. In a year, thought I—in a year....

With overwhelming force came the thought of myself, of my

wife, and the old life of hope and tender helpfulness that had ceased for ever.

IX.
WRECKAGE

And now comes the strangest thing in my story. And, perhaps, it is not altogether strange. I remember, clearly and coldly and vividly, all that I did that day until the time that I stood weeping and praising God upon the summit of Primrose Hill. And then I forget....

Of the next three days I know nothing. I have learned since that, so far from my being the first discoverer of the Martian overthrow, several such wanderers as myself had already discovered this on the previous night. One man—the first—had gone to St. Martin's-le-Grand, and, while I sheltered in the cabmen's hut, had contrived to telegraph to Paris. Thence the joyful news had flashed all over the world; a thousand cities, chilled by ghastly apprehensions, suddenly flashed into frantic illuminations; they knew of it in Dublin, Edinburgh, Manchester, Birmingham, at the time when I stood upon the verge of the pit. Already men, weeping with joy, as I have heard, shouting and staying[1] their work to shake hands and shout, were making up trains, even as near as Crewe, to descend upon London. The church bells that had ceased a fortnight since suddenly caught the news, until all England was bell-ringing. Men on cycles, lean-faced, unkempt, scorched along every country lane shouting of unhoped deliverance, shouting to gaunt, staring figures of despair. And for the food! Across the Channel, across the Irish Sea, across the Atlantic, corn, bread, and meat were tearing to our relief. All the shipping in the world seemed going Londonward in those days. But of all this I have no memory. I drifted—a demented man. I found myself in a house of kindly people, who had found me on the third day wandering, weeping, and raving through the streets of St. John's Wood. They have told me since that I was singing some insane doggerel[2] about "The Last Man Left Alive! Hurrah! The Last Man Left Alive!" Troubled as they were with their own affairs, these people, whose name, much as I would like to express my gratitude to them, I may not even give here, never-

---

1   Stopping.
2   Loosely styled and irregular verse.

theless cumbered themselves[1] with me, sheltered me and protected me from myself. Apparently they had learnt something of my story from me during the days of my lapse.

Very gently, when my mind was assured again, did they break to me what they had learnt of the fate of Leatherhead. Two days after I was imprisoned it had been destroyed, with every soul in it, by a Martian. He had swept it out of existence, as it seemed, without any provocation, as a boy might crush an ant hill, in the mere wantonness of power.

I was a lonely man, and they were very kind to me. I was a lonely man and a sad one, and they bore with me. I remained with them four days after my recovery. All that time I felt a vague, a growing craving to look once more on whatever remained of the little life that seemed so happy and bright in my past. It was a mere hopeless desire to feast upon my misery. They dissuaded me. They did all they could to divert me from this morbidity. But at last I could resist the impulse no longer, and, promising faithfully to return to them, and parting, as I will confess, from these four-day friends with tears, I went out again into the streets that had lately been so dark and strange and empty.

Already they were busy with returning people; in places even there were shops open, and I saw a drinking-fountain running water.

I remember how mockingly bright the day seemed as I went back on my melancholy pilgrimage to the little house at Woking, how busy the streets and vivid the moving life about me. So many people were abroad everywhere, busied in a thousand activities, that it seemed incredible that any great proportion of the population could have been slain. But then I noticed how yellow were the skins of the people I met, how shaggy the hair of the men, how large and bright their eyes, and that every other man still wore his dirty rags. The faces seemed all with one of two expressions—a leaping exultation and energy or a grim resolution. Save for the expression of the faces, London seemed a city of tramps. The vestries were indiscriminately distributing bread sent us by the French Government. The ribs of the few horses showed dismally. Haggard special constables with white badges stood at the corners of every street. I saw little of the mischief wrought by the Martians until I reached Wellington Street, and

---

1 Took on the burden.

there I saw the Red Weed clambering over the buttresses of Waterloo Bridge.

At the corner of the bridge, too, I saw one of the common contrasts of that grotesque time: a sheet of paper flaunting against a thicket of the Red Weed, transfixed by a stick that kept it in place. It was the placard of the first newspaper to resume publication—the *Daily Mail*. I bought a copy for a blackened shilling I found in my pocket. Most of it was in blank, but the solitary compositor who did the thing had amused himself by making a grotesque scheme of advertisement stereo[1] on the back page. The matter he printed was emotional; the news organization had not as yet found its way back. I learned nothing fresh except that already in one week the examination of the Martian mechanisms had yielded astonishing results. Among other things, the article assured me what I did not believe at the time: that the "Secret of Flying," was discovered. At Waterloo I found the free trains that were taking people to their homes. The first rush was already over. There were few people in the train, and I was in no mood for casual conversation. I got a compartment to myself, and sat with folded arms, looking grayly at the sunlit devastation that flowed past the windows. And just outside the terminus the train jolted over temporary rails, and on either side of the railway the houses were blackened ruins. To Clapham Junction the face of London was grimy with powder of the Black Smoke, in spite of two days of thunderstorms and rain, and at Clapham Junction the line had been wrecked again; there were hundreds of out-of-work clerks and shop-men working side by side with the customary navvies, and we were jolted over a hasty relaying.

All down the line from there the aspect of the country was gaunt and unfamiliar; Wimbledon particularly had suffered. Walton, by virtue of its unburned pine-woods, seemed the least hurt of any place along the line. The Wandle, the Mole, every little stream, was a heaped mass of Red Weed, in appearance between butcher's meat and pickled cabbage. The Surrey pine-woods were too dry, however, for the festoons of the red climber. Beyond Wimbledon, within sight of the line, in certain nursery grounds, were the heaped masses of earth about the sixth cylinder. A number of people were standing about it, and some sappers were busy in the midst of it.

---

1   Short for stereotype, a printer's use of permanent type for text that was printed over and over again.

Over it flaunted a Union Jack,[1] flapping cheerfully in the morning breeze. The nursery grounds were everywhere crimson with the weed, a wide expanse of livid colour cut with purple shadows, and very painful to the eye. One's gaze went with infinite relief from the scorched grays and sullen reds of the foreground to the blue-green softness of the eastward hills.

The line on the London side of Woking station was still undergoing repair, so I descended at Byfleet Station and took the road to Maybury, past the place where I and the artilleryman had talked to the hussars,[2] and on by the spot where the Martian had appeared to me in the thunderstorm. Here, moved by curiosity, I turned aside to find, among a tangle of red fronds, the warped and broken dog cart with the whitened bones of the horse scattered and gnawed. For a time I stood regarding these vestiges....

Then I returned through the pine-wood, neck-high with Red Weed here and there, to find the landlord of the Spotted Dog had already found burial, and so came home past the College Arms. A man standing at an open cottage door greeted me by name as I passed.

I looked at my house with a quick flash of hope that faded immediately. The door had been forced; it was unfastened and was opening slowly as I approached.

It slammed again. The curtains of my study fluttered out of the open window from which I and the artilleryman had watched the dawn. No one had closed that window since. The smashed bushes were just as I had left them nearly four weeks ago. I stumbled into the hall, and the house felt empty. The stair-carpet was ruffled and discoloured where I had crouched soaked to the skin from the thunderstorm, the night of the catastrophe. Our muddy footsteps I saw still went up the stairs.

I followed them to my study, and found lying on my writing-table still, with the selenite paper-weight upon it, the sheet of work I had left on the afternoon of the opening of the cylinder. For a space I stood reading over my abandoned arguments. It was a paper on the probable development of Moral Ideas with the development of the civilizing process; and the last sentence was the opening of a prophecy: "In about two hundred years," I had written,

---

1 The British national flag.
2 Light cavalry, named after the fifteenth-century Hungarian units on which they were modeled. See Appendix I for a photo of Hussars.

"we may expect——" The sentence ended abruptly. I remembered my inability to fix my mind that morning, scarcely a month gone by, and how I had broken off to get my *Daily Chronicle* from the newsboy. I remembered how I went down to the garden gate as he came along, and how I had listened to his odd story of the "Men from Mars."

I came down and went into the dining-room. There were the mutton and the bread, both far gone now in decay, and a beer bottle overturned, just as I and the artilleryman had left them. My home was desolate. I perceived the folly of the faint hope I had cherished so long. And then a strange thing occurred. "It is no use," said a voice. "The house is deserted. No one has been here these ten days. Do not stay here to torment yourself. No one escaped but you."

I was startled. Had I spoken my thought aloud? I turned, and the French window was open behind me. I made a step to it, and stood looking out.

And there, amazed and afraid, even as I stood amazed and afraid, were my cousin and my wife—my wife white and tearless. She gave a faint cry.

"I came," she said. "I knew—knew—"

She put her hand to her throat—swayed. I made a step forward, and caught her in my arms.

X.
THE EPILOGUE

I cannot but regret, now that I am concluding my story, how little I am able to contribute to the discussion of the many debatable questions which are still unsettled. In one respect I shall certainly provoke criticism. My particular province is speculative philosophy. My knowledge of comparative physiology is confined to a book or two, but it seems to me that Carver's suggestions as to the reason of the rapid death of the Martians is so probable as to be regarded almost as a proven conclusion. I have assumed that in the body of my narrative.

At any rate, in all the bodies of the Martians that were examined after the war, no bacteria except those already known as terrestrial species were found. That they did not bury any of their dead, and the reckless slaughter they perpetrated, point also to an entire ignorance of the putrefactive process. But probable as this seems, it is by no means a proven conclusion.

Neither is the composition of the Black Smoke known, which the Martians used with such deadly effect, and the generator of the Heat-Rays remains a puzzle. The terrible disasters at the Ealing and South Kensington laboratories have disinclined analysts for further investigations upon the latter. Spectrum analysis of the black powder points unmistakably to the presence of an unknown element with a brilliant group of three lines in the green, and it is possible that it combines with argon to form a compound which acts at once with deadly effect upon some constituent in the blood. But such unproven speculations will scarcely be of interest to the general reader, to whom this story is addressed. None of the brown scum that drifted down the Thames after the destruction of Shepperton was examined at the time, and now none is forthcoming.

The results of an anatomical examination of the Martians, so far as the prowling dogs had left such an examination possible, I have already given. But everyone is familiar with the magnificent and almost complete specimen in spirits at the Natural History Museum, and the countless drawings that have been made from it; and beyond that the interest of their physiology and structure is purely scientific.

A question of graver and universal interest is the possibility of another attack from the Martians. I do not think that nearly enough attention is being given to this aspect of the matter. At present the planet Mars is in conjunction,[1] but with every return to opposition I, for one, anticipate a renewal of their adventure. In any case, we should be prepared. It seems to me that it should be possible to define the position of the gun from which the shots are discharged, to keep a sustained watch upon this part of the planet, and to anticipate the arrival of the next attack.

In that case the cylinder might be destroyed with dynamite or artillery before it was sufficiently cool for the Martians to emerge, or they might be butchered by means of guns so soon as the screw opened. It seems to me that they have lost a vast advantage in the failure of their first surprise. Possibly they see it in the same light.

Lessing has advanced excellent reasons for supposing that the Martians have actually succeeded in effecting a landing on the planet Venus. Seven months ago now, Venus and Mars were in

---

1   It is far away from earth, but will be "in opposition" again.

alignment with the sun; that is to say, Mars was in opposition from the point of view of an observer on Venus. Subsequently a peculiar luminous and sinuous marking appeared on the unillumined half of the inner planet, and almost simultaneously a faint dark mark of a similar sinuous character was detected upon a photograph of the Martian disk. One needs to see the drawings of these appearances in order to appreciate fully their remarkable resemblance in character.

At any rate, whether we expect another invasion or not, our views of the human future must be greatly modified by these events. We have learned now that we cannot regard this planet as being fenced in and a secure abiding-place for Man; we can never anticipate the unseen good or evil that may come upon us suddenly out of space. It may be that in the larger design of the universe this invasion from Mars is not without its ultimate benefit for men; it has robbed us of that serene confidence in the future which is the most fruitful source of decadence, the gifts to human science it has brought are enormous, and it has done much to promote the conception of the commonweal of mankind. It may be that across the immensity of space the Martians have watched the fate of these pioneers of theirs and learned their lesson, and that on the planet Venus they have found a securer settlement. Be that as it may, for many years yet there will certainly be no relaxation of the eager scrutiny of the Martian disk, and those fiery darts of the sky, the shooting stars, will bring with them as they fall an unavoidable apprehension to all the sons of men.

The broadening of men's views that has resulted can scarcely be exaggerated. Before the cylinder fell there was a general persuasion that through all the deep of space no life existed beyond the petty surface of our minute sphere. Now we see further. If the Martians can reach Venus, there is no reason to suppose that the thing is impossible for men, and when the slow cooling of the sun makes this earth uninhabitable, as at last it must do, it may be that the thread of life that has begun here will have streamed out and caught our sister planet within its toils. Should we conquer?

Dim and wonderful is the vision I have conjured up in my mind of life spreading slowly from this little seed-bed of the solar system throughout the inanimate vastness of sidereal[1] space. But that is a remote dream. It may be, on the other hand, that the destruction

---

1   Having to do with the stars.

of the Martians is only a reprieve. To them, and not to us, perhaps, is the future ordained.

I must confess the stress and danger of the time have left an abiding sense of doubt and insecurity in my mind. I sit in my study writing by lamplight, and suddenly I see again the healing valley below set with writhing flames, and feel the house behind and about me empty and desolate. I go out into the Byfleet Road, and vehicles pass me, a butcher-boy in a cart, a cabful of visitors, a workman on a bicycle, children going to school, and suddenly they become vague and unreal, and I hurry again with the artilleryman through the hot, brooding silence. Of a night I see the black powder darkening the silent streets, and the contorted bodies shrouded in that layer; they rise upon me tattered and dog-bitten. They gibber[1] and grow fiercer, paler, uglier, mad distortions of humanity at last, and I wake, cold and wretched, in the darkness of the night.

I go to London and see the busy multitudes in Fleet Street and the Strand, and it comes across my mind that they are but the ghosts of the past, haunting the streets that I have seen silent and wretched, going to and fro, phantasms in a dead city, the mockery of life in a galvanised body. And strange, too, it is to stand on Primrose Hill, as I did but a day before writing this last chapter, to see the great province of houses, dim and blue through the haze of the smoke and mist, vanishing at last into the vague lower sky, to see the people walking to and fro among the flower-beds on the hill, to see the sightseers about the Martian machine that stands there still, to hear the tumult of playing children, and to recall the time when I saw it all bright and clear-cut, hard and silent, under the dawn of that last great day....

And strangest of all is it to hold my wife's hand again, and to think that I have counted her, and that she has counted me, among the dead.

THE END

---

1   To speak rapidly, inarticulately, and often foolishly

Appendix A: H.G. Wells on The War of the Worlds

1. H.G. Wells. From *Strand Magazine* 109 (1920): 154.

[In this 1920 interview, Wells traces the origin of *The War of the Worlds* to a conversation with his brother Frank. Wells dedicated the book to Frank and consistently credited him with suggesting the original idea. Wells felt his book was a warning to his Victorian readers that was borne out by the horrors of the First World War, which had ended two years earlier.]

The book was begotten by a remark of my brother Frank. We were walking together through some particularly peaceful Surrey scenery. "Suppose some beings from another planet were to drop out of the sky suddenly," said he, "and begin laying about them here!" Perhaps we had been talking of the discovery of Tasmania by the Europeans—a very frightful disaster for the native Tasmanians! I forget. But that was the point of departure.

In those days I was writing short stories, and the particular sort of short story that amused me most was to do vivid realizations of some disregarded possibility in such a way as to comment on the false securities and fatuous self-satisfaction of the everyday life—as we knew it then. Because in those days the conviction that history had settled down to a sort of jog-trot comedy was very widespread indeed. Tragedy, people thought, had gone out of human life forever. A few of us were trying to point out the obvious possibilities of flying, of great guns, of poison gas, and so forth in presently making life uncomfortable if some sort of world peace was not assured, but the books we wrote were regarded as the silliest of imaginative gymnastics. Well, the world knows better now.

The technical interest of a story like *The War of the Worlds* lies in the attempt to keep everything within the bounds of possibility. And the value of the story to me lies in this, that from first to last there is nothing in it that is impossible.

2. H.G. Wells. From "Preface to Volume III." *The Works of H.G. Wells Vol. 3: The Invisible Man, The War of the Worlds, A Dream of Armageddon*. [Atlantic Edition] New York: Charles Scribner's Sons, 1924, ix-x.

[Wells wrote brief introductions for the Atlantic edition of his collected works. In this extract from Volume 3, Wells describes the destruction of Woking in ironic terms, but his use of recognizable towns and landmarks gave his story tremendous impact for Victorian readers.]

The War of the Worlds was suggested to the writer by his elder brother, Frank, to whom the first edition was dedicated. Mr. Frank Wells is a practical philosopher with a disbelief even profounder than that of the writer in the present ability of our race to meet a great crisis either bravely or intelligently. The Great War, the Mean Peace, the Russian Famine and the present state of the world's affairs have but confirmed our early persuasion. Our present civilization, it seems, is quite capable of falling to pieces without any aid from the Martians....

The scene is laid mainly in Surrey in the country round about Woking, where the writer was living when the book was written. He would take his bicycle of an afternoon and note the houses and cottages and typical inhabitants and passers-by, to be destroyed after tea by Heat-Ray or smothered in the red weed. He could sit by the way-side imagining his incidents so vividly that now when he passes through that country these events recur to him as though they were actual memories....

Appendix B: Wells's Publications Related to The War of the Worlds

1. H.G. Wells. From "Zoological Retrogression," *Gentleman's Magazine* 271 (Sept. 1891): 246-53.

[The opposite of evolution in the Victorian period was "degeneration." Originally a biological concept proposed by E. Ray Lankester, the term became widely used as both a social and political category (see also Ruddick, *The Time Machine* pp. 157-83, and Danahay, *Dr. Jekyll and Mr. Hyde* pp. 160-73). Wells shows clearly his debt to both Darwin and Huxley in this essay. Wells takes Victorian society to task for making "evolution" into an idea of inevitable progress and cites numerous examples of species "degenerating." In conclusion, he lectures his Victorian readership on their groundless optimism.]

Perhaps no scientific theories are more widely discussed or more generally misunderstood among cultivated people than the views held by biologists regarding the past history and future prospects of their province—life. Using their technical phrases and misquoting their authorities in an invincibly optimistic spirit, the educated public has arrived in its own way at a rendering of their results which it finds extremely satisfactory. It has decided that in the past the great scroll of nature has been steadily unfolding to reveal a constantly richer harmony of forms and successively higher grades of being, and it assumes that this "evolution" will continue with increasing velocity under the supervision of its extreme expression—man. This belief, as effective, progressive, and pleasing as transformation scenes at a pantomime, receives neither in the geological record nor in the studies of the phylogenetic embryologist[1] an entirely satisfactory confirmation.

On the contrary, there is almost always associated with the suggestion of advance in biological phenomena an opposite idea, which is its essential complement. The technicality expressing this would, if it obtained sufficient currency in the world of culture, do

---

1   An embryologist specializing in the evolution of the phylum or primary biological division of organisms.

much to reconcile the naturalist and his traducers. The toneless glare of optimistic evolution would then be softened by a shadow; the monotonous reiteration of "Excelsior"[1] by people who did not climb would cease; the too sweet harmony of the spheres would be enhanced by a discord, this evolutionary antithesis—degradation.

Isolated cases of degeneration have long been known, and popular attention has been drawn to them in order to point well-meant moral lessons, the fallacious analogy of species to individual being employed. It is only recently, however, that the enormous importance of degeneration as a plastic process[2] in nature has been suspected and its entire parity with evolution recognized.

It is no libel to say that three-quarters of the people who use the phrase, "organic evolution," interpret it very much in this way:—Life began with the amoeba, and then came, jelly-fish, shell-fish, and all those miscellaneous invertebrate things, and then real fishes and amphibian reptiles, birds, mammals, and man, the last and first of creation. It has been pointed out that this is very like regarding a man as the offspring of his first cousins; these, of his second; these, of his relations at the next remove, and so forth—making the remotest living human being his primary ancestor. Or, to select another image, it is like elevating the modest poor relation at the family gathering to the unexpected altitude of fountain-head—a proceeding which would involve some cruel reflections on her age and character. The sounder view is, as scientific writers have frequently insisted, that living species have varied along divergent lines from intermediate forms, and, as it is the object of this paper to point out, not necessarily in an upward direction.

In fact, the path of life, so frequently compared to some steadily-rising mountain-slope, is far more like a footway worn by leisurely wanderers in an undulating country. Excelsior biology is a popular and poetic creation—the *real* form of a phylum, or line of descent, is far more like the course of a busy man moving about a great city. Sometimes it goes underground, sometimes it doubles and twists in tortuous streets, now it rises far overhead along some viaduct, and, again, the river is taken advantage of in these varied journeyings to and fro. Upward and downward these threads of pedigree interweave, slowly working out a pattern of accomplished

---

1   The word means "higher" in Latin. Wells turns the spiritual references of "higher" as a synonym for progress into a literal climbing of a mountain.
2   A shaping or molding process.

things that is difficult to interpret, but in which scientific observers certainly fail to discover that inevitable tendency to higher and better things with which the word "evolution" is popularly associated....

[Wells cites numerous examples of "degeneration"]

...These brief instances of degradation may perhaps suffice to show that there is a good deal to be found in the work of biologists quite inharmonious with such phrases as "the progress of the ages," and the "march of mind." The zoologist demonstrates that advance has been fitful and uncertain; rapid progress has often been followed by rapid extinction or degeneration, while, on the other hand, a form lowly and degraded has in its degradation often happened upon some fortunate discovery or valuable discipline and risen again, like a more fortunate Antaeos,[1] to victory. There is, therefore, no guarantee in scientific knowledge of man's permanence or permanent ascendancy. He has a remarkably variable organisation, and his own activities and increase cause the conditions of his existence to fluctuate far more widely than those of any animal have ever done. The presumption is that before him lies a long future of profound modification, but whether that will be, according to present ideals, upward or downward, no one can forecast. Still, so far as any scientist can tell us, it may be that, instead of this, Nature is, in unsuspected obscurity, equipping some now humble creature with wider possibilities of appetite, endurance, or destruction, to rise in the fullness of time and sweep *homo* away into the darkness from which his universe arose. The Coming Beast must certainly be reckoned in any anticipatory calculations regarding the Coming Man.

2. H.G. Wells. "On Extinction," *Chambers's Journal of Popular Literature, Science and Art* 10 (30 September 1893): 623-24.

[Wells is in prophetic mode at the end of this article in which he moves from dinosaurs, to the dodo and the bison, to the human

---

1   A mythical king of Libya and a giant who would gain strength when thrown to the earth. He would challenge strangers to wrestling matches and win because of his unusual power. He was defeated by Hercules who prevented him from touching the ground.

species. The article echoes many of the narrator's comments in *The War of the Worlds* about the complacency of human attitudes and the inevitability of humans following the dodo and bison to extinction. This kind of attitude produced Tennyson's famous protests against a "nature red in tooth and claw" that apparently consigned species to oblivion with utter indifference. See also Ruddick, *The Time Machine* p. 173 for the relevance of this piece to Wells's other texts.]

The passing away of ineffective things, the entire rejection by Nature of the plans of life, is the essence of tragedy. In the world of animals, that runs so curiously parallel with the world of men, we can see and trace only too often the analogies of our grimmer human experiences; we can find the equivalents to the sharp tragic force of Shakespeare, the majestic inevitableness of Sophocles,[1] and the sordid dreary tale, the middle-class misery, of Ibsen.[2] The life that has schemed and struggled and committed itself, the life that has played and lost, comes at last to the pitiless judgment of time, and is slowly and remorselessly annihilated. This is the saddest chapter of biological science—the tragedy of Extinction.

In the long galleries of the geological museum are the records of judgments that have been passed graven upon the rocks. Here, for instance, are the huge bones of the "Atlantosaurus,"[3] one of the mightiest land animals that this planet has ever seen. A huge terrestrial reptile this, that crushed the forest trees as it browsed upon their foliage, and before which the pigmy ancestors of our present denizens of the land must have fled in abject terror of its mere might of weight. It had the length of four elephants, and its head towered thirty feet—higher, that is, than any giraffe—above the world it dominated. And yet this giant has passed away, and left no children to inherit the earth. No living thing can be traced back to these monsters; they are at an end among the branchings of the tree of life. Whether it was through some change of climate, some subtle disease, or some subtle enemy, these titanic reptiles dwindled in numbers, and faded at last altogether among things mundane. Save

---

1   One of the great dramatists of fifth century B.C. Athens, author of more than 100 plays including *Oedipus Rex*.
2   Henrik Ibsen (1828-1906), famous Norwegian playwright who wrote realistic psychological dramas, including *A Doll's House* (1879) and *Hedda Gabler* (1890).
3   Named in 1877, this dinosaur is now known as Apatosaurus.

for the riddle of their scattered bones, it is as if they had never been.

Beside them are the pterodactyls, the first of vertebrated animals to spread a wing to the wind, and follow the hunted insects to their last refuge of the air. How triumphantly and gloriously these winged lizards, these original dragons, must have floated through their new empire of the atmosphere! If their narrow brains could have entertained the thought, they would have congratulated themselves upon having gained a great and inalienable heritage for themselves and their children forever. And now we cleave a rock and find their bones, and speculate doubtfully what their outer shape may have been. No descendants are left to us. The birds are no offspring of theirs, but lighter children of some clumsy "deinosaurs."[1] The pterodactyls also have heard the judgment of extinction, and are gone altogether from the world.

The long roll of palaeontology is half filled with the records of extermination; whole orders, families, groups, and classes have passed away and left no mark and no tradition upon the living fauna of the world. Many fossils of the older rocks are labelled in our museums, "of doubtful affinity." Nothing living has any part like them, and the baffled zoologist regretfully puts them aside. What they mean, he cannot tell. They hint merely at shadowy dead subkingdoms, of which the form eludes him. Index fingers are they, pointing into unfathomable darkness, and saying only one thing clearly, the word 'Extinction.'

In the living world of to-day the same forces are at work as in the past. One Fate still spins, and the gleaming scissors cut. In the last hundred years the swift change of condition throughout the world, due to the invention of new means of transit, geographical discovery, and the consequent 'swarming' of the whole globe by civilised men, has pushed many an animal to the very verge of destruction. It is not only the dodo that has gone; for dozens of genera and hundreds of species, this century has witnessed the writing on the wall. In the fate of the bison extinction has been exceptionally swift and striking. In the forties' so vast were their multitudes that sometimes, "as far as the eye could reach," the plains would be covered by a galloping herd. Thousands of hunters,

---

1 This is the technically correct way of spelling "dinosaur" which has lost its "e" over the years. Sir Richard Owen coined the word in 1842, combining the Greek words for "terrible lizard."

tribes of Indians, lived upon them. And now! It is improbable that one specimen in an altogether wild state survives. If it were not for the merciful curiosity of men, the few hundred that still live would also have passed into the darkness of non-existence. Following the same grim path are the seals, the Greenland whale, many Australian and New Zealand animals and birds ousted by more vigorous imported competitors, the black rat, endless wild birds. The list of destruction has yet to be made in its completeness. But the grand bison is the statuesque type and example of the doomed races.

Can any of these fated creatures count? Does any suspicion of their dwindling numbers dawn upon them? Do they, like the Red Indian, perceive the end to which they are coming? For most of them, unlike the Red Indian, there is no alternative of escape by interbreeding with their supplanters. Simply and unconditionally, there is written across their future, plainly for any reader, the one word "Death."

Surely a chill of solitude must strike to the heart of the last stragglers in the rout, the last survivors of the defeated and vanishing species. The last shaggy bison, looking with dull eyes from some western bluff across the broad prairies, must feel some dim sense that those wide rolling seas of grass were once the home of myriads of his race, and are now his no longer. The sunniest day must shine with a cold and desert light on the eyes of the condemned. For them the future is blotted out and hope is vanity. These days are the days of man's triumph. The awful solitude of such a position is almost beyond the imagination. The earth is warm with men. We think always with reference to men. The future is full of men to our preconceptions, whatever it may be in scientific truth. In the loneliest position in human possibility, humanity supports us. But Hood, who sometimes rose abruptly out of the most mechanical punning to sublime heights, wrote a travesty, grotesquely fearful, of Campbell's "The Last Man."[1] In this he probably hit upon the most terrible thing that man can conceive as happening to man: the earth desert through a pestilence, and two men, and then one man, looking extinction in the face.

---

1 Thomas Campbell wrote a poem "The Last Man" in which the last man alive professes a belief in God, while Thomas Hood's "The Last Man," with its pessimistic tone, is closer to reality, according to Wells.

3. H.G. Wells. From "The Advent of the Flying Man: An Inevitable Occurrence," *The Pall Mall Gazette* (December 8, 1893): 1-2.

[Wells shows his and his society's interest in flying and also demonstrates why the job of prophet can be tricky; his vision of men (no women) flying from the dome of St. Paul's is wildly different from the prosaic reality of commercial flight. The article also shows his love of cycling, which serves as an analogy for flight, and his belief in the continued advance of technology.]

In the Twentieth Century

The real flying man will certainly be an imposing figure when he arrives. He will have to spread great fans of China silk fifty or sixty feet across. One may fancy him at last—his initial difficulties conquered—flapping serenely through the nether air, all the streets agape as he pursues his way. And the pleasure of such travelling! Locomotion free from friction; the earth spread out below one, and the sweet air rushing by! Only those who have travelled downhill on a pneumatic tyre with a broad landscape extended in front, and nothing in the way, can even fancy the free delight of it. And the cyclist is ever bounded by hedges and tied to a road. Besides, the swiftest cycling is mere snail's crawling, to the possibilities of speed in flight. The mechanical conditions of flight render possible a velocity almost as swift as falling. Plovers, according to Herr Gatke, can do their 240 miles an hour, and the swift[1] can outstrip an express train. And moreover, consider the wide sweeps, the circles and spiral curves of it, besides which skating is clog dancing, and dancing a mere cripple's gait!...

A Forecast

So by Anno Domini 2000 or so we may hope in the greater part of humanity learning to fly. The teaching of this art itself will become an art, and so the first excursion into the air will be robbed of its terror. We may also foresee small flying machines

---

1 European bird (*apus apus*) with a shrieking call that nests in caves or under the eaves of houses and is famous for its incredible speed and agility in the air.

adventured upon for little boys and girls; and the knack learnt early will lose its element of effort and danger, and become at last as easy and habitual as walking erect, just as swimming comes by nature in the South Sea Islands. Then with assurance of safety will come the loosening of the decorative instinct, instead of the vast windmill sails covered with oiled silk of the first flight of humanity we shall spread fantastically gorgeous and beautiful wings across the heavens, cunningly constructed to catch and reflect the light and to delight and dazzle the eyes. So at last will man conquer and rejoice in the empire of the air. And to conclude let us imagine what an observer might see watching the City of London one red evening in the year 2100 A.D.

At the stroke of five, the daily business of thousands of men ceases and forthwith a vast cloud of winged figures will begin to erupt from among the grimy roofs of the crowded business houses and hang for a moment eddying and circling in the air after the cramping labours of the day. The dome of St. Paul's will be covered with the fathers and sons of suburban families, poising themselves for their homeward flight; they will cling to the Monument like bats; and obscure the outlines of every steeple. Then presently the vast crowd will begin to separate. One swarm will flap its way like homeward bound rooks in a long column northwards towards Willesden and Wembley Park and Pinner and Harrow; another westward to Richmond, Kingston and Staines; another southward to Sutton, Dorking and Reigate. Each will carry his inseparable bag and umbrella beneath him as an owl might carry a mouse. And so home to their rookeries and nests, where the domestic angel,[1] her wings laid aside after shopping, has prepared the dinner of the day. And as paterfamilias swoops, downward, little winged cherubs flutter up to meet him with shrill cries of "Papa, papa!"

It reads fantastic, perhaps, but not more so than a description of a cycling tour or an account of a modern railway could have done a hundred years ago. At any rate, while the sceptic scoffs, the scientific man is silent, or gives us guarded encouragement. Practically, the only serious bar between humanity and flying is the extreme danger of the initial attempts. There are no other difficulties that modern science may not reasonably hope to overcome. And even in this matter of danger, Mr. Head, for instance, has suggested sev-

---

1 Victorian women were often referred to as "angels" after the famous
   Coventry Patmore poem "The Angel in the House" (1854–56).

eral possible ways of breaking the fall of the experimenter. A parachute, for instance might be automatically released in case of accident. No, in spite of dull incredulity, the flying man is hard upon us; so close, indeed, that even now the imaginative person may hear the beating of his wings.

4. H.G. Wells. From "The Man of the Year Million," *Pall Mall Gazette* 57 (6 November 1893): 3.

[This early piece by Wells is written in a facetious style that imitates and parodies the methods of Thomas Carlyle. Wells uses the device of a fictitious professor from Germany who is an expert on evolution. The article makes explicit, however, Wells's acceptance of the theory of evolution which he then applies, in a comic tone, to humans of the future. The evolution of the future human shows some of the thinking behind Wells's projection of what a highly evolved Martian would look like. Technology plays a crucial role in this evolution. The article is especially helpful in explaining why the Martians no longer eat. See also Ruddick p. 176 for the relevance of this piece to *The Time Machine*.]

....."The theory of evolution," writes the Professor, "is now universally accepted by zoologists and botanists, and it is applied unreservedly to man. Some question, indeed, whether it fits his soul, but all agree it accounts for his body." Man, we are assured, is descended from ape-like ancestors, moulded by circumstances into men, and these apes again were derived from ancestral forms of a lower order, and so up from the primordial protoplasmic jelly. Clearly then, man, unless the order of the universe has come to an end, will undergo further modification in the future, and at last cease to be man, giving rise to some other type of animated being. At once the fascinating question arises, What will this being be? Let us consider for a little the plastic influences at work upon our species.

"Just as the bird is the creature of the wing, and is all moulded and modified to flying, and just as the fish is the creature that swims, and has had to meet the inflexible conditions of a problem in hydrodynamics, so man is the creature of the brain; he will live by intelligence, and not by physical strength, if he live at all. So that much that is purely 'animal' about him is being, and must be, beyond all question, suppressed in his ultimate development. Evolution is no mechanical tendency making for perfection, according to the ideas current in the year of grace 1892; it is simply the continual adaptation of plastic life, for good or evil, to the circumstances that surround it.... We notice this decay of the animal part around us now, in the loss of teeth and hair, in the dwindling hands and feet of men, in their smaller jaws, and slighter mouths and ears. Man now does by wit and machinery and verbal agreement what he once did by bodily toil; for once he had to catch his dinner, capture his wife, run away from his enemies, and continually exercise himself, for love of himself, to perform these duties well. But now all this is changed. Cabs, trains, trams, render speed unnecessary, the pursuit of food becomes easier; his wife is no longer hunted, but rather, in view of the crowded matrimonial market, seeks him out. One needs wits now to live, and physical activity is a drug, a snare even; it seeks artificial outlets, and overflows in games. Athleticism takes up time and cripples a man in his competitive examinations, and in business. So is your fleshly man handicapped against his subtler brother. He is unsuccessful in life, does not marry. The better adapted survive."

The coming man, then, will clearly have a larger brain, and a slighter body than the present. But the Professor makes one exception to this. "The human hand, since it is the teacher and interpreter of the brain, will become constantly more powerful and subtle as the rest of the musculature dwindles." Then in the physiology of these children of men, with their expanding brains, their great sensitive hands and diminishing bodies, great changes were necessarily worked...

"Furthermore, fresh chemical discoveries came into action as modifying influences upon men. In the prehistoric period even, man's mouth had ceased to be an instrument for grasping food; it is still growing continually less prehensile, his front teeth are smaller, his lips thinner and less muscular; he has a new organ, a mandible not of irreparable tissue, but of bone and steel—a knife and fork. There is no reason why things should stop at partial artificial division thus afforded; there is every reason, on the contrary, to believe my statement that some cunning exterior mechanism will presently masticate and insalivate[1] his dinner, relieve his diminishing salivary glands and teeth, and at last altogether abolish them." Then what is not needed disappears. What use is there for external ears, nose, and brow ridges now? The two latter once protected the

---

1 Chew and mix with saliva.

eye from injury in conflict and in falls, but in these days we keep on our legs, and at peace. Directing his thoughts in this way, the reader may presently conjure up a dim, strange vision of the latter-day face: "Eyes large, lustrous, beautiful, soulful; above them, no longer separated by rugged brow ridges, is the top of the head, a glistening, hairless dome, terete[1] and beautiful; no craggy nose rises to disturb by its unmeaning shadows the symmetry of that calm face, no vestigial ears project; the mouth is a small, perfectly round aperture, toothless and gumless, jawless, unanimal, no futile emotions disturbing its roundness as it lies, like the harvest moon or the evening star, in the wide firmament of face." Such is the face the Professor beholds in the future.

Of course parallel modifications will also affect the body and limbs. "Every day so many hours and so much energy are required for digestion; a gross torpidity, a carnal lethargy, seizes on mortal men after dinner. This may and can be avoided. Man's knowledge of organic chemistry widens daily. Already he can supplement the gastric glands by artificial devices. Every doctor who administers physic implies that the bodily functions may be artificially superseded. We have pepsine, pancreatine, artificial gastric acid[2]—I know not what like mixtures. Why, then, should not the stomach be ultimately superannuated[3] altogether? A man who could not only leave his dinner to be cooked, but also leave it to be masticated and digested, would have vast social advantages over his food-digesting fellow. This is, let me remind you here, the calmest, most passionless, and scientific working out of the future forms of things from the data of the present. At this stage the following facts may perhaps stimulate your imagination. There can be no doubt that many of the Arthropods,[4] a division of animals more ancient and even now more prevalent than the Vertebrata, have undergone more phylogenetic modification"— a beautiful phrase—"than even the most modified of vertebrated[5] animals. Simple forms like the lobsters display a primitive structure parallel with that of the fishes. However, in such a form

---

1 Smooth and round.
2 Like today's antacids and other medicines, these were substances that helped digest food.
3 Made redundant, superfluous.
4 Includes insects, spiders and crustaceans.
5 Having a spine or backbone, like humans.

as the degraded "Chondracanthus,"[1] the structure has diverged far more widely from its original type than in man. Among some of these most highly modified crustaceans the whole of the alimentary canal—that is, all the food-digesting and food-absorbing parts—form a useless solid cord: the animal is nourished—it is a parasite—by absorption of the nutritive fluid in which it swims. Is there any absolute impossibility in supposing man to be destined for a similar change; to imagine him no longer dining, with unwieldy paraphernalia of servants and plates, upon food queerly dyed and distorted, but nourishing himself in elegant simplicity by immersion in a tub of nutritive fluid....?"

5. H.G. Wells. From "Another Basis for Life," *The Saturday Review* 78 (Dec. 22, 1894): 676–77.

[Wells was reviewing Sir Robert Stawell Ball's book *The Possibility of Life in Other Worlds* (1894) in which the astronomer searched for planets that had carbon, nitrogen and oxygen and could support life similar to that on earth. Wells asks why confine oneself to these elements, and fantasizes about a life form based on silicon and aluminium.]

Very attractive is the question whether life extends beyond the limits of this little planet of ours. The latest contribution to this branch of speculation is that made by Sir Robert Ball, who, like his predecessors, starts from the hypothesis that the phenomena of life are inseparably associated with certain complex combinations of the chemical elements carbon, nitrogen, hydrogen, and oxygen, and proceeds to search space for these elements under conditions of temperature that admit of vitality. Undeniably, so far as our assured knowledge goes, this association is forced upon us; protoplasm, the common basis of all terrestrial life, is a highly unstable and complicated grouping mainly of the atoms of these four elements and sulphur, and all the phenomena we call vital, up to and including the processes of mind, are associated with the decomposition of some of this substance and the oxidation of carbon and hydrogen. Yet it is certainly open to question whether this connexion of life with the five elements specified above is absolutely inevitable, whether there are not other groups to be found which may be

---

1   The scientific name of a seaweed.

conceived of as running through a series of combinations and decompositions that would afford the necessary material basis for a quasi-conscious and even mental superstructure....

One is startled towards fantastic imaginings by such a suggestion: visions of silicon–aluminium organisms—why not silicon–aluminium men at once?—wandering through an atmosphere of gaseous sulphur, let us say, by the shores of a sea of liquid iron some thousand degrees or so above the temperature of a blast furnace. But that, of course, is merely a dream. The possibility of a material evolution of an analogue to protoplasm in the past history of our planet upon a silicon–aluminium basis is, however, something more than a dream. And in this connexion it is interesting to remark, as bearing upon their relative importance in extra-terrestrial space, that silicon is a far more abundant and frequent constituent of meteorites than carbon, and that the photosphere of the sun, which is frequently spoken of as incandescent carbon, is just as probably silicon in the incandescent state.

6. H.G. Wells. "The Extinction of Man: Some Speculative Suggestions," *Pall Mall Gazette* 59 (25 September 1894): 3.

[Following the thread of "On Extinction," this article, after rehearsing the extinction of animal species, goes on to consider what might topple humans from their contemporary ascendancy. Wells, applying a pessimistic Huxleyian view of the struggle for survival and the march of evolution, considers where a rival species might emerge to challenge human hegemony. His discussion of the effects of a kind of super octopus prefigures the narrative of innumerable horror movies. Most strikingly, Wells at the end of the article considers the possibilities of new diseases. Where viruses helped humans in *The War of the Worlds*, they kill them in this article. Given the rise of new diseases in the late twentieth century, the prescience of Wells's remarks here shows why he achieved such a reputation as a prophet of the future. See also Ruddick p. 181 for the relevance of the speculation on "giant land crabs" for *The Time Machine*.]

It is part of the excessive egotism of the human animal that the bare idea of its extinction seems incredible to it. "A world without *us!*" it says, as a heady young Cephalapsis might have said it in the old Silurian sea. But since the Cephalapsis[1] and the Coccosteus[2] many a fine animal has increased and multiplied upon the earth, lorded it over land or sea without a rival, and passed at last into the night. Surely it is not so unreasonable to ask why man should be an exception to the rule. From the scientific standpoint at least any reason for such exception is hard to find.

No doubt man is undisputed master at the present time—at least of most of the land surface; but so it has been before with other animals. Let us consider what light geology has to throw upon this. The great land and sea reptiles of the Mesozoic period,[3] for instance, seem to have been as secure as humanity is now in their preeminence. But they passed away and left no descendants when the new orders of the mammals emerged from their obscurity. So, too, the huge Titanotheria[4] of the American continent, and all the powerful mammals of Pleistocene[5] South America, the sabre-toothed lion, for instance, and the Machrauchenia[6] suddenly came to a finish when they were still almost at the zenith of their rule. *And in no case does the record of the fossils show a really dominant species succeeded by its own descendants.* What has usually happened in the past appears to be the emergence of some type of animal hitherto rare and unimportant, and the extinction, not simply of the previously ruling species, but of most of the forms that are at all closely related to it. Sometimes, indeed, as in the case of the extinct giants of South America, they vanished without any considerable rivals, victims of pestilence, famine, or, it may be, of that cumulative inefficiency that comes of a too undisputed life. So that the analogy of geology, at any rate, is against this too acceptable view of man's certain tenure of the earth for the next few million years or so.

And, after all, even now man is by no means such a master of the kingdoms of life as he is apt to imagine. The sea, that mysterious nursery of living things, is for all practical purposes beyond his

---

1 A crab from the Paleozoic era, 300 million years ago.
2 An armored fish from the Middle Devonian period.
3 The Mesozoic period is divided into the Triassic (245–208 million years ago), the Jurassic (208-146 million years ago) and the Cretaceous (146-65 million years ago).
4 Titanotheres were huge mammals that are the ancestors of the modern horse and rhinoceros.
5 1.8 million to 11,000 years ago.
6 An extinct ancestor of the guanaco and llama.

control. The low-water mark is his limit. Beyond that he may do a little with seine[1] and dredge, murder a few million herrings a year as they come in to spawn, butcher his fellow air-breather, the whale, or haul now and then an unlucky king crab or strange sea urchin out of the deep water in the name of science; but the life of the sea as a whole knows him not, plays out its slow drama of change and development unheeding him, and may in the end, in mere idle sport, throw up some new terrestrial denizens, some new competitor for space to live in and food to live upon, that will sweep him and all his little contrivances out of existence, as certainly and inevitably as he has swept away auk, bison, and dodo during the last two hundred years.

For instance, there are the crustacea. As a group the crabs and lobsters are confined below the high-water mark. But experiments in air-breathing are no doubt in progress in this group—we already have tropical land crabs—and as far as we know there is no reason why in the future these creatures should not increase in size and terrestrial capacity. In the past we have the evidence of the fossil Paradoxides[2] that creatures of this kind may at least attain a length of six feet, and, considering their intense pugnacity, a crab of such dimensions would be as formidable a creature as one could well imagine. And their amphibious capacity would give them an advantage against us such as at present is only to be found in the case of the alligator or crocodile. If we imagine a shark that could raid out upon the land, or a tiger that could take refuge in the sea, we should have a fair suggestion of what a terrible monster a large predatory crab might prove. And so far as zoological science goes we must, at least, admit that such a creature is an evolutionary possibility.

Then, again, the order of the Cephalopods, to which belong the cuttlefish and the octopus (sacred to Victor Hugo[3]), may be, for all we can say to the contrary, an order with a future. Their kindred, the Gasteropods, have, in the case of the snail and slug, learnt the trick of air-breathing. And not improbably there are even now genera of this order that have escaped the naturalist, or even well-

---

1 A fishing net.
2 A type of trilobyte, an early form of crustacean.
3 Hugo (1802–85) was a famous French novelist, whose works include *The Hunchback of Notre Dame* (1831) and *Les Misérables* (1862). His 1866 novel, *Les Travailleurs du Mer* (*Toilers of the Sea*), describes an octopus that attacks the central character, the fisherman Gilliatt.

known genera whose possibilities in growth and dietary are still unknown. Suppose some day a specimen of a new species is caught off the coast of Kent. It excites remark at a Royal Society *soirée*, engenders a Science Note, "A Huge Octopus!" and in the next year or so three or four other specimens come to hand and the thing becomes familiar. "Probably a new and larger variety of *Octopus* so-and-so, hitherto supposed to be tropical," says Professor Gargoyle, and thinks he has disposed of it. Then conceive some mysterious boating accidents and deaths while bathing. A large animal of this kind coming into a region of frequent wrecks might so easily acquire a preferential taste for human nutriment, just as the Colorado beetle acquired a new taste for the common potato and gave up its old food-plants some years ago. Then perhaps a school or pack or flock of *Octopus Gigas* would be found busy picking the sailors off a stranded ship, and then in the course of a few score years it might begin to stroll up the beaches and batten on excursionists.[1] Soon it would be a common feature of the watering-places, possibly at last commoner than excursionists. Suppose such a creature were to appear—and it is, we repeat, a possibility, if perhaps a remote one—how could it be fought against? Something might be done by torpedoes; but so far as our past knowledge goes man has no means of seriously diminishing the numbers of any animal of the most rudimentary intelligence that made its fastness in the sea.

Even on land it is possible to find creatures that, with a little modification might become excessively dangerous to the human ascendancy. Most people have read of the migratory ants of Central Africa, against which no man can stand. On the march they simply clear out whole villages, drive men and animals before them in headlong rout, and kill and eat every living creature they can capture. One wonders why they have not already spread the area of their devastations. But at present no doubt they have their natural checks, of ant-eating birds, or what not. In the near future it may be that the European immigrant, as he sets the balance of life swinging in his vigorous manner, may kill off these ant-eating animals, or otherwise unwittingly remove the checks that now keep these terrible little pests within limits. And once they begin to spread in real earnest it is hard to see how their advance could be stopped. A world devoured by ants seems incredible now, simply

---

1 Eat tourists, like the shark in the film *Jaws*.

because it is not within our experience; but a naturalist would have a dull imagination who could not see in the numerous species of ants, and in their already high intelligence, far more possibility of strange developments than we have in the solitary human animal. And no doubt the idea of the small and feeble organism of man triumphant and omnipresent would have seemed equally incredible to an intelligent mammoth or a paleolithic cave bear.

And finally there is always the prospect of a new disease. As yet science has scarcely touched more than the fringe of the probabilities associated with the minute fungi that constitute our zymotic[1] diseases. But the bacilli have no more settled down into their final quiescence[2] than have men; like ourselves, they are adapting themselves to new conditions and acquiring new powers. The plagues of the Middle Ages, for instance, seem to have been begotten of a strange bacillus engendered under conditions that sanitary science, in spite of its panacea[3] of drainage, still admits are imperfectly understood, and for all we know even now we may be quite unwittingly evolving some new and more terrible plague—a plague that will not take ten or twenty or thirty per cent, as plagues have done in the past, but the entire hundred.

No; man's complacent assumption of the future is too confident. We think, because things have been easy for mankind as a whole for a generation or so, we are going on to perfect comfort and security in the future. We think that we shall always go to work at ten and leave off at four and have dinner at seven forever and ever. But these four suggestions out of a host of others must surely do a little against this complacency. Even now, for all we can tell, the coming terror may be crouching for its spring and the fall of humanity be at hand. In the case of every other predominant animal the world has ever seen, I repeat, the hour of its complete ascendancy has been the eve of its entire overthrow. But if some poor story-writing man ventures to figure this sober probability in a tale, not a reviewer in London but will tell him his theme is the utterly impossible. And when the thing happens, one may doubt if even then one will get the recognition one deserves.

---

1 A generic term for germs that cause fermentation.
2 Ultimate end, or in this case extinction.
3 A cure-all; a single remedy proposed for a range of ills.

7. H.G. Wells. From "The Stolen Bacillus," *Pall Mall Budget* (June 21 1894), then published as part of *The Stolen Bacillus and Other Stories* (November), Methuen & Co., 1895.

[This extract comes from a longer short story. The story ends in farce as the mysterious visitor to whom the Bacteriologist is talking turns out to be a very inept terrorist. He steals a vial from the Bacteriologist, but takes the wrong one and instead of releasing cholera in London he swallows a virus that will make him break out in blue patches. Biological warfare, however, is very much on Wells's mind in this story, and the death of the Martians in *The War of the Worlds* can be seen as an inadvertent piece of biological warfare by humans against the invaders. From British experiences in both succumbing to and transmitting viruses throughout the Empire, Wells and his readers would be well aware of the consequences of releasing a new virus in London.]

"This again," said the Bacteriologist, slipping a glass under the microscope, "is a preparation of the celebrated Bacillus of cholera—the cholera germ."

The pale-faced man peered down the microscope. He was evidently not accustomed to that kind of thing, and held a limp white hand over his disengaged eye. "I see very little," he said.

"Touch this screw," said the Bacteriologist; "perhaps the microscope is out of focus for you. Eyes vary so much. Just the fraction of a turn this way or that."

"Ah! Now I see," said the visitor. "Not so very much to see after all. Little streaks and shreds of pink. And yet those little particles, those mere atomies, might multiply and devastate a city! Wonderful!"

He stood up, and releasing the glass slip from the microscope, held it in his hand towards the window. "Scarcely visible," he said, scrutinising the preparation. He hesitated. "Are these alive? Are they dangerous now?"

"Those have been stained and killed," said the Bacteriologist. "I wish, for my own part, we could kill and stain every one of them in the universe."

"I suppose," the pale man said with a slight smile, "that you scarcely care to have such things about you in the living—in the active state?"

"On the contrary, we are obliged to," said the Bacteriologist.

"Here, for instance——" He walked across the room and took up one of several seated tubes. "Here is the living thing. This is a cultivation of the actual living disease bacteria." He hesitated. "Bottled cholera, so to speak." A slight gleam of satisfaction appeared momentarily in the face of the pale man. "It's a deadly thing to have in your possession," he said, devouring the little tube with his eyes. The Bacteriologist watched the morbid pleasure in his visitor's expression. This man, who had visited him that afternoon with a note of introduction from an old friend, interested him from the very contrast of their dispositions. The lank black hair and deep grey eyes, the haggard expression and nervous manner, the fitful yet keen interest of his visitor were a novel change from the phlegmatic deliberations of the ordinary scientific worker with whom the Bacteriologist chiefly associated. It was perhaps natural, with a hearer evidently so impressionable to the lethal nature of his topic, to take the most effective aspect of the matter.

He held the tube in his hand thoughtfully. "Yes, here is the pestilence imprisoned. Only break such a little tube as this into a supply of drinking-water, say to these minute particles of life that one must needs stain and examine with the highest powers of the microscope even to see, and that one can neither smell nor taste say to them, 'Go forth, increase and multiply, and replenish the cisterns,' and death—mysterious, untraceable death, death swift and terrible, death full of pain and indignity—would be released upon this city, and go hither and thither seeking his victims. Here he would take the husband from the wife, here the child from its mother, here the statesman from his duty, and here the toiler from his trouble. He would follow the water-mains, creeping along streets, picking out and punishing a house here and a house there where they did not boil their drinking-water, creeping into the wells of the mineral-water makers, getting washed into salad, and lying dormant in ices. He would wait ready to be drunk in the horse-troughs, and by unwary children in the public fountains. He would soak into the soil, to reappear in springs and wells at a thousand unexpected places. Once start him at the water supply, and before we could ring him in, and catch him again, he would have decimated the metropolis."

8. H.G. Wells. "Intelligence on Mars," *Saturday Review* 8 (1 April 4, 1896): 345-46.

[Wells's piece is written in direct response to the notice of a "strange light" on Mars reproduced in Appendix G. Wells concludes this piece by saying it is wildly anthropomorphic to suppose that life on Mars would in any way resemble humans. Having discounted the possibility of intelligent life on Mars being anything recognizable to humans, he goes on, of course, in *The War of the Worlds*, to imagine that bipeds similar to humans have in fact evolved on Mars and that these beings provide the Martians with the blood that is their primary source of nutrition.]

Year after year, when politics cease from troubling, there recurs the question as to the existence of intelligent, sentient life on the planet Mars. The last outcrop of speculations grew from the discovery by M. Javelle[1] of a luminous projection on the southern edge of the planet. The light was peculiar in several respects, and, among other interpretations, it was suggested that the inhabitants of Mars were flashing messages to the conjectured inhabitants of the sister-planet, Earth. No attempt at reply was made; indeed, supposing our Astronomer-Royal, with our best telescope, transported to Mars, a red riot of fire running athwart the whole of London would scarce be visible to him. The question remains unanswered, probably unanswerable. There is no doubt that Mars is very like the earth. Its days and nights, its summers and winters differ only in their relative lengths from ours. It has land and oceans, continents and islands, mountain ranges and inland seas. Its polar regions are covered with snows, and it has an atmosphere and clouds, warm sunshine and gentle rains. The spectroscope, that subtle analyst of the most distant stars, gives us reason to believe that the chemical elements familiar to us here exist on Mars. The planet, chemically and physically, is so like the earth, that, as protoplasm, the only living material we know, came into existence on the earth, there is no great difficulty in supposing that it came into existence on Mars. If reason be able to guide us, we know that protoplasm, at first amorphous and unintegrated, has been guided on this earth by natural forces into that marvellous series of forms and integrations we call the animal and vegetable kingdoms. Why, under the similar guiding forces on Mars, should not protoplasm be the root of as fair a branching tree of living beings, and bear as fair a fruit of intelligent, sentient creatures?

Let us waive objections, and suppose that, beginning with a simple protoplasm, there has been an evolution of organic forms on

---

1   This report by the French astronomer is described in Appendix G.

the planet Mars, directed by natural selection and kindred agencies. Is it a necessary, or even a probable, conclusion that the evolution would have culminated in a set of creatures with sense-perception at all comparable to that of man? It will be seen at once that this raises a complicated, and as yet insoluble, problem—a problem in which, to use a mathematical phrase, there are many independent variables. The organs of sense are parts of the body, and, like bodies themselves and all their parts, present forms which are the result of an almost infinite series of variations, selections, and rejections. Geographical isolation, for instance, has been one of the great modifying agencies. Earth movements, the set of currents, and the nature of rocks acting together have repeatedly broken up land-masses into islands, and, quite independently of other modifying agencies, have broken up groups of creatures into isolated sets, with the result that these isolated sets have developed in diverging lines.[1] He would be a bold zoologist who should say that existing animals and plants would have been as they are to-day had the distribution of land and water in the cretaceous age been different. Since the beginning of the chalk, all the great groups of mammals have separated from the common indifferent stock, and have become moulded into men and monkeys, cats and dogs, antelopes and deer, elephants and squirrels. It would be the wildest dream to suppose that the recurrent changes of sea and land, of continent and islands, that have occurred since the dawn of life on the earth, had been at all similar on Mars. Geographical distribution is only one of a vast series of independently varying changes that has gone to the making of man. Granted that there has been an evolution of protoplasm upon Mars, there is every reason to think that the creatures on Mars would be different from the creatures of earth, in form and function, in structure and in habit, different beyond the most bizarre imaginings of nightmare.

If we pursue the problem of Martian sensation more closely, we shall find still greater reason for doubting the existence of sentient beings at all comparable with ourselves. In a metaphysical sense, it is true, there is no external world outside us; the whole universe from the furthest star to the tiniest chemical atom is a figment of our brain. But in a grosser sense, we distinguish between an external reality and the poor sides of it that our senses perceive. We think of a something

---

1   This line of thought was initiated by Darwin after his visit to the Gala-
    pagos islands off South America.

not ourselves, at the nature of which we guess; so far as we smell, taste, touch, weigh, see, and hear. Are these senses of ours the only imaginable probes into the nature of matter? Has the universe no facets other than those she turns to man? There are variations even in the range of our own senses. According to the rate of its vibrations, a sounding column of air may be shrilled up, or boomed down beyond all human hearing; but, for each individual, the highest and lowest audible notes differ. Were there ears to hear, there are harmonies and articulate sounds above and below the range of man. The creatures of Mars, with the slightest anatomical differences in their organs, might hear, and yet be deaf to what we hear—speak, and yet be dumb to us. On either side the visible spectrum into which light is broken by a prism there stretch active rays, invisible to us. Eyes in structure very little different to ours might see, and yet be blind to what we see. So is it with all the senses; and, even granted that the unimaginable creatures of Mars had sense-organs directly comparable with ours, there might be no common measure of what they and we hear and see, taste, smell, and touch. Moreover it is an extreme supposition that similar organs and senses should have appeared. Even among the animals of this earth, we guess at the existence of senses not possessed by ourselves. Our conscious relations to the environment are only a small part of the extent to which the environment affects us, and it would be easy to suggest possible senses different to ours. With creatures whose evolution had proceeded on different lines, resulting in shapes, structures and relations to environment impossible to imagine, it is sufficiently plain that appreciation of the environment might or must be in a fashion inscrutable to us. No phase of anthropomorphism[1] is more naive than the supposition of men on Mars. The place of such a conception in the world of thought is with the anthropomorphic cosmogonies and religions invented by the childish conceit of primitive man.

9. H.G. Wells. "Through a Microscope." From *Certain Personal Matters: A Collection of Materials, Mainly Autobiographical*. London: Lawrence & Bullen, 1897, 244-45.

[In this extract from a longer essay on microscopes, Wells describes an amoeba unaware of being observed under a microscope, just as

---

1   Literally means treating a deity as having a human form, but here meaning treating all natural phenomena in terms of human development.

the narrator says that humans are unaware of being observed by superior beings on Mars.]

And all the time these creatures are living their vigorous, fussy little lives in this drop of water they are being watched by a creature of whose presence they do not dream, who can wipe them all out of existence with a stroke of his thumb, and who is withal as finite, and sometimes as fussy and unreasonably energetic, as themselves. He sees them, and they do not see him, because he has senses they do not possess, because he is too incredibly vast and strange to come, save as an overwhelming catastrophe, into their lives. Even so, it may be that the dabbler himself is being curiously observed.... The dabbler is good enough to say that the suggestion is inconceivable. I can imagine a decent Amoeba saying the same thing.

Appendix C: Extracts from Wells's Correspondence

[The following extracts offer insight into H.G.Wells's work and life in the period up to and including publication of *The War of the Worlds*. All are taken from *The Correspondence of H.G. Wells*, ed. David C. Smith, 4 vols. (London: Pickering & Chatto, 1998). The punctuation, dating (conjectural and otherwise), and numbering of letters are Smith's. Parenthetical volume and page references follow each extract.]

1. From Letter 203 to Joseph Wells, 10 August 1894.

... About my work. The *PMG*, is still my bread and cheese. I do from six to ten columns a month and get two guineas a column. I have been doing work for Briggs that brings in about 60 pounds a year but it takes too much time and I am resigning that. I am also dropping the *Journal of Education* which comes to about 12 pounds a year and takes nearly a day a month. I do *Educational Times* work from 2 to 5 or more cols. a month at half a guinea col. and in addition drop articles at *Black and White* and the *National Observer*, when I get the time free. Then there are short stories which are difficult to plant at present, but I expect this series in *P.M. Budget* will get my name up. They are paid at a slightly higher rate than articles but are much more profitable in the end because they can be republished as a book. Besides that I have been writing a longer thing on spec. and have been treating through an agent to get some of my *P.M.G.* articles published as a book.

I think that is a pretty complete statement of my affairs. Naturally things are a little tight with me at present as the divorce business is heavy but after that bill is settled I see no reason why things should not get easier with all of us. I shall have to pay Isabel 100 pounds a year or more, but my income by hook or by crook can always be brought up to 350 pounds and it may be more in future. Mrs. Robbins is going to raise the ready money for our furniture by a small mortgage on her house and the interest on that with the ground rent will come to 30 pounds out of her 90 pounds. Still I don't expect to be pinched and I have no doubt that I shall be able to do my filial duty by mother and yourself all right.

My health hasn't given me any trouble, save for one cold and a bit of over-work this year. (1: 219-20)

2. From Letter 224 to T.H. Huxley, May 1895 (with copy of *The Time Machine*).

I am sending you a little book that I fancy may be of interest to you. The central idea—of degeneration following security—was the outcome of a certain amount of biological study. I daresay your position subjects you to a good many displays of the range of authors but I have this much excuse, I was one of your pupils at the Royal College of Science and finally: the book is a very little one. (1: 238)

3. From Letter 238 to Grant Richards, 6 November 1895.

It's awfully good of you to go writing up a reputation for me, and I will gladly do what you ask of me. I was born at a place called Bromley, in Kent, a suburb of the damnedest, in 1866, educated at a beautiful little private school there until I was thirteen, apprenticed on trial to all sorts of trades, attracted the attention of a man named Byatt, headmaster of Midhurst Grammar School, by the energy with which I mopped up Latin—I went to him for Latin for a necessary examination while apprenticed (on approval, of course!) to a chemist there, became a sort of teaching scholar to him, got a scholarship at the Royal College of Science, S. Kensington (1884), worked there three years, started a students' journal, read abundantly in the Dyce and Foster Library, failed my last year's examinations (Geology), wandered in the wilderness of private school teaching, had a lung haemorrhage, got a London degree B.Sc. (1889) with first and second class honours, private coaching, *Globe* turnovers, article in the *Fortnightly*, edited an obscure educational newspaper, had haemorrhage for the second time (1893), chucked coaching and went for journalism. *P.M.G.* took up my work, then Henley (*N. Obs.*), Hind (*P.M. Budget*), set me on to short stories. Found *Saturday Review* when Harris bought the paper. *Review of Reviews* first paper to make a fuss over *Time Machine*—for which I shall never cease to be grateful. *Referee*, next. Brings us up to date.

Books published—

Textbook of Biology. A cram book—and pure hackwork (illustrated grotesquely bad—facts imagined).

Time Machine
Wonderful Visit
Stolen Bacillus
Forthcoming-
The Island of Dr. Moreau Jan. 1896

I am dropping all journalism now, and barring a few short stories to keep the wolf from the door am concentrating upon two long stories—one of these is a cycling romance (I am a cyclist), the other a big scientific story remotely resembling *The Time Machine*. I am trying to secure a serial publication of these in 1896—if ever I get them finished. (1: 249-50)

4. From Letter 250 to Elizabeth Healey, [late Spring 1896].

... I hope you've read The Island of Dr Moreau, and I do hope that you don't think [it] merely a festival of 'orrors. You may perhaps have seen that the good Jerome has joined the select band of my believers, and that I've got a serial in To Day illustrated with incredible violence and vulgarity—Also between ourselves I'm doing the dearest little serial for Pearson's new magazine, in which I completely wreck and destroy Woking—killing my neighbours in painful and eccentric ways—then proceed via Kingston and Richmond to London, which I sack, selecting South Kensington for feats of peculiar atrocity.... (1: 261)

5. From Letter 297 to the Editor, *Critic*, 21 January 1898.

I have received a rather startling cutting from the Boston *Post* through the Author's Clipping Bureau. The cutting is dated 27 November, the accompanying invoice is dated 31st December, the Boston post-mark is 7th January and it has reached me here today. From it I learn that my story *The War of the Worlds* "as applied to New England, showing how the strange voyagers from Mars visited Boston and vicinity," is now appearing in the *Post*. This adaptation is a serious infringement of my copyright and has been made altogether without my participation or consent. I feel bound to protest in the most emphatic way against this manipulation of my work in order to fit it to the requirements of the local geography... (1: 300)

6. From Letter 336 to Harry Quilter [December 1898?].

I will show you someday certain private copies of my "works."
They are black with revision & remorse. I've spent weeks over the
penmarked book of the *Wheels of Chance* & given it up at last. That
young woman is a dummy of wood, & the construction reeks of
the amateur. It's beyond repair. And the *War of the Worlds* is a clot-
ted mass of fine things spoilt. The serial that's beginning in the
Graphic is almost intolerably wrong & I am rewriting & cutting
whole chapters from the book.... (1: 333)

Appendix D: Reviews of The War of the Worlds

1. John St. Loe Strachey. *Spectator* 29 January 1898, lxxx, 168–69.

[Originally unsigned, this review was written by John St. Loe Strachey (1860-1927), an Anglo-Irish politician, editor of *The Spectator*. In later years he criticized Wells for his political and social views, but this review is enthusiastic in its appreciation of *The War of the Worlds*. Strachey singles out for praise Wells's use of well-known local towns such as Woking.]

In *The War of the Worlds* Mr. Wells has achieved a very notable success in that special field of fiction which he has chosen for the exercise of his very remarkable gift of narration. As a writer of scientific romances he has never been surpassed. Poe[1] was a man of rare genius, and his art was perhaps greater than Mr. Wells's, though Mr. Wells has a well-cultivated instinct for style. But in Poe there is a certain vein of pedantry which makes much of even his best work tame and mechanical. The logical method which he invented, or at any rate perfected, is too clearly visible in his stories, and appears to cramp his imagination. Besides, in Poe there is always a stifling hothouse feeling which is absent from Mr. Wells's work. Even when Mr. Wells is most awful and most eccentric, there is something human about his characters. *The Invisible Man* is in many ways like one of Poe's creations; but yet we feel that Poe would have stiffened the invisible man into a splendidly ingenious automaton, not left him a disagreeable, but still possible, medical student. Both Poe and Mr. Wells are, of course, conscious or unconscious followers of Swift,[2] but Mr. Wells keeps nearest to the

---

1   Edgar Allen Poe (1809-49), American author who wrote many famous short stories that laid the groundwork for the later horror and mystery genres.
2   Jonathan Swift (1667-1745), considered one of the greatest prose stylists and satirists in English, is most famous for his work *Gulliver's Travels* (1726).

human side of the author of Gulliver.[1] In manner, however, as in scheme and incident, Mr. Wells is singularly original, and if he suggests any one in externals it is Defoe.[2] There are several passages in *The War of the Worlds* which seem to recall the *History of the Plague*. Nevertheless, we should not be surprised to hear that Mr. Wells had never read Defoe's immortal book. In any case, the resemblance comes, we are certain, not from imitation, but from the parallel action of two very acute and sincere intelligences. Each had to get into something like the same mental attitude towards the things to be related, and hence the two narrations are something akin. We say 'sincere intelligences' advisedly. We feel that in spite of the wildness of Mr. Wells's story it is in no sort of sense a 'fake.' He has not written haphazard, but has imagined, and then followed his imagination with the utmost niceness and sincerity. To this niceness and sincerity Mr. Wells adds an ingenuity and inventiveness in the matter of detail which is beyond praise. Any man can be original if he may be also vague and inexpressive. Mr. Wells when he is most giving wings to his imagination is careful to be concrete and specific. Some sleights of chiaroscuro,[3] some tricks of perspective, some hiding of difficult pieces of drawing with convenient shadows,— these there must be in every picture, but Mr. Wells relies as little as possible on such effects. He is not perpetually telling us that such-and-such things could not be described by mortal pen.

Mr. Wells's main design is most original. As a rule, those who pass beyond the poles and deal with non-terrestrial matters take their readers to the planets or the moon. Mr. Wells does not 'err so greatly' in the art of securing the sympathy of his readers. He brings the awful creatures of another sphere to Woking junction, and places them, with all their abhorred dexterity, in the most homely and familiar surroundings. A Martian dropped in the centre of Africa would be comparatively endurable. One feels, with the grave-digger in *Hamlet*,[4] that they are all mad and bad and awful there, or, if not, it is no great matter. When the Martians come fly-

---

1   Gulliver, the hero of *Gulliver's Travels*, is used by Swift to satirize many targets, including science.

2   Daniel Defoe (1660-1731) is considered one of the founders of the modern novel. His most famous works are *Robinson Crusoe* (1719), *A Journal of the Plague Year* (1722), and *Moll Flanders* (1722).

3   The use of white and black shading to give the impression of three dimensionality in a painting.

4   Grave digger in *Hamlet*, v.i. 149-52.

ing through the vast and dreadful expanses of interplanetary space hid in the fiery womb of their infernal cylinders, and land on a peaceful Surrey common, we come to close quarters at once with the full horror of the earth's invasion. Those who know the valleys of the Wey and the Thames, and to whom Shepperton and Laleham are familiar places, will follow the advance of the Martians upon London with breathless interest. The vividness of the local touches, and the accuracy of the geographical details, enormously enhance the horror of the picture. When everything else is so true and exact, the mind finds it difficult to be always rebelling against the impossible Martians. We shall not attempt here—it would not be fair to Mr. Wells's thrilling book—to tell the story of the Martian war. We may, however, mention one point of detail. Many readers will be annoyed with Mr. Wells for not having made his Martians rather more human, and so more able to receive our sympathy of comprehension, if not of approbation. A little reflection will, we think, show that this was impossible. This is the age of scientific speculation, and scientific speculation, rightly or wrongly, has declared that if there are living and sentient creatures on Mars they will be very different from men.[1] Mr. Wells, whose knowledge of such speculations is obviously great, has followed the prevailing scientific opinion, and hence his appalling Martian monster—a mere brain surrounded by a kind of brown jelly, with tentacles for hands—a creature which, by relying upon machinery, has been able to dispense with almost everything connected with the body but the brain. Mr. Wells has made his Martians semi-globular and bisexual. Had he, we wonder, in his mind the passage in Plato's Symposium which describes how man was once two sexes in one, and had a round body?[2] If he was not relying upon Plato's legend, it is curious to note how the scientific imagination has twice produced a similar result.

In Mr. Wells's romance two things have been done with marvellous power. The first is the imagining of the Martians, their descent upon the earth and their final overthrow. They were terribly difficult figures to bring on and keep on the stage, but the difficulty of managing their exit with a reasonable deference to the

---

1 See Wells's "Intelligence on Mars" in Appendix B, and Lowell in Appendix G.
2 Plato (c. 427–347 BC), one of the most important philosophers of the ancient world, wrote the *Symposium* which considers the nature of love.

decencies of fictional probability was nothing but colossal. Yet Mr. Wells turns this difficulty triumphantly, as our readers will discover for themselves. The second thing which Mr. Wells has done with notable success is his description of the moral effects produced on a great city by the attack of a ruthless enemy. His account of the stampede from London along the great North Road is full of imaginative force.

[Quotes Book 1, Chapter 6, from "So much as they could see" to "The Martians are coming!"]

That is a most remarkable piece of literary workmanship, and therefore we quote it, though far more sensational is the account of how the Martians turned their heat-ray on their victims, how they fed themselves by sucking into their own veins the blood of the men and women they caught, how they threw the canisters of black powder that blasted half London, and how they died in the end because they were not, like men, the descendants of those who have survived after millions of years of struggle with the bacteria that swarm in air, earth, and water. These, however, we must leave our readers to read about by themselves. That they will read with intense pleasure and interest we make no sort of doubt, for the book is one of the most readable and most exciting works of imaginative fiction published for many a long day. There is not a dull page in it, and virtually no padding. One reads and reads with an interest so unflagging that it is positively exhausting. *The War of the Worlds* stands, in fact, the final test of fiction. When once one has taken it up, one cannot bear to put it down without a pang. It is one of the books which it is imperatively necessary to sit up and finish. We will add one word of personal comment. Our readers may remember that some three or four months ago we tried to work out, apropos of Mr. Wells's book, which was then appearing serially, the possible results on mankind of a Martian invasion. Mr. Wells enters upon a similar inquiry, though on somewhat different lines. And now, before we leave Mr. Wells's book, we will add our one piece of adverse criticism. Why did he cumber his pages with such a hopelessly conventional figure as the poor, mouthing, silly curate? A weak-minded curate of this kind is the sort of lay figure that any second-rate novelist might have borrowed out of a fictional costumier's cupboard. Mr. Wells should have been above so poor and strained a device. If it was necessary for him to use a stalking-horse[1] of this kind, why not an editor, a publisher, an author, or an architect? Even a rector[2] would have been a little fresher. One has had so many seriocomic curates in fiction that the mind really refuses to bite upon them.

2. From an unsigned review, *Academy* 29 January 1898, liv, 121-22.

... Mr. H.G. Wells has probably a greater proportion of admirers among people actively engaged in scientific work than among any other section of the reading public. It is not difficult to understand the reason of this. Nothing irritates a man of science more than incorrect assertions with reference to natural facts and phenomena; and the writer who essays to use such material must obtain information from Nature herself, or he will provoke the derision of better informed readers. Mr. Wells has a practical familiarity with the facts of science, and this knowledge, combined with his imaginative mind, enables him to command the attention of readers who are not usually interested in romance.

The fact that Mr. Wells has been able to present the planet Mars in a new light is in itself a testimony to originality. The planet has been brought within the world of fiction by several writers, but in the *War of the Worlds* an aspect of it is dealt with altogether different from what has gone before.[3] We have had a number of stories of journeys to Mars, but hitherto, so far as we remember, the idea of an invasion by inhabitants of Mars has not been exploited. Astronomers can make out just enough of the planet's surface to justify the conclusion that water and ice or snow exist there, and that the land areas are at times traversed by a network of canals or channels more or less enigmatical in origin. According to Mr. Percival Lowell,[4] who made an exhaustive study of Mars in 1894, these canals are really belts of fertilised land, and are the only

---

1 A cover, mask or pretense.
2 A parson, lower in the hierarchy than a vicar.
3 Mars had figured in imaginative works from Jonathan Swift's (1667-1745) *Gulliver's Travels* (1726) on, and was used in Robert Cromie's *A Plunge into Space* (1891), Genone Hudor's *Bellona's Bridegroom: A Romance* (1887) and Greg Percy's *Across the Zodiac* (1880). Wells combined Mars with the genre of invasion narrative described in Appendix F.
4 See Appendix G.

habitable tracts on Mars, the remainder of the land surface being desert. The view that the Martians—it is less unreasonable to think that Mars is inhabited than that it is not—would look towards our earth with longing eyes is thus quite within the bounds of legitimate speculation; and the fact that Mr. Wells put it forward before Mr. Lowell had brought before the attention of British astronomers the reasons for thinking that Mars at the present time is mostly a dreary waste from which all organic life has been driven, is a high testimony to his perceptive faculties. In other words, the reasons given for the invasion of the Earth by Mars are perfectly valid from a scientific point of view, and are supported by the latest observations of the nature of the planet's surface.

Then, as to the intellectual status of whatever inhabitants there may be on Mars, there is every reason for thinking that it would be higher than that of man. On this matter the following words, written by a distinguished observer of Mars—M.E.M. Antoniadi[1]—in July last, give evidence to the view of the Martians presented by Mr. Wells. Referring to the origin of the canal systems, M. Antoniadi wrote:

Perhaps the least improbable—not to say the most plausible—clue to the mystery still attaches to the overbold and almost absurd assumption that what we are witnessing on Mars is the work of rational beings immeasurably superior to man, and capable of dealing with thousands and thousands of square miles of grey and yellow material with more ease than we can cultivate or destroy vegetation in a garden one acre in extent.

Naturally, the view that beings immeasurably superior to man exist upon Mars is repugnant, but we see by the words quoted that astronomers are being forced to accept it as the easiest method of explaining the phenomena observed. Mr. Wells's idea of the invasion of the earth by emigrants of a race possessing more effective fighting machinery than we have is thus not at all impossible; and the verisimilitude of the narrative appeals more strongly, perhaps, to scientific readers than to others not so familiar with accepted opinion upon the points deftly introduced.

---

1   An astronomer of Greek descent who worked as an assistant to Camille Flammarion (1842-1925), the famous French astronomer.

The most striking characteristic of the work is not, however, the description of the Martians, but the way they are disposed of after they had invaded the Earth. We venture to assert that scientific material has never been more cleverly woven into the web of fiction than it is in the epilogue of this story. The observations of Pasteur, Chaveau, Buchner, Metschnikoff,[1] and many others, have made the germ theory of disease an established truth. In the struggle for existence man has acquired, to a certain extent, immunity against the attacks of harmful micro-organisms, and there is little doubt that any visitors from another planet would not be able to resist these insidious germs of disease. The Earth itself furnishes analogous instances: Englishmen who migrate to the West Coast of Africa, or the strip of forest land in India known as the Terai, succumb to malarial disease, and the Pacific Islander who comes to reside in London or another large British city, almost certainly perishes from tuberculosis. Mr. Wells expresses the doctrine of acquired immunity so neatly that not to quote his words would be to do him an injustice.

[Quotes Book 11, Chapter 8, from "These germs of disease" to "die in vain."]

The book contains many other paragraphs which happily express scientific views, but we must refrain from quoting them. Not for an instant, however, do we think that Mr. Wells owes his success to mere correctness of statement. Science possesses a plethora of facts and ideas, yet not once in a generation does a writer arise competent to make use of them for purposes of romance. Already Mr. Wells has his imitators, but their laboured productions, distinguished either by prolixity or inaccuracy, neither excite the admiration of scientific readers nor attract the attention of the world in general.

3. R.A. Gregory. From *Nature* 10 February 1898, lvii, 339-40.

[Sir Richard Gregory (1864-1952), a lifelong friend, had been a student at the Normal School of Science in South Kensington

---

1   Louis Pasteur (1822-95), Pierre Chaveau (1820-90), Eduard Buchner (1860-1917) and Elias Metschnikoff (1845-1916) were scientists who worked either on germs or the human immune system and helped establish the germ theory of infection as fact.

at the same time as Wells. He was a writer on scientific issues for the popular press and editor of *Nature* from 1919-39. Like the previous reviewer, Gregory emphasizes Wells's knowledge of science and praises the realism of his narrative.]

Many writers of fiction have gathered material from the fairy-land of science, and have used it in the construction of literary fabrics, but none have done it more successfully than Mr. H.G. Wells. It is often easy to understand the cause of failure. The material may be used in such a way that there appears no connection between it and the background upon which it is seen; it may be so prominent that the threads with which it ought to harmonise are thrown into obscurity; or (and this is the worst of all) it may be employed by a writer whose knowledge of natural phenomena is not sufficient to justify his working with scientific colour. Mr. Wells makes none of these mistakes. Upon a groundwork of scientific fact, his vivid imagination and exceptional powers of description enable him to erect a structure which intellectual readers can find pleasure in contemplating ...

The invasion of the earth by inhabitants of Mars is the idea around which the present story is constructed. The planet is, as Mr. Percival Lowell puts it, older in age if not in years than the earth; and it is not unreasonable to suppose that if sentient beings exist upon it they would regard our world as a desirable place for occupation after their own globe had gone so far in the secular cooling as to be unable to support life. Mr. Wells brings the Martians to the earth in ten cylinders discharged from the planet and precipitated in Surrey. The immigrants are as much unlike men as it is possible to imagine, and only a writer familiar with the lines of biological development could conceive them. The greater part of their structure was brain, which sent enormous nerves to a pair of large eyes, an auditory organ, and sixteen long tactile tentacles arranged about the mouth; they had none of our complex apparatus of digestion, nor did they require it, for instead of eating they injected into their veins the fresh living blood of other creatures. Their organisms did not sleep any more than the heart of man sleeps; they multiplied by budding; and no bacteria entered into the scheme of their life. When they came to the earth they brought with them a means of producing a ray of intense heat which was used in connection with a heavy vapour to exterminate the inhabitants of London and the neighbourhood.

This bald outline does not, however, convey a good idea of the narrative, which must be read before the ingenuity which the author displays in manipulating scientific material can be appreciated. The manner in which the Martians are disposed of is undoubtedly the best instance of this skill. As the Martians had eliminated micro-organisms from their planet, when they came to the earth their bodies were besieged by our microscopic allies, and they were destroyed by germs to which natural selection has rendered us immune. This is a distinctly clever idea, and it is introduced in a way which will allay the fears of those who may be led by the verisimilitude of the narrative to expect an invasion from Mars. Of course, outside fiction such an event is hardly worth consideration; but that the possibility of it can be convincingly stated, will be conceded after reading Mr. Wells' story. A remarkable case of the fulfilment of fiction is furnished by the history of the satellites of Mars. When Dean Swift wrote *Gulliver's Travels* (published in 1726), he made the astronomers on the island of Laputa not only observe two satellites, but caused one of these to move round the planet in less time than the planet itself takes to rotate on its axis. As every student of astronomy knows, the satellites were not discovered until 1877, and one of them actually does revolve round Mars three times while the planet makes a rotation. The coincidence is remarkable; but it is to be hoped, for the sake of the peace of mind of terrestrial inhabitants, that Mr. Wells does not possess the prophetic insight vouchsafed to Swift.

In conclusion, it is worth remark that scientific romances are not without a value in furthering scientific interests; they attract attention to work that is being done in the realm of natural knowledge, and so create sympathy with the aims and observations of men of science.

4. Basil Williams. From *Athenaeum* 5 February 1898, 178.

Mr. Wells has evidently studied and attempted to imitate the methods of Jules Verne[1] in this account of an attack from Mars on earth. But while perceiving that Jules Verne's plausibility comes largely from a scrupulous exactitude in matter-of-fact details, he has not seen that matter-of-fact details need not necessarily be vulgar and commonplace. There is too much of the young man from

---

1 French writer of science fiction (1828-1905) famous for such stories as *From the Earth to the Moon* (1865) and *Twenty Thousand Leagues Under the Sea* (1869-70).

Clapham[1] attitude in the book ... For example, what a splendid opportunity is lost in the description of the exodus from London! One thinks what a writer with a great eye for poetical effect like Mr. Meredith[2] would have made with such an idea; whereas Mr. Wells is content with describing the cheap emotions of a few bank clerks and newspaper touts, and the jostling in the road which might very well do for an account of a Derby crowd going to Epsom.[3] Mr. Wells must look carefully to his writing; he began well, but he evidently writes too much now, and is too apt to trust solely to the effect of his blood-curdling ideas, without taking the trouble to give them distinction.

---

1 The "man on the Clapham omnibus" was shorthand for "the common man" and is used to suggest how ordinary Wells and his characters seem to this critic.

2 George Meredith (1828–1909), English novelist, poet and journalist was a famous master of style and author of such novels as *The Egoist* (1879) and *Diana of the Crossways* (1885).

3 The Epsom Derby has been an annual horse-racing event since 1780 and attracts large and often raucous crowds. William Powell Frith (1819–1909) made a famous painting called *Derby Day* (1858) that shows the range of social classes attending such an event.

Appendix E: Influences on Wells

1. Winwood Reade. From *The Martyrdom of Man*, 1872, 2nd ed. London: Trubner & Co., 1875.

[Wells read *The Martyrdom of Man* while at Up Park and frequently cited it as an influence on his thinking. The book is an attempt to give a cosmic history, both natural and human, and then extrapolate this into the far future. Less grounded than Wells in science, Reade's text is written in a more visionary and apocalyptic style. Several themes that preoccupied Wells in his fiction and non-fiction are touched upon briefly in Reade. See also Ruddick p. 204 for the influence of Reade's vision of the future of London on Wells's *The Time Machine*.]

The whole world will be united by the same sentiment which united the primeval clan, and which made its members think, feel, and act as one. Men will look upon this star as their fatherland; its progress will be their ambition; the gratitude of others their reward. Those bodies which now we bear, belong to the lower animals; our minds have already outgrown them! Already we look upon them with contempt. A time will come when Science will transform them by means which we cannot conjecture, which, even if explained to us, we could not now understand, just as the savage cannot understand electricity, magnetism, steam. Disease will be extirpated; causes of decay will be removed; immortality will be invented. And then, the earth being small, man-kind will migrate into space, and will cross the airless Saharas which separate planet from planet, and sun from sun. The earth will become a Holy Land which will be visited by pilgrims from all the quarters of the universe. Finally, men will master the forces of nature; they will become themselves architects of systems, manufacturers of worlds. Man will then be perfect; he will then be a creator; he will therefore be what the vulgar worship as a god.

2. T.H. Huxley. From "Evolution and Ethics" [The Romanes Lecture, 1893]. *Collected Essays.* Vol. IX. *Evolution and Ethics and Other Essays.* New York: D. Appleton, 1902. 46–116.

[This extract comes from T.H. Huxley's *Evolution and Ethics*, which was the published version of a lecture he gave at Oxford University in May, 1893. The text abounds with gardening references, and in the metaphor below Huxley links gardening and colonization. His choice of Tasmania could not help but raise images of extinction in the minds of his audience, well aware of the fate of the original inhabitants of the island at the hand of British colonizers, and so the image speaks to both colonization and extinction. Like Wells's aliens, the colonizing English wish to subjugate the native inhabitants to their will. The Martians carry out a similar process by introducing the Red Weed. The image of a hostile universe wiping out all remains of the colonizers also echoes many of Wells's own pessimistic views on the longevity of humanity and its works.]

The process of colonization presents analogies to the formation of a garden which are highly instructive. Suppose a shipload of English colonists sent to form a settlement, in such a country as Tasmania was in the middle of the last century. On landing, they find themselves in the midst of a state of nature, widely different from that left behind them in everything but the most general physical conditions. The common plants, the common birds and quadrupeds, are as totally distinct as the men from anything to be seen on the side of the globe from which they come. The colonists proceed to put an end to this state of things over as large an area as they desire to occupy. They clear away the native vegetation, extirpate or drive out the animal population, so far as may be necessary, and take measures to defend themselves from the re-immigration of either. In their place, they introduce English grain and fruit trees; English dogs, sheep, cattle, horses; and English men; in fact, they set up a new Flora and Fauna and a new variety of mankind, within the old state of nature. Their farms and pastures represent a garden on a great scale, and themselves the gardeners who have to keep it up, in watchful antagonism to the old regime. Considered as a whole, the colony is a composite unit introduced into the old state of nature; and, thenceforward, a competitor in the struggle for existence, to conquer or be vanquished.

Under the conditions supposed, there is no doubt of the result, if the work of the colonists be carried out energetically and with intelligent combination of all their forces. On the other hand, if they are slothful, stupid, and careless; or if they waste their energies in contests with one another, the chances are that the old state of nature will have the best of it. The native savage will destroy the immigrant civilized man; of the English animals and plants some will be extirpated by their indigenous rivals, others will pass into the feral state and themselves become components of the state of nature. In a few decades, all other traces of the settlement will have vanished.

3. H.G. Wells. From "Huxley," *Royal College of Science Magazine* 13 April 1901, 210-11.

[In this brief reminiscence of T.H. Huxley, Wells turns their meeting into comedy. In the middle of a dissection class in which he was cutting into a rabbit, Wells tries to impress the great man and instead makes a gory mess. The only communication between them, Wells reveals later, was when Huxley once said "good morning" to him. Nonetheless Wells is obviously deeply proud of his connection to Huxley and says that he and other students at the Science School read everything that Huxley wrote and viewed him as their leader.]

And then, presently, it was, when we were all deeply imbued with blood and watercolours, that Huxley appeared. I was not aware of him till he was abreast of my table, and then I saw first his drab spatterdashes.[1] He was surveying the class without any passionate approval on his face, and his hands were deep in his pockets. It was his peculiarity to look like his photographs, only in these one did not catch the bright alertness of the little nut brown eyes that sheltered deep under his portentous eyebrows. When I saw him so close, so familiarly present to me, I became excessively agitated with pride, and my respect for him. Possibly he might in a moment speak to me, or look at the gory mess before me. He might proffer instruction! I pretended to be absorbed in that gory mess and not particularly aware of his presence. I consulted my Zootomy and scrutinized these bowels, then with elaborate delicacy and a certain air of concentrated attention I made a little cut that meant neither good nor harm, and pricked a hole in the main branch of the portal vein! When I looked up presently out of the enormity

---

1 Leggings to cover trousers to protect them from stains.

of this thing, I perceived his back receding leisurely up the room. It still worries me at times whether he saw what happened or no....

I believed then he was the greatest man I was ever likely to meet, and I believe all the more firmly to-day. And when people ask, "Were you not at South Kensington in Huxley's time?" I answer, with a great amount of dishonest implication in my off-handed manner, "Oh yes, *I was one of his men!*"

Appendix F: Invasion Narratives

1. William Le Queux. From *The Great War in England in 1897*. London: Tower Publishing, 1894.

[While this book deals with the destruction of London, as does *The War of the Worlds*, it tells the story in a very detached narrative. Like *The War of the Worlds* it refers to well-known London sites, but it does not convey the same emotional impact as the narrator's brother's description of the gradual panic that engulfed London as news of the Martian approach spread.]

CHAPTER XXXV.

LONDON BOMBARDED.

The Hand of the Destroyer had reached England's mighty metropolis. The lurid scene was appalling.

In the stormy sky the red glare from hundreds of burning buildings grew brighter, and in every quarter flames leaped up and black smoke curled slowly away in increasing volume.

The people were unaware of the events that had occurred in Surrey that day. Exhausted, emaciated, and ashen pale, the hungry people had endured every torture. Panic-stricken, they rushed hither and thither in thousands up and down the principal thoroughfares, and as they tore headlong away in this *sauve qui peut*[1] to the northern suburbs, the weaker fell and were trodden under foot.

Men fought for their wives and families, dragging them away out of the range of the enemy's fire, which apparently did not extend beyond the line formed by the Hackney Road, City Road, Pentonville Road, Euston Road, and Westbourne Park. But in that terrible rush to escape many delicate ladies were crushed to death, and numbers of others, with their children, sank exhausted, and perished beneath the feet of the fleeing millions.

Never before had such alarm been spread through London; never before had such awful scenes of destruction been witnessed. The French Commander-in-Chief, who was senior to his Russian

---

1 French for "every man for himself."

colleague, had been killed, and his successor being unwilling to act in concert with the Muscovite staff, a quarrel ensued. It was this quarrel which caused the bombardment of London, totally against the instructions of their respective Governments. The bombardment was, in fact, wholly unnecessary, and was in a great measure due to some confused orders received by the French General from his Commander-in-chief. Into the midst of the surging, terrified crowds that congested the streets on each side of the Thames, shells filled with melinite dropped, and, bursting, blew hundreds of despairing Londoners to atoms. Houses were shattered and fell, public buildings were demolished, factories were set alight, and the powerful exploding projectiles caused the Great City to reel and quake. Above the constant crash of bursting shells, the dull roar of the flames, and the crackling of burning timbers, terrific detonations now and then were heard, as buildings, filled with combustibles, were struck by shots, and, exploding, spread death and ruin over wide areas. The centre of commerce, of wealth, of intellectual and moral life was being ruthlessly wrecked, and its inhabitants massacred. Apparently it was not the intention of the enemy to invest[1] the city at present, fearing perhaps that the force that had penetrated the defences was not sufficiently large to accomplish such a gigantic task; therefore they had commenced this terrible bombardment as a preliminary measure.

Through the streets of South London the people rushed along, all footsteps being bent towards the bridges; but on every one of them the crush was frightful-indeed, so great was it that in several instances the stone balustrades were broken, and many helpless, shrieking persons were forced over into the dark swirling waters below. The booming of the batteries was continuous, the bursting of the shells was deafening, and every moment was one of increasing horror. Men saw their homes swept away, and trembling women clung to their husbands, speechless with fear. In the City, in the Strand, in Westminster, and West End streets the ruin was even greater, and the destruction of property enormous.

Westward, both great stations at Victoria, with the adjoining furniture repositories and the Grosvenor Hotel, were burning fiercely; while the Wellington Barracks had been partially demolished, and the roof of St. Peter's Church blown away. Two shells falling in the quadrangle of Buckingham Palace had smashed every window

---

1   Enter and seize control.

and wrecked some of the ground-floor apartments, but nevertheless upon the flagstaff, amidst the dense smoke and showers of sparks flying upward, there still floated the Royal Standard. St James's Palace, Marlborough House, Stafford House, and Clarence House, standing in exposed positions, were being all more or less damaged; several houses in Carlton House Terrace had been partially demolished, and a shell striking the Duke of York's Column soon after the commencement of the bombardment, caused it to fall, blocking Waterloo Place.

Time after time shells whistled above and fell with a crash and explosion, some in the centre of the road, tearing up the paving, and others striking the clubs in Pall Mall, blowing out many of those noble time-mellowed walls. The portico of the Athenaeum had been torn away like pasteboard, the rear premises of the War Office had been pulverised, and the Carlton, Reform, and United Service Clubs suffered terrible damage. Two shells striking the Junior Carlton crashed through the roof, and exploding almost simultaneously, brought down an enormous heap of masonry, which fell across the roadway, making, an effectual barricade; while at the same moment shells began to fall thickly in Grosvenor Place and Belgrave Square, igniting many houses, and killing some of those who remained in their homes petrified by fear.

Up Regent Street shells were sweeping with frightful effect. The Café Monico and the whole block of buildings surrounding it was burning, and the flames leaping high, presented a magnificent though appalling spectacle. The front of the London Pavilion had been partially blown away, and of the two uniform rows of shops forming the Quadrant many had been wrecked. From Air Street to Oxford Circus, and along Piccadilly to Knightsbridge, there fell a perfect hail of shell and bullets. Devonshire House had been wrecked, and the Burlington Arcade destroyed. The thin pointed spire of St. James's Church had fallen, every window in the Albany was shattered, several houses in Grosvenor Place had suffered considerably, and a shell that struck the southern side of St. George's Hospital had ignited it, and now at 2 A.M., in the midst of this awful scene of destruction and disaster, the helpless sick were being removed into the open streets, where bullets whistled about them and fragments of explosive shells whizzed past.

As the night wore on London trembled and fell. Once Mistress of the World, she was now, alas, sinking under the iron hand of the invader. Upon her there poured a rain of deadly missiles that caused appalling slaughter and desolation. The newly introduced long-range guns, and the terrific power of the explosives with which the French shells were charged, added to the horrors of the bombardment; for although the batteries were so far away as to be out of sight, yet the unfortunate people, overtaken by their doom, were torn limb from limb by the bursting bombs.

Over the roads lay men of London, poor and rich, weltering in their blood, their lower limbs shattered or blown completely away. With wide-open haggard eyes, in their death agony they gazed around at the burning buildings, at the falling debris, and upward at the brilliantly-illumined sky. With their last breath they gasped prayers for those they loved, and sank to the grave, hapless victims of Babylon's downfall.

2. "Grip" (pseudonym). From *How John Bull Lost London*. London: Sampson Low, Marston, Searle & Rivington, 1882.

[Like the earlier *The Battle of Dorking*, this story used familiar town names, like that of Guildford in Surrey, to give verisimilitude to its descriptions. This narrative makes the capture of London an anti-climax, and focuses on the repercussions of losing the capital. The story makes clear the rivalry for Empire between England and France at this time in the list of demands that include giving up territory in Egypt and India.]

The Battle of Guildford and Capture of London

Nearly 40,000 men of both nationalities lay dead and wounded on the ground at the conclusion of the battle of Guildford; but though the defenders still held the ground, they had gained no victory, for the foe had given them the slip, and was upon the back of London.

By morning the French army had passed through Kingston-on-Thames, Wimbledon, and Wandsworth, and had entered the metropolis, meeting with hardly more resistance than a single division might with ease have overcome.

The English had not been beaten in the open field, they had simply been out-manoeuvred.

London was at the mercy of the invader.

The army facing the French who had landed upon Southend had nothing for it but to retreat, lest it should be taken in rear by the force that had passed into London, and was fain to fall back northwards; so that the next day saw nearly 400,000 Frenchmen in possession of the metropolis, the shipping of the great port, with all the vast stores of London in their hands, and their ships now in a position to push the rest of the way up the Thames. No such disaster had ever befallen a nation as that which now well-nigh overwhelmed this one; and the heart of the country was nearly broken.

The capital was placed under a requisition immediately; the troops were billetted upon the inhabitants as we have seen in the case of John Smith; orders of the most stringent kind were issued condemning to instant death any one who tampered with the communications of the invader between London and Dover. Torpedoes were placed in the Thames below where the invading fleet was stationed, in order to prevent any surprise from English vessels of war; and finally, propositions of peace were sent to York, whither the Government of England had with much precipitancy fled.

They were concise and clear. They included the surrender of Egypt to France, the cession of a considerable stretch of territory in Southern India, the giving up of all rights to the New-Foundland fishery, the cession of certain islands in the Pacific and of the Gold Coast of Africa, a large war indemnity, and an acknowledgment of the right of France to erect and hold for ever a fortress of such strength as might be deemed necessary on the English side of the Channel Tunnel.

Failing the acceptance of these terms, the French army would advance northward forthwith, and exact a heavier penalty.

Appendix G: Mars in 1898

1. Anonymous. *Nature* **2 August 1894, No. 1292, Vol. 50, p. 319.**

Since the arrangements for circulating telegraphic information on astronomical subjects was inaugurated, Dr. Krueger, who is in charge of the Central Bureau at Kiel, certainly has not favoured his correspondents with a stranger telegram than the one which he flashed over the world on Monday afternoon:

> Projection lumineuse dans région australe du terminateur de Mars observée par Javelle 28 juillet 16 heures Perrotin.[1]

This relates to an observation made at the famous Nice Observatory, of which M. Perrotin is the Director, by M. Javelle, who is already well known for his careful work. The news therefore must be accepted seriously, and, as it may be imagined, details are anxiously awaited; on Monday and Tuesday nights, unfortunately, the weather in London was not favourable for observation, so whether the light continues or not is not known.

It would appear that the luminous projection is not a light outside the disc of Mars, but in the region of the planet not lighted up by the sun at the time of observation. The gibbosity[2] of the planet is pretty considerable at the present time. Had there been evidence that the light was outside the disc, the strange appearance might be due to a comet in the same line of sight as the planet. If we assume the light to be on the planet itself, then it must either have a physical or human origin; so it is to be expected that the old idea that the Martians are signalling to us will be revived. Of physical origins we can only think of Aurora (which is not improbable, only bearing in mind the precise locality named, but distinctly improbable unless we assume that in Mars the phenomenon is much more intense than with us), a long range of high snow-capped hills, and forest fires burning over a large area.

---

1 "Flash of light in the region of the southern terminator of Mars observed by Javelle July 28 at 4 O'clock" (my translation).
2 More than half of the planet, but not all of it, illuminated by sun.

Without favouring the signalling idea before we know more of the observation, it may be stated that a better time for signalling could scarcely be chosen, for Mars being now a morning star, means that the Opposition, when no part of its dark surface will be visible, is some time off. The Martians, of course, find it much easier to see the dark side of the earth than we do to see the dark side of Mars, and whatever may be the explanation of the appearances which three astronomers of reputation have thought proper to telegraph over the world, it is worth while pointing out that forest fires over large areas may be the first distinctive thing observed on either planet from the other besides the fixed surface markings.

2. Percival Lowell. From *Mars*. Boston: Houghton Mifflin and Co., 1895.

[Lowell conjectures that the "canals" of Mars show the presence of a civilization, and that Mars being older geologically than Earth means that this civilization would probably be more advanced than humans. He also conjectures that Martians would be giants compared to humans given the lower gravity. Finally he warns that there may not necessarily be "men" on Mars; there could just as well be lizards or frogs as the dominant species.]

To review, now, the chain of reasoning by which we have been led to regard it probable that upon the surface of Mars we see the effects of local intelligence. We find, in the first place, that the broad physical conditions of the planet are not antagonistic to some form of life; secondly, that there is an apparent dearth of water upon the planet's surface, and therefore, if beings of sufficient intelligence inhabited it, they would have to resort to irrigation to support life; thirdly, that there turns out to be a network of markings covering the disk precisely counterparting what a system of irrigation would look like; and, lastly, that there is a set of spots placed where we should expect to find the lands thus artificially fertilized, and behaving as such constructed oases should. All this, of course, may be a set of coincidences, signifying nothing; but the probability points the other way. As to details of explanation, any we may adopt will undoubtedly be found, on closer acquaintance, to vary from the actual Martian state of things; for any Martian life must differ markedly from our own.

The fundamental fact in the matter is the dearth of water. If we keep this in mind, we shall see that many of the objections that spontaneously arise answer themselves. The supposed herculean task of constructing such canals disappears at once; for, if the canals be dug for irrigation purposes, it is evident that what we see, and call by ellipsis the canal, is not really the canal at all, but the strip of fertilized land bordering it—the thread of water in the midst of it, the canal itself, being far too small to be perceptible. In the case of an irrigation canal seen at a distance, it is always the strip of verdure, not the canal, that is visible, as we see in looking from afar upon irrigated country on the Earth.

We may, perhaps, in conclusion, consider for a moment how different in its details existence on Mars must be from existence on the Earth. One point out of many bearing on the subject, the simplest and most certain of all, is the effect of mere size of habitat upon the size of the inhabitant; for geometrical conditions alone are most potent factors in the problem of life. Volume and mass determine the force of gravity upon the surface of a planet, and this is more far-reaching in its effects than might at first be thought.

Gravity on the surface of Mars is only a little more than one third what it is on the surface of the Earth. This would work in two ways to very different conditions of existence from those to which we are accustomed. To begin with, three times as much work, as for example, in digging a canal, could be done by the same expenditure of muscular force. If we were transported to Mars, we should be pleasingly surprised to find all our manual labor suddenly lightened threefold. But, indirectly, there might result a yet greater gain to our capabilities; for if Nature chose she could afford there to build her inhabitants on three times the scale she does on Earth without their ever finding it out except by interplanetary comparison. Let us see how.

As we all know, a large man is more unwieldy than a small one. An elephant refuses to hop like a flea; not because he considers the act undignified, but simply because he cannot bring it about. If we could, we should all jump straight across the street, instead of painfully paddling through the mud. Our inability to do so depends upon the size of the Earth, not upon what it at first seems to depend, on the size of the street.

To see this, let us consider the very simplest case, that of standing erect. To this every-day feat opposes itself the weight of the body simply, a thing of three dimensions, height, breadth, and thickness, while the ability to accomplish it resides in the cross-section of the muscles of the knee, a thing of only two dimensions, breadth and thickness. Consequently, a person half as large again as another has about twice the supporting capacity of that other, but about three times as much to support. Standing therefore tires him out more quickly. If his size were to go on increasing, he would at last reach a stature at which he would no longer be able to stand at all, but would have to lie down. You shall see the same effect in quite inanimate objects. Take two cylinders of paraffine wax, one made into an ordinary candle, the other into a gigantic facsimile of one, and then stand both upon their bases. To the small one nothing happens. The big one, however, begins to settle, the base actually made viscous by the pressure of the weight above.

Now apply this principle to a possible inhabitant of Mars, and suppose him to be constructed three times as large as a human being in every dimension. If he were on Earth, he would weigh twenty-seven times, but on the surface of Mars, since gravity there is only about one third of what it is here, he would weigh but nine times as much. The cross-section of his muscles would be nine times as great. Therefore the ratio of his supporting power to the weight he must support would be the same as ours. Consequently, he would be able to stand with as little fatigue as we. Now consider the work he might be able to do. His muscles, having length, breadth, and thickness, would all be twenty-seven times as effective as ours. He would prove twenty-seven times as strong as we, and could accomplish twenty-seven times as much....

Mars being thus old himself, we know that evolution on his surface must be similarly advanced. This only informs us of its condition relative to the planet's capabilities. Of its actual state our data are not definite enough to furnish much deduction. But from the fact that our own development has been comparatively a recent thing, and that a long time would be needed to bring even Mars to his present geological condition, we may judge any life he may support to be not only relatively, but really older than our own. From the little we can see, such appears to be the case. The evidence of handicraft, if such it be, points to a highly intelligent mind behind it. Irrigation, unscientifically conducted would not give us such truly wonderful mathematical fitness in the several parts to the whole as we there behold. A mind of no mean order would seem to have presided over the system we see—a mind certainly of considerably more comprehensiveness than that which presides over the various departments of our own public works. Party politics, at all events, have had no part in them; for the system is planet wide. Quite possibly, such Martian folk are possessed of inventions of which we have not dreamed, and with them electrophones and kinetoscopes[1] are things of a bygone past, preserved with veneration in museums as relics of the clumsy contrivances of the simple childhood of the race. Certainly what we see hints at the existence of beings who are in advance of, not behind us, in the journey of life....

To talk of Martian beings is not to mean Martian men. Just as the probabilities point to the one, so do they point away from the other. Even on this Earth man is of the nature of an accident. He is the survival of by no means the highest physical organism. He is not even a high form of mammal. Mind has been his making. For aught we can see, some lizard or batrachian[2] might just as well have popped into his place early in the race, and been now the dominant creature of this Earth. Under different physical conditions, he would have been certain to do so. Amid the surroundings that exist on Mars, surroundings so different from our own, we may be practically sure other organisms have been evolved of which we have no cognizance. What manner of beings they may be we lack the data even to conceive....

If astronomy teaches anything, it teaches that man is but a detail in the evolution of the universe, and that resemblant though diverse details are inevitably to be expected in the host of orbs around him. He learns that, though he will probably never find his double anywhere, he is destined to discover any number of cousins scattered through space.

---

1   Electrophones were early electrified instruments, and kinetoscopes were precursors to cameras.
2   The family that includes frogs and toads.

Appendix H: Woking and Surrey

1. A.R. Hope Moncrieff. From *Black's Guide to Surrey*. London: Adam and Charles Black, 1898.

[One of innumerable guide books for day trippers from London, *Black's Guides* gave thumbnail descriptions of towns, sights and walks in the surrounding countryside. The guide for Surrey mentions Chertsey, the Woking Junction Station, Woking, and other Surrey towns mentioned in *The War of the Worlds*. Woking is described chiefly in terms of the Oriental Institute and the London Necropolis, a huge cemetery with which the town was often linked, even though it was closer to the town of Brookwood. The cemetery grounds would have been a familiar sight for anybody traveling by train from London to Woking Junction.]

Chertsey (Hotels: Crown, Bridge) lies among pleasant meadows a little way back from the river. It consists chiefly of two main streets that cross at right angles, with a wide fringe of new red dwellings chiefly towards the station on the south side. The Church, at the central meeting of ways, rebuilt in 1806–1808, contains some fragments of old stained glass, a good modern east window, and one or two monuments worth noting. Of these the best is a bas-relief by Flaxman—the raising of Jairus's daughter—to the memory of Eliza Mawbey, in the Chancel, where also is a plain memorial to Laurence Tomson, whose translation of the New Testament was first published in 1576. In the south aisle an oval tablet recalls the residence of Charles James Fox in this neighbourhood, though he was buried in Westminster Abbey. The tower contains six bells of various dates, and one is thought to have come from the destroyed Chertsey Abbey.

Cowley House, formerly Porch House, on the left of Guildford Street, coming from the station, was once the abode of Cowley the poet, as shown by the inscription on the oval tablet outside.

Just short of **Woking Junction** (station) a remarkable red building is passed on the left, an institution for Indian students, with a mosque at one end balanced by a Hindoo temple at the other.

Woking lies stranded 1 1/2 mile south of the Junction, round which a considerable new town has sprung up. The old place has a picturesque Early English church on the bank of a tributary of the Wey. (Take the road opposite subway on down side of station;

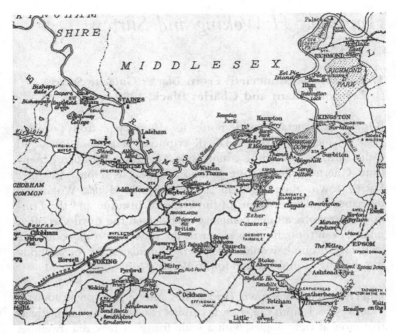

From *Black's Guide to Surrey*, 1898

in ten minutes, beyond bottom of a descent, look out for second stile, where finger-post on lamp points out a broad path as shortest way.) It may be visited as a stepping-stone to one of Surrey's rare ruins, Newark Priory, also to be reached by road from **Byfleet** or from **Ripley**.

Newark Priory lies half an hour's walk east of old Woking, among the channels of the Wey. Crossing the bridge near Woking Church, one finds a path running between the tortuous river and its canalised branch till these unite. A little way above are the ruined walls, composed of grouted flints and gravel, apparently of an Early English structure which it is difficult to trace. Though these ruins are not very imposing, they mark the spot as a favourite one for summer picnics, often reached by water from **Guildford** or **Weybridge**.

Pyrford, on the hill immediately north of the ruin, is a pretty little village, with an interesting church. A fine oak-tree and the village school combine with it to make a pleasing group, and from the churchyard the view of the meads surrounding Newark Priory, here seen at its best, is soft and peaceful.

On the other side of the line, above **St. John's**, a new out-growth of Woking, rises Knap Hill, the site of more than one public institution, the best known of which, Woking Prison, has now been turned into barracks.

2. Eric Parker. From *Highways and Byways in Surrey*. London: Macmillan and Co., 1908.

[Another of the guides for visitors like *Black's Guides*, this extract goes into more detail about Woking and is explicit about its bad reputation as a nondescript town. The guide then describes Old Woking, which is quiet and picturesque in contrast to the noisy and congested area around the train station.]

In whatever way you may choose to travel through Surrey, it is difficult to avoid making Woking a centre and a rendezvous. All the trains stop there; at least, I cannot remember ever passing through the station without stopping, either to change trains, which generally takes three quarters of an hour, or to wait in the station until it is time to go on again, which usually takes eleven minutes. I never found anything else to do at Woking, unless it were at night, when the railway lights up wonderful vistas and avenues of coloured lamps. Then the platform can be tolerable. Once when I had a long time to wait I walked out to the church which stands rather finely on the ridge north of the railway. I thought then it was Woking church: it belongs to Horsell. It was that Woking, the Woking of the station, which for many years I imagined to be the only Woking in Surrey. One did not wish for another.

But there is another Woking, and it is as pretty and quiet as the railway Woking is noisy and tiresome. It stands with its old church on the banks of the Wey two miles away, a huddle of tiled roofs and old shops and poky little corners, as out-of-the-way and sleepy and ill-served by rail as anyone could wish. I found it first on a day in October, and walked out from the grinding machinery of the station by a field-path running through broad acres of purple-brown loam, over which plough-horses tramped and turned. It was a strange and arresting sight, for over the dark rich mould there was drawn a veil of shimmering grey light wider and less earthly than any mist or dew. The whole plough land was alive with gossamer; and Old Woking lay beyond the gossamer as if that magic veil were meant to shield it from the engines and the smoke.

More to the east, 3 miles from the station, are Waterer's

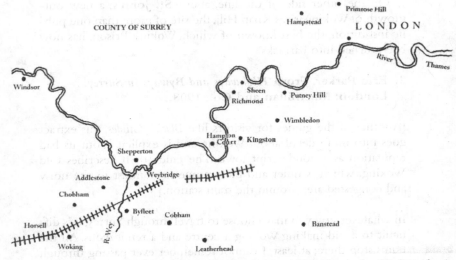

From Eric Parker, *Highways and Byways in Surrey*, 1908 (drawn by M. Danahay)

Nursery Gardens, the rhododendrons of which in early summer make them, like those at Bagshot belonging to another branch of the same family, one of the sights of the neighbourhood. The principal avenue, three-quarters of a mile long, is a fine show of American plants in bloom at the same season. The little church of Horsell, passed on the way to these gardens, about a mile from the junction, is an interesting one. In the tower is preserved a huge spit used for roasting oxen whole in the good old days of revelry.

Woking has some reason to complain of the way in which its scattered name has been identified with gloomy associations. It would have us know that the vast burying ground the railway now traverses should take its name rather from Brookwood, the station for it, but Woking Cemetery this is in the popular voice.

The London Necropolis, as its title is, can boast to be the largest burying ground in the Kingdom. Laid out in 1860, it consists of 500 acres of sandy land, prettily varied with clumps of wood, patches of heather, banks of rhododendrons and other shrubs, that form a paradise of death, owned by a Company, where funerals are carried out with as much regard to sentiment as is consistent with the conditions of crowded city life.

Appendix I: The Victorian Military

[The following images (with the exception of Figure 5) come from issues of the magazine *Army and Navy Illustrated*. The magazine was published from 1895 until 1903 (by Hudson and Kearns) when it was merged with another magazine called *The King of Illustrated Papers*. The new joint magazine was named *The King and His Navy and Army*. Intensely patriotic and jingoistic, the magazine contained stories of the latest technology employed by the armed forces, descriptions of military life in various parts of the Empire, and descriptions of exotic people and locales that were under British military control. The magazine covered the Boer War (1899-1902) extensively, describing at length the actions of the British army and navy in the conflict in South Africa. The captions reproduced with some of the images are from the magazine. Figure 5 was provided by Mr. David Clammer author of *The Victorian Army in Photographs* (London: David & Charles, 1975).]

Figure 1. Field Artillery. (Vol. 1, Number 5. February 21st 1896, p. 113).

FIELD ARTILLERY AWAITING ORDERS TO GO TO THE FRONT

The gun detachment in the picture are some of the men of the Aldershot batteries which took part in the New Forest Manoeuvres last year. They are in Field Service order, and are shown drawn up just before going forward to come into action, in fact, whilst waiting for orders to take up position and unlimber.

Figure 2. Gunners of Field Artillery. (Vol. 1, Number 1. Friday, December 20th 1895, p.15).

GUNNERS OF FIELD ARTILLERY DRILLING WITH A 12-POUNDER

Here we have a 12-pounder gun, which a squad of gunners, in field service uniform, are pointing at an imaginary enemy during the New Forest operations in late August. This is one of the weapons with which the Royal Artillery, both field and horse batteries, have recently been supplied. It is claimed for the 12-pounder that as a light field gun it is second to none. It weighs under the third of a ton, and with a service charge of 4 lbs., if given 25 degrees of elevation, has a range just under five miles. The caliber of the piece or size of the bore is three inches. The drill is taking place in camp.

Figure 3. High-Angle Firing. (Vol. 1, Number 43. August 6th 1897, p. 185).

HIGH-ANGLE FIRING

This is a very interesting picture. It shows one of the more recent pieces of Service ordnance—a wire-wound gun of 9.2 inch caliber, weighing 19 tons, on an expanding mounting, placed for high-angle fire. The gun is of great power, range, and penetration … it was calculated that the extreme height attained by the projectile was about 16,000 ft., or three miles. The time occupied by the flight was slightly over one minute. The result is one of the achievements of modern gunnery.

Figure 4. Machine Gun Detachment. (Vol. 1, Number 11. May 15th 1896, p. 253).

THE MACHINE GUN DETACHMENT OF THE 3rd BATTALION KING'S ROYAL RIFLES

Under the mobilization scheme for Home Defence a machine gun detachment is attached to every Brigade of Infantry, which detachment is drawn from the men of one Battalion of the four, which together constitute the Brigade. Each machine gun detachment consists of one officer, one sergeant, and thirteen men, and is provided with two guns, each drawn by one horse, and two horsecarts ... Our photograph shows the detachment and the two Maxim guns belonging to the 3rd Battalion of the King's Royal Rifle Corps.

Figure 5. Heliograph Operators. (Courtesy of Mr. David Clammer).

Figure 6. 1st Dragoons. (Vol. 7, Number 84. September 10th 1898, p. 580).

1st DRAGOONS, 7th HUSSARS, 16th LANCERS

Figure 7. H.M.S. Thunderer. (Vol. 1, Number 7. March 20th 1896, p. 169).

H.M.S. THUNDERER—PORTGUARD SHIP AT PEM-BROKE

The "Thunderer" is an iron second-class battleship completed for sea in 1877.... She carries, as her principal armament, four 10-in. 29-ton guns; and six 6-pounder and eight 3-pounder quick-firers, and has a partial belt of armour of from 12 to 10 ins.

Figure 8. H.M.S. Ramilles. (Vol. 6, Number 26. September 18th 1896, p. 308).

H.M.S. RAMILLES IN DOCK

A ship in dry dock showing the ram prow.

Selected Bibliography

[This bibliography offers suggestions for further reading to those interested in H.G. Wells and *The War of the Worlds*. It does not attempt to be exhaustive.]

Wells Bibliographies

Hammond, J.R. *Herbert George Wells: An Annotated Bibliography of His Works.* New York and London: Garland, 1977.

H.G. Wells Society. *H.G. Wells: A Comprehensive Bibliography.* 4th ed. (revised). London: H.G. Wells Society, 1986.

Hughes, David Y. "Criticism in English of H.G. Wells's Science Fiction: A Select Annotated Bibliography." *Science Fiction Studies* 6.3 (November 1979): 309-19.

Scheick, William J. and J. Randolph Cox. *H.G. Wells: A Reference Guide.* Boston: G.K. Hall, 1988.

Wells Autobiographies and Biographies

Coren, Michael. *The Invisible Man: The Life and Times of H.G. Wells.* London: Bloomsbury Press, 1993.

Foot, Michael. *H.G.: The History of Mr. Wells.* London: Doubleday, 1995.

Hammond, J.R. *An H.G. Wells Chronology.* New York: St. Martin's, 1999.

—, *H.G. Wells and Rebecca West.* New York: St Martin's, 1991.

—, ed. *H.G. Wells: Interviews and Recollections.* London and Basingstoke: Macmillan, 1980.

Mackenzie, Norman and Jeanne. *H.G. Wells: A Biography.* New York: Simon and Schuster, 1973.

Smith, David C. *H.G. Wells: Desperately Mortal: A Biography.* New Haven and London: Yale UP, 1986.

Wells, G.P., ed. *H.G. Wells in Love: Postscript to An Experiment in Autobiography.* Boston and Toronto: Little, Brown, 1984.

Wells, H.G. *Experiment in Autobiography: Discoveries and Conclusions of a Very Ordinary Brain (Since 1866).* 1934. Philadelphia and New York: J.B. Lippincott, 1967.

West, Anthony. "H.G. Wells." In Anthony West, ed. *Principles and Persuasions.* New York: Harcourt, 1957. Reprinted in *H.G.*

Wells: A Collection of Critical Essays. [Twentieth-Century Views] Ed. Bernard Bergonzi. Englewood Cliffs, NJ: Prentice-Hall, 1976. 8-24.

—. *Aspects of a Life.* New York, Random House, 1984.

West, Geoffrey [Geoffrey H. Wells.]. *H. G. Wells.* [Intro. H.G. Wells.] New York: Norton, 1930.

Wells Correspondence

Crossley, Robert, ed. "The Correspondence of Olaf Stapledon and H.G. Wells, 1931-42." *Science Fiction Dialogues.* Ed. Gary Wolfe. Chicago: Academy Chicago, 1982. 27-57.

Edel, Leon and Gordon N. Ray, eds. *Henry James and H.G. Wells: A Record of Their Friendship, Their Debate on the Art of Fiction, and Their Quarrel.* London: Hart-Davis, 1959.

Gettmann, Royal A., ed. *George Gissing and H.G. Wells: Their Friendship and Correspondence.* Urbana: U of Illinois P, 1961.

Ray, Gordon N. *H. G. Wells and Rebecca West.* London: Macmillan, 1974.

Smith, David C., ed. *The Correspondence of H. G. Wells.* 4 vols. London: Pickering & Chatto, 1998.

Smith, J. Percy, ed. *Bernard Shaw and H.G. Wells.* [Selected Correspondence of Bernard Shaw.] Toronto, Buffalo and London: U of Toronto P, 1995.

Wilson, Harris, ed. *Arnold Bennett and H.G. Wells: A Record of a Personal and Literary Friendship.* London: Hart-Davis, 1960.

Annotated Editions of *The War of the Worlds*

Holmsten, Brian and Alex Lubertozzi. *The Complete War of the Worlds: Mars's Invasion from H.G. Wells to Orson Welles.* Naperville, IL: Sourcebooks; Northam: Roundhouse, 2001.

Hughes, David Y. and Harry M. Geduld. *A Critical Edition of The War of the Worlds: H.G. Wells's Scientific Romance.* Bloomington: Indiana UP, 1993.

McConnell, Frank D. *The Time Machine. The War of the Worlds: A Critical Edition.* New York: Oxford UP, 1977.

Stover, Leon E. *The War of the Worlds: A Critical Edition of the 1898 London First Edition, with an Introduction, Illustrations and Appendices.* Jefferson, NC: McFarland, 2001.

Criticism

Aldiss, Brian W., with David Wingrove. "The Great General in Dreamland: H.G. Wells." *Trillion Year Spree: The History of Science Fiction*. London: Gollancz, 1986. 117–33.

Batchelor, John. *H.G. Wells*. [Introductory Critical Studies]. Cambridge: Cambridge UP, 1985.

—. "The Referee of *The War of the Worlds*" *Foundation* 28 (Autumn, 1999): 7–14.

Bellamy, William. *The Novels of Wells, Bennett and Galsworthy 1890-1910*. London: Routledge & Kegan Paul, 1971.

Beresford J.D. *H.G. Wells*. London: Nisbet, 1915.

Bergonzi, Bernard. *The Early H.G. Wells: A Study of the Scientific Romances*. Manchester: Manchester UP, 1961.

Borges, Jorge Luis. "The First Wells." *Other Inquisitions, 1937 - 1952*. Trans. Ruth L.C. Simms. Intro. James E. Irby. Austin and London: U of Texas P, 1975. [Trans. of *Otras Inquisiciones*. 1952. 86–88.]

Carey, John. *The Intellectuals and the Masses: Pride and Prejudice Among the Literary Intelligentsia, 1880-1931*. London: Faber, 1992. 118–5l.

Caudwell, Christopher. "H.G. Wells: A Study in Utopianism." *Studies in a Dying Culture*. London: John Lane The Bodley Head, 1938. 73–95.

Costa, Richard Hauer. *H.G. Wells*. 1967. 2nd ed. New York: Twayne, 1985.

Crossley, Robert. *H.G. Wells*. [Starmont Reader's Guide 19.] Mercer Island, WA: Starmont House, 1986.

Draper, Michael. *H.G. Wells*. [Macmillan Modern Novelists]. Basingstoke and London: Macmillan, 1987.

Fitting, Peter. "Estranged Invaders: The War of the Worlds." In *Learning from Other Worlds: Estrangement, Cognition and the Politics of Science Fiction*. Ed. Patrick Parrinder. Durham, NC: Duke UP, 2001.

Gailor, Denis. "Wells's War of the Worlds, the 'Invasion Story' and Victorian Moralism." *Critical Survey* 8(3): 270–76. 1996.

Gannon, Charles E. "'One Swift, Conclusive and Smashing End': Wells, War, and the Collapse of Civilization." *Foundation* 28 (Autumn 1999): 7–14.

Hammond, J.R. *An H.G. Wells Companion: A Guide to the Novels, Romances and Short Stories*. London and Basingstoke: Macmillan, 1979.

Haynes, Roslynn D. *H.G. Wells: Discoverer of the Future: The Influence of Science on His Thought.* New York and London: New York UP, 1980.

Hillegas, Mark R. "Cosmic Pessimism in H.G. Wells's Scientific Romances." *Papers of the Michigan Academy of Science, Arts, and Letters* 46 (1961): 655-63.

—. *The Future as Nightmare: H.G. Wells and the Anti-Utopians.* New York: Oxford UP, 1967.

Hughes, David Y. "Bergonzi and After in the Criticism of Wells's SF." *Science Fiction Studies* 3 (1976): 165-74.

—. "The Garden in Wells's Early Science Fiction." In *H.G. Wells and Modern Science Fiction.* Eds. Darko Suvin and Robert M. Philmus. Lewisburg: Bucknell UP, and London: Associated UP, 1977. 48-69.

Huntington, John. *The Logic of Fantasy: H.G. Wells and Science Fiction.* New York: Columbia UP, 1982.

—. "The Science Fiction of H.G. Wells." *Science Fiction: A Critical Guide.* Ed. Patrick Parrinder. London: Longman, 1979. 34-50.

Kagarlitski, J. *The Life and Thought of H.G. Wells.* London: Sidgwick and Jackson, 1966. Trans. of *Herbert Wells: ocherk zhizni i tvorchestva.*

Kemp, Peter. *H.G. Wells and the Culminating Ape.* (Revised Edition) New York: St. Martin's, 1996.

Lake, David. "The Current Texts of Wells's Early SF Novels: Situation Unsatisfactory." *Wellsian* 11 (Summer 1988): 3-12.

McCarthy, Patrick A. "Heart of Darkness and the Early Novels of H.G. Wells: Evolution, Anarchy, Entropy." *Journal of Modern Literature* 13.1 (March 1986): 37-60.

McConnell, Frank D. *The Science Fiction of H.G. Wells.* Oxford: Oxford UP, 1981.

Morton, Peter R. "Biological Degeneration: A Motif in H.B. [sic] Wells and Other Late Victorian Utopianists." *Southern Review* [Australia] 9 (1976): 93-112.

—. *The Vital Science: Biology and the Literary Imagination, 1860-1900.* London, Boston and Sydney: Allen & Unwin, 1984.

Murray, Brian. *H.G. Wells.* [Literature and Life: British Writers.] New York: Continuum, 1990.

Nicholson, Norman. *H.G. Wells.* [The English Novelists.] Denver: Alan Swallow, 1950.

Parrinder, Patrick. *H.G. Wells.* 1970. New York: Capricorn, 1977.

—. "From Mary Shelley to *The War of the Worlds*: The Thames

Valley Catastrophe." In *Anticipations: Essays on Early Science Fiction and Its Precursors*. Ed. David Seed. Syracuse, NY: Syracuse UP, 1995.

—. "How Far Can We Trust the Narrator of *The War of the Worlds?" Foundation* 28 (Autumn, 1999): 46-58.

—. "Science Fiction: Metaphor, Myth or Prophecy?" In *Science Fiction, Critical Frontiers*. New York: St. Martin's, 2000.

—. "H.G. Wells and the Fall of Empires." *Foundation* 57 (Spring 1993): 48-58.

—, ed. *H. G. Wells: The Critical Heritage*. London and Boston: Routledge & Kegan Paul, 1972.

—. "Science Fiction as Truncated Epic." *Bridges to Science Fiction*. Ed. George E. Slusser, George R. Guffey and Mark Rose. Carbondale and Edwardsville: Southern Illinois UP, 1980. 91-106.

—. *Shadows of the Future: H. G. Wells, Science Fiction and Prophecy*. Liverpool: Liverpool UP, 1995.

—, and Robert M. Philmus, eds. *H. G. Wells's Literary Criticism*. Brighton: Harvester P, and Totowa, NJ: Barnes & Noble, 1980.

Philmus, Robert M. and David Y. Hughes, eds. *H. G. Wells: Early Writings in Science and Science Fiction*. Berkeley: U of California P, 1975.

—. "Wells and Borges and the Labyrinths of Time." *Science Fiction Studies* 1.4 (Fall 1974): 237-48. [As "Borges and Wells and the Labyrinths of Time." In *H. G. Wells and Modern Science Fiction*. Eds. Darko Suvin and Robert M. Philmus. Lewisburg: Bucknell UP and London: Associated UP, 1977. 159-78.]

Pritchett, V.S. "The Scientific Romances." [from *The Living Novel*, 1946]. In *H. G. Wells: A Collection of Critical Essays* [Twentieth-Century Views.] Ed. Bernard Bergonzi. Englewood Cliffs, NJ: Prentice-Hall, 1976. 32-38.

Raknem, Ingvald. *H. G. Wells and His Critics*. Trondheim: Universitetsforlaget, 1962.

Renfroe, Craig S. Jr. "*The War of the Worlds*: Wells's Anti-Imperialist Support of Empire." *Postscript* 15: 43-51. 1998.

Ruddick, Nicholas. "The Wellsian Island." *Ultimate Island: On the Nature of British Science Fiction*. Westport and London: Greenwood P, 1993. 62-71.

Showalter, Elaine. "The Apocalyptic Fables of H.G. Wells." *Fin de Siecle/Fin du Globe: Fears and Fantasies of the Late Nineteenth Century*. Ed. John Stokes. Basingstoke and London: Macmillan, 1992. 69-84.

Sommerville, Bruce and Michael Shortland. "Thomas Henry Huxley, H.G. Wells, and the Method of Zadig." *Thomas Henry Huxley's Place in Science and Letters: Centenary Essays*. Ed. Alan P. Barr. Athens and London: U of Georgia P, 1997. 296-322.

Stableford, Brian. "H.G. Wells." *Scientific Romance in Britain 1890-1950*. New York: St. Martin's P, 1985. 55-74.

Stover, Leon. "H.G. Wells, T.H. Huxley and Darwinism." *H.G. Wells: Reality and Beyond: A Collection of Critical Essays Prepared in Conjunction with the Exhibition and Symposium on H.G. Wells*. Ed. Michael Mullin. Champaign, IL: Champaign Public Library, 1986. 43-59.

Suvin, Darko. *Victorian Science Fiction in the UK: Discourses of Knowledge and Power*. Boston: G.K. Hall, 1983.

—. "Wells as the Turning Point of the SF Tradition" and "*The Time Machine* Versus *Utopia* as Structural Models for SF." *Metamorphoses of Science Fiction: On the Poetics and History of a Literary Genre*. New Haven and London: Yale UP, 1979. 208-42.

Weeks, Robert P. "Disentanglement as a Theme in H.G. Wells's Fiction." *Papers of the Michigan Academy of Science, Arts, and Letters* 39 (1954): 439-44. Reprinted in *H.G. Wells: A Collection of Critical Essays*. [Twentieth-Century Views.] Ed. Bernard Bergonzi. Englewood Cliffs, NJ: Prentice-Hall, 1976. 25-31.

Williamson, Jack. *H.G. Wells: Critic of Progress*. Baltimore: Mirage P, 1973.

Zamyatin, Evgenii. "Wells's Revolutionary Fairy Tales." [Abridged from *Herbert Wells*, 1922]. In *H.G. Wells: The Critical Heritage*. Ed. Patrick Parrinder. London and Boston: Routledge & Kegan Paul, 1972. 258-74.

From the Publisher

A name never says it all, but the word "Broadview" expresses a good deal of the philosophy behind our company. We are open to a broad range of academic approaches and political viewpoints. We pay attention to the broad impact book publishing and book printing has in the wider world; for some years now we have used 100% recycled paper for most titles. Our publishing program is internationally oriented and broad-ranging. Our individual titles often appeal to a broad readership too; many are of interest as much to general readers as to academics and students.

Founded in 1985, Broadview remains a fully independent company owned by its shareholders—not an imprint or subsidiary of a larger multinational.

For the most accurate information on our books (including information on pricing, editions, and formats) please visit our website at www.broadviewpress.com. Our print books and ebooks are also available for sale on our site.

broadview press
www.broadviewpress.com